THE DEATH AND LIFE OF SUPERMAN

THE DEATH AND LIFE OF

A NOVEL
ROGER STERN

Superman created by Jerry Siegel and Joe Shuster

BANTAM BOOKS
NEW YORK • TORONTO • LONDON • SYDNEY • AUCKLAND

THE DEATH AND LIFE OF SUPERMAN

A Bantam Book / September 1993

Superman and all related characters, slogans, and indicia are
trademarks of DC Comics

ISBN 0-553-09582-X

Published simultaneously in the United States and Canada

Bantam Books are published by Bantam Books, a division of Bantam
Doubleday Dell Publishing Group, Inc. Its trademark, consisting of the
words "Bantam Books" and the portrayal of a rooster, is Registered in
U.S. Patent and Trademark Office and in other countries. Marca
Registrada. Bantam Books, 1540 Broadway, New York, New York
10036.

PRINTED IN THE UNITED STATES OF AMERICA

BVG   0 9 8 7 6 5 4 3 2 1

To my mother and father,
who encouraged me in all things . . .

To David Purvis,
teacher extraordinaire,
who encouraged me to write and to think . . .

To Charles Kochman and Carmela Merlo,
who kept telling me I could do it . . .

To Jerry Siegel and Joe Shuster,
who created a legend . . .

And to George Reeves,
who first made me believe that a man could fly . . .

. . . this book is respectfully dedicated.

The Death and Life of Superman was primarily adapted from the story serialized in the following comic books, originally published by DC Comics:

Superman: The Man of Steel #17–26 (1992–93)
Superman #73–82 (1992–93)
Adventures of Superman #496–505 (1992–93)
Superman in Action Comics #683–92 (1992–93)
Supergirl and Team Luthor #1 (1993)

Editor:	Mike Carlin		Inkers:	Brett Breeding
				Jackson Guice
Assistant				Doug Hazlewood
Editors:	Jennifer Frank			Dennis Janke
	Frank Pittarese			Denis Rodier
Writers:	Dan Jurgens		Colorist:	Glenn Whitmore
	Karl Kesel			
	Jerry Ordway		Letterers:	John Costanza
	Louise Simonson			Albert DeGuzman
	Roger Stern			Bill Oakley
Pencillers:	Jon Bogdanove			
	June Brigman			
	Tom Grummett			
	Jackson Guice			
	Dan Jurgens			

With additional material adapted from:

Man of Steel #1–6 (limited series, 1986)

Editor:	Andrew Helfer		Colorist:	Tom Ziuko
Writer/Penciller:	John Byrne		Letterer:	John Costanza
Inker:	Dick Giordano			

Justice League America #69 (1992)

Editor:	Brian Augustyn		Inker:	Rick Burchett
Assistant Editor:	Ruben Diaz		Colorist:	Gene D'Angelo
Writer/Penciller:	Dan Jurgens		Letterer:	Willie Schubert

Action Comics #650 (1990)

Editor:	Mike Carlin		Artist:	George Pérez
Assistant Editor:	Jonathan Peterson		Colorist:	Glenn Whitmore
Writer:	Roger Stern		Letterer:	Bill Oakley

Star-Spangled Comics #7 (1942)
Written and drawn by Joe Simon and Jack Kirby

ACKNOWLEDGMENTS

Before we get started, there's one thing you should know about this book.

I didn't write it all by myself.

The story within these pages was first published by DC Comics in some forty comic books from the autumn of 1992 through the summer of 1993. It represents a fine collaborative effort on the part of the nearly two dozen comic-book creators who see to it that a new installment in the never-ending story of Superman appears on the newsstands and comic-book racks of North America virtually every week. For over half a decade, yours truly has been privileged to be a part of this superteam; I can truthfully say that a wackier, more wildly creative group of men and women would be hard to find. Their names appear on the preceding page, and the debt that this book owes them cannot be stressed enough. Without their good works, the story that you are about to read would not exist.

But the collaboration that produced *The Death and Life of Superman* isn't limited solely to the present Superman team. Some six decades of source material from various media have shaped and influenced the personality of Superman.

It all began in the comics with the genius of Jerry Siegel and Joe Shuster, who created Superman and gave a new industry its first major star.

It continued with the work of Joe Simon and Jack Kirby, who together created the Guardian and the Newsboy Legion . . . with the work of Julius Schwartz, Gardner Fox, and Mike Sekowsky, who breathed life into the Justice League and gave us new heroes when we so desperately needed them . . . and with the work of Wayne Boring, Curt Swan, Murphy Anderson; of Edmond Hamilton, Otto Binder, Dennis O'Neil, and so many more who added to the legend of Superman.

It's a legend that, I'm happy to say, continues to grow.

In 1986, my good friend John Byrne went back to the basics and, as both writer and artist, launched Superman's second fifty years with the *Man of Steel* miniseries. John's work laid a solid foundation for the entire *Superman* family of comic-book titles and was a major influence on this novel.

As a child of the fifties, I also must mention the contributions of George Reeves, Noel Neill, Phyllis Coates, Jack Larson, John Hamilton, and Robert Shayne. The images and voices of these people, the cast of the original *Adventures of Superman* television series, will forever be a part of my memory. They have been and continue to be a constant inspiration whenever I sit down at the keyboard to put words in the mouths of Superman and his friends.

In writing this book, I also drew upon a small network of folks who provided invaluable advice and support.

Thanks then to the real-life Mark Spadolini, who generously shared the knowledge he has gained as a paramedic . . . to Christie "Walt" Davenport for her medical expertise, and to Joe Davenport, for his geological advice.

Thanks to my military affairs advisors, former Petty Officer Second Class Lou Ann Batts and Army Reserve Sergeant William Val Kone . . . to Richard "Scratch" Lauterwasser for lending technological verisimilitude and other constructive support . . . and to Joseph Collins Edkin who lent time, office space, and his laptop computer and who occasionally supplied dinner to fellow writers who might otherwise have forgotten to eat.

Thanks to Curtis King of DC Comics, and to Ari Kissiloff and the folks at Public Communications, Inc., of Ithaca, New York, for computer logistic support.

And thanks to my copy editor, Zoë Kharpertian, who labored long and hard under the crunch of deadlines to catch my typos and keep my spelling in line.

I must give special thanks to Mike Carlin, my comics editor of many years, who suggested me as the writer of this book. As editor of the *Superman* line of comics, Mike has displayed uncommon strength and patience. Without his guidance, the stories that led to this novel could never have happened. Mike has been a friend as well as an editor. I hope that I will always be worthy of his trust.

In addition, I owe a great debt to all the people at DC Comics and Bantam Books who worked so hard behind the scenes to produce this book.

Finally, there are two people who—more than any others—got me through the writing process alive and with a minimum of scars.

The first is my book editor, Charles Kochman. Working both in person and over the phone, Charlie provided a clarity of guidance (if not always of penmanship), as well as a wonderfully goofy sense of humor that sustained us both through the often difficult process of birthing a novel. Writing this book has been a constant learning experience, and Charlie has been a most generous instructor. My hat's off to him.

The second is my wife, Carmela Merlo. Carmela organized my notes, kept track of outlines and time-lines, proofread my rough drafts, found problems and devised solutions, and suggested scenes and dialogue. She checked my science, ran down research, and held my hand (often literally) as I battled my way through this, my first novel. Correction, *our* first novel. I couldn't have done this without Carmela's love and help. She has been my strength and inspiration; and after eleven years of marriage, she still laughs at my jokes.

So, you see, I really did have quite a bit of help in writing this book. I hope that you enjoy the result.

—Roger Stern

SECTION ONE

DOOMSDAY

Prologue

It was dark as pitch, the place where he awoke, and the air was stale. The Creature tried to flex his stiff muscles and discovered that he could not move.

The Creature was bound tight, his face covered. Both arms were lashed behind his back, and his feet were manacled. Even the rise and fall of his massive chest was restrained.

The rage grew inside him. From deep within his great chest, a low, muffled growl built to a mighty, defiant bellow. The sound that echoed back seemed to suggest that he was enclosed in a small place, a room with metal walls.

Who had imprisoned him? Where was he, and how long had he been there? He did not know, nor did he care. All that mattered was that he be free.

The Creature began to thrash about wildly, and the bonds that held him began to creak and groan under the strain.

He would be free . . . oh, yes! It was just a matter of time. . . .

1

The sun was still burning the early morning fog off Metropolis Harbor, but it was clearly going to be a beautiful day. There was just a hint of a breeze in the air, and the sky was forming a bright blue dome over the city's skyscrapers.

Henry Johnson eased his big frame down onto the high steel of what would soon become the fifty-third story of the Newtown Plaza and sat staring off into the canyons of Metropolis. The big ironworker's mood was anything but bright. He looked out at the gleaming towers before him and wondered if he deserved to live. *It would be so easy,* he thought, *just to push off and fall. Everybody'd say it was an accident. It's not as if anyone would miss another single black male. Probably wouldn't rate more than a mention on the evening news. How long could it take? Fifty-three stories . . . twelve feet per story . . . acceleration of thirty-two feet per second per second.* A mathematic equation whizzed through his head—*a shade over six seconds.* He frowned, realizing how effortlessly he had computed the figure. *Always were too damn smart for your own good,* came the inner voice. *Just remember, you're not an engineer anymore . . . that was a different Henry. You're not a weapons engineer anymore. You're working CONstruction now, not DEstruction.* Henry removed his hard hat to wipe his brow, angry with himself. As he grabbed the cable to pull himself up, he heard someone yell, one story above him.

Pete Skywalker had tripped and tumbled over the edge. Without thinking, Henry pushed off from the girder, grabbing for Pete's belt. The metal strands of the inch-thick cable cut into Henry's hand as it drew taut under the weight of the two men, but he would not let go. For an instant, they were suspended in midair, with the whole city beneath them. And then they went swinging back in over a completed floor. Henry shoved the big Mohawk to safety, but his own wrist had become enwrapped in the cable. His pendulum swing carried him back out into space. Then the cable came loose.

In the split second he began his fall, Henry knew for certain that he was a dead man, and he mourned, less for himself than for those people he had wronged in his life. *Sorry, Grandma . . . Grandpa. Wish I could've told you how sorry—*

Suddenly, he was not alone. At the fifty-story level, Henry felt a jolt as a powerful arm reached out, grabbing him by the wrist with a hand as strong as steel. A calm, confident voice rang out, "Don't worry, I have you!" For an awful moment the fall continued, and Henry felt his guts start to clench. No! *I've pulled another man down with me.* But then the sting of rushing air began to ease, and by the forty-sixth floor the fall had stopped. Hanging in midair, Henry craned his head around to look at his rescuer.

He was a big man, as big as Johnson, and the dark blue overshirt fit him as snugly as a second skin. Emblazoned across his chest was a pentagonal shield of red and yellow, and tucked in at his collar was a bright, flowing red cape. His jaw was firm and wide, and a lock of unruly black hair curled down over his forehead.

"Superman!" Henry choked on the name.

The big man smiled back. "Relax. You're going to be all right!" Before Henry could draw another breath, Superman effortlessly swung about and set them both down onto the solid flooring of the forty-fifth story.

"You . . . you . . ." Henry couldn't make his mouth work right.

"Easy does it!" Superman put a hand on his shoulder. "Take a deep breath and let it out." His voice was soothing, reassuring, and Henry reflexively did as the caped man said.

"You're Superman! You're really Superman . . . the Man of Steel!" The words finally came tumbling out. "You saved me—!"

"My pleasure," said Superman, clapping him on the back. "You know, I saw how you helped that other man. I'd say that your efforts were more impressive than mine. You certainly took a much bigger risk than I just did."

"Doesn't matter, man. I owe you my life!"

Superman smiled gently and shook his hand. "Then make it count for something!"

With a wave, Superman leapt into the air, soaring away across the city skyline. Johnson watched him disappear behind a maze of high rises. For a second, all was deathly still, save for the whistle of the wind through the high steel. Did that really happen? Henry looked down at his lacerated hand, inspecting the cable cut for the first time. And then a crowd of workers came rushing up around him.

"Henry!"

"You okay, man?"

"Geez, I thought you was a goner for sure!"

Henry rubbed his hand. "For a second there, I *was* a goner." *I was a dead man. But I'm not anymore. Superman's given me a second chance at life, and I can't blow it this time.* Henry stared off across the skyline. *Got to make it count for something. It's the only way I'll ever pay him back!*

Superman flew in a long, lazy loop out over the West River. He loved spring days in the city, and any morning that started with saving a life seemed especially sweet. *I got back from Tokyo just in time for that one,* he thought. *Another few seconds—!* Superman repressed a shudder. Early in his career, he'd had to recognize the simple fact that he couldn't save every life.

It was an unpleasant realization he had gradually come to accept, much as he'd adjusted to the growth of his superhuman powers throughout early adulthood. The more powerful he became, and the more he tried to do, the more it became apparent that he couldn't do everything. Still, he'd resisted facing his limits until that hellish week nearly a decade ago. . . .

Superman had been away from the city for three days, helping to put out a forest fire in Northern California, and returned barely five minutes after a jet crashed shortly after takeoff from Metropolis International. The flight crew had done a heroic job of bringing the plane down in a nearby field, but three passengers had died. For days after that, Superman had maintained an almost constant presence in the city's skies. He'd brooded over those three deaths to the point at which it put a strain on his double life.

His boss was fit to be tied. "Kent, you were supposed to cover the mayor's speech. Where the blazes were you?"

"Sorry, Mr. White." Clark Kent straightened his glasses. He'd been patrolling the skies, but he couldn't say that. "I guess I lost track of the time."

"Step into my office. Now!" Perry White closed the door behind them. "For the past week, you've been walking around the City Room like a zombie—no, more like a ghost. It's become a rare occasion when you show up! What in blazes is wrong with you, Kent?"

"It's . . . personal, Chief." Clark couldn't very well tell the managing editor of the *Daily Planet* that his newest reporter was also Superman. "I'm having to adjust to a lot of things."

"Well, adjust faster!" White slammed both palms down hard on his desk top, and Clark could sense the increase in his editor's blood pressure. "I hired you on the basis of that Superman exclusive you got for the *Planet.* It was a damn fine piece of reporting, but you can't coast on one story. Not at this paper!"

"No, sir."

"My reporters work for a living! I won't put up with any slackers."

"No, sir. I'm sorry, sir. It won't happen again."

"See that it doesn't!"

Clark got up to go.

"Kent?"

"Sir?"

"I meant what I said about that exclusive. It was one of the best-written pieces I've seen in twenty-five years of newspaper work." Perry's gruff voice softened. "I know it can be tough . . . to suddenly burst on the scene, making a big splash. You've made a lot of people jealous. They're all out there, waiting for you to fall on your face. They think you're a flash in the pan. Well, I think they're wrong. I think you have the makings of a great reporter."

"Thank you, sir. That means a lot. You—"

"Aw, I'm just an old beat reporter who got some lucky breaks." Perry opened a desk drawer. "Cigar?"

"No, thank you. I don't smoke."

"Oh. That's right. I forgot." Perry stuffed a Corona in his vest pocket for later. "Look, Clark, if something's troubling you—"

"It really is personal, Mr. White. I'd rather not talk about it."

"Fair enough." Perry came around from behind his desk. "We all have a life outside these walls, and what you do with yours is none of my damn business . . . as long as it doesn't reflect badly on the *Planet.* But I want you to know that my door will always be open to you. If you have a problem, I'll listen. If you don't feel like telling me, fine . . ." Perry paused and looked Clark in the eye, ". . . but tell someone, someone you can trust. It doesn't pay to keep things bottled up inside."

It had been good advice. That night Clark had flown home to Kansas and poured his heart out to the two people in this world whom he trusted above all others . . . the couple who had raised him as their own son.

"Dear, you mustn't do this to yourself!" Martha Kent's worry lines became deep furrows in her ivory skin. "Mercy sakes, Superman can't be everywhere. Even if you'd been in Metropolis at the time, there's no guarantee you could've saved those people."

"Your ma has a point, son." Jonathan Kent pulled an old red bandanna from the right rear pocket of his overalls and began polishing his glasses. It was a contemplative mannerism that Clark had seen so many times before—when his father had sat him down to explain the facts of life, when Aunt Sal had died, when Jon had showed Clark the craft that had brought him to Earth. "From the way you described it, that plane crashed on takeoff, without more'n a few seconds' warning. Why, you'd have had to been right there at the scene to have done any good. On the other hand, who knows how many lives you saved by putting out that forest fire!"

"That's right. You're able to do so many wonderful things with your powers, Clark, but even you can't solve all the world's problems." He could tell Martha was upset. She had practically twisted the hem of her apron into a knot. "Don't dwell on what might have been, or you'll worry yourself into a terrible state! Think of what you've already accomplished. You're just one man . . . and you manage to do so much good. And we're so very proud of you. Don't you ever forget that!"

Superman hadn't forgotten. He couldn't forget anything. That's the blessing and the curse of a good memory, Pa had once said, and his memory was just about perfect. Jonathan and Martha had done their best to set him straight, bless them, and time had proven them right.

A growing chorus of car horns cut into Superman's consciousness. Five hundred feet below him, rush-hour traffic was already backing up through the borough of Queensland Park along the Burnley Expressway. A quick scan showed him the problem . . . about three miles away, a late-model sedan sat stalled in the express lane, its emergency lights blinking. As Superman sped to the scene, his ears picked up a high-pitched wail coming from the vehicle.

"MOMMEEEE!"

In the driver's seat, Rosemary Carson kept trying the ignition in a vain hope that the engine would turn over. In the back, strapped into a child seat, was the two-year-old source of the wail.

"MOMMEEE! I gotta POTTEEE!"

"Honey, I asked you if you needed to go before we left."

"Didn't need to then."

"We'll get you to day care soon, Benjamin, and then you can go. Okay?"

"Whennnn?"

"It won't be long." *I hope.* "First, Mommy has to get the car started." *And later Mommy has to remind Daddy that he didn't get the car serviced, like he promised.*

"Need to go nowww!"

Benjamin's whine was reaching the point where it was just slightly less annoying than the miles of car horns. Rosemary had to grit her teeth. *No, don't yell at him, he's just a kid. This isn't his fault.* "Try not to think about it, sweetie. Let's . . . let's sing a song. What shall we sing?"

" 'She'll Be Comin' Round the Mountain' was always one of my favorites, when I was his age!"

Rosemary sat up with a start at the sound of the rich baritone. She hadn't heard anyone approaching, but suddenly—there he was, leaning down to look into her car!

"Superman! SUPERMAN!" Benjamin had instantly forgotten the pressure on his bladder. The man he'd seen fly on TV was now smiling at him.

"Hello, Benjamin."

Superman knew his name!

"Don't worry, we'll have things taken care of before you know it."

Benjamin's mother just nodded, not quite sure whether to believe this was happening or not. Still, the horn honking seemed to have stopped. Rosemary checked her mirror. Yes, drivers in the cars backed up behind her looked as surprised as she felt. When she looked ahead again, Superman was staring at the front end of her car and stroking his chin. *Of course, X-ray vision. He can see right through the hood.* Superman came back to her window, and this time she cranked it all the way down.

"I don't think I can fix it. At least not right here."

"You can't? I thought you could do anything!"

"Not quite." He grinned, perhaps a little self-consciously, and she realized how intently she was staring at him. She dropped her eyes, a bit embarrassed.

"Tell you what, how about if I give you and Ben a lift to day care? Then we can call a tow truck."

"Sure, I . . ." Her jaw dropped. "How did you know where we were going?"

Now it was his turn to look embarrassed. She found it charming.

"I, ah, overheard. We'd probably better get going, if we want to avoid any more emergencies." Superman glanced pointedly back at the boy.

"Oh. Yes! Yes, of course."

"Who's your day-care provider?"

"The Little Pitchers Children's Center . . . on Melrose."

"I know the place. Do either of you suffer from acrophobia?"

10

"No." *What an odd thing to ask,* thought Rosemary. "In fact, Benjamin loves heights."

"Fasten your belts, then. This won't take a minute."

Suddenly Superman literally dropped out of sight. For a second, Rosemary wondered if he'd fallen. But then the car gently began to rise into the air.

"We're flying, Mommy! Superman is making the car fly! WHEEEE!"

"Flying . . . yes, of course." Rosemary was amazed by the even timbre of her voice. Just the same, she clutched the end of her seat belt and cinched it tighter. No wonder he asked about acrophobia! She turned in her seat to see Benjamin bouncing happily in his car seat and trying to undo its harness. "Don't do that, Benjamin!"

"Wanna look out the window! WANNA LOOK OUT THE WINDOW!"

"No, honey. Superman wants us both to stay buckled up. Just sit still and you'll see—!"

"Don't wanna sit still! DON'T WANNA!"

"Ben!" The boy froze in the seat as his name echoed through the car. Superman's voice was deep, much deeper than his father's. The whole car vibrated with the sound. "Do as your mother says!"

"I will." Benjamin's voice was a bare whisper.

"That's what I like to hear." Superman lowered his voice to a more conversational volume. "Your mother wants only what's best for you . . . it's important to listen to what your parents say! Understand?"

"Uh-huh." The boy nodded almost reverentially.

Rosemary smiled. They were already descending toward the day-care center. *No one at the office will ever believe this,* she thought. *Not in a million years.* "What a baby-sitter he would make!" Her words came out as a wistful sigh, but Superman heard her all the same.

Coming from a farming family, he knew all about the problems working couples faced in raising their children. The Kents had faced them all, and more. *Thank God my powers developed slowly,* he thought. *Imagine the hell Ma and Pa would have had with a super toddler going through the Terrible Twos!* Superman shook his head and smiled. He hoped his folks liked the surprise he'd left for them.

At that moment, one time zone to the west, Jonathan Kent padded into the kitchen of the old family farmhouse and gave his wife a peck on the cheek as she stood stirring a pot at the stove. "Morning, love. Why'd you let me sleep so late?"

"It does you good to sleep in, dear. You are supposed to be retired, after all!"

"Semiretired, Martha. You ought to know by now that a real farmer never completely retires. I intend to work until I fall over in the field and they plow me under for fertilizer."

"Jonathan Kent! What a thing to say!"

"Well, it makes more sense than pickling a man in formaldehyde and burying him in a box." He looked down into the pot and made a face. "Oatmeal again?"

"I thought you liked oatmeal."

"I do, but I also like a little variety. Seems like forever since I last had steak and eggs . . . with home fries and biscuits."

"Now, you know what Doc Lanning said! You have to be careful with your heart. And it does us both good to eat smarter and cut down on fats." Martha considered her husband's sour expression. "I could see about getting some of those egg substitutes at the market."

"Can you fry 'em sunny-side up?"

"I don't think so."

"I'll stick with the oatmeal, then. We got any brown sugar and cinnamon to put on it?"

"There on the table. I bought raisins, too. Raisins are good in oatmeal!"

"Uh-huh. The morning paper come yet?"

"I haven't checked."

Jonathan opened the door to the back porch, and a brown-paper-wrapped package toppled in onto the floor. "Jehoshaphat! What's this?"

He turned the package over. There were no postal or delivery service markings, but a small envelope had been taped to one side. Jonathan fished out a note.

"Martha, it's from our boy! 'Dear Ma and Pa, I saw this when I was in Tokyo and thought you might like it. Sorry I couldn't stop in, but I had to get back to the city. All my love, Clark.' " Jonathan handed the package to his wife. "Here, you open it!"

Martha carefully pried loose the package's sealing tape with the corner of one fingernail and slowly unfolded the brown paper. "Oh, Jonathan, look! It's a framed watercolor of . . . what's that mountain?"

"Mount Fuji, as I live and breathe! I visited it when I was in Japan on leave, back during the war. You remember, I brought back that postcard. Oh, but this is a real beauty!" He looked at his wife, watching her start to tear up. "Almost as beautiful as you."

"You're full of malarkey, Jonny Kent." But as she said it, she smiled, and in that smile he saw the girl he'd first fallen in love with, all those years ago.

"And you're full of salt water." He handed her his bandanna. "Here, take this before you rust up on me!" *It hasn't always been an easy life, but it's been a happy one for the most part,* thought Jonathan. *I'm glad we've shared it.* He looked again at the watercolor. *And I couldn't love that son of ours more if he was really our own.*

The memory of the night they'd found him remained one of the most vivid in his recollection.

It was November, and a big storm was blowing in out of the west. Martha and he had just secured the last of the shutters when it happened. A brilliant, dazzling light had shot across the sky, passing so low over the house that Martha had cried out in alarm. The light disappeared behind the barn, and there followed a low, echoing thud that reminded Jonathan of nothing so much as the impact of an unexploded mortar round.

"Jonathan, was that—?"

"A meteor! By gum, it had to be! It must've hit somewhere in the back forty! C'mon, Martha, let's go see!"

"Now? But the storm—"

"From the feel of the wind, that storm's gonna drop snow. If there's an honest-to-god meteorite on our land, I want to know *where* before it gets buried. You don't have to come if you don't want to."

But she did, of course. Martha was every bit as curious as her husband, and the two of them jumped into their old pickup and set out across the fields.

They soon found the source of the mysterious light. In a remote section of their property, in the midst of a surprisingly shallow crater, sat what appeared to be a huge, glistening egg mounted onto a set of smoking metal fins.

"Jonathan, what in the world is it?"

"I don't know. Looks almost as if it's some kind of little rocket or satellite or something! Better stay clear, Martha."

"But . . . look, Jonathan!" Dark as the egg was, it was still translucent, and Martha could see signs of movement. "There's something inside! Something alive!"

"You think so? It's awfully small. Maybe this is some sorta test craft?" Jonathan gingerly reached out to touch the smooth surface of the egg. "That's funny . . . it's cool. I read these things were supposed to get hot on reentry an' . . . what the hey?!"

The outer surface of the egg seemed to melt away beneath Jonathan's hand, revealing its precious cargo within.

"Oh! Ohhh, Jonathan! It's a baby!" Martha pushed past her amazed husband and gathered the squirming newborn infant into her arms.

"And so small! Those . . . those monsters! They put a poor little baby into a rocket ship! And then they shot him off to the moon or somewheres! What kind of people are they?"

"Now, you be careful, Martha! We don't know that this baby came from Earth! He could be some kind of—I don't know—Martian or something!"

"Oh, now you hush, Jonathan Kent. You've been reading too many of those science-fiction magazines! Just look at him, he's as human as you or me!" The baby boy seemed to smile up at Martha and then shiver as the cold wind picked up. Martha pulled her coat close around him and headed for the truck. "Well, little one, whoever the monsters were who shot you into space, I'm going to make sure that they never get their hands on you again!"

"Martha!" Jonathan had to scramble to catch up to his wife. He started to protest, but before he could open his mouth again, she turned and fixed him with a stare.

"We can't just leave him here, now can we?"

Jonathan scratched the back of his neck for a moment, then went around the truck and held open the door for his wife.

All during the bumpy ride back to the house, Martha kept the infant cradled in her arms, alternately cooing to the child and arguing with her husband. From the moment she'd laid eyes on the boy, Martha had wanted to keep him. She and Jonathan had been trying for eight years to have a child of their own, but after two miscarriages and a stillbirth they had just about given up. Neither of them were regular churchgoers, but Martha believed in destiny, and she felt that this child was meant to be theirs. She was determined to keep him, and Jonathan was hard-pressed to counter her arguments. By the time they got home, they'd already decided to name him Clark, Martha's maiden name.

That's when the storm hit. Actually, it was the first of many storms. A whole series of fronts swept across Kansas that winter, effectively isolating the Kents from friends and relatives in the surrounding area. It was five months before they were again seen in town. Being farmers, they had a full larder and were able to survive in relative comfort, if in solitude, when the phones periodically failed. For his part, the tiny infant thrived under his new parents' care.

With the spring thaw, the Kents finally made it into the nearby town of Smallville, where they proudly displayed Clark as their own natural son. Their friends were thrilled and happy that at last they had the child they'd so long wished for. Knowing Martha's medical history, their families willingly accepted their story that she'd kept another attempted pregnancy a secret. And Jonathan had helped deliver so many calves, they knew that he could easily have played midwife. When questioned further, the new father just beamed and said, "It was a good birth . . . easier than a cat dropping kittens," which, as a matter of fact, it had been.

Young Clark Kent at first exhibited no extraordinary powers or abilities. To all outward appearances, he was growing up to be just another normal, healthy American boy.

But Clark was not like other children. Years later, the Kents would learn that Jonathan had been right, that their son was not of this Earth. He had, in fact, been conceived on the dying world of Krypton, some fifty light-years from our planet. His genetic father, the Kryptonian scientist-historian Jor-El, had sent the gestating child to Earth within an artificial womb, so that Krypton's last son would have a chance for survival.

As Clark grew older, he also grew increasingly stronger. When he was just eight years old, the boy was trampled by an angry bull. His clothes were left in tatters, but Clark himself didn't suffer so much as a scratch. A few months later, Martha looked out her kitchen door to see her son nonchalantly lift up the back end of their truck to retrieve a softball that had rolled just out of his reach. As he reached puberty, Clark discovered that he could see farther and in far greater detail than any of his friends. And if he concentrated, he was able to actually see through solid objects. Finally, in the summer of his seventeenth year, Clark found that he could step off into space and defy gravity. His joy at discovering that he could fly was as boundless as his parents' amazement.

Throughout Clark's adolescence, Martha and Jonathan kept his incredible abilities a secret and cautioned their son to do the same. They feared that if the boy's powers became public knowledge and the authorities learned the truth about his birth, he might be taken away from them. They suspected that some people might be afraid of Clark or consider him a monster, and that unscrupulous people would want to exploit his powers. And they knew that, at the very least, they would all become part of an unending series of stories in the supermarket tabloids.

The Kents counseled Clark to think of his powers as a great gift. Martha and Jonathan both impressed upon the boy that being stronger or able to fly didn't necessarily make him better than anyone else. "Power carries a lot of responsibilities, son, and it's up to each of us to use whatever talents we have to leave this world a better place than we found it." And they stressed to Clark that he should never use his special powers to make other people feel useless.

Clark took their lessons to heart, and when he reached manhood and left Smallville, he was careful to keep his powers a secret. For seven years, he wandered around the world, working covertly to help people. But finally circumstances forced him to use his powers in public.

An experimental NASA space plane had become involved in a midair collision over Metropolis. With only seconds to act, Clark had leapt into the sky to catch the ship and guide it down to a safe landing. No one was able to get a clear photograph of his face, so quickly did he move, but there were thousands of witnesses to the rescue. After he'd brought the space plane safely to the ground, Clark had been mobbed. People were clutching and pulling at him, their voices becoming a roar of offers and demands and desperate pleas for help. It was as if they all wanted a piece of him.

Appalled, Clark shot into the air to flee the mob and didn't stop until he'd flown halfway around the world. He finally came to rest on a remote mountaintop in Tibet, where he sat and shook with shock and revulsion.

Unsure of what to do, Clark returned to Smallville to seek the guidance of his parents. Recalling the legendary mystery-men of the 1940s, Jonathan suggested that his son adopt a separate identity through which he could publicly use his powers. Within a few days, Clark and the Kents had devised his new persona of Superman, taking the name used in newspaper articles to describe the unknown rescuer of the space plane.

Working with Jonathan, Clark developed certain subtle tricks of appearance—using horn-rimmed glasses and changes of voice, posture, and body language—by which he could divert any attention from his resemblance to Superman. The Kents reasoned that if he appeared unmasked as Superman, most people would never even consider that he might spend part of his time as someone else.

Martha had stitched up his first costume on her old sewing machine.

"I made the fit nice and snug," she explained. "When you were a boy —just about twelve, I think—I started noticing that cloth right up close against you never seemed to tear or get dirty. Besides, it shows off your muscles."

Martha was especially proud of her work on the long, flowing cape, designed to emulate the costumed heroes of an earlier era. But as her son put it on, she began to have second thoughts. "Oh, dear. It hangs so nicely, but it's sure to tear . . . not being skintight, I mean."

"Don't worry, Ma. I'll try to be careful with it." Clark's voice seemed to have gone down an octave. Martha and Jonathan were astounded. In the costume, their son seemed to be a whole different person.

"The whole outfit works just fine. It has exactly the symbolic look I wanted." And then, to reassure his mother, Superman bent down and kissed her on the forehead.

.   .   .

Wish I had a picture of that moment, thought Jonathan. *Could've knocked us both over with a feather, I'll bet.* Just the thought brought a smile to his face.

"That boy, Jonathan . . . that boy!" Martha wiped away her last few tears, still marveling over the gift of the watercolor.

Jonathan hugged her to him. "Yeah, we raised us a good one, hon. We surely did."

Barely five hundred miles east of the Kents' Kansas farmhouse, the Creature pulled at his bonds. His massive, hulking body was covered from head to toe by a hooded garment three times as thick as the thickest cowhide and more than fifty times as strong and tough. It muffled his snarls of frustration, reducing them to a low feral murmur.

Thick cables—forged of the strongest metal alloys—encircled his limbs and torso. They ranged from three to twelve centimeters in diameter and were attached to a great metal harness that was somehow bonded to the material of the garment. The harness held him upright and his limbs motionless.

Considerable time had passed since the Creature had awakened, but just how long—days? weeks? months?—he had no way of knowing. He knew that he had not slept since, and that he had spent every moment fighting against the bonds that held him. And now . . . now he felt some of the restraints beginning to weaken. The Creature thrashed all the more wildly, and one of the smaller cables snapped. With a roar of triumph, he pulled even harder, his strength seeming to feed off his rage. With a groan, more cables parted, and the Creature yanked his left arm free of the harness!

He reached out with his free arm. He could touch the wall. In the darkness, he still could not see it, but he knew where it was. And he knew it was hard.

It was, in fact, forged of the same metal as his bonds. The wall was but one of six that formed a vault around the Creature. The walls were eighteen centimeters thick, and above them lay a mile of rock and clay. No one alive was aware of the buried vault . . . no one, save for the Creature inside.

All was quiet and motionless. Then he began beating at the wall.

2

Superman soared high above the sprawl of Queensland Park and headed north, across the river into Metropolis's central borough, the island of New Troy. Separated from the other five boroughs by two rivers and a deep harbor, New Troy was what out-of-towners thought of when you told them you were from Metropolis.

To Superman's left stretched street after street of five- to ten-story buildings, some of them fine old brownstones and apartments with first-floor storefronts. Others were old factory buildings, slowly being retrofitted into condominiums, lofts, and studios, as the last of the small manufacturers continued their exodus to the industrial parks of the outer boroughs and the suburbs. Beyond that, at the northwest part of New Troy, lay the greenery of Centennial Park and the adjacent campus of the University of Metropolis.

Alma mater, we shall not falter . . . Dear old U. Met, we all hail you! The school fight song which had so appalled his literature professor—for attempting to rhyme mater with falter—immediately sprang, unbidden, to Clark Kent's mind. He had earned his bachelor's degree in journalism at U. Met, astounding his faculty advisor by fulfilling all the requirements for the four-year program in just two years. It wasn't that difficult if you could get by on one hour of sleep a night. *Ah, the resiliency of youth,* he thought with a smile. *I could never do that now! These days, if I don't get at least two hours, I'm wasted.*

Off to Superman's right lay Metropolis's central business district, its skyline dominated by the ninety-six-story L-shaped tower that served as the world headquarters of LexCorp International.

Over the past quarter century, LexCorp had grown from a feisty young aerospace engineering firm into one of the world's largest, most diversified multinational corporations. LexCorp was into everything from banking and brewing to robotics and sanitation. Nearly two-thirds of Metropolis's citizens were employed by companies owned—either in whole or in part—by LexCorp.

LexCorp had been named for its vainglorious founder, Lex Luthor. Luthor had generally been considered the most powerful man in Metropolis.

Until Superman came along.

That was the big problem, thought Superman, *wasn't it?* Luthor couldn't stand being second best at anything, and he hated anything he couldn't own or control. Taken together, those two qualities had made Luthor Superman's greatest enemy.

During his first year and a half as Superman, the Man of Steel had been fortunate to avoid contact with the billionaire industrialist. Luthor had left the country to inspect business holdings in South America shortly after Superman's public debut.

At first Luthor had dismissed reports of a superstrong flying man as media hype and exploitation. But in the course of his travels abroad, Luthor had become at first bemused and then intrigued by satellite news stories of Superman's exploits.

Upon his return to Metropolis, Luthor received information that a terrorist cell planned to hijack his yacht, the *Sea Queen,* the next time he took it out of port. Where other men might have felt threatened or outraged, Luthor saw only opportunity and connived to provide an irresistible target for the terrorists. Luthor organized a lavish party aboard the ship, inviting the elite of Metropolis society. He ordered his security team to hold back in case of trouble. His hope was that Superman would show up, and that he could see for himself if all the wild stories he'd heard were true.

The terrorists went for Luthor's bait, just as he'd planned, and Superman indeed intervened. The billionaire was greatly impressed and attempted to hire Superman on the spot, handing him a check for twenty-five thousand dollars. "Consider that a retainer. Everyone who's anyone in Metropolis works for me. And you're far too valuable a resource to leave undirected."

He thought he could buy me. Luthor always treated people as commodities.

But Luthor had gone too far this time. Among the partygoers was Frank Berkowitz, the mayor of Metropolis, and he was outraged that they'd all been placed in jeopardy just to satisfy Luthor's curiosity. "Superman, as mayor I hereby appoint you a special deputy. I want you to arrest that man. The charge is reckless endangerment!"

"Don't be absurd, Frank!" The big, balding man hadn't even tried to hide his contempt. "You can't arrest me. I'm Lex Luthor. I'm the most powerful man in Metropolis."

"No you're not, Lex." Mayor Berkowitz looked at Superman. "Not anymore."

Luthor was photographed and fingerprinted like any common criminal. Despite the fact that he was one of the world's wealthiest men, he was then locked up behind bars. His attorneys immediately sprang into action and arranged his release. All charges were subsequently dropped, but the public humiliation gnawed at Luthor. He again sought out Superman, confronting him privately outside Metro General Hospital.

"You've made a mistake, Superman . . . a big mistake. Metropolis belongs to me. Its people are mine, to nurture or destroy as I see fit. They've just forgotten that. They've looked at you, with your costume and your flashy superhuman powers, and they've forgotten who their real master is. Well, I intend to remind them, Superman. I'm going to show them that you're nothing. I'm going to destroy you, but no one will ever be able to prove me responsible. I'll not be arrested again, Superman . . . not ever again!"

From that day on, Lex Luthor had devoted much of his time and energy, and a considerable amount of his fortune, toward fulfilling his threat. The industrialist even went so far as to outfit an elite LexCorp security team with jet-propelled body armor, forming his so-called Team Luthor in a vain try to overshadow the Man of Steel. Superman survived countless attempts to discredit and kill him, but was never able to prove that Luthor was behind the attacks.

Then Luthor had gotten his hands on a chunk of kryptonite.

Kryptonite was the common ore of kryptonium, an unusually stable transuranic element which had been created in the thermonuclear destruction of Superman's ancestral world of Krypton. The two-pound chunk of glowing ore was the only such specimen on the planet. Ironically, it had come to Earth on the tail section of the same drive vehicle that had brought Krypton's last son to our world. The rock had passed through several hands before it came into Luthor's possession and he discovered that its radiations were deadly to Superman.

Ecstatic over his find, Luthor had a fragment of the kryptonite cut, polished, and set in a signet ring which he wore for many months. He taunted Superman with the ring and used it to keep the last son of Krypton at bay. But the kryptonite was not as harmless to terrestrial life-forms as Luthor's physicists had thought. The ring's radiation slowly poisoned him. His doctor was forced to amputate Luthor's right hand, although even that drastic measure proved in vain. He managed to avoid a slow, wasting death from kryptonite poisoning, however, when his plane crashed in the Andes. Superman himself recovered Luthor's remains, but he could never determine whether the crash had been an accident or if his old enemy had planned it.

I never thought of Luthor as being the kind to take his own life, but you just never know. He was a complicated man, thought Superman. He stared long and hard at the LexCorp Tower but was unable to discern much. The old man had retrofitted the building with a fine mesh of lead that frustrated Superman's X-ray vision and installed elaborate sound baffles to keep him from hearing sounds spoken inside. Still, it was a different world without Lex Luthor around. Without the first Lex Luthor, anyway.

LexCorp had momentarily floundered in the wake of Luthor's death, the value of its stock plummeting on the open market as members of its board of directors vied for power. The corporation was looking like a prime candidate for downsizing and restructuring when Luthor's son arrived to take control.

Accompanied by Sydney Happersen, the elder Luthor's chief aide, Lex Luthor II had taken the city by storm. As his father's only heir, he had access to both a personal fortune and a controlling interest in LexCorp, and he used both to put the recession-strapped Metropolis back to work. Young Lex proved every bit as wily as his father in handling the board of directors, and within days he had himself approved as LexCorp's chief executive officer. It was now generally acknowledged that he had turned the company around. Just twenty-one years old, Lex Luthor II was a genuine wunderkind. Until he had been recognized as both heir and son in Luthor's will, it was claimed, his existence had been kept hidden for his own protection. The boy had apparently been fathered by Luthor with his personal physician, Dr. Gretchen Kelley, and brought up by LexCorp employees in Australia.

A son, raised in secret. Superman shook his head at the thought. *Even now it sounds like something out of a soap opera. But, Lord knows, Luthor had plenty of enemies from whom he might need to protect a son. It was just the sort of Byzantine scheme he and Happersen would concoct.* Superman had personally flown overseas, using both his powers and the contacts he'd made over the years as Clark Kent, to investigate young Luthor's background. All the stories checked out.

When young Lex became aware that there'd been bad blood between Superman and his father, he had gone out of his way to apologize to the Man of Steel. *He seemed utterly sincere, but . . . I don't know. Maybe it's just me, but there's still something about the man that bothers me. He's almost too good.* Superman turned away from downtown, trying to put LexCorp Tower and its young owner out of his mind.

Straight ahead of Superman lay a ten-square-block area known officially as Hob's Bay. Named for Elias Hob, an early Metropolis landowner, it had been a prosperous, middle-class neighborhood at the turn of the century. With the beginning of the Great Depression, it began a slide into poverty and decay from which it never recovered. Now only City Hall and the Chamber of Commerce referred to the neighborhood as Hob's Bay. To the rest of Metropolis, it was Suicide Slum.

Suicide Slum was a hellhole. Its most famous sons and daughters were those who had escaped to a better life. Despite numerous attempts over the years at urban renewal and Superman's best efforts, it remained a venue for X-rated theaters and adult bookstores, for run-down tenements, and for crime-infested streets. Life was cheap in Suicide Slum. On the other hand, so was the rent.

On the edge of Suicide Slum stood a blocky five-story brick building whose single distinguishing characteristic was an oversized satellite dish. The sole tenant of the building's top floor was an eccentric former college professor by the name of Emil Hamilton.

Professor Hamilton was an inventive genius whose unorthodox work habits had resulted in his being fired from a score of commercial research laboratories. Like his boyhood idol Nikola Tesla, Hamilton was able to design circuitry in his head, visualizing it so vividly that he sometimes neglected to commit his preliminary notes to paper. While still a young man, Emil had conceptualized a magnetic field generator that he theorized could provide protection from nuclear attack. He spent much of the next twenty years laboring on his own to develop a working prototype. During that time, he repeatedly tried to interest the Defense Department in his proposed generator but was able to obtain only an occasional small federal grant to continue his work. For the most part, government bureaucrats considered Emil a crank and dismissed his work as impractical. The one man who had seen possibilities in his work was Lex Luthor.

Luthor began funding the professor's work through a dummy corporation with an eye toward eventually discrediting him and claiming full ownership of his device. Under extreme stress from the pressure put on him by Luthor's people, Emil had suffered a nervous breakdown. He became obsessed with proving the effectiveness of his invention, and irrationally set out to test its power against that of Superman. In doing so, Hamilton pushed his prototype device beyond its limits, requiring Superman to use his own invulnerable body to protect the professor from the explosion of the overloaded generator.

Hamilton was remanded to a mental health facility for treatment and counseling. He later served a few months of a sentence in a minimum security prison before being paroled on Superman's recommendation. Upon his release, he managed to secure enough funding to set up a small, independent lab in the old building, where he began to eke out a modest living as a technical consultant. In that capacity, the professor had aided Superman on numerous occasions and had eventually come to serve as the Man of Steel's unofficial science advisor.

The big double windows on the fifth floor swung open, apparently of their own volition, at Superman's approach. *That's new,* he thought, landing silently inside the lab. As the windows began to ratchet closed, he heard the whir of tiny servomotors mounted onto their hinges. Looking more carefully, Superman saw where the new wiring connections passed through the wall into a conduit leading to the roof, and from there to a new array of equipment mounted just under the eaves. A glance at the circuitry within confirmed what he already expected. "Ah-ha! Infrared motion detectors!"

"What about them?" The voice came from beneath a nearby computer console and was immediately followed by the squeaking of wheels. A gray-haired figure emerged from beneath the console astride an old mechanic's dolly, soldering gun in hand. A quizzical look beneath the man's safety glasses quickly brightened. "Superman! How good to see you!"

"And you, Professor!" Superman reached out a hand and pulled the lanky scientist to his feet. "Overhauling the mainframe?"

"Just making a few alterations." Emil ran a hand through his beard, discovering a few flecks of solder.

"I was just admiring your new window opener."

"Like it, do you?" Emil beamed. "I noticed that you usually fly in from that direction when you visit, so I decided to make things a bit easier. I'm glad to see that it worked so well." He winced as a clump of hair came out with the solder from his beard. "I had the devil's own time getting the proper setting for the motion detectors. When I first installed it, it admitted a flock of pigeons to the lab. What a mess!"

"I can imagine!" Superman tried mightily to stifle a laugh but was only marginally successful. If his host noticed, he did not mention it.

"So," asked Emil, "what brings you here?"

"I was wondering if you'd finished analyzing the data we'd compiled on my powers."

"Ah, yes! Your physical! Come right this way!" Emil led his visitor past several cluttered worktables.

"Professor? What the devil is this?" Superman paused before a lathe, upon which was centered a ruby-red translucent tube, six inches in diameter and nearly four feet long.

"Eh? Oh, that. Just a new synthetic I'm experimenting with, as a component for a laser cannon."

"A laser cannon? Who are you working on that for?"

"Oh, nobody. The idea just intrigued me . . ." Emil let that thought trail off. "Watch your footing. I upset a box of ball bearings around here the other day, and I'm afraid I still haven't recovered them all."

Superman shook his head. *Same old Emil. He just can't let an idea pass him by without exploring it.*

The professor came to yet another console. Plopping down into an old swivel chair, he hit a series of switches and pushed his safety glasses up onto his forehead. Graphs began to appear on the monitor screen as Emil's fingers danced across the keyboard.

Superman stared intently at the screen. His "physical," as the professor called it, had been a series of tests they'd put the Man of Steel through over the past few months, in an attempt to determine just how his powers worked.

"Here we go," said Emil, pointing out a series of intersecting lines. "While I've been unable to determine the exact cellular mechanism, there is something about your Kryptonian physiology that stores and channels solar energy."

"We already knew that, Professor. I'm essentially a living solar capacitor. My body's converted all the energy I've absorbed over the years, amplifying my senses, boosting my strength, and so on."

"Exactly! It's the sun that made a Superman of you. Your body holds vast energy reserves, but they're not inexhaustible. See here." An inverted bell curve appeared on the screen. "This represents the twenty-four-hour period during which you towed a disabled Amtrak train through the Rockies, flew several tons of food and medical supplies into Central Africa, repositioned a falling communications satellite, and thwarted a terrorist bombing in Rome, among other things."

"I remember. It wasn't the busiest day I've ever had, but I was kept on my toes."

Hamilton's safety glasses fell back down onto his nose as he gaped at his friend. " 'Kept on your toes?' Egads, you were shot at and blown up! You endured extremes of temperature, radiation, and hard vacuum! You flew nearly a million miles, often at speeds far faster than that of sound, and I've just barely been able to estimate how many ergs you expended!"

Superman shrugged. "I did feel a little weary by the end of that day."

"Well . . . I . . . I should think so!" Emil removed the safety glasses and tucked them into his shirt pocket. The very act of doing so seemed to calm him. "That's the point I was making. The public looks upon you as an indestructible champion, and they're right—up to a point. Certainly, your body is invulnerable to harm from a wide array of weaponry, but there is no such thing as absolute invulnerability. Look at this."

Emil hit a series of keys, and the graph on the monitor was enlarged. "At the end of that day, the readings I took showed a noticeable energy deficit. By that point, you were drawing heavily on your body's energy reserves. If you had continued to exert yourself beyond that point, your strength would have continued to ebb, your senses would have dulled— and, of course, use of your heat vision would have accelerated the process. The greater the expenditure, the weaker you would become. Eventually, the bioelectric aura that accounts for much of your body's invulnerability would begin to break down. That being the case, you could find yourself in mortal danger."

"It wouldn't be the first time, Professor. Twice, I've survived thermo-nuclear explosions in the forty-megaton range."

Emil looked at him thoughtfully. "We must talk more about that."

"Some other time, Professor?" An oddly plaintive tone came to Superman's voice. "Neither experience was very pleasant."

"I'm not surprised. The fact that you lived was miraculous. It must have put a terrible drain on your system."

"I felt . . . awful afterward."

"Yes . . ." Emil made some quick calculations. "Such an ordeal would severely affect your invulnerability. Still, the fact that you suffered no lasting effects is testimony to your body's resiliency." Emil turned back to the monitor. "Looking back at our testing period . . . by this point"—Emil's finger traced the upward curve on the screen— "on the following day, you had already recovered nearly a third of the energy you'd expended."

Superman studied the graph. "Then, according to your readings, within a day and a half I was back to normal? That sounds about right. I remember feeling much more on top of things by the end of that week."

"Really? That is reassuring. My figures are, unfortunately, still the roughest of approximations. When it comes to measuring the limits of your power, I'm afraid my instruments are woefully inadequate." A gleam came to Emil's eyes. "How I'd love to have another opportunity to use the equipment in that wondrous Antarctic Fortress of yours!"

Superman considered that. The Fortress did have a lot to offer. In addition to an array of advanced analysis systems, its vast halls held holographic dioramas commemorating the history of his home planet Krypton, as well as working models of Kryptonian battle suits and robots. The robots, in fact, served to maintain his hideaway. Superman flinched inwardly at the thought of the Fortress as "his." He rarely went there. Intellectually, he saw it as a memorial to the world of his genetic parents. On an emotional level, the place gave him the willies. *Visiting the Fortress,* he thought, *is like walking through a tomb . . . a cold, sterile tomb.*

To be sure, Superman was the last son of Krypton, the sole survivor of that dead world. Had Krypton not exploded, his predetermined birth name would have been Kal-El. But he had not been born on Krypton. He had been born in a Kansas field, when Martha Kent had lifted him from the birthing matrix that had carried him to Earth. It was only in his eighteenth year that the Kents told him they weren't his natural parents. He was over thirty before he knew of his Kryptonian heritage. Since then he had learned much about Krypton—its entire history was locked in his subconscious; however, he still thought of himself—first and foremost— as an Earthman and an American.

To Superman that Fortress of Solitude was like an unwanted inheritance from a distant relative, something to keep buried in the basement. It had been constructed beneath the ice of Antarctica, without his knowledge, by an ancient artifact called the Eradicator.

The Eradicator had been created millennia ago by one of his Kryptonian ancestors. It had been passed on to Superman by a dying alien cleric, who'd recognized him as Krypton's last son. Its possession had been an endless nightmare for the Man of Steel. The Eradicator had proven to possess an artificial intelligence, programmed to preserve all things Kryptonian. To that end, it had manipulated Superman's mind, submerging his emotions to remake him in the image of what its programming had come to consider the perfect Kryptonian. Superman had finally overcome the Eradicator's influence, smashing the infernal device and hurling it into the sun.

But that had been a mistake.

Although the Eradicator's physical substance was destroyed by the intense solar heat, its intelligence had somehow managed to survive. Slowly, this independent "mind" had managed to tap into the thermonuclear reactions of the sun's core, using that immense energy source to re-create itself as a humanoid entity. This new Eradicator, possessing incredible solar energies, had returned to Earth, determined to transform the planet into a second Krypton. When Superman had tried to stop the Eradicator, it had nearly killed him. Superman had just barely managed to survive, pulling himself together enough to confront the Eradicator deep within the Antarctic Fortress. There, with the aid of Professor Hamilton, the entity had finally been defeated, its intelligence dissipated and its energies dispersed.

Superman looked at Professor Hamilton. The Eradicator had put Emil through hell while he was in the Fortress, but he'd come through all that without any lasting trauma. Typically, what was foremost in the scientist's mind was the vivid memory of the Fortress's Kryptonian technology.

"The things I could learn down there . . ." Emil's voice trailed off dreamily.

Superman suppressed a smile. "Maybe we can arrange that, Professor."

"Emil? Where are you?" A new voice echoed off the brick walls.

"Over here, Mildred. We're just past the lathe! Watch your step—!"

The last warning came too late. Mildred Fillmore stepped onto an errant ball bearing, and her feet flew out from under her. Like a shot, Superman was across the room, catching the woman and sparing her a painful landing.

Mildred gaped at her rescuer as he set her back down on firmer footing. "Th-thank you." She'd heard the professor mention working with Superman once or twice—and she'd of course seen the Man of Steel flying over the city—but she'd never expected to see him in person. *I didn't realize he was so . . . tall.*

"Mildred! Mildred, are you all right?" Emil came dashing forward, almost tripping over his own feet in the process.

"Fine . . . I'm fine, Emil. Just a bit startled, that's all." She straightened her waitress's cap and tried to compose herself. "When you didn't show up at the diner at your usual time, I figured you were working on something, so I brought you some breakfast."

"Really?" Emil rummaged through the bag she offered. "Coffee black . . . large grapefruit juice . . . head cheese and liverwurst on pumpernickel with mustard and extra onions . . . and a giant kosher dill! Mildred, you shouldn't have!"

"I know. Still, you always seem to survive."

"Survive?!" Emil looked mildly offended. "A man can thrive on such a repast!"

Mildred smiled gently as Emil eagerly took a big bite of the sandwich. She gave Superman a wry look and shook her head. "I don't know how he can stand that stuff, especially at this hour of the morning!"

"And I thought *I* had a cast-iron stomach." Superman chuckled. He glanced at a clock on the wall. *Eight-oh-five . . . it's getting late!* "Well, Professor, I have to be moving on."

"Mmmph . . . oh, yes," mumbled Emil. He swallowed his mouthful with a contented sigh. "Could you excuse us just a moment, Mildred?"

"Of course."

Emil casually switched off the computer screen and accompanied Superman back across the lab. The big windows opened automatically at their approach. The Man of Steel grinned appreciatively as he clapped Hamilton on the shoulder.

"Thanks for all your time and effort, Professor."

"My pleasure, Superman. I am so indebted to you. If not for your support, I would no doubt still be behind bars. I am honored by the confidence you have in me."

"You've returned the favor a hundredfold. I know I can trust you to keep your findings secret."

Emil made a zippering motion across his lips. "Mum's the word!"

With a nod and a wink, Superman leapt out into the skies. As the windows ratcheted shut behind him, he could hear the professor turn and walk back across the lab to his visitor.

"Sorry for the interruption, Mildred. What do I owe you for breakfast?"

"Consider it on the house, Emil."

"That's very kind, but . . . are you certain I can't give you anything in return?"

"Well . . . you could take me dancing again."

Superman immediately focused his senses in a different direction. *Better watch that eavesdropping, Kent.* He did his best to respect other people's privacy, but it wasn't always easy for someone who could see and hear as well as he.

Superman was glad to see that Mildred had taken an interest in Emil. And if he knew anything at all about human nature, the professor was interested in her, in his own way. *Well, good. Everyone needs a little love in their life.* Superman banked sharply to the west, picking up speed. *And if I don't step on it, I'll miss meeting the love of MY life!*

3

"US Air 793, service from Ottawa, has arrived at gate twenty-three."

Lois Lane walked up the jetway, carry-on bag in hand. It sometimes seemed to her that she spent most of her life in airports. *That's what happens when you're born into the military,* she thought ruefully. Her father had been transferred to base after base on the road to promotion, and the family had dutifully followed. Before she was twelve, Lois had lived on three different continents. Captain Sam Lane had clearly enjoyed the constant change of scenery during the years when his daughters were growing up; the family had adapted as best they could. To this day, Lois's mother, Ella, had boxes that she had never unpacked. Lois's sister, Lucy, seemed unable to stay in any one place for long and had found work as an airline flight attendant. And Lois herself had become a reporter, her job often taking her across the country or out of it.

It wasn't until the girls were grown and out on their own that Sam surprised everyone by opting for early retirement and settling in Metropolis. *For Mom's sake, I'm glad he did,* Lois reflected. *Things are finally a little easier for her. But it figures that the Captain would turn into a homebody after teaching his daughters to be vagabonds.*

That wasn't all he'd taught them. Complications with Lucy's birth had prevented Ella from having any more children, and Sam had never bothered to hide his disappointment.

"All my life I've wanted a boy . . . a son to carry on my name. Your mother has let me down twice, but I'll make do."

The memory of her father's words still stung Lois. *You "made do" all right, Dad.* The Captain had drilled her and Lucy in hand-to-hand combat, and even put them through a course in survival training. *You were determined to make us as tough as any boy.* Lois grinned wryly. *The problem was, you did too good a job.* During her last year of high school, Lois had stood up to her father, told him off, and moved out. It was years before they even spoke to each other again.

"Pardon me, ma'am . . ." Lois was suddenly aware of a tall figure behind her. " . . . but 'would you believe in a love at first sight'?"

She turned and smiled at a square-jawed man in a double-breasted suit. " 'Yes I'm certain that it happens all the time.' Lennon and McCartney, 1967."

"Mostly Paul, y'know," he lapsed into a Liverpool accent, "though I think I read where John helped out with a lyric here or there."

Lois tried unsuccessfully to choke back her laughter. "Clark Kent, you're terrible!"

"I am?" He assumed a look of mock dismay. "And here I thought my accent was pretty good."

"Oh, it's spot-on. No, I meant your using an old Beatles song to pick up strange women in airports!"

"Correction—one particular strange woman!" He bent down, and their lips met.

"Mmm, I stand corrected. You're a great kisser, you know that?"

"So you say. I guess I can trust your judgment."

"You'd better!" she teased. "After all, I did say that I'd marry you." Lois slipped her arm through his and they headed for the main terminal.

"So, how was your interview with the prime minister?"

"It went great. Honestly, Clark, she is so funny. I just wish we could print some of the stories she told me off the record."

"Do you have any pressing need to get back to the office?"

"No, I already faxed in the interview."

"Any baggage to claim?"

She shook her head. "Just this carry-on. Why? What do you have in mind?"

"Well, I faxed my story in earlier, too. So, I thought we could get some breakfast, and you could tell me all about your Canadian adventure."

"You're on, Clark! Come on, my car's in the short-term lot."

The glass double doors of the terminal hissed open, and they were greeted by sunny skies, a warm breeze, and the whine of jet engines. As they waited for traffic to clear the crosswalk, Lois traced the contour of Clark's bicep with the tip of her finger.

He beamed down at her. "Remember the first time I picked you up at this airport?"

"Remember? That's something I'll never forget . . ."

Lois had been working full-time for the *Daily Planet* barely five years, but she'd already made quite a name for herself as an investigative reporter. The power and prestige of the *Planet* had given her work national exposure and led to her being chosen as a civilian crew member for the maiden flight of NASA's experimental space plane, the *Constitution.*

The launch went off on schedule without a hitch, and Lois had made history as the first journalist ever to file her stories from out in space. Her daily reports on the flight of the space plane saw print in newspapers throughout the world, inspiring interest in space the likes of which hadn't been seen since the days of the first Apollo mission to the moon. As a result of all the public attention, an enormous crowd, numbering in the hundreds of thousands, had turned out to see the *Constitution* land at Metropolis International Airport.

The unusual landing site had been agreed upon thanks to a serendipitous joining of forces. NASA wanted a landing at a civilian airport to maximize publicity and display the commercial potential of its space plane project. The city's movers and shakers had wanted a big event to cap off a series of celebrations of the 250th anniversary of the founding of Metropolis. And the presence of a *Daily Planet* reporter in the flight crew had sealed the deal.

Even with all the hassles involved in rescheduling the scores of commercial flights to provide ready clearance, everything had gone like clockwork. It looked as though the *Constitution* would complete her maiden flight in picture-perfect style.

But then suddenly, despite all precautions, a small civilian jet aircraft somehow slipped into the restricted airspace, though whether by accident or by design was never determined. The small plane slammed into the *Constitution*'s tail section, metal locking onto metal. For one surreal moment, the two ships seemed to hang motionless in the air. And then, fused together, they tumbled Earthward.

Aboard the space plane, Colonel Howard Morrow let out a string of curses as he fought for control of his ship. Two seats back, Lois wondered if she would live to file another story, and the plane went into a spin. *It's like being inside a clothes dryer,* she thought numbly, *just cooler.*

Up front, the white-haired Morrow felt his stomach clench. "This thing is going to hit just like a brick."

But then, inexplicably, the spinning ceased.

"We're leveling off . . . we're slowing down!" Morrow turned to his copilot. "Callahan, did you—?"

Major Adam Callahan shook his head. "Not me, boss. We're still dead stick and power down. I don't know what's going on."

"I . . . I do." Lieutenant Anne West, the ship's navigator, looked up from her monitor station, her eyes wide. "I've got it on our belly camera, but I don't believe it for a minute."

Lois looked at the video display. There was someone under the *Constitution*. And he looked as though he was holding the ship aloft!

"It can't be! A flying man?!"

"Don't argue with it!" barked Morrow. "He's saved us! Start cranking . . . we've got to get the landing gear down."

The instant they were down and had come to a halt, Lois was out of her seat and headed for the forward hatch. She knew that she'd found the kind of story that reporters dreamed of. That man was news—the story of the decade, maybe of the century—and she wasn't about to let him get away. Scrambling from the space plane, she spotted the tall stranger as he emerged from under the fuselage.

Lois put all the authority she could muster into a shout. "Hold it right there, buster!"

It worked. The young man froze in his tracks. Lois dashed up to him, and then a strange thing happened. Their eyes met, and the brash young auburn-haired reporter found herself speechless.

Thus far in her career, Lois Lane had already interviewed three heads of state and a number of Nobel Prize winners. Moreover, she'd just returned from a three-day flight on the edge of space. She was not easily impressed. But . . . there was something about this man.

It wasn't just that he was tall and handsome, which admittedly he was. Lois stood five foot six, and the stranger towered over her a good head taller. Six-two at the least, she thought. His eyes were a deeper blue than any she'd ever seen. And his hair was very dark, with an errant lock that boyishly curled down across his forehead, almost forming the letter S.

No, aside from his striking appearance—even aside from the astounding fact that he'd flown through the air and saved their lives—there was something very different about this man. There was nothing distinguishing about his clothing. He was dressed quite simply in slacks and a jacket. Yet he had a presence about him.

Lois opened her mouth but found that she still couldn't speak. The stranger appeared to be similarly affected. They stood just inches apart, staring at each other for what seemed like hours.

Gradually, Lois became aware of a distant roar which grew in volume and intensity. The roar suddenly turned into voices . . . cheering, shouting, screaming voices. Across the runways streamed hundreds of people who had broken through a chain link fence and overwhelmed the security barricades. Before Lois could gather her wits, the crowd surged around her, separating her from the handsome stranger. A look of panic flashed across his face, and he leapt straight up into the air . . . and kept going.

Stunned silent by the flying man's sudden departure, the mob fell back and began to disperse. In the confusion, Lois made her way nearly unnoticed to a pay phone and called through to the *Planet's* city desk.

"Morrie? This is Lois."

"Lois? What's goin' on? The TV just showed—"

"Don't say another word. Just take this down." She paused to collect herself. "The crew of the *Constitution*, NASA's experimental space plane, was saved from certain death this afternoon by a mysterious flying . . . Superman."

Within minutes, the story went out over the wire, and newspeople across the country seized upon the name Lois had given her rescuer. To the media, he became Superman, and neither his life nor hers would ever be the same again.

It was just three days later that Superman reappeared in the skies over Metropolis, and this time he was not trying to escape notice. Wearing the red, yellow, and blue costume that would become his trademark, he seemed to be everywhere. He was the one who swooped from the heavens to stop the purse thief, pull people from the burning building, or prevent a terrorist bombing.

And for that first week, Lois Lane found herself one step behind him. No matter how quickly she moved, Superman was always gone by the time she arrived at the scene of the crime or the rescue.

"Fine thing," she groused. "Everyone's using the name I gave the guy, and I can't find out the first thing about him! I've chased him all over Metropolis, and all I have to show for my trouble is sore feet."

Determined to interview Superman, Lois finally devised a phony emergency to attract his attention. Taking the precaution of stashing a scuba tank under her front seat, she actually drove her car off a city pier and into the river. As she'd hoped, Superman responded to her "danger," fishing her and the car from the waters.

In costume, Superman cut an even more striking figure, the tight fit of the garment accentuating every ripple of muscle as he opened the car door. *Not just tall*, thought Lois, *he's BIG*.

"Are you all right, Ms. Lane?" His voice was a deep baritone.

"A . . . a bit waterlogged, but otherwise fine . . . thanks to you!"

"Don't mention it." His mouth widened into a smile that actors would kill for. Every tooth was perfect. "It'd probably be wise if you got into some dry clothes as soon as you could. Here, let me fly you home."

In a matter of moments, Lois found herself whisked through the air to her midtown apartment.

"You . . . know where I live?"

"Of course, Ms. Lane. I know where everyone lives."

Everything was happening so fast, but this time Lois kept her wits about her. She asked her rescuer to wait and rushed to make herself more presentable. As Lois threw on dry clothes, she fought back a giddiness she hadn't felt since she was a girl. *Let's keep this professional, Lois. That's the story of the century sitting out there in your living room.* She started to reach for the hair dryer, then stopped and wrapped a towel around her hair. *Mustn't keep him waiting.* Taking a deep breath, Lois returned to find her visitor scratching her young cat, Elroy, behind the ears. *He likes cats. That's a good sign,* she thought and promptly shifted into reporter mode.

Superman was not a difficult interview, but neither was he very forthcoming. Lois was able to pin him down on the specifics of his amazing powers but not much else.

"Okay, you can obviously fly . . . you're very strong and very fast . . . you can see through anything . . . and you can produce some kind of heat-ray zap with your eyes."

"Yes. But as I've already said, Ms. Lane, I don't think knowing all this will be of much use to you."

"You're too modest. You happen to be the story of the century, Mr. . . . Mr. . . . just what should we call you?"

"I think the name you gave me is quite appropriate, Ms. Lane."

"Superman?" *So, he won't admit to any other name?* "All right, Superman it is. Now, is there any way I can get you to call me 'Lois'?"

"I'd be delighted . . . Lois."

"Thank you." *Now maybe there's a chance I can pry more details out of you.* "Just where are you from, Superman? Are you a Metropolis native, or are you from out of town?"

"Out of town. To be honest, I don't know exactly where I'm from originally. I guess it doesn't really matter. Let's just say I'm an American."

Try as she might, Lois couldn't get him to talk about his private life. He remained in complete control of the interview, even in bringing it to a close.

"There's nothing more I can tell you, Lois. And as I said, what I have told you isn't going to be of much use." He rose to his feet. "So I'll say good-bye for now." He crossed the room, covering the distance to the balcony with an even, effortless stride. There, he paused for a moment and looked back, shooting her a wry grin. "Just out of curiosity, Lois . . . do you always drive around with a scuba tank under your front seat?"

"I never could keep anything a secret from you."

"What was that, Lois?" Clark's clear, even tenor was a marked contrast to the deeper voice he used as Superman.

"Nothing." She unlocked the passenger door for him and walked around to the driver's side of her car. "Just thinking out loud."

"You think wrong, kemo sabe! In all the time I've known you, you've kept plenty of secrets. In fact, you continue to surprise me!"

"Good!" Lois tossed her carry-on bag into his lap. "You kept me in the dark about so many things for so long, it's only fair that I occasionally return the favor."

"Now, Lois, we've been over this before. I couldn't very well tell you that I led a double life . . . not during that first little . . . discussion."

"Interview!" Lois could feel her face growing hot. "It was an interview, not a discussion! It would have been the story of the century if it'd ever seen print!"

"Honey . . . I told you when we talked that it wouldn't be of much use."

"You didn't tell me that you'd already written up the story yourself!"

"I know. Looking back, I should have said that I'd already talked to another reporter. Except I wasn't officially a reporter at that point. That story got me my job at the *Planet*." Clark put a hand on her shoulder. He was relieved that she didn't pull away. "I never meant to steal your glory. Don't be angry with me."

"I'm not. I'm just . . . well, yes—I guess I still am." She stopped just short of turning the key in the ignition. *No good sense in driving while I'm mad. That's how accidents happen.* She turned in her seat to face him. "Two hours! Two hours I spent at the keyboard, whipping that story into shape. And it was good—Pulitzer material for certain!"

"I believe it. You were a better reporter than I was—!"

"And still am!"

Clark let the challenge slide. "But ask yourself this. If our positions had been reversed, what would you have done?"

Lois looked down at the wheel. It was a question she'd put to herself many times, even before she'd learned his secret. "Probably the same thing." Her voice was barely a whisper.

"Uh, what was that, Lois? Did you say something?"

"You heard me, Mr. Super-hearing!" She playfully elbowed him in the ribs and instantly felt an electric tingle shoot up her arm. "Ow!"

"Honey, are you all right?"

"No! I hit my funny bone on you!" Lois gingerly rubbed her arm. "Might as well have tried to elbow a brick wall!"

"Here, let me." Clark moved closer, gently rubbing her elbow and applying pressure to certain nerves.

"Oh, that's good!" The pins and needles feeling faded. "You're very good at that."

"My back rubs aren't bad, either. They're almost as good as yours."

She looked into his eyes. His glasses had a dulling effect, muting the color of his irises so that they looked more gray than blue.

"I love you, Lois."

"And I love you." She sighed. "That's why it's so infuriating! If you hadn't scooped me with the Superman story, we might not have become such rivals. And then we might have gotten together a lot sooner."

"Maybe . . . maybe not." He planted a little kiss on the tip of her nose. "Things might have been different, but there's no way of knowing for certain that they'd have been better." He kissed her right cheek. "As it was, there was competition between us, sure, but we also got to work alongside each other . . ." He kissed her left cheek. ". . . got to know each other better . . . and fell in love."

Clark gazed into her eyes. "Besides, anticipation makes the heart grow fonder."

"I thought that was 'absence.' "

"No, absence just makes it sadder."

Their lips met, and no further words were exchanged.

4

Days passed, but they might as well have been minutes to the imprisoned Creature. As he flailed away at the wall of the vault that held him, he seemed neither to weaken nor to tire. Again and again he struck at his prison wall. And with each strike, the heavy gauntlet that encased his free hand gradually began to shred and fall apart.

Bony spurs, protruding from the huge knuckles of the Creature, began to emerge from the tattered glove. With each succeeding impact, the spurs scored deeper grooves into the thick metal wall. Although ever so slightly, the metal began to deform under the assault of his ceaseless pounding. Trailing strands of cable whipped about like maddened snakes as the Creature continued, his huge arm working like a trip-hammer.

And then, finally, the tips of his bony knuckles pierced the wall. Four tiny little points, none bigger than the tip of a finely sharpened pencil, broke through solid alloy.

A satisfied growl rumbled beneath his hood, and the Creature redoubled his efforts.

Northwest of Metropolis, far beneath the surface of Mount Curtiss, another heavily fortified structure lay buried, far bigger than the vault that held the Creature. This structure was a sprawling underground complex of research laboratories and test facilities of the federal government's top-secret Cadmus Project.

On this particular morning, Project Security Chief Jim Harper was, as usual, in the middle of his calisthenics. Every day without fail, Harper started out with five minutes of stretching and thirty minutes of sit-ups, push-ups, pull-ups, and jumping jacks, followed by another thirty minutes of working out with weights. The other men and women on his staff might use the more high-tech workout equipment, but Jim preferred the old standbys. He'd first begun his daily regimen over fifty years ago, while working with the Metropolis Police Department. The regimen had stood the test of time. *Better than I have,* thought Harper. Though he prided himself on staying fit, time and circumstances had eventually taken their toll. *I'd be long dead, if not for the boys.*

The boys . . . Harper set down his hundred-pound weights and walked across the room to where an old framed photograph sat on his desk. The photo was yellowing around the edges, but it still brought a smile to his face. There he was in his old police uniform with four boys clustered around him. They were grown men now, each one of them near the top of his chosen field, but in Jim's heart of hearts they'd always be his boys. *We've all come a long way from Suicide Slum. Hard to believe that it's been so long.*

Over half a century ago, Jim Harper had been a young rookie cop, newly assigned to the precinct that encompassed Suicide Slum. Then, as now, it was the toughest neighborhood in Metropolis. That point was driven home one day when, after going off duty, Jim was beaten by a band of hoodlums who had lain in wait for him. Satisfied that they'd taught the rookie a lesson, his attackers left him lying bruised and battered in an alley. But Jim Harper was a stronger, far tougher man than they'd realized. His clothing in tatters, he pulled himself to his feet and lurched down the darkened street after the hoodlums. Leaning against the threshold of a local costume shop to catch his breath, he was surprised when the door, left unlocked by a careless cashier, swung open. Harper's eyes settled on a prominently displayed crash helmet. Seized by a sudden inspiration, he cobbled together a mystery-man outfit complete with gloves, boots, and mask. Easing the helmet onto his aching head, he topped off the look with an ornamental metal shield that he found hanging on the wall. Leaving behind cash to cover his late-night purchase, the disguised Harper secured the storefront and ran off in pursuit of his attackers.

He found them in a neighborhood pool hall. With the protection of his helmet and shield, and the advantage of surprise, Harper made fast work of the hoodlums. Checking their wallets for identification, the masked man discovered thick wads of cash, bearing serial numbers identical to the numbers on the money paid in the ransom of a recent kidnapping. As he tied up the groggy thugs, one of them stared at him in disbelief.

"Who *are* you?"

"Why, I'm . . ." Harper hesitated. The question surprised him. The mask worked better than he'd thought; they really hadn't recognized him. "I'm . . . sort of a . . . *guardian*, I guess. Yes, that's it. I guard society from the likes of you!"

And then, as the wailing sirens of approaching patrol cars grew louder, the Guardian slipped away into the night.

The next day, back in his normal uniform and back on duty patrolling the streets, Harper was still mulling over his Lone Ranger–like adventure of the night before. He could almost have dismissed it as a dream or perhaps an hallucination if not for the costume he'd hidden in the back of his closet.

"Hooligans! Thieves! Stop them!" The angry cry roused Patrolman Harper from his reverie. He bolted down the sidewalk and ran right into four young street urchins who were in the act of fleeing a hardware store with stolen goods.

The four were a motley crew of orphans who had banded together to live on their own, in defiance of continued attempts by authorities to find them foster homes. The boys—the soft-spoken, athletic Tommy, talkative Gabby, short and feisty Scrapper, and tall, thin Big Words, the thinker of the group—tried to make ends meet by hawking newspapers on the corner and occasionally supplementing their income with petty theft.

When Harper brought the boys before Judge Charles Benjamin Collins, the jurist was not happy to see them. "According to past records, you boys have stolen radiator caps, tires, and other goods. And now this!" Collins paused to remove his pince-nez glasses and rub the bridge of his nose. "I have no recourse but to find you guilty. These crimes brand you as potential enemies of society. As you have no families, it is my sad duty to commit you to the State Institution for Boys, where you will remain until you reach the age of twenty-one."

"W-w-what?" stammered Big Words. "Institution—? Imprisonment—?"

"Till we're twenty-one?!" Tommy couldn't believe it.

"You can't do that to us!" yowled Scrapper.

Gabby strained to hold him back. "Holy geez, Scrap, don't go startin' nothin' now. We're in enough trouble as it is!"

"Your Honor?" Harper stepped forward. "I'd like to say a few good words on behalf of these boys."

"We don't need your help, copper!"

"Scrapper! Geez!"

Judge Collins gaveled for silence. "Well, Patrolman?"

"I know these boys, Judge Collins. Just about everyone in Hob's Bay does. They're basically good boys. They've had to fight and steal their way through life to avoid starving. If you send them to that reform school, they'll associate with tougher, more hardened offenders . . . and become more hardened themselves. I wish you'd reconsider your decision."

The judge gave Harper a quizzical look. "I take it that you have another plan to help these boys, Patrolman?"

"Yes, Your Honor." Jim Harper looked at the boys. He'd been an orphan himself, not so different from them. Jim knew that he might just as easily have grown up to be a criminal as a cop, if not for a few good breaks. Now he saw a way to pass those breaks along to a new generation. Harper looked back at the judge. "I ask that you release the boys into my custody. Give me a chance to prove that they can become useful, productive citizens."

Judge Collins stroked his mustache. So many officers who appeared before him were hardened and cynical about life in Suicide Slum. The judge was frankly astounded by the young patrolman's plea. Here was obviously an idealist! "I'd like to see you in my chambers, young man."

Alone with the judge in his paneled office, Harper again made his case.

"Do you know what you're asking, Harper? Do you realize the responsibilities involved?"

"Yes, sir."

"All right, your point about the State Institution is well-taken. It probably breeds more young criminals than it reforms, and it's horribly overcrowded. And, at this point, so are the orphanages." The judge studied the young rookie. "Normally, policy prohibits assigning the guardianship of a child to any single man or woman who is not a blood relative, but our state law does allow me a certain amount of leeway. Still, all *four* of them—?"

"They're all the family they know, sir. Breaking them up would be a mistake."

"A mistake is probably what I'm about to make, but . . . all right, Harper. They're yours for now. But I don't ever want to see them in my court again! Is that clear?"

"Absolutely, Your Honor."

In the years that followed, Jim Harper saw to it that his ragtag "Newsboy Legion," as he came to call them, stuck to the straight and narrow. Often, he used his other identity as the Guardian to help them out of rough spots. They eventually caught on to his double life, but they'd never betrayed Harper to another living soul. In time, the boys grew up and moved out of the old neighborhood, and the patrolman put his Guardian outfit away.

Harper had done a good job in helping his boys turn their lives around. Big Words graduated from the University of Metropolis to become Dr. Anthony Rodrigues and gained fame for his expertise in quantum mechanics. Scrapper dropped his street name long before he became the much-sought-after engineer Patrick MacGuire. John "Gabby" Gabrielli's talent for public speaking contributed to his success in the business world. And Dr. Tommy Tompkins's research in genetics led to the creation of the Cadmus Project, which had ultimately brought them all together again.

Along with the renowned geneticist Reginald Augustine and his eccentric colleague Dabney Donovan, Dr. Tompkins had founded the Cadmus Project after decades of independent research. The idea of the founders was to launch a study of DNA and the human genetic code with the same degree of intensity and support that the Manhattan Project had garnered during the Second World War. When, after years of lobbying, they finally got government funding, Tompkins called upon his three boyhood friends for assistance in making the Project work.

It was Pat MacGuire who remembered an old, abandoned aqueduct, stretching from far beneath the streets of Metropolis to distant Mount Curtiss, and developed the underground site plan for what became the Cadmus Project. Tompkins and his friends became so involved in the design and construction of Cadmus that they all stayed on the job, eventually becoming high-ranking department heads within the Project.

Years after the four friends got the Cadmus Project up and running, they received word that their old mentor, Jim Harper, was dying. Pulling every string available to them, they had Harper brought into the Project. Utilizing still-experimental processes developed by Cadmus's amazing genetics laboratories, they cloned him a powerful new body, literally giving him a new lease on life.

Jim picked up his weights and continued with his reps. *Not bad for an old man,* he thought. It felt good to be strong and vital again. And, of course, after all the boys had done for him, he could hardly turn down their offer to head the Project's Security Team.

As it turned out, there'd been considerable problems brought about by some controversial experiments started by Dabney Donovan. Before his death, the eccentric geneticist caused a major scandal, which the department heads were still trying to put behind them. They'd desperately needed their old mentor's help in getting the Cadmus Project back on the up and up.

Harper shook his head and chuckled to himself. *One way or another, I always wind up playing the Guardian.*

. . .

In a plush penthouse apartment on the ninetieth floor of the LexCorp Tower, Lex Luthor II tossed and turned in his sleep, dreaming.

In his dream, Lex was running for his life. Something was chasing him down a long series of twisting corridors. His chest burned from the effort, and every muscle ached. Why . . . do I feel . . . so tired . . . so old? Even his thoughts were labored. An old familiar pain seized him, and he looked down to see an ugly prosthetic hand clamped to the end of his right arm. My hand! No! He stopped and pulled at the metal hand. It came away, revealing the reddened, irritated skin of the stub of his arm. It was a fat, flabby arm.

The wall suddenly became a mirror, and Luthor screamed. The man who stared out at him was old and fat and bald. Behind him the shadows laughed.

"You shouldn't run so hard, Lex. You're not a young man anymore."

"Who is it? Who's there?" Luthor's voice was a tortured wheeze.

"Don't you recognize me, Lex? I'm disappointed." A gaunt and gangly figure shambled forward, a soiled and tattered lab coat flapping about his ankles. A week's growth of beard crawled along his jaw, and a disreputable brush of a mustache grew beneath his hook of a nose. Above, a scraggly wisp of hair was all that was left of the widow's peak that had once topped his forehead. His eyes were all but hidden behind the thick lenses of gogglelike glasses.

Luthor swallowed hard. "Dabney Donovan. I don't believe it."

Donovan laughed. "Is that any way to greet the man who made you what you are?"

"But you're dead, I killed you!"

"You killed one of my clones, Luthor. You see, I trusted you even less than you trusted me."

"You bastard, what have you done to me?" Luthor grabbed Donovan by the lapel of his lab coat and shook him.

Donovan's mouth gaped wide in a grotesque smile, and then his jaw fell loose from his head and clattered across the floor. Luthor let go of the lapel and jumped back as Donovan's body fell apart, collapsing into a bleeding, oozing heap.

"Oh, my God!"

"God had nothing to do with it!"

Lex whirled around. There was another Donovan right behind him.

"Genetic engineering, Lex. If you know the right molecules to tweak on the chromosomal matrix, you can create anything. You don't need to rely upon any deity."

Donovan's breath smelled like rotting meat. Luthor tried to turn away but found himself back against a wall.

"That's how we saved your miserable life, after all!" Donovan poked a bony finger against his chest. "First, we faked your death by letting your body-double die in the plane crash. Then, while the world was mourning the passing of the great Lex Luthor, we got you on the table and scraped away all the tainted tissue."

Donovan took a step back and began fishing around in his coat pocket. "Now, where did I put that—? Ah, here it is!" He pulled what looked like a television remote control from the pocket and flipped a switch. In response, an image appeared in midair . . . a ghastly image of a brain and two staring eyes floating in a chemical bath within a huge glass retort. Donovan assumed a professorial demeanor.

"There wasn't much left of you by the time we got through, Lex. Just a brain, a bit of the spinal column, and two eyes . . . and they were slightly astigmatic! Ah, but we fixed all that. There was more than enough DNA to play with. With the proper manipulation, it took us only a few months to make a new man of you . . . stronger, taller, younger . . . we even did something about that annoying pattern baldness." Donovan ran a hand through his own thinning mop. "Must remember to do something about that myself."

"Then what went wrong?" Luthor demanded. "What's happened to me? Why am I old again?"

"You were young only in body." A new voice echoed from down the corridor, drawing nearer. "Inside, you were still the same old Luthor. You might have convinced the rest of the world that you were your own son, but you couldn't fool me . . . not for long."

From out of the shadows came a tall, powerful figure that Luthor knew all too well.

"Superman!"

"Yes, Lex, and I have something for you." From beneath the folds of his cape, Superman produced a heavy lead canister.

"What's that?"

"Oh, I think you know what it is, Lex."

"Keep away from me!"

"Why, Lex, I want only to give you a hand!" He opened the end of the canister with a twist, revealing a withered human hand. It was Luthor's hand. On one finger was the ring with its dimly glowing kryptonite gem . . . the ring that had nearly cost him his life!

"This is what you want, isn't it?"

"No . . . no . . ."

"Take it, Lex. Take it!"

The hand flew from the canister, grabbed Luthor by the throat, and began to squeeze.

"No! NOOOOO!!!"

Lex awoke with a start, clutching at his throat. His heart racing, he raised a good right hand to his head. The neatly cropped beard, the long, flowing mane of hair was still there. He hit a switch on the nightstand and a soft diffused light illuminated the far corner of the room. He arose from his bed and walked toward the light, regarding his reflection in the window. A rugged young man with broad shoulders and a tight, firm gut looked back at him. He breathed a sigh of relief.

"Lex?" A body stirred behind him. "What is it? What's wrong?"

"Nothing, love. Just had m'self a bit of a nightmare 'sall."

A lithe, athletic young woman emerged from beneath the covers and padded across the room to join him at the window. Her long blond hair fell across his chest as she snuggled close to him.

"Why, I can feel your heart pounding. That must have been a real horror."

"Wasn't any fun, to be sure. I . . . I dreamt that I'd lost m'hand . . . like m'father had."

"Oh! How awful!" She kissed his hand and gently caressed it. "What do you think could have caused such a terrible dream?"

Lex shrugged. "I think about Father all the time." That was no lie. "Guess m'mind just jumbled things up, and made me imagine what it must've been like . . . to be in his shoes. Nothing to really worry about."

Except for Dabney Donovan, thought Luthor. *The one I killed did turn out to be a clone . . . that much of the dream was true. He's the only one outside of Kelley and Happersen who knows my secret.* Gretchen Kelley had been his personal physician for years and had been willing—however reluctantly—to play the part of his mother. In her own way, she loved Luthor, and he knew that he could trust her with his life. Syd Happersen was a valued aide who had been with him since LexCorp's founding. Happersen couldn't betray Luthor without exposing his own part in a number of capital crimes. Only Donovan was a potential danger to him . . . *He's the only one beyond my control.*

"Are you sure it's nothing?" The young woman's face was a picture of concern.

"Would I lie to you, love?"

"No, of course not." She smiled. "Come on, let's go back to bed."

They slipped back under the covers and she cuddled close to him, softly crooning in his ear.

"Mmm, lovely tune." He stifled a yawn and looked at the clock: 3:47. " 'S the hour, love, not the comp'ny."

"Shhh, that's all right. You need your sleep." She kissed him, more affectionately than passionately. "Sweeter dreams, Lex."

"An' to you . . . m'darlin' . . . Supergirl."

Within moments, Lex Luthor was once again fast asleep. It was, he had once told her, a talent he had inherited from his father. For nearly half an hour she watched as his chest slowly rose and fell and his eyelids twitched rapidly through REM sleep and beyond. Then, satisfied that his nightmares had passed, Supergirl silently arose, floating free of the covers and gliding across the room. She stopped at the door, looking back once more at her slumbering lover before slipping out into the hall. There she glanced down at her clinging nightgown. *Can't go out like this,* she thought, as the cloth began to flow about her, changing in both form and color. In an instant, she stood attired in a bright red skirt with matching cape and boots—layered over a royal-blue leotard. Across her chest stretched a red and yellow pentagonal shield, forming a familiar stylized letter S. She paused but a moment to check her reflection in the window at the end of the dimly lit hall before leaping from a nearby window and flying out over the city of Metropolis.

Hundreds of feet above the streets, Supergirl swooped and soared to her heart's content. She hoped she hadn't made a mistake, leaving Lex alone tonight, but she needed far less sleep than he did. And it wasn't as if she hadn't slipped away many times before. She loved to fly at night, with the lights of Metropolis spread out before her.

It's so beautiful at night, thought Supergirl, *like a huge Christmas tree, going on for miles and miles.* The city, with its millions of residents, held a constant fascination for her. There were no cities where she had come from, only ruins. *This is what my world would have been like, if not for General Zod.*

Supergirl had come to Earth not just from another planet but from another universe. That extradimensional realm had been an altered copy of our own reality, a kind of pocket universe created by a mysterious cosmic entity.

There was a duplicate of Earth in that pocket universe. But that world had possessed no Superman and had been all but defenseless when attacked by a trio of superpowered terrorists led by the murderous General Zod. Zod's forces effectively subjugated that world, forcing the native resistance forces to go underground.

Although that other-Earth had no Superman, it did claim among its residents a doppelganger of Lex Luthor. That alternate-version of

Luthor was a younger, more vital man than the aging industrialist of our world, but he was no less ambitious. He was a scientific genius without equal, and he quickly became the leader of the resistance forces. In an attempt to devise a means of combatting the superterrorists, he made two remarkable discoveries. The first was a substance of his own invention that he called "protomatter," and the second was the existence of our universe and its Superman. Despite being able to observe our world, he was at first unable to make contact with it. And so he set out to create his own superpowered champion.

The other-Luthor deduced that protomatter could be manipulated to duplicate the human form right down to the molecular level. After much grueling work, he finally managed to create an artificial life-form inspired by his observations. . . a Supergirl. Luthor was her Pygmalion, and she his Galatea. He had created in his Supergirl a being able to levitate and fly at incredible speeds. While not as strong as Superman, she wielded powerful psychokinetic energies and could generate energy shields capable of cloaking her presence, effectively rendering her invisible. And due to the fluidity of her protomatter substance, Supergirl could also alter her appearance at will.

But even with her amazing powers, Supergirl was no match for Zod and his partners. They ran roughshod over the planet, boiling away its oceans and depleting its atmosphere. Soon they rendered it all but uninhabitable.

In desperation the other-Luthor tried transporting Supergirl to our world to locate and enlist Superman's help in ending Zod's reign of terror. The complicated transfer left Supergirl dazed and disoriented, but her quest finally proved successful, and Superman returned with his young namesake to aid the resistance fighters.

But Superman's help came too late. Before they could be stopped, Zod's terrorists left Supergirl gravely injured and destroyed all other native life within that other-universe. In the name of the resistance, Superman was forced to execute the terrorists. It was the only way he could keep their killing spree from crossing over to our world.

Superman gathered up the injured Supergirl and left the dead duplicate of Earth, carrying her back to our reality and entrusting her to his own parents. Although her injuries had affected her mind, leaving her childlike and simple, under the care of Jonathan and Martha Kent she slowly began to recover. Supergirl came to love the Kents dearly, but—in her attempts to regain mastery of her powers—she feared that she had inadvertently put the Kents in danger. Afraid that she was too dangerous to remain around normal human beings, she flew off into space.

After some time spent wandering among the stars, Supergirl finally came to realize that Earth was the closest thing to a home that she might find. Locating a small abandoned starship, she put her doubts behind her and set a course for our world.

But something went wrong.

Supergirl's ship went off course, crash-landing in the New Mexico desert. There it was spotted and recovered by a research team from the aeronautics division of LexCorp International. The first face that Supergirl saw upon regaining consciousness was that of Lex Luthor II. He was the very image of the man who had created her, and she had fallen hopelessly in love with him.

I was so lucky to find him, thought Supergirl, as she looped around the *Daily Planet* Building. *I wish Superman could understand that.* She frowned, remembering the awful scene with Superman when he had learned that she was living with Lex. *He said that he didn't want to see me hurt, but he was just as worried that I'd spill the beans about his double life. As if I'd ever reveal anything that would jeopardize him or the Kents! I just wish I hadn't lost my temper.*

Their argument had escalated, and she'd wound up blasting Superman into a landfill halfway across the city. He had not been physically injured, of course, but they'd both been embarrassed by the altercation.

We've hardly spoken since. He knows I'm sorry, and I know he's not the type to carry a grudge, but I still feel awful about it. We should be . . . well, not partners . . . and certainly not lovers! I have Lex and he has Lois. But I wish we could be closer. She briefly considered dropping by Clark's apartment but decided against it. *He might have company. He is engaged, after all! Besides, there'll be other times to talk.*

Supergirl turned in a wide loop back toward the LexCorp Tower. She loved to soar over Metropolis and tried never to miss her nighttime flights. But dawn was now just a few hours away, and she had to be there for her darling Lex when he awoke.

5

"Hey, Mr. Kent! Wait up!"

Clark stopped in midstride and turned as a red-haired young man dashed toward him from a nearby subway entrance, a camera case slapping against his leg.

"Hello, Jimmy. And how goes things in the borough of Bakerline this fine morning?"

"Okay, I guess, for Bakerline." Jimmy Olsen shrugged. "I'd still rather live here on the big island—like you do, Mr. Kent—but it's so hard to find an apartment I can afford."

"Jim, I've told you, I really don't mind if you use my first name. Every time you call me 'Mr. Kent,' I feel like looking around to see if my father's there."

"Yeah, I know. Ms. La—I mean, Lois has been after me about the same thing. I still feel funny about it, though."

"I'll make you a deal. If you don't call me Mr. Kent, I won't call you Mr. Olsen."

Jimmy chuckled. "Okay, Clark . . . I'll try."

"Good. As to your apartment problem, have you considered finding a roommate?"

"Aw, I tried that once and it didn't work out."

"Maybe you just didn't find the right roommate. It's worth another try, don't you think?"

"Yeah, I guess so." Jimmy absentmindedly smacked his hand with a rolled-up magazine as they waited for the traffic lights to change.

"What do you have there, Jim?"

"This? It's the latest *Newstime.*"

"Ah. Did they pick up another of your photos?"

"Not this week. No, I was reading an article about Guy Gardner, you know, the ex–Green Lantern."

"I'm . . . familiar with Gardner's exploits, Jimmy."

"Boy, I don't know why the Justice League puts up with that jerk. Seems to me, when I was in high school—which wasn't that long ago— the Justice League used to go after butt-heads like him; they didn't admit 'em as members!"

"Well, the world turns and times change, Jim."

"Yeah, and not always for the better."

The WALK light came on, and they started across the street.

"It doesn't pay to be negative, James. Besides, you're much too young to be a curmudgeon."

"Well, if I were Superman, I'd bounce Gardner out of the League so hard, he'd come down in Australia."

"Maybe Superman has a good reason for keeping him in the Justice League. Maybe he thinks it's better to have Gardner around people who stand a chance of keeping him in line, rather than letting him run off and get himself into trouble."

Jimmy considered that. "I suppose. But I still don't like the idea of him and that Maxima woman being considered super-heroes. Heck, Maxima gave Superman all kinds of grief, and now she's his teammate?" The young photographer shook his head. "The Justice League used to stand for something, but now they're just a bunch of joke-heroes . . . except for Superman, of course. I don't know why he let himself get mixed up with those guys!"

"I'm sure Superman has asked himself that question many times, Jimmy. I suppose it seemed like a good idea to him at the time. Maybe he feels . . . responsible for them."

"Responsible? For the Justice League? How so?"

Okay, Kent, explain your way around that one. Clark scratched the back of his neck. "Well, Jim, wasn't Superman the first hero with extraordinary powers to go public since the end of the Second World War? Certainly there were earlier costumed heroes, people like the Hourman and Dr. Mid-Nite, but they'd mostly retired by midcentury. It wasn't until after Superman came on the scene that we started to see a lot of new super-heroes. I guess he really started something."

"I see what you mean. I remember reading an interview with the Black Canary once, where she said that most of today's heroes would probably never have gotten started if it hadn't been for Superman. I'm not even sure there was such a term as 'super-hero' before he came along. From what my Uncle Phil once told me, the wartime heroes were mainly called crime fighters or mystery-men."

"Exactly. You might say that Superman was the first of a new generation. He was followed by the Batman over in Gotham, the Flash in Central City, Green Lantern out on the West Coast . . . Aquaman, the Canary, J'Onn J'Onzz. And with all those heroes running around, they eventually founded the Justice League as an organization to take on the menaces that were too big for any one of them to handle."

"Yeah, and the League was really something back then. It's too bad Superman couldn't have been a member of that original team!"

Well, they did *ask me,* thought Clark.

Superman had been flying over the Aleutian Islands when he spotted a strange series of flashing lights. He'd followed the lights into Alaska's Valley of the Ten Thousand Smokes when he saw the five founding members of the Justice League. They were fighting among themselves.

One moment, the Flash was punching Aquaman, and the next he suddenly turned and tried to tackle Green Lantern. There was no rhyme or reason to their actions. Each of them was striking randomly, and they were rapidly wearing themselves down. *What are they trying to do,* he wondered, *kill each other?*

And then Superman spotted the robot.

It stood twenty feet tall and looked like a high-tech metal gorilla. It was a formidable construct, but he noticed that it kept a prudent distance from the superpowered combatants. He also noticed a strange ripple in the air which seemed to be originating from a sort of turret in the robot's midsection. And behind the turret, secreted within a heavily reinforced control chamber, he could see a strange little gnome of a man.

He's doing something to them, playing with their minds maybe, thought Superman. *I have to put an end to this before one of them is seriously injured.*

Staying out of range, Superman trained his heat vision on the turret. Under the bombardment, it began to glow red, then white. With a flash of energy the turret turned to slag.

The heroes of the Justice League froze in their tracks, looking on in wonder at the red and blue blur that dove from the sky, slamming into the big robot like a runaway train. Within moments, Superman gutted the walking tank and confronted its controller.

"No! NO!" screamed the gnome. "You couldn't have destroyed my illusion maker!"

"Illusion maker?" If the situation hadn't been so serious, Superman would have laughed. The weird little man had a strange accent, unlike any he'd ever heard, but he spoke like a mad scientist from one of those old movie serials Clark used to watch in college. "What is going on here?"

The little man cowered in the back of the control chamber. "There was no mention of this in the histories!" His voice rose to a high, thin shriek, and to Superman's astonishment he began to fade away. "I was supposed to win—to WIN! What went wrong? What went wro . . ."

With that, he disappeared completely, and Superman was left alone amid the wreckage of the robot. He scanned every last bit of the metal hull with his X-ray vision, but he could find no trace of the little man.

"Superman, you did it! You stopped Xotar!"

Superman turned to find himself suddenly face-to-face with a masked man wearing a crimson bodysuit. "I beg your pardon?"

"Xotar . . . that's what the fellow who ran this contraption called himself. He claimed that he was from ten thousand years in the future."

"Ten thousand—?"

"That's what he said. Personally, I think he was fudging his dates to impress us." There was the slightest hint of a midwestern drawl in the masked man's voice. "Oh, say, we haven't really been introduced. I'm the Flash!"

"I've heard of you."

"Really?" The Flash fairly vibrated in his excitement. "Well, hey, you've got to meet the others."

"Wait a minute." Superman held up a hand. "What about Xotar? He just . . . vanished on me."

"Can't say that I'm surprised." The Flash looked thoughtful. "I think he had some sort of fail-safe device to send him back to his own time. Don't worry, we'll check it out."

As they walked out of the robot's metal shell, the other members of the Justice League gathered around them.

Another masked man, this one lanky and dark haired, stepped forward, offering his hand. "An honor, Superman. They call me Green Lantern." As they shook hands, Superman swore he could feel an endless wave of energy surging within the glowing emerald ring on the Lantern's second finger.

"I need your help with this wreck, Lantern," said the Flash. "We want to make certain that Xotar hasn't pulled a fast one on us!"

Green Lantern nodded and followed the Flash back into the remains of the robot. As they disappeared from view, a nimble young blond woman dressed in black and navy spoke up. "I'm Black Canary, and this tall drink of water"—she gestured to a muscular, fair-haired man—"is Aquaman."

The fifth and final member of the League towered over Superman. His skin was an unusual shade of green, and his eyes were shadowed by the ridge of his brow. "I am J'Onn J'Onzz, a detective of sorts. And to answer your unasked question . . . no, I am not of this world. My planet of origin is Mars."

"I didn't think there was any life on Mars."

"That is unfortunately correct . . . in this era."

Before Superman could question J'Onzz further, Green Lantern and the Flash returned, looking pleased.

"Xotar's gone back to his own time," the Lantern reported. "My power ring detected a deviation in the"—he turned to his teammate—"what did you call it?"

"Quantum field," said the Flash. "Anyway, G. L.'s ring traced him through the field into the future. Get this . . . Xotar beamed himself right back into the hands of his own time period's police. And he's no problem there. Thanks to Superman here, he had to bug out without any of his fancy weapons . . . not that there's much left of them now!" The Flash began pumping Superman's hand. "That was great! Superman, this is a real pleasure."

"The pleasure is mine, Flash. This Justice League of yours has made a lot of news in the past few weeks. I'm glad I finally got the chance to meet you." Superman glanced back at the wreckage of the robot. "I just wish it could have been under more sociable circumstances."

"Well, with Xotar gone, I'd say we all have reason to celebrate," said Black Canary. She gazed admiringly at Superman. "We have a place back east where we meet in private. Why don't you join us?"

Unable to turn down such an intriguing invitation, Superman accompanied the Justice League back to their hidden sanctuary. It was an impressive hideaway, from its extensive computerized library to its satellite uplink. *This group is full of surprises,* thought Superman. But the biggest surprise came when the Flash gaveled a meeting to order and nominated the Man of Steel for membership, a nomination immediately seconded by Aquaman.

"Flash . . . Aquaman . . . I'm very flattered. And I'd be honored to join . . . if I could devote the time to your League that membership demands." Superman paused. "But my time is not my own. I'm afraid I cannot accept your nomination."

Superman regretted the decision, but he could see no way to be an active member of the Justice League in addition to his other activities.

Just being Superman is as much a full-time job as working for the Daily Planet. *I wonder how these people manage to find time for private lives? Maybe they don't. After all, as far as the public knows, I'm Superman all the time.*

Superman could see the disappointment in the Flash's face, even without peering beneath his mask—and he respected the privacy of his fellow heroes too much to do such a thing. All five of them looked disappointed, even the big poker-faced Martian.

"Look," he said, "you've created a well-organized team. I doubt that you really need me as a member. But rest assured, if you ever truly do need me, I'll be there."

In the years that followed, Superman proved true to his word. He stood by the Justice League as a faithful ally in fighting and defeating threats to this planet and others.

But time did not remain kind to the Justice League. There were countless changes in membership and two major reorganizations, and eventually the League disbanded. Shortly after the group's dissolution, Superman enlisted the aid of former members to organize a superpowered fighting force to combat an alien invasion. The success of that mission led him to reassess his standing in what the media was starting to call "the super-hero community." Finally, Superman agreed to become a member of a new American division of the Justice League.

Since then, it's been one hassle after another, thought Clark. It would have been different, if he'd been working alongside the original members. They knew how to work together. But his new partners, on the other hand, were not all team players. New League members Fire and Ice had once been part of a European supergroup and could be counted on to the fullest extent of their powers of heat and cold. Likewise, the Blue Beetle was an expert hand-to-hand combatant and a highly skilled engineer. But if you put him in the same room with Booster Gold, there was trouble. Together, Booster and the Beetle became insufferable practical jokers.

Guy Gardner was even worse. Guy had belonged to an intergalactic corps of Green Lanterns, as had one of the League founders, but he was nothing like the Green Lantern whom Superman had first met. Guy was a loose cannon who shot his mouth off as readily as he did his power ring. He was, frankly, an obnoxious, egotistical oaf. After finally being drummed out of the Green Lantern Corps, he managed to acquire a golden power ring which allowed him to continue operating as a member of the League.

Clark grimaced inwardly. Gardner was a far cry from his idea of a super-hero, but as long as he worked with the League, they could conceivably keep him reined in.

Maxima was yet another matter. The heir to the throne of an interstellar empire based on the distant planet Almerac, Maxima had first come to Earth looking for a suitable consort with whom to enrich the bloodline of the royal family. Arrogant, self-righteous, and quick-tempered, she had set her sights on Superman. He had done his best to persuade her that he wasn't interested in fathering any future galactic despots. But thanks to the part she'd played in stopping the alien invasion, she had been inducted into the Justice League. Her physical strength and her extensive psychokinetic powers made her a valuable addition to the group, but her imperious attitude continually put her at odds with other League members.

And then there was Bloodwynd. Clark still wasn't sure what to make of him. None of the others in the Justice League really knew anything about the tall, powerfully built black man, but he had proven to be a valuable ally. Bloodwynd seemed nearly as strong as Superman and claimed to be a sorcerer. As Superman, Clark had had dealings with supernatural entities in the past, and Bloodwynd certainly fit the mold; he was more aloof even than Maxima.

They are *an unruly lot,* thought Clark. But—barring a massive change in membership—they were *his* unruly lot, and he'd just have to make the best of things. After all, the Justice League had a history nearly as long and distinguished as his own. And there *was* only so much one man, even a Superman, could do on his own. That was why he had welcomed the emergence of the other heroes in the first place.

"If we're lucky, they'll all pull together eventually."

"What was that, Mr. Ken—Clark?"

"Eh? Oh, just thinking out loud, Jimmy . . . about the Justice League. For all their eccentricities, they're still very capable people. I don't think we should be so ready to write them off just yet. After all, the original founding members weren't very experienced when they started out."

"I suppose so." Jimmy didn't sound very convinced. "I just hope that Superman's as optimistic as you are."

"I'm sure he is, Jim. I don't think that Superman would stay with the League if he didn't think they had promise."

"Yeah, well, if he'd come out and say so, I'd feel a lot better about it."

"Maybe he will, Jimmy. Maybe he will."

As the alarm Klaxon went off in the Cadmus Security Office, Jim Harper crossed the room in three giant strides and hit a switch on the comlink.

"Guardian here. What's going on?"

"It's those blasted kids," choked a voice which Harper recognized as belonging to one of the Project's resident mechanics. "Those Newsboy clones! They set off a stink bomb in the motor pool and made off with the all-terrain wagon."

Not again, thought Harper. "All right, I'll take care of it. Have my bike ready." He quickly fitted his helmet into place. *"Those blasted kids," eh?*

The "kids" were, in fact, the result of an experiment in human cellular replication that had gone awry, producing young teenage doppelgangers of the five Cadmus Project department heads. The young clones had adopted their progenitors' old street names, and "Flip"—the clone of Cadmus biochemist Walter Johnson—had been welcomed as a new member of this second-generation Newsboy Legion.

Scooping up his shield on the run, the Guardian sprinted down a corridor. *They're even more of a handful than their fathers were . . . and now there are five of them!* The Guardian shook his head. *A stink bomb . . . I'm getting too old for this.*

By the time he reached the Project's motor pool, exhaust fans had already drawn off the worst of the stink bomb's residue. But there was still an acrid stench in the air and more than a few puffy-eyed mechanics. One grease monkey was suddenly seized with a coughing fit. When it had subsided, he glared at the helmeted man through his tears. "Guardian, you have to do something about those brats!"

Harper straddled the gleaming motorcycle that had been wheeled out for him. "What do you suggest we do?"

The man shrugged. "I don't know. Find them and lock them up, I guess."

"We already keep them locked away in this Project as if they were prize guinea pigs. They're young teenage boys . . . they didn't ask to be born into this."

"None of us asks to be born." The new voice was low and even and unnaturally distinct. All activity ground to a halt as its speaker stepped into the chamber.

He stood just under six feet tall, and his skin was a light gray. His green eyes were elliptical, like those of a cat. But by far his most striking features were the two hornlike protuberances that grew from his high, wide forehead. He was called Dubbilex, and though he had been a fixture at the Project for many years, there were still many who felt uncomfortable around him.

Jim Harper was never one of those. Quite to the contrary, he found Dubbilex fascinating. The gaunt gray man reminded Jim of a benevolent alien from an old science-fiction pulp of his youth, and that image wasn't far from wrong. Dubbilex, he knew, was the creation of Dr. Dabney Donovan.

One of the Cadmus Project's three original founders, Donovan was a brilliant and—unfortunately—highly unstable genius who had become obsessed with the idea of creating whole new species through genetic engineering. Dubbilex had been the first survivor of a series of experiments to produce a race of what the doctor called his DNAliens. When the other Project heads had begun to raise questions about Donovan's ethics and place restrictions on his research, he committed suicide.

If it was *a suicide,* thought the Guardian.

Dubbilex looked at the Guardian quizzically. *"Then you also have doubts about my creator's supposed death?"*

The Guardian looked around him. He had heard the DNAlien's thought as clearly as if it had been spoken aloud, but no one else in the room seemed aware of it.

"Sorry," came another thought, *"I didn't mean to pry. But the thought was so strong in your mind, I couldn't help but 'hear' it."*

That's all right, Dubbilex, thought the Guardian. *I guess I'm still not used to working with a telepath.*

"I quite understand," came the reply. *"It hasn't been all that easy for me, either. Mastering the powers of the psyche is a bit like learning to master Rollerblading. You fall on your tail a lot."*

The Guardian grinned, tickled by the very image of Dubbilex on Rollerblades. *I read you.*

Dubbilex nodded toward the staring mechanics. *"I believe they're feeling a bit ill at ease. Perhaps we should say something?"*

Ah, yes. The Guardian broke the silence. "We could use your help, Dubbilex. The youngsters have taken off on a joyride. Any ideas as to where they might be headed?"

Dubbilex cocked his head to one side and stared off into space . . .
Trying to hear beyond hearing, to see beyond sight, thought the Guardian.

The lanky DNAlien slowly brought his hands to his temples. "I think that they are not far away. Yes, I can feel their exuberance. I feel . . . freedom."

The underground vault rang like a blacksmith's anvil under the force of the Creature's hammering blows.

The Creature kept pounding.

Sparks flew from the metal, sporadically lighting the tiny chamber.

The Creature kept pounding.

Finally, the tortured metal of the wall began to give, curling away as if trying to escape from that pounding fist.

With a muffled bellow, the Creature tore at his bonds, and more of the thick metal cables snapped. Now more mobile, he threw himself against the tiny opening, pushing the twisted metal farther apart. Then, when he'd widened the hole enough for his shoulders to slip through, the Creature began to claw at the compacted clay and rock beyond.

"Free at last, free at last!" Young Flip Johnson punched the air, feeling the slipstream sting his fists, as an experimental high-performance vehicle emerged from a cave near the base of Mount Curtiss.

"Hey, Johnson, keep yer mitts inside this Whiz Wagon, if ya don't wanna lose 'em!"

"Aw, lay off 'im, Scrapper! Ain't a guy entitled to celebrate a little? I mean, geez Louise, this's been our first chance to go outside, since . . . since the last time we ran off to the city." Gabby stopped only briefly to take a breath before rambling on. "I mean, I feel like celebratin'! Don't you feel like celebratin'? You oughtta! I think this is great, really!"

"Hey-hey! Turn off the faucet, will ya?" Scrapper peered out from under the brim of his cap at Gabby, fixing his buddy with a look of exasperation. "I was jus' tryin' to give a li'l friendly advice. It ain't safe to stick a hand out, not as fast as we're goin'!"

Big Words nodded judiciously. "Our colleague is quite astute, gentlemen."

"What?!" Scrapper lunged toward Big Words, straining against his safety harness. "Who's a stupe?! C'mere an' say that again, ya four-eyed, walkin' encyclopedia!"

The gangly teenager pressed a big, bony hand against Scrapper's chest, holding him at arm's length. "I merely meant that you spoke wisely."

"Well, why din't ya say so?"

"I believed that I had." Big Words scanned the array of indicators before him. "As a matter of fact, our present velocity is a hundred and seventy kilometers per hour. At such a speed, a chance encounter with another object, whether in motion or at rest, would prove quite injurious, not to mention painful."

Flip, who'd fought to keep a straight face through the exchange, nodded in mock imitation of Big Words. "I can dig it. So, Tommy, how long till we get to Metropolis?"

From behind the wheel of the Whiz Wagon, Tommy just grinned. "We're not going to Metropolis."

"Huh?"

"Not goin'—?!"

"Oh, man—!"

Tommy downshifted, and the silvery vehicle began to decelerate. "Tell 'em, Words."

"Well, simply put . . ."

"That'll be a good trick fer you," Scrapper grumbled.

" . . . our previous attempts at freedom met with failure when we were intercepted either in or *in transit* to the city. Clearly, a change of destination is in order, if we are to succeed."

"Okay, okay, I can see that, sorta, but if we're not going to Metropolis, where are we gonna go? Where else is there? Around here, I mean?"

"Gabby's got a point, man. We have the wheels and the fuel to get us to Philly or Gotham or . . . heck, even all the way out to California, if we wanted. But the Whiz Wagon ain't exactly a Chevy." Flip gazed appreciatively out past the windscreen and patted the padded dash. "Not to put her down, but she does look like a cross between a grand prix racer and somethin' outta *Star Trek.* We're gonna attract attention wherever we go."

"Oh, most assuredly. There is, however, within close proximity an arboreal sanctuary wherein we can conceal ourselves for the preparation of any further course of action."

Scrapper pulled his cap low over his eyes and sank back into his seat. "Can anybody put that into plain English?"

"Arboreal?" Flip looked skeptical. "You mean we're gonna hide out in some trees?"

"Not just some trees . . . *those* trees!" Tommy pointed across a small clearing. Big Words smiled smugly, as three sets of jaws dropped in amazement. Ahead of them loomed wooden towers, terraces, and avenues.

"Holy cow." For once Gabby had trouble finding his voice. "It's . . . it's . . ."

"It's dat big tree city what the Project built! I remember now . . . they called it 'Have-a-trap' or somethin'."

"*Habitat,* Scrapper! And it wasn't built, it was grown—right into the shapes of buildings and streets."

"Correct, Flip. But Habitat wasn't exactly a product of the Project *per se*. Strictly speaking, it was more of a by-product or offshoot of allied research into—!"

"Yeah, yeah. We get the picture, Words. The Project don't keep close tabs on the joint, do they? So we can hide out here for as long as we want, wit' no one the wiser."

"Well, within reason, Scrapper. By the time they've exhausted their normal search patterns, we shall be—!"

"Nuts!"

"What's wrong, Tommy?"

"I don't know."

"Then why're you slowing down?" asked Flip.

"I'm not. We're losing power. The Whiz Wagon's turbines just shut down."

"Don't tell me . . . we're gonna have to get out and push." Scrapper was already starting to unbuckle his seat belt.

Tommy fiddled with the starter. "Maybe. But we're still on a bit of an incline. With a little luck we can coast the rest of the way into—uh-oh."

" 'Uh-oh?' " Flip gave Tommy a worried look. "What're you 'uh-oh'in' about?"

"Him!"

Straight ahead of them, the Guardian sat astride his motorcycle, arms folded across his chest. Tommy hit the brakes, and their vehicle rolled to a stop barely a foot in front of the man clad in blue and gold.

"Going somewhere?" In a half century of police work Harper had developed the ability to assume a very businesslike monotone.

"Oh, man, he's Jack Webbin' us," whispered Flip. "We're in trouble now."

"Guardian, we . . . uh . . . we were just catchin' a little air. Ain't we, guys? Guys?"

"Yeah, Gabby's right," insisted Scrapper. "We're growin' boys, after all. The docs said we needed more fresh air."

"I see." The Guardian drummed his fingers against the side of the long silver vehicle. "And these . . . doctors . . . advised a nice long drive in the country?"

"Yeah. Sure!"

"In a stolen car?"

"Yeah, we . . . no!"

"We din't steal no car! Tell 'em, Words."

"Yes, well . . . ahem . . . there may have been a slight lapse in acquiring the proper requisitions, sir, but I assure you, it was never our intent to abscond with the Whiz Wagon. We have the greatest respect for all Project equipment."

"Yeah, we didn't *mean* to break it!"

Scrapper clamped a hand over Gabby's mouth. "Will you pipe down?"

Tommy slumped glumly behind the wheel as Big Words nervously cleared his throat. "I'm sure you realize, sir, that some of our progenitors worked on the design of this vehicle, so naturally we would have a proprietary interest in it."

The Guardian towered over them. "But you don't own it, do you?"

"Well, technically . . . we . . . ah . . . no."

"And did any of you ask permission to use it?"

"No."

The Guardian locked eyes with Tommy. "I didn't realize you were even old enough to have a driver's permit."

"I-I'm not sure how old I am, sir." Tommy tried—and failed—to keep from blinking. "It's hard for a clone to know. Sometimes, I feel almost thirty."

"How do you feel right now?"

"Like mud."

"And how do you think your fathers will feel when they find out what you've done?"

"I don't know, sir. Surprised?"

"I doubt that. You're too much like them." *Entirely too much like them!*

"Well, if our pops turned out okay, then there must be hope for us! Right, Guardian?" Flip was thinking fast and talking faster. "I mean, we can't help being the way we are."

"Yeah!" Scrapper set his jaw at a determined angle that the Guardian knew all too well. "We're just livin' out our genetical hermitage . . . doin' what our old men woulda done under the same soicumstances."

" 'Soicumstances'?" Under his helmet, Jim Harper raised an eyebrow. *I'd like to know how that Bowery Boys accent managed to become genetically programmed.*

"What he's trying to say, sir . . ." Gabby was making a feeble attempt to choke back mock tears. ". . . is that we're just poor, misguided youths, trying to find our way in the world. We didn't mean to cause any trouble."

"What about the stink bomb, boys?"

They all looked at Big Words.

"Ah, yes . . . well . . . that was the result of an experiment in organic chemistry, sir. And like many experiments, it was none too successful."

"I'd say it was very successful in clearing your way through the motor pool."

"Guardian—?"

"Yes, Tommy?"

"We just *had* to get out for a while. We were going stir crazy in there."

The Guardian sighed. "I know, but that doesn't excuse—!"

"Oh, you 'know.' Right!" Scrapper's face was a study in disgust. "You can waltz outta the Project anytime you like. You get to pal aroun' wit' yer buddy Sooperman, an' help 'im fight aliens, an' have all kinda great adventures—an' all wit'out us!"

"I've aided Superman a few times, yes. But those were dangerous missions. There's no way you could've gone along."

"Hey, man, it doesn't matter." Flip sounded just as disgusted as Scrapper. "The fact remains that you're allowed to leave the Project, and we're not."

"Ain't fair," sniffed Gabby. "Ain't fair at all . . . keepin' us cooped up all the time."

The Guardian nodded. "You're right. It isn't fair."

"Huh?"

"We are?"

"It's not?"

"I've been working on getting approval to take you characters into Metropolis for extended periods—"

"All right!"

"—but if you keep setting off stink bombs and causing mayhem, I'm never going to get that approval. Paul Westfield takes a very dim view of such shenanigans!"

"Dat bum? He don't like nothin'! He don't even like Sooperman!"

"Mr. Westfield's likes and dislikes are beside the point. The fact remains that he is the administrator of the Cadmus Project, and what he says goes!" *Whether we like it or not,* thought the Guardian. He was none too keen on Westfield's hard-nosed approach himself. "Do me a favor, guys. Try to toe the straight and narrow for a while, and I'll do my best to get some vacation time for you all. Do we have a deal?"

"Well . . ."

"Tommy?"

"Yes, sir."

"Flip?"

"Yeah, I guess."

"Gabby?"

"Yeah, yeah. Sure, sure."

"Scrapper?"

"You promise to get us some free time?"

"I'll do everything in my power."

The young tough gave the Guardian a toothy grin. "Okay, Officer Harper, ya got me!"

"And I shall be most happy to make it unanimous." Big Words's ear-to-ear grin looked to rival even Scrapper's.

"Good. Now, what do you say we turn this wagon around and head home?"

"Uh, we have a problem there, sir." Tommy tugged nervously at his collar. "The Whiz Wagon seems to have stalled out, and I haven't been able to restart it."

"No problem." The Guardian pulled a small wireless microphone from behind his shield and spoke into it. "Override stall-out command. Initiate power-up and ignite turbines."

The Whiz Wagon's engines suddenly roared to life.

"Holy smokes!"

"Do you mean to say—?"

"You shut us down . . . by remote control?!"

"Well, don't look so surprised." The Guardian no longer tried to hide his own grin. "You're not the only ones who can play it sneaky!"

6

Hundreds of miles away, in a remote section of the Midwest, the ground began to shudder. Spooked by the underground rumbling, a flock of crows abandoned their perches, filling the sky like a living cloud. A stag stood stock-still, listening for the sound, and then bolted as he realized it came from beneath his hooves. The ground itself began first to shake and then to heave, as the Creature pounded and dug his way to the surface, his progress impeded by the bonds still immobilizing his right arm. And then, with a final, wrenching punch, he broke through to the surface.

Sinking his knuckle spurs into the compacted soil, the Creature slowly inched his way up out of the newly hewn hole. Little of the fresh air filtered through the material of his restraining garment, but he did not seem to care. He strode to the top of a nearby hillock, surveying the surrounding wilderness through the thick goggles of the enshrouding hood. For nearly an hour he just stood there in the dwindling sunlight, as still and unmoving as a rock.

As twilight came, a tiny goldfinch, its curiosity getting the better of it, fluttered in for a landing on the outstretched hand of this strange figure. For a moment, a pair of crimson eyes glared out through the goggles at the peeping little bird. Then, like a vise, his fist snapped shut, crushing the life from the goldfinch. A horrible growl of laughter echoed from beneath the hood.

Dropping into a crouch, the Creature bounded skyward, his leap carrying him thousands of feet into the air and fully a mile away. He landed in the midst of an old-growth forest, squirrels scattering at his approach.

The Creature lurched forward toward a huge oak which stood in his path. In minutes the tree, which had stood on that spot for well over a hundred years, lay in splinters on the ground.

Again the Creature leapt, this time covering nearly two miles, and then again. From the apogee of one leap, he caught sight of something shining far to the east, and he set out to discover what it was.

Night had fallen when the Creature finally came to rest on a high embankment overlooking an interstate highway. The small cluster of speeding vehicles fascinated him, and he leapt directly into their path.

A late-model Ford pickup braked and swerved in an attempt to miss the hulking form that had suddenly appeared on the roadway. The Creature seemed to take this as a challenge, lashing out with a punch that sent truck and driver rolling over and over into oncoming traffic. A cacophony of squealing brakes and car horns was quickly joined by the crunch of metal and the whoosh of igniting gasoline. An approving howl came from the Creature as he charged headlong at the abutment of the highway overpass. With one arm still tied behind him, he struck and clawed at the reinforced concrete, slamming into the weakened supports with his back and shoulders until, finally, the entire overpass fell in a mass atop the crash scene. The Creature looked around him. No signs of life came from the crushed cars and trucks. No other shiny challenges were to be seen. With almost an air of disappointment, the Creature leapt on, following the highway.

Chuck Johnston stifled a yawn as his rig flashed past the road sign. TOLEDO: SIXTY MILES. He'd have to hustle if he was going to make it there by daybreak. *These overnight hauls're gonna be the death of me!* He shook his thermos. Empty. *Dang! I shoulda got a refill back in Wapokeneta.* Chuck rubbed the bridge of his nose. No time to stop now. He stifled another yawn. He'd need some conversation if he was going to keep himself awake. He thumbed the mike switch of his CB. "Yo! Breaker! This's Chuckie-Jay, anybody got their ears on? C'mon!"

"Chuckie, baby! This's Moon Pie, where you been keepin' yerself, bro?"

Chuck smiled. It'd been a good six months since he'd last seen Donny Moon. Donny was one of the few white men he knew who called him "bro" and meant it.

"Yo, Moon! Been down runnin' Houston to St. Loo. Got me a load on for Dee-troit this mornin', though. 'M headed north on I–75 just outside'a Beaverdam."

"Shoot, good buddy, you must be just 'bout breathin' down my neck. What d'ya say we hit J. C.'s at Toledo for steak an' eggs?"

"Okay, man, but I'm buyin'!"

"Woo! Texas musta been good to you, bro! I can't wait to—what the heck?!"

Chuck's grin faded. "Moon? What is it?"

"Don't know. Some big cuss just lit in the middle of the—!"

Chuck heard the weird double-echo of Donny's horn—half over the CB and half through his partially open window—and realized with a start that he'd almost caught up with his friend's rig. He, too, could see a huge figure lurching onto the roadway.

"Hey, buddy," Moon's voice sounded oddly strained over the speaker, "get outta the way!"

Chuck hit the brakes reflexively as he saw Moon's rig slam into the hulking figure and flip over! "Moon!" The radio let out an ungodly squeal as the upended tractor-trailer burst into flames.

"Oh, man . . . Moon . . ."

And then a huge, dark figure emerged from the fire, laughing.

Rolling to a stop, Chuck hit the dial of his radio. "State troopers!" he screamed the words. "Chuck Johnston calling state troopers!"

"I read you, Mr. Johnston. What—?"

"Big monster flipped Moon's rig . . . one hand tied behind its back!"

"Excuse me?"

"A monster, man—on I–75 just south'a Bluffton! It just wrecked my friend's eighteen-wheeler! It's burnin'—!"

"Did you say . . . monster?"

"Yeah . . . big as a damn house! It's tearin' up the whole interstate!"

Miles away, at the nearest highway patrol post, an alarmed dispatcher immediately put out a call to all cars in the vicinity and punched up an emergency code. If the report coming over was true, they'd need special help.

Dawn was just beginning to break over Manhattan when the call came through. In the shadow of the United Nations Plaza, a low glass and granite complex jutted out into the East River. Deep within that complex a little man sat before a bank of communications equipment, a Manhattan Yellow Pages directory on the seat beneath him. The soft amber lights of the display screen were reflected in his bald pate. Oberon was the only name he answered to, though whether that was his first name or his last, nobody knew for certain.

Oberon was a dwarf. He had spent half a lifetime in show business, first as a clown in a traveling circus and then as sideman to the renowned escape artist Thaddeus Brown. When Thaddeus died, Oberon had gone on to work with his successor, a young man who called himself Scott

Free. But Scott was no ordinary young man. He possessed amazing powers and knowledge, and as Mr. Miracle, he became not just a super-escape artist, but a super-hero. When Scott eventually joined with the other heroes in the Justice League, Oberon had tagged along. Before the little man could realize what was happening, he had become second-in-command to the League's administrator. Scott was gone now, off to God knows where on some wild adventure, but Oberon stayed on. Through changes in operations and membership, he had remained a fixture in the management of the League.

This particular morning, Oberon was enjoying a cup of ginseng tea when the police monitor bank began to warble electronically. Oberon grimaced. *Why can't they program a decent bell tone into these things? The last thing a man ought to hear at this hour is that infernal chirping.* The little man hit the monitor switch, and command codes started crawling across the soft amber of the screen. Ohio. Oberon smiled. *Haven't played Ohio in over ten years. What was the name of that place . . . the Richland County Fairgrounds? Yes, good crowd . . . nice audience.* His curiosity piqued, he hit a second switch, and a tiny microphone emerged out of the console. "Good morning, this is Justice League Command. What is your situation?"

"This is Captain Brian Stang, Ohio Highway Patrol. We're not certain, but we may have a problem involving a metahuman or superbeing of some sort."

"You're not certain—?"

"Reports are still sketchy, but something's tearing up sections of highway in the northeast quadrant of the state . . . something big. We recorded a call just a few minutes ago."

Oberon listened intently as Stang relayed the tape of Chuck Johnston's call for help. "A monster . . . big as a house, eh? Now, this *does* sound like a job for the Justice League."

Less than five minutes after Oberon hit the priority alert, a strange flying object lifted off from the Justice League compound. Outwardly, it appeared to be a giant, thirty-foot water bug. It was, in fact, a supersonic aircraft of a highly sophisticated design. Its creator, Ted Kord, sat in the pilot's seat, his face masked by the hood and goggles of the Blue Beetle.

"Next stop, eastern Ohio! Hold on to your hats, kiddies!"

"I am not wearing a hat," said Maxima, looking disdainfully at the Beetle, "and I am not a 'kiddie.' "

"Chill out, Max, it's just an expression."

"My name is Maxima, Mr. Gold. You may address me as 'my lady.' "

"Whatever you say, 'your lady,' but you don't have to call me 'Mr. Gold.' You can call me 'Mr. Booster Gold, sir'!"

"Could you please hold it down?" Fire raised her hand to cover a yawn. "It's too early in the morning for all this noise."

"It's not that early, Fire!" The snowy-haired young woman seated beside her gave Fire a gentle nudge in the ribs. "Of course, if you hadn't been up all night—!"

"Ice, please! Don't remind me." Fire stifled a second yawn and ran her fingers back through her mane of green hair. "Is there any coffee service on this flight?"

"Coming right up!" Blue Beetle flipped a switch on his control board, and a china mug popped up from the armrest of Fire's seat.

"Yuck! This coffee . . . it's tepid."

"Sorry. I've been having a little trouble with the dispenser. I can try to reheat it."

"Never mind. I'll do it myself." As Fire clutched the mug tightly, a gout of emerald flame flared up from her hands, bringing her beverage to a quick simmer. "Mmm, now that's coffee!"

"Neat trick, Fire. If the hero biz ever gets slow, you and Ice could always become caterers!"

"If I might interrupt?" The sepulchral tones of Bloodwynd's voice brought Booster's needling to a sudden halt. "Have we received any further word on this monster whom we've been asked to find?"

"Not so far . . ." Beetle paused to enter a code into his communications console. ". . . but we should be getting a fax from the Ohio Highway Patrol soon . . . hopefully before we arrive."

"I wish Superman was with us." Ice looked uncertainly toward the forward view port, worry lines deepening beneath her bangs.

"Hey, we don't need that Boy Scout!" The new voice emanated from a glowing wall in the aft section. From out of the light, a tall man clad in leather and denim materialized through the side of the craft. His sharp features were topped by an unruly mop of red hair that was cut close on the sides. Upon the middle finger of his right hand glowed a golden ring. "You don't need nothin' but your favorite Guy!"

Oh, fine, thought Beetle. "Morning, Gardner. Nice of you to make it."

"Guy, I was wondering where you were!" Ice's eyes sparkled as Guy Gardner folded down the jump seat next to her.

Fire just shook her head as he brushed past. *I wonder what Ice sees in that self-centered louse?*

"Hey, as America's foremost hero, I'm one busy Guy!" Gardner settled in next to Ice and took her hand in his. "Ever since those jerks in the Green Lantern Corps decided that they were too good for yours truly, I've been twice as busy—"

"Trying to convince people that you're not as worthless as they thought?" Fire suggested sweetly.

"—teaching lowlifes that I still have what it takes to kick their behinds!" Gardner favored the green-haired woman with his best sneer. "Yeah, my new power ring is just as effective as the ones the Green Lanterns use, maybe more so. After all, it does respond to my willpower . . . and there's nothin' that's stronger."

"Except maybe your socks!" needled Booster.

"You're a real funny man, aren't ya, Gold? Well, I'll put this ring up against all the fancy microcircuits in that battle suit of yours, any day of the week."

"Hey, everybody," called Beetle from the front of the cabin, "that fax is coming across now. Sketchy stuff, but this monster sounds like one tough hombre."

"Bring 'im on! I'm ready for 'im." Guy put his boots up against the seat in front of him. "You'll see, Ice. We don't need Superman to put one lousy monster in his place!"

7

In his third-floor apartment at 344 Clinton Street, Clark Kent stepped from the shower and slipped into a gray terry cloth robe, whistling the theme from *Star Wars*. Wiping the condensation from the mirror, he reached into the medicine cabinet, removing a small, curved piece of polished metal that he'd long ago scavenged from the stardrive that had brought him to Earth. He stopped whistling to concentrate his attention on the metal, directing a slender beam of radiant heat from his eyes. The curved metal reflected the beam back at his chin, neatly searing away the exposed whiskers. In a matter of seconds, Kent was clean-shaven.

The sound of a key being inserted into the lock of his apartment door caught Clark's attention. He glanced at the far wall, and it seemed to dissolve away as he focused past it to the rooms beyond. As he watched, Lois entered the apartment, shifting a brown paper bag from hand to hand as she dropped the keys back into her handbag. "Oh—" The word escaped her lips as the bag slipped from her grasp.

The next instant, Clark was at her side, deftly snagging the bag in midfall, even as she finished, "—darn it."

The big man grinned at her. "Consider it darned!"

Lois stood there with her mouth open for a second. Then her hands went to her hips and she assumed a look of mock exasperation. "Mr. Kent, I don't think I am ever going to get used to that!"

"No? Well, how about this?" He leaned down and planted a kiss full on her lips.

"Mmm." Lois smiled. "Maybe not . . . but it'll be fun finding out!"

"Same here." Clark glanced down at the bag. "Oh, boy! Cinnamon bagels and . . . What's that? Neufchâtel cheese? You're such a good provider!"

Lois heaved a sigh. "I can see where coming up with ways to surprise you will be one of the bigger challenges of married life, Mr. X-ray Vision!"

"I have every faith that you'll find a way, dear." He gathered her up in his arms. "You're very resourceful. That's why I asked you to marry me!"

"It is? And here I thought it was because you liked my hair."

"Oh, I do." His smile softened. "Have I told you lately how much I love you?"

"Not since last night." She snuggled closer. "I wish we had time for a more leisurely breakfast."

"So do I, but this is going to be a busy day. Superman has a live interview with Cat Grant today, and I have to get into the office early enough to set up my cover story."

"What did you finally settle on? What will the great reporter supposedly be off investigating?"

"Gun smuggling."

"Sounds very sexy."

"Potentially very deadly." He frowned. "From the tips I've picked up, some street gangs are trying to get their hands on a shipment of extremely sophisticated ordnance. I'll actually be checking it out as soon as I finish Cat's show."

Lois looked Clark over, as if seeing him for the first time. "I'll never know how you managed to juggle two identities for so many years."

"It hasn't always been easy." He nuzzled her ear. "But things have improved considerably since I found a fiancée to help cover for me."

"Just keep thinking that way."

"Believe me, Lois, I will."

On the western edge of Metropolis's central business district stood the thirty-seven-floor *Daily Planet* Building. Though long since dwarfed by larger office towers, the building, with its signature rooftop globe, was still one of the most recognizable landmarks in the Metropolis skyline.

As the elevator doors were closing on the lobby floor, a red-haired young man rushed to get on. He broke into a wide grin. "Morning, Mr. Kent, Ms. Lane!"

Clark and Lois winked at each other, then turned and answered in unison, "Good morning, Mr. Olsen, sir!"

Jimmy Olsen blinked, then blushed, turning almost as red as his hair. "I did it again, didn't I? Sorry, Clark . . . Lois."

"Jimmy, we've known each other how long?" Lois fixed him with a world-weary look. "Almost a decade, for heaven's sake! I remember when you were just a runny-nosed kid hanging around the City Room."

"That's just the point, Ms. . . . Lois! I was just a kid, and you were already a hotshot reporter! I still feel like a kid next to you two!"

"Next to us old folks, you mean?" asked Clark.

"Yeah. No! It's just that . . . it's a habit, you know? Mom brought me up to show respect for my elders—!"

"Deeper and deeper, James!"

"I don't mean that you guys are old like Mom . . . I mean—"

"I'm going to tell her you said that!" Lois scolded.

Jimmy blanched. "You wouldn't!"

Lois and Clark gave the young photographer their most serious looks for at least fifteen seconds before they both broke up.

"Aw, gimme a break, you guys!" Jimmy thrust his hands into his pockets and slouched back against the side of the elevator. "I've got enough on my mind without having to get the needle from my friends."

The elevator door opened with a ping, and the three filed out, entering the bustle of the *Daily Planet* City Room.

"What's the problem, Jim? If you're a little short, I can float you a loan until payday."

"Money's no big deal, Clark . . . not now, anyways. The problem is time! Remember that contract I signed to play Turtle Boy?"

Clark nodded. There'd been some serious cutbacks at the *Planet* earlier in the year, and Jimmy had been temporarily laid off. One of the many odd jobs he'd taken in the interim had been playing the part of the Godzilla-like "Turtle Boy" in a pizza commercial.

Jimmy lowered his voice. "Well, WGBS made a deal with the pizza shop owner to produce a Turtle Boy kids' show . . . and the contract I signed made me part of the deal. Now I've got to juggle my regular assignments with playing a monster on a kids' show!"

Clark leaned over his desk and punched up his computer monitor, checking his messages. "Surely the contract has some sort of escape clause?"

"I don't know. Mom's lawyer is checking it over for me. In the meantime, I've managed to talk the production team into scheduling my scenes for my lunch hour."

"Maybe you should talk to someone on the paper's legal staff." Lois stopped and looked at Jim pointedly. "Does Perry know about this?"

Jimmy looked around guiltily at the mention of their managing editor. "No. I haven't had the nerve to tell him. I mean, I'm not all that recognizable in the makeup, and they're not using my name in the credits or anything. But I don't think the Chief would be too keen on having one of his photographers playing a monster on TV. I'm hoping to get the whole mess settled before he finds out. You won't tell him, will you?"

Clark clapped Jimmy on the back. "Don't worry, Turtle Boy! Your secret is safe with me!" He winked at Lois.

"And me! Clark and I are very good at keeping secrets!"

"Well, I've got to go," announced Clark. "Big story brewing in midtown."

"Is that the street gang story?"

"Uh-huh."

"Well, be careful."

"I always am." He leaned down and gave Lois a peck on the cheek. "At least as careful as you are, m'dear!"

"See you later, Mr. . . . Clark!"

"Later, James."

No sooner had Clark passed through the double doors of the City Room than a bell went off on the wire service machine. Curious, Jimmy wandered over and tore loose the latest printout.

"Anything interesting, Jimmy?"

"Not unless you're into stories about Bigfoot."

"I beg your pardon?"

Jimmy chuckled. "According to this, there's some monster tearing up part of Ohio. Unbelievable!"

Exiting the City Room, Clark headed toward the elevator bank. When he was certain no one was watching, he slipped into the stairwell and started up, three steps at a time. Moments later, he was standing on a metal catwalk within the hollow globe atop the building. There he removed his glasses and began to doff his street clothes. In seconds, Clark Kent had disappeared, replaced by the bold figure of Superman!

Glancing around, he used his X-ray vision to make certain that the coast was clear. And then, when he was satisfied that no one would see him, he exited through a cleaning port in the side of the globe and launched himself heavenward.

Superman soared over the city, indulging himself by making a few loops as he went. It was a bright, sunny morning, a good day to be alive, another great day for flying.

The arc of his flight carried Superman high over Hob's River toward the northwest borough of Park Ridge. From five miles away, he spotted the flag flapping majestically from the pole on the roof of Roosevelt High School and the WGBS broadcast van with its microwave uplink dish parked just outside. Inside, he knew that Catherine Grant would be waiting for him to arrive for his interview.

Superman frowned. He hated taking such a high public profile. He knew that his activities made news—much of Clark Kent's career as a journalist had been built on reporting Superman's exploits. But ordinarily he avoided personal publicity in his costumed identity. That first awful experience after the rescue of the space plane had driven home to him the importance of maintaining his privacy. It was simply a matter of self-preservation to keep the Man of Steel a figure of mystery rather than of celebrity. It kept people from suspecting that Superman might live among them under another identity.

It's worked pretty well, he thought, as he landed on the school grounds. *Of course, it helps that I try to keep Clark Kent's and Superman's personal associations as separate as possible.* His relationship with Lois had been the one weak spot in his armor. She had come close to seeing through his deception, but his parents had helped conspire to make her doubt her own judgment. When Clark had finally told Lois of his double life after they were engaged, she was initially taken aback. But she couldn't truly admit to being surprised. *That problem's over now. She's already become my partner in life.*

Striding into the school's main building, Superman tried to ignore the sudden silence that his presence inspired. He could not help but be aware, though, of the turning heads and the nervous whispers. Inwardly, he was embarrassed by the attention. He'd long since learned to deal with the fame Clark had garnered as a journalist and author, but that kind of fame was nothing compared to what he engendered as Superman. *Like living in the proverbial goldfish bowl. If I couldn't keep my lives separate, I'd go crazy. How on Earth do rock stars cope?*

"Superman! This is a great honor!" The officious little man who approached him, hand outstretched, had a girth that suggested too many years spent behind a desk. "I'm Morton Wolf, principal of Roosevelt High. We're so happy to have you here."

Superman shook the offered hand, wishing that Wolf wouldn't stare at him so intently. "Happy . . . to be here, Mr. Wolf," he lied. The principal nodded, paying no notice to the caped man's hesitation. *Bet he'd have noticed it in one of his students,* thought Superman. He hated deceiving the man, but it was a small deception, and he knew how hurt Wolf would be if he told him how he really felt.

"Superman, over here!"

He turned, glad for the interruption, and suddenly found himself being led away by a young woman wearing jeans that were one size too tight and a cowl-necked sweater three sizes too big.

"Hi, Ann McNally. I'm Cat's producer. She's been wearing a groove in the floor, afraid you wouldn't make it. I told her not to worry, but that's Cat for you. Auditorium's back this way. It's really just a glorified gymnasium, but there's a stage with a proscenium at one end. We're set up around here. When we start the show, Cat will introduce you and start the interview. Sometime after the second commercial break, we'll start taking questions from kids in the audience."

Superman nodded, wondering how she managed to get through all that in one breath.

"Cat! He's here!" The volume of Ann's voice suddenly increased by a factor of five, drawing the attention of a statuesque blonde who nervously paced back and forth in the wings of the stage area.

Catherine Jane Grant looked up, turning in midstride, the anxiety melting away from her face. "Superman, darling, so good to see you again! It was so good of you to finally consent to an interview."

"Well, I've never appeared on a talk show before, Ms. Grant. I hope I don't wind up boring your audience."

"You? Boring?! Never! Why, the network is already talking about rerunning the show next week in prime time!"

" 'Scuse me, Cat," Ann interrupted, "but the kids are filing in and we really need to start the warm-up!"

"Be right there!" Cat fixed the Man of Steel with her most dazzling smile. "We'll be starting shortly. If there's anything you need, Ann will see to it." In a swirl of fabric, she was gone through the curtain.

With his X-ray vision, Superman watched Cat work the crowd. *She's very good at this, very smooth. And much brighter than anyone gives her credit for.*

Cat Grant had first made her mark in the newspaper trade as a West Coast gossip columnist. She'd gained fame through a series of in-depth interviews with leading Hollywood celebrities, sometimes becoming romantically linked with several of her more famous male subjects. Eventually, Cat moved to Metropolis, writing features and columns for the *Daily Planet* in the same breezy style that had made her the talk of Los Angeles. Her fame and reputation had led to additional work for Galaxy Communications, first as cohost of WGBS's *Hollywood Tonight* and finally to her own talk show.

Superman looked out at all the eager young faces on the students fidgeting in their seats. They looked like a bright bunch. He was struck by the memory of the one interesting assembly he'd attended in high school, when astronaut Pete Conrad had visited Smallville. Clark and his friends had been so excited to meet and hear a man who had actually walked on the moon. It had made him want to go into space himself . . . and eventually he had.

Superman smiled. Perhaps this wouldn't be so bad after all. Still, he never would have agreed to such an interview, in any forum, if it hadn't been for the Justice League.

No, not the League . . . not directly. I doubt that I'd be doing this if not for Guy Gardner. The former Green Lantern saw himself as leader of the group and carried a chip on his shoulder a mile wide. There had been unpleasant confrontations between the two of them, some of them in public. There were already dozens of rumors flying about the League— rumors that the UN was thinking of canceling their charter, even that the federal government was considering putting restrictions on the exercise of superpowers. Things were getting out of hand, and Superman couldn't let that continue. The Justice League was just too important to the world. Cat's show was an opportunity for him to reassure the public on that count. *I just hope that I've seen the last of the trouble with Gardner. I don't have time to go on TV every week.*

On U.S. Highway 30 just outside of Bucyrus, Ohio, a LexOil tanker truck lay twisted and burning around a late-model Subaru. The drivers of the two vehicles were pinned within the wreckage. Both had mercifully lost consciousness.

They could not see the two glowing figures who dropped through the curtain of fire. Nor did they hear the wrench of metal as the wreckage was ripped open by powerful gauntleted hands.

In an instant, the Lady Maxima had lifted the unconscious trucker from the cab of the tanker. "Quickly, Booster! These men require immediate medical attention."

Booster Gold nodded, carefully cradling the other driver as he extended the electromagnetic force field of his battle suit to cover them. "Let's get out of this inferno!"

As they rushed the injured men to safety, Ice thrust out her arms and through force of will began to draw heat from the surrounding air. The air appeared to thicken as moisture began condensing. Then, as if by magic, a wall of ice formed around the perimeter of the fire, momentarily halting its spread.

Guy Gardner circled overhead, using the energies of his ring to form a lid over the blaze. "Yeah, I'll have this little campfire snuffed out faster than you can say weenie roast."

Less than fifty feet away, the Blue Beetle's bug-ship hovered silently over a highway patrol car. A state trooper mopped his brow uneasily as Bloodwynd and Fire administered first aid to the rescued men.

"We appreciate the help, Justice Leaguers. I guess that Ohio is a little out of your normal jurisdiction."

"Not at all, Officer." The Beetle's manner was uncommonly serious. It was no time to be flippant. "We go where we're needed."

"We surely needed you today. Whatever it is that's responsible for this . . ." The trooper stopped, gesturing toward the smoldering wreckage, and swallowed hard. "Well, it's more than we're used to handling."

Fire looked up from her work. "These men both have concussions and some minor fractures, but I think they'll be all right. Maxima and Booster got to them just in time."

The trooper nodded. "Best news I've had all morning. Dispatch says the ambulances should be here within another couple minutes."

A dark, caped figure arose from Fire's side. "We must find the beast."

"I agree, Bloodwynd." Blue Beetle waved to get Gardner's attention. "Everybody back into the Bug and we'll be on our way."

In seconds, the strange ship was circling the area. "Keep your eyes on the ground, people. The sooner we spot our monster, the better." The Beetle glanced from his craft's infrared scanners to the countryside below. "Uh-oh. Looks like we've found our man's trail of crumbs."

A freshly hewn path cut through a wooded area to the east. Trees were splintered and in some cases completely uprooted.

Booster let out a long, low whistle. "Looks like a tornado came through here."

Beetle turned in his seat. "Bloodwynd, Maxima . . . you two have all those psychic powers. Any chance you can scan ahead and tap into this thing's mind?"

Bloodwynd shrugged. "I will try. But it will be difficult."

"Speak for yourself." Maxima settled back into her seat and began to concentrate.

Ice looked out of the ship, staring down at the path of destruction. "This is terrible. Such pointless, needless devastation."

Gardner drummed his fingers impatiently. "Let's just find the sucker, okay?"

For several long minutes, the ship was silent. Then Maxima stiffened and let out a cry. "I've found the Creature. He is east of here, perhaps no more than fifty miles. Yes, his presence is very strong . . . He . . ." She shook her head and her eyes narrowed. "He is hate . . . death and bloodlust personified. Nothing more."

Gardner laughed, and his ring glowed all the more brightly. "Sounds like my kinda guy." He leaned over and patted Ice's hand. "Don't worry, doll. We'll kick his butt!"

Ice shuddered involuntarily. *Guy, I don't care what you say, I still wish that Superman was here.*

In the Roosevelt High auditorium, a floor manager held up a hand, fingers wide as he ticked off the seconds to the end of the first commercial break. Four, three, two, one. The tally light atop camera one burned red.

"Welcome back!" Cat smiled. "We're coming to you live from Roosevelt High with an incredible show." She paused for effect. "He is perhaps the most celebrated man of our time! He's been called the Man of Tomorrow, the Last Son of Krypton, and the Man of Steel! But he's most appropriately known as—Superman!"

The auditorium erupted into thunderous applause—and not a few cheers—as Superman stepped through the curtain. Waving in acknowledgment, he strode across the tiny stage, taking Cat's hand. As they waited for the response to die down, Superman felt relieved that she was willing to accept a handshake rather than an air kiss. *People always look so damned foolish when they do that.* The applause showed no sign of ending, and he finally held out his hands, gesturing for calm.

Following his example, Cat added her own admonition. "Please! This is only a ninety-minute show! If we don't get to the interview soon, Principal Wolf will make us all stay after school!" The gag got the cheap laugh she was looking for from her audience, and they at last settled down.

"I can't thank you enough for joining us here, Superman." Cat finetuned her smile. "Interviews with you are a true rarity! You so seldom speak for the public record."

"I seldom have the time, Ms. Grant."

"Yes, well, let's cross our fingers and hope that any natural disasters hold off for the next hour and a half."

"That would be fine by me. I could use the rest."

"All right then . . . Superman, like others of your colleagues—Booster Gold, the Elongated Man, Wonder Woman—you've led a fairly public life, but we still know so very little about you! As leader of the Justice League—"

"Pardon me for interrupting, Ms. Grant, but I have to correct you on that point. It's unfair to the other members to paint me as the leader of the League. Every member has a say on issues . . . and a vote as well."

"Surely, though, you have a greater influence than some, Superman. Longtime observers suggest you've provided a quality of strength and focus that the League has been lacking for some time."

"I don't know who these 'observers' are, or how qualified they are to speak. But I've found the members of the Justice League to be a talented, dedicated group of individuals. They have a long, proud history, and I'm honored to be in their ranks."

"Superman, I'm sure no one disputes the long-standing reputation of the Justice League. But aside from yourself, this new League is relatively inexperienced."

"So were the original members, when the League was first founded."
"That may well be. But the original members seemed on the whole more . . . oh . . . even-tempered? Certainly, if they had any disagreements, they kept them private. That clearly isn't the case with the new League. As the whole country must know by now, you and Guy Gardner exchanged blows just a few weeks ago! What about that?"

Superman shook his head. *I knew she'd get to that sooner or later.*

"Reports of that incident were greatly exaggerated, Ms. Grant. In point of fact, I never struck Mr. Gardner."

"But he did hit you?"

"I allowed him to, yes. There had been an unfortunate misunderstanding involving the alarm system at the Justice League Compound in New York. Some members believed they were under attack, and Guy was caught up in the middle. He lost his temper . . . and I let him take it out on me." It was the truth, as far as it went.

"He must have quite a temper. It still doesn't sound as though he gets along with anybody."

"I can't say. I don't know the man that well. We're obviously not the closest of friends. But we're both professionals. When the chips are down, we work together and get the job done." He stole a glance at his image in the monitor and felt relieved. His nose hadn't grown at all. *Lord, but I'll be glad when this is over.*

While Superman diplomatically parried Cat Grant's questions, a big bear of a man lay sprawled facedown across an old, swaybacked bed in a second-floor walk-up over a Suicide Slum tavern known as the Ace o' Clubs. His last name was Bibbowski, and his first name was known only to a handful of police officers who had required it for their reports. To friends and acquaintances, he was simply Bibbo.

A fly settled tentatively on Bibbo's puffy left ear, causing it to twitch involuntarily. Still asleep, Bibbo rolled onto his back, his mouth flew open, and a window-rattling snore filled the room. His close-cropped gray hair and prominent beer gut suggested a man on the far side of fifty, but just how far was uncertain. His cauliflower ears and battered nose were mute evidence that Bibbo had once supported himself as a boxer.

To hear some people talk, Bibbo might have once been a serious heavyweight contender. Others dismissed him as just another lowlife, the veteran of too many barroom brawls. Bibbo had a reputation as a man who could clear a saloon in a matter of minutes. And it was rumored that on one occasion it had taken a dozen burly policemen to hold him down.

Bibbo had supported himself by working the docks as a longshoreman until the day when a gust of wind literally blew a lottery ticket into his face. The ticket won him a fourteen-million-dollar jackpot. Others might have taken the money and run as far from Suicide Slum as they could, but not Bibbo. With the first year's worth of his winnings, Bibbo bought the Ace o' Clubs and set about silently helping his more down-and-out buddies.

"Yo, Bibbo! You in there, man?" A knock came at the door of the apartment, answered only by a loud, beery snore. The pounding on the door became more insistent. "Bibbo? Hey, man, it's me . . . Lamarr! Hey, wake up! The beer truck's here!"

Bibbo awoke with a snort. "Beer truck? Oh, yeah . . . mus' be delivery day." He stumbled to the door and yanked it open so suddenly that Lamarr Powell all but fell into the room.

"Bibbo, are you—? Hooeee!" Lamarr pulled back from his friend, his nose wrinkling so that it appeared to bury itself deeper into his face. "Man, you smell like a sour keg!"

"Hey, your breat' ain't exactly daisies! What time is it?"

"I dunno. 'Bout a quarter to eleven, I guess."

"Quarter to 'leven?!" Bibbo came fully awake, his eyes fairly popping out of his head. "Oh, no! I'm missin' it!"

Bibbo shoved past Lamarr and bolted down the stairs, two steps at a time. He sprinted down the back hall like a crazed bull, knocking over the man from the beer truck. "Outta my way! I'm missin' my fav'rit!"

Following in his friend's wake, Lamarr helped the delivery man to his feet. "You all right?"

"Yeah, I think so. What got into him?"

"Beats me. I ain't seen Bibbo so agitated since the night Milwaukee was down two runs to Seattle in the bottom of the ninth."

Cautiously, they entered the back of the tavern to find Bibbo up on a stool hastily changing channels on the bar's old television.

"Yo, Bib. You won't find any game on this time o' day."

"Ain't lookin' for a game. What channel's the *Cat Grant Show* on?"

"Channel two. Since when do you follow talk shows?"

"I don't. But my fav'rit's s'posed to be on today! An' I been missin' 'im!" Bibbo hopped down from the stool.

"His favorite?" The delivery man regarded Bibbo with a fishy stare. "His favorite what?"

"Oh, I get it now!" Lamarr gave the delivery man a reassuring grin. "Superman must be on."

"Superman? But he doesn't do talk shows!"

"Well, he's doin' this one!" Bibbo glanced impatiently at the screen, waiting for the commercial break to end. "It said so, right in yesterday's *Planet*!"

"Okay. Whatever you say. But in the meantime, can I get you to sign for this delivery?"

"Yeah, sure." Bibbo scribbled his name on the proffered bill.

"Thanks. So . . . you like Superman, eh? Ever see him? Up close, I mean?"

"See 'im?" Bibbo let out a raspy laugh. "I almos' busted my knuckles on 'im once!"

"Excuse me?"

"Yeah, before I bought this place . . . Sooperman came in here one night lookin' for info on some crumbum. I thought 'e was just some jerk wearin' a phony costume, but 'e was real! An' 'e was tough! C'mere—!" Bibbo threw an arm around the delivery man and steered him to the middle of the barroom. "See here where we replaced the tile? Y'know why we hadda do that?"

"Uh, look, I really have to be going—!"

" 'Cause this is where Sooperman pulled me through the floor!"

"He what?!"

"Pulled me through the floor! Me an' some other guys! See, we was hasslin' this pal o' his, Olsen . . . only we din't know him an' Sooperman was buddies, see? Anyways, this Olsen kid was askin' a lotta nosy questions, an' we din't know 'im from Adam, so we was givin' 'im a hard time . . . not really leanin' on 'im, but lettin' 'im think we was. When all of a sudden, these hands come smashing up through wood, tiles, an' everything, an' pulled us right down through the floor! Haw-haw-haw!" Bibbo merrily slapped the confused delivery man on the back. "Sooperman, 'e's my fav'rit!"

"Let me get this straight. You nearly broke your hand punching Superman . . . and another time, he pulled you through a floor . . . and now you like him?"

"Like 'im? Ain't you been payin' attention? 'E's—!"

"He's your favorite . . . yeah, right. But . . . why?"

"Why?!" Bibbo looked at the delivery man in amazement. " 'Cause 'e's tough! 'E's the toughest guy I ever met! Ya gotta respect that!"

"Yo, Bibbo!" Lamarr called for his friend's attention. "Commercials're over! The show's comin' on!"

Bibbo pointed proudly at the caped figure on the screen. "Ya see? I tolja Sooperman was on!"

"Yeah, I—"

"Shaddup! I wanna hear what he hasta say!"

"Hello! We're back with Superman and the students of Roosevelt High." Cat stood in the central aisle of the auditorium bleachers, a wireless microphone in hand. "And I think it's high time that we let these students ask a few questions." She nodded to one young man who rose uncertainly from his seat. "And your name is—?"

"Kenny. I was wonderin' what you super-heroes do when you're not bashing the bad guys. I mean, do you get together and party all the time or what?"

"The members of the Justice League have a variety of interests, Ken, just as you and your friends do. The Blue Beetle, for example, is an inventor who enjoys spending his free time in the lab. Ice grew up in an isolated section of Norway and as a result likes to travel and learn about other cultures. Booster Gold is a sports buff. Maxima is busy adjusting to life on Earth. And Guy Gardner . . . well, Guy tends to be a bit more private with his free time. We don't see him much when he's on his own."

A freckle-faced boy approached the mike. His hair was an unruly mop that had been cut close on the sides. "Yeah, I have a question for Superman about Guy Gardner. Why won't you let him be a Green Lantern anymore? Why did you fire him?"

Superman cleared his throat. *Be diplomatic, Clark. The boy obviously idolizes Gardner enough to have his hair cut the same way.* "I can assure you that we didn't 'fire' Guy." *Much as we might like to.* "We really had no say regarding his status as a Green Lantern. You may not be aware of it, but all the many Green Lanterns are part of a much larger Green Lantern Corps. Guy's retirement as a Green Lantern was an internal matter of the corps . . . and I'm not qualified to speak on their behalf. Nor would I wish to second-guess them."

Three hundred miles away, students in Noah Swanson's third-period history class sat fidgeting in their seats as the interview played out on a classroom monitor. Noah himself was getting annoyed. "Look, this interview is taking place in Metropolis for the benefit of high school students nationwide. I want you kids to pay attention!"

Daryl Warner rolled his eyes and held his voice down to a whisper. "If you ask me, Mitch, this is turning into a real yawner."

Across the aisle, Mitch Andersen nodded wearily. "No kiddin'! If they're going to talk about Guy Gardner, why don't they get Guy Gardner on there with that Boy Scout? But no . . . they wouldn't do that! Besides, Guy wouldn't waste his time with some stupid talk show!"

"Mr. Andersen? Mr. Warner?"

Nuts! Old Man Swanson caught us.

"Is there something you wish to share with the class?"

"Uh . . . no, sir."

"No."

"Let's keep it down, then, shall we? Some of us, at least, want to hear what Superman has to say!"

As Cat came up the aisle, a boy in a battered old leather jacket rose and leaned over the microphone. "Hey, Superman, I got a question about Fire. Does she score as high on the babe-o-meter as she seems?" The boy plopped back into his seat, to the amusement of his friends seated nearby.

Ah, yes. Sophomore, no doubt. Superman tried to maintain a poker face, but it was a battle not to grin. "Fire is good at her job and a terrific person. You'd like her. Next question?"

Cat stepped down a few rows and held the microphone out to an earnest young girl. "I was, y'know, wondering, Superman, if there's anything out there that, y'know, really frightens you? I mean, I'd get scared facing all that stuff if I were you."

"That's a very good question, miss. One way or another, fear is always part of my job. Mainly, there's the fear of failure. There are criminals who have eluded me, and there have been people whom I was unable to save." *Like the crew of the* Excalibur.

Several months before, the space shuttle *Excalibur* had crash-landed outside Metropolis, its crew the victims of an orbital radiation experiment. Of the four crash survivors, Superman had been able to save only one, Terri Henshaw. The Man of Steel had watched helplessly as her husband, shuttle commander Hank Henshaw, succumbed to the radiation. Henshaw's body had failed, and then—!

Mustn't dwell on that, he reminded himself. *Answer the question.*

"Aside from that, I'm also afraid of unintentionally hurting innocent people. And, to be candid, there have been times when I have feared for my own life. On numerous occasions, I have encountered forces powerful enough to kill me." Superman noticed some doubting expressions in the audience. *They wouldn't look so skeptical if they'd ever met Mongul or Darkseid.*

The girl pressed on. "What about all that, y'know, hitting and violence? Don't you get tired of it? I mean, aren't there better ways to work things out, other than caving in someone's head?"

Superman nodded appreciatively. *She sounded a little uncertain at first, but she's obviously given a lot of thought to this.* "There certainly are better ways, and we must use them whenever possible. The Reverend Dr. Martin Luther King, Jr., spoke of the need for humanity 'to overcome oppression and violence without resorting to oppression and violence.' That's a goal that every one of us must strive to meet." He paused. The school auditorium had grown unnaturally quiet. "I wish that the use of force would never be necessary. But experience has taught me that there are some opponents who cannot be stopped any other way. I have torn apart tanks and planes with my bare hands, and I have used these hands to render other people unconscious. Believe me when I say that I am not proud of that. It is something that I find necessary to do to protect others, to accomplish a greater good, a common good. It is that common good that we choose to protect with our powers . . . and our lives."

8

The Justice League did not find the Creature. He found them.

The shadow of the bug-ship passed over the Creature as he stalked through a small wooded glen not far from Canton, Ohio. Intrigued by the odd flying craft, he hurled a good-sized rock through it.

"Everybody assume crash positions!" Beetle frantically fought the controls. "Our hydraulics are shredded! We're going down!"

Thousands of feet in the air, the bug-ship began to break apart. The seven Justice Leaguers suddenly found themselves in free-fall.

"I'm gonna find the creep who whacked us and sew his eyelids shut!"

"Give us nonfliers a hand first, Guy!" The Beetle's plea had its hoped-for effect.

Guy swung about and swooped under Ice, while Booster grabbed hold of Beetle and slowed his fall. "Gotcha, ol' buddy. Nothing to worry about now!"

"There's plenty to worry about! What's left of my Bug is about to slam into Route 62! When it hits—!"

"It will not!" Maxima stood in midair, a ripple of energy swirling around her. As she gestured, the ship's wreckage came to a slow stop.

While Maxima occupied herself with holding the wreckage together and lowering it to Earth, the other members of the League assembled along the shoulder of the highway. No sooner had they caught their breath than the ground shook and a gout of flame roared up beyond the adjoining grove.

"Before we were hit I saw—!" Beetle swallowed hard. "That is, I think . . . there's a LexOil refinery over there!"

"All right! That does it!" Guy Gardner shot away from the group, headed for the fiery glow. Flying over the grounds of the refinery, he quickly spotted the heavily shrouded figure emerging from the ruin of one huge tower. Ring blazing, Gardner swooped down to confront the Creature.

"What'll it be, fella—burial or cremation? Your pick!"

The Creature seemed at first startled by the appearance of a glowing, flying man. But his surprise was short-lived. Despite Gardner's ring-generated force field, the Creature grabbed hold of the cocky former Green Lantern and threw him headfirst to the ground. A huge boot came down hard on Guy's head, again and again. And then, with his one free hand, the Creature picked Guy up by the head and shook him like an old rug.

"Let go of him, you . . . monster!" Fire streaked across the sky, awash in emerald flame. *Guy may be a jerk, but he's* our *jerk.* She directed her flame in a searing stream at the Creature. He dropped Guy and stood there for a moment, flames crackling all around him, staring silently at the blazing woman. And then he simply turned and walked away.

Fire pursued him, pouring on the heat until the Creature's bonds began to smoke and smolder. "I don't believe it! No matter how much flame I throw at this goon, it doesn't seem to faze him in the least!"

"I will deal with him, Fire!" Bloodwynd dropped from the sky directly into the Creature's path. Calling upon all the eldritch power at his command, the sorcerous warrior channeled that energy into one single devastating punch. The Creature hardly appeared to feel it. He barely paused as he returned the blow tenfold, punching Bloodwynd and sending him through the side of a massive oil storage tank.

The Blue Beetle ran onto the refinery grounds, trying to help the downed Bloodwynd. But before he could reach his injured teammate, a monstrous hand grabbed him from behind. The Creature turned the Beetle around and slammed the Leaguer against the side of a metal tank. So hard was the impact that the Beetle's goggles shattered and his protective mask peeled away from half his face. Then the Creature tossed the unconscious hero to the side.

"Cut!"

"Cut?" Cat Grant turned to confront her director. "What do you mean, 'Cut'?!"

"I mean, we're off the air." He clutched his headset tightly to his ear as the monitors set up around the auditorium flashed the familiar Galaxy

Broadcasting G. "We're being preempted by network news. There's something weird going on in the Midwest . . . some sort of trouble."

"Trouble?" Superman was on his feet and across the stage in an instant.

The director reached for the volume control. "You want me to turn up the sound?"

"If you want. I can hear it fine as is."

"Turn it up, Mickey." Cat joined them by the central monitor. "If I'm being preempted, I want to know by what!"

". . . reports at this hour of intense fighting between members of the Justice League and what authorities are calling a monster at an oil refinery near Canton, Ohio." The voice of a WGBS news announcer suddenly boomed out across the chamber. "Initial indications are that the League has been unable to halt the destructive rampage of the as-yet-unidentified creature."

"I have to go, Ms. Grant." Superman became a blur.

"Superman—?" Cat ran after him, but by the time she reached the exit door, he was already several miles away.

The Blue Beetle landed hard and did not move. Ice and Booster Gold were the first to reach him.

"My God, Ice, is he breathing?"

"I think so. But he's so still . . ."

"Do everything you can for him. I'm going after that thing!"

Booster streaked after the Creature, catching up to him at the perimeter of the burning refinery. "No more games, Ugly. Not after what you did to my buddy!" Thumbing the microcontrols on his battle suit, Booster peppered the Creature with high-intensity energy blasts from his gauntlets.

The Creature gave out an angry snort and charged at the hero full tilt. Booster just barely had time to divert power to his force field before the thing struck. With a blow that cracked like thunder, the Creature sent Booster flying out of control.

The sound of the wind sluicing off his force field was almost deafening as Booster arced several miles into the sky. *Never been hit like that before.* The thought came to him slowly. Even with the cushioning effect of his protective field, Booster was seeing stars. *That thing smacked me so hard . . . flight circuits are overpowered. Don't know if I can stop.*

"Drop your field, Booster! I'll catch you."

"What—?" Booster's eyes went wide, but he recognized the voice almost immediately and did as he was told. A mighty hand reached out, firmly grabbing hold of him.

"Superman? Where'd you come from?"

"I heard that the League was having some trouble."

" 'Trouble' isn't the word for it!" Booster took a deep breath and shook his head. "It's more like Doomsday has arrived!"

Mitch Andersen sailed down the sidewalks of his neighborhood atop his skateboard, a warm breeze blowing through his hair. *This sure beats hanging out with the dweebs in the cafeteria, getting ptomaine from the City Chicken or whatever today's Mystery Meat was.* Mitch hated school. He especially hated it on such a bright and sunny day. In the back of his mind, he weighed his chances for cutting his afternoon classes without getting caught. His stomach rumbled. *Better grab some lunch first.*

Mitch jumped the curb and kicked his way down the street to the two-story tract house at the end of a cul-de-sac. The "War Zone," he called it. He hated that house almost as much as he did school, but until he was ready to move out on his own, he was stuck there . . . with a mother and baby sister who were slowly driving him nuts. He already knew what his mother would say when he walked in the door: "Mitch, dear, is that you? How's your day been?" That's what she always said. He'd heard the same thing—day after day, week after week, month after month. It was like some corny, sickeningly sweet mantra. That was his mother all right. That's what people were always telling him. "Your mother is so nice . . . so sweet and sincere." *Yeah, as if being sincere could excuse anyone for being* that *sweet!* Mitch skidded to a halt and kicked the skateboard up into his hands. He sometimes wondered if his father had left them because he just couldn't take the sweetness anymore.

Mitch opened the back door, his skateboard under one arm.

"Mitch, dear, is that you?"

Why doesn't she just record it and save her voice? It's not like anyone would ever notice. "No, it's Axl Rose."

Mitch's baby sister, Becky, was in her high chair, getting fed something that looked even more disgusting than usual. Mitch surveyed the kid and his mother. He could never understand why his mom had wanted to have another baby at her age. Had she thought it would hold the family together? Mitch shrugged to himself. "We got anything worth eating around here?"

"Help yourself to whatever's in the fridge. How was school this morning?"

Mitch almost blinked. His mother had actually said something different for a change! He answered with a snort.

"How did you do on your algebra test?"

"Like you care." Mitch stuck his head in the refrigerator. "Hey! What happened to all the soda?!"

"Mitch! Of course I care." She paused, a spoon of strained squash in hand. "Say, wasn't today the day that Superman was going to address high school students on TV? It must have been a thrill to see that!"

"No way. The superweasel was called away on some case and he bailed out early. Probably had to yank a cat from a tree." Mitch shoved the refrigerator door shut and leaned back against it in disgust. "Why do we always run out of soda around here? Why can't you ever buy enough to last?"

"Look, I'm sorry, but your sister isn't feeling well. I haven't had time to go shopping—"

"I am really tired of that baby being the only one who rates around here! I mean, Dad always has soda waiting for me at his apartment!"

"I'm sorry, Mitchell, but I cannot keep up with everything here. This house isn't perfect and neither am I. We just have to do the best we can!"

"Jeez, if this is the best you can do, it's no wonder Dad left. No wonder he wants a divorce."

Claire Andersen opened her mouth to speak, but not a word came out. She turned away from her only son, tears welling up in her eyes.

What is the matter with her? Why doesn't she say something? Why does she just sit there and take it? Mitch could feel his stomach knotting up. *Why doesn't she yell and scream? Other mothers would. Why is mine such a wimp?* "I'm goin' over to Aaron's." He turned and headed for the door. He tried to sound cool, but his voice had all of a sudden gotten husky. "See you later."

Becky made a gurgling noise and reached out to her mother. Claire brushed away her tears and was attempting to smile for her daughter when an odd cracking noise came from somewhere outside.

"Mitch, wait! Did you hear that—?"

Suddenly Ice came crashing through their big kitchen window.

As Ice tumbled across the room, Claire instinctively threw herself in front of Becky, shielding the baby from the shower of flying glass. She pulled Becky from the high chair and turned to her son, who stood frozen in the doorway. "Mitchell, call 911! Hurry!" Then something beyond the shattered window caught her eye, and she froze as well.

The Creature came striding straight toward their house. Only the family car stood in his way. With one sweep of his hand, he batted it aside.

"Our car!" Still unable to move, Claire clutched the baby to her.

Mitch was moving, but slowly, as if he were caught in some movie filmed in slow motion. Behind the looming Creature, he could see a row of uprooted trees and, far beyond, a darkening cloud of smoke. *Whoa! That dude did all this—with one hand tied behind his back?!*

Less than ten feet from the house, the Creature stopped and looked up. Something was approaching . . . something up in the sky.

Booster Gold and Superman landed directly in the Creature's path. "That's the guy, Superman. He's the one who took the Justice League apart at the seams."

Superman quickly sized the Creature up. *Seven feet tall if he's an inch.* With his X-ray vision, Superman looked beneath the heavy shroud. *No, not a robot . . . but dense, very dense . . . and ugly.* "What was it you called him, Booster? Doomsday?"

The newly named Doomsday saw a challenge in the caped man who stood so boldly in his path. He cocked back his free arm and delivered a powerful blow to Superman's midsection.

Superman did not budge, but he felt the blow. *If I hadn't seen it coming, hadn't tensed my abdominals, that could have hurt.*

Booster flinched. "Superman . . . are you all right?"

Superman looked back at Booster, and in that moment, Doomsday struck again, wheeling around and this time kicking him in the midsection. Caught off guard, Superman went flying backward through one side of the Andersen house and out the other. The entire house sagged to one side as he crashed into an old oak in the side yard. The Man of Steel sprawled back across the toppled tree, stars swimming before his eyes.

Booster made a grab for Doomsday, but the creature evaded his lunge and slammed him into a large sycamore. As the tree cracked and fell, Booster's force field flickered out.

The Andersens were just starting to pick themselves up from the rubble of what had been their kitchen when Doomsday bashed his way in. Mitch froze in slack-jawed disbelief, not that this monster was ripping apart their house, but that his mother—*his mother!*—was standing her ground.

"Why?" Claire's voice shook with indignation. "Why are you doing this to our house? What do you want from us?"

Doomsday's only answer was a muffled snort. His attention was drawn to Ice, who lay semiconscious amid the remains of a kitchen counter. Gleefully, Doomsday pounded her, laughing at the sound of breaking ribs. Behind him, little Becky found her voice and began to wail. Doomsday turned, fist raised. Claire's eyes went wide with fear.

"No! Not my baby! Please, not my baby!"

Doomsday raised his arm to strike, but suddenly Superman was there. With a punishing combination of blows, he drove the creature away from the Andersens and back out of the swaying house.

"Get your family out of here!" Superman shouted over his shoulder. "I'll cover your escape as long as I can!"

"You won't have to do it alone, Supes! The Cavalry is on the scene."

Superman didn't need to risk a glance this time. *Booster*—who else would call him "Supes"?—*back on his feet. And from the sound of things, he's rallied some of the others.*

" 'S'matter, Boy Scout?" Guy Gardner sounded unsteady, his words spit from painfully swollen lips. His eyes were nearly swollen shut. "Is that guy too tough even for you?"

"Guy, that monster might be too tough for all of us!" Fire's usual confidence was missing.

"No way, babe!" Booster had never sounded more serious. "I say we hit him with everything we got!"

"All our powers in a combined, concerted effort." Bloodwynd looked to Superman. "Agreed?"

Superman nodded. "Let's do it!"

Five beams of incredible energy shot out at Doomsday. Fire aimed another searing blast of green flame at the creature. From Superman's eyes came a tightly focused beam of radiant heat. Likewise, Bloodwynd trained the coherent energy of his eye-beams on Doomsday, even as he helped the half-blinded Guy Gardner aim his power ring's golden beam. Booster Gold went into a crouch, routing all the energy of his power cells into his gauntlets, adding their blasting power to his teammates' miniature fire storm.

"Give it everything you've got!" yelled Booster, squinting into the glare. "We'll show this dude what kind of trouble he buys when he takes on the Justice League!"

Mitch's head swung back and forth as though it were mounted on a spring; he literally didn't know which way to turn.

"Mitch, get hold of yourself! I need you!"

He looked at his mother with something akin to shock. *Did she really say that?* She'd never said a single, solitary assertive thing for as long as he could remember. "Mom—?" Before he could finish his question, she thrust the baby into his hands and stooped down to grab Ice by the shoulders. "Mom, what're you doing?"

"What's it look like I'm doing?" Claire slowly eased the unconscious Justice Leaguer across the linoleum. "You heard Superman! We have to get out of here, and we can't very well leave this poor woman behind!"

"Yeah. I guess not." Mitch numbly fell in alongside his mother, holding Becky in one arm and using the other to shove debris out of their path.

Superman peered down the length of his heat beam. "Amazing. I can't even see him anymore, but I think he's still standing!"

"Don't stand there blabbin', Boy Scout. Just turn up the juice!" Guy's voice had become a raspy growl.

Fire began to sway, her flame flickering out. "I'm spent . . . can't go on anymore!"

"Me neither." Sweat was running down Booster's face. "My power cells are shot . . . drained!"

Bloodwynd looked pained. "I . . . am weakened myself."

"Okay, let's give it a rest!" Though he'd never admit it, Guy was about to collapse. "After all this there's no way the creep could still be standin'!"

But as the smoke and fire of their barrage dissipated, it became all too clear that Doomsday was indeed still standing. He had stood his ground throughout their high-energy attack. The ground around him, however, was scorched and smoldering. Doomsday's heavy suit was partially burnt away, and his left arm was completely free of its bonds.

All they had succeeded in doing was destroying the last of his restraints.

Doomsday launched himself at the assembled Justice Leaguers, scattering them like tenpins. He battered the powerless Booster Gold unconscious and then used Gold's body as a weapon, hurling him headlong at Guy Gardner. Superman and Bloodwynd tried to surround Doomsday in a flanking maneuver, but the creature lashed out unexpectedly, stunning them both. Groggy, Bloodwynd tried again to focus his eye-beams on the creature but succeeded only in accidentally igniting the ruin of the Andersens' house. Stumbling away from the battle, Fire tried to give Claire Andersen a hand with the injured Ice.

That's when the house fire touched off a gas line. Already severely weakened, the house blew apart. A huge burning section of roof and wall fell toward Mitch and his family, separating them from the stunned Justice League.

Amid all the chaos and confusion he had caused, Doomsday leapt away, laughing madly.

With that awful laughter ringing in his ears, Superman scrambled to his feet, a look of horror on his face. All his life, ever since he'd reached maturity and realized the extent of his powers, he had held himself in check whenever circumstances forced him to fight another living being.

If my holding back has resulted in this—! The thought terrified him. *No . . . no way is that maniac escaping me!* With a spring and a leap, Superman shot into the sky. The others could deal with the fire—he had to stop Doomsday!

Mitch came to, surrounded by smoke and scattered debris. "Where . . . where is everybody? Mom? Becky—?!" He had been holding his baby sister. Now where was she? *My God, did I drop her?*

Then he saw them. They were just a few feet away, but they might as well have been on the moon. A burning beam separated him from his family. Through the wall of flame, Mitch could see Becky sitting huddled next to their mother's body. *No, don't think that. She's alive, she's got to be!* A wave of heat forced Mitch back and he stumbled from the wreckage. The Justice Leaguers lay sprawled around him like broken dolls. Mitch looked around wildly. *There's only one guy who can help us . . . Where is he?*

"Superman! Please, Superman, you gotta hear me! Help us! Please!"

Superman was already many miles away. He caught up to Doomsday at the apex of his second leap and struck the creature in the side so hard that the sound of his punch echoed like a thunderclap. Stunned, Doomsday fell from the sky, landing like a rock in the fields far below.

Superman glanced back toward the ravaged suburban subdivision. He could hear the distant wail of sirens and the cry of a desperate young man.

"Superman! Please—you've got to help us! My mom . . . my baby sister . . . they're trapped! Please!"

Scanning the scene with his super-vision, Superman discovered to his horror that the rest of the Justice League were in no shape to help, and civilian rescue workers were still several minutes from the scene. *Good Lord! I've got to get back there!*

But in that moment's distraction, Doomsday launched himself skyward, slamming into Superman like a guided missile. The Man of Steel tumbled backward, the creature holding on to him.

This creature's fast and strong, but it seems to leap rather than fly! As long as I can hold it, it's at my mercy as to where we go.

Clutching Doomsday tight around the shoulders, Superman dove beneath the waters of nearby Westville Lake. There he forced the creature deep into the silt at the bottom of the reservoir. Superman then shot up out of the lake. *That should keep the monster out of trouble. I just pray there's still time to help that family!*

Claire Andersen regained consciousness amid the fiery rubble of what had been her home, her baby crying plaintively by her side. She picked up her daughter and cradled her in her arms, trying to shield the child from the blistering heat with her own body. "It's okay, Becky. It's okay. We'll get out somehow."

Then came an awful cracking noise. Claire looked up to see another huge beam toppling toward them.

Suddenly, a crimson and blue flash swept through the fire, and a pair of powerful arms scooped up Claire and her baby.

"Come on, let's get you out of here."

"S-Superman?"

They soared out of the wreckage, high and away from the heat and flame. Claire looked down and saw what was left of her home going up in smoke. *Down below . . . mother's china, the family photos . . . everything's burning . . . it doesn't seem possible.* Becky squirmed in her arms, and she hugged her tighter. *But it doesn't matter . . . they were just—things. We'll get by . . . as long as the kids are safe. The kids—!*

"Where's my son? Where's Mitch?"

"Don't worry, ma'am, he's all right. An EMS crew's just arrived . . . I can see him down there with them."

Mitch Andersen looked up in wonderment as Superman descended. "He did it! He saved my mom and baby sister."

Superman handed the Andersens over to the paramedics and then looked about him. Booster Gold, Fire, and Guy Gardner were being laid out on stretchers. One rescue worker was starting to tape Ice's ribs, even as she was trying to get Guy to lie still. Bloodwynd was standing, but he didn't seem all that steady on his feet. Finally able to take a head count, Superman realized that two members were missing.

"Where are the others?"

Ice looked up tearfully. "Before you ever arrived . . . Beetle was beaten . . . horribly. I . . . I convinced Maxima that she should rush him to the hospital."

Superman looked grim. "You should all go to the hospital. None of you is in any shape to carry on."

"Yeah, but you are." Guy Gardner reached up, tugging on his cape. "Don't wuss out on us, Boy Scout! Get that Doomsday creep. Put him in a pine box for me . . . or I'll crawl off this stretcher and kick both your butts!"

"I'll take care of things, Guy. You just let the doctors help you."
Superman turned to the nearest paramedic. "Have your local hospital
contact the Justice League Compound in New York City. They'll supply
you with the medical records for these people."

And then Superman was gone, rocketing off into the heavens.

9

Doomsday emerged from the lake, growling like an angry bear. The previous attacks had blasted away part of the goggled hood that masked his hideous face, and now he stared with his exposed eye, scanning the skies for signs of the flying man who had tried to bury him in the lake bottom. But where was he?

High overhead, an air force jet fighter shot across the sky, its contrail marking its flight path. Doomsday regarded the fast-moving speck for a moment. Was that the flying man?

Crouching low, Doomsday leapt nearly a mile into the sky. It was not high enough. The contrail drifted far higher. The creature let out an angry snort as he arced Earthward. If his target flew higher, he would just leap higher. It would not escape him.

Doomsday landed feetfirst on a rocky cliffside, and immediately sprang skyward again. Higher and higher he climbed . . . two miles, then three . . . but still not high enough. Again he fell to Earth, and again he leapt into the sky. His third leap carried him well into the wilds of Pennsylvania, and still he did not stop. He would not stop—not until he had caught up to his quarry and brought it down.

Superman scoured the bottom of Westville Lake, finding no sign of the creature. He emerged to find a highway patrolman waving to him from the shoreline.

"Superman! Superman, if you're looking for that monster, it's gone!"

"Any idea of where he went?"

"Not for certain. Some kids playing near here say they saw it jump up into the air and just keep going. Can—can it fly, too?"

"Not exactly. Did they say which direction it was headed?"

"Sure did. It took off to the east."

Superman looked eastward and instantly noticed the contrail. "Oh, no!"

Captain Joyce Miller cruised eastward in her F–15, appreciating the day and the fine weather, and simply appreciating being alive and in flight. She had thoroughly enjoyed taking part in the Wright-Patterson air show, had been sorry even to see it end. *Too bad Will had to cancel at the last minute. Two F–15s make for an even better show than one. Oh, well, there's always next year.*

She was eight miles high and twenty miles south of Lancaster, Pennsylvania, when a blip suddenly appeared on her short-range radar.

"Dover Control . . . Dover Control, this is Momma Bird, do you copy? Over."

"This is Dover Control. We read you, Momma Bird. What is your situation? Over."

Captain Miller frowned at her screens. "Not clear. Short-range is showing a bogey on my tail . . . no, wait, it's falling off screen." For a moment it had looked like the simulations of a surface-to-air shot. *But that's ridiculous! Who'd be firing a SAM in southern Pennsylvania?* "Wait a minute! There it is again!" A warning buzzer sounded in the cockpit. "It's gaining on me!"

Miller yanked the stick sharply to the side and hit the afterburners, taking evasive action, but it was too late. "I'm hit! Repeat, I'm hit!" She looked back over her shoulder and saw an apparition out of her worst nightmares crawling down the fuselage toward her. The air tore at the monster's tattered hood, exposing a huge red eye that stared out at her through a cage of craggy bone. More bone protruded, tusklike, from around the gaping mouth.

"What the hell is that?!"

"Momma Bird? What is your—?"

"I've got some refugee from the *Twilight Zone* on my back!" She could swear she heard it bellow, even over the roar of the jets.

"Momma Bird? We didn't copy that—!"

"I don't believe it myself!" Miller pulled back on the stick. She was losing power fast. But, hallucination or not, as long as she had some degree of control, she was determined to bring her craft down.

The F–15 shook as Doomsday sank his fists into the fuselage, defiantly hanging on against the force of the onrushing gale. Inch by inch he worked his way toward the helmeted figure beneath the canopy. It was not the flying man who lurked within the falling metal craft, but it lived. He would kill it before he moved on.

Miller mouthed a silent curse. She was losing control and that . . . thing seemed to be getting closer. She looked down. The Susquehanna River stretched out before her, emptying into the upper Chesapeake Bay. At least she wouldn't have to worry about crashing into some town. The jet shook again. This time, when she looked back, the creature was scraping at the edges of the canopy. *That does it!*

"Dover Control, this is Momma Bird! You may ground me for this, but I have a monster on my back!" Her voice suddenly calm, she gave her location and initiated procedures for ejection.

The canopy suddenly exploded out of Doomsday's grasp, and the next instant Captain Miller shot up and out of the damaged craft. When her parachute finally opened, she was still high enough to watch as the monster rode her ship down into the bay.

Several minutes after the jet disappeared beneath the waters of the bay, the air overhead was chopped by the rotors of an Apache helicopter from nearby Fort Schiff.

"I don't get it, Marcus." The copilot looked up from the instrument array and shot his buddy a quizzical look. "An F–15 goes down and some fly-boy bails, but we're not looking for him?"

"Her. We're not looking for her, Ralph."

"Whatever. So what *are* we looking for?"

"A monster."

"Oh, a monster! Why didn't you say so? A monster . . . get serious!"

"The CO seemed very serious. The jet pilot claimed that some monster lit on her bird and forced it down. Air rescue's already been dispatched to scoop up the pilot."

"And we drew boogeyman duty."

"You might say that, Ralph . . . but I wouldn't. At least not to the CO."

"Well, if you ask me . . ." Ralph Greenwood let the thought trail off. "What the hell is that?!"

Below, the surface of the bay began to swirl and churn. And then Doomsday erupted from the waters.

"Holy—! That's our target down there, Ralph! Launch the Hellfires."

But as the missile-launch cycle was triggered, Doomsday's leap carried him straight up through the helicopter. The Apache lurched sickeningly to one side, sending the two army airmen tumbling helplessly Earthward.

In a blur of motion, Superman suddenly dropped down over the bay, plucking the wayward Hellfire missile from the air and turning it back on course toward the soaring Doomsday. The Man of Steel then executed a perfect 180–degree turn and swooped beneath the falling airmen, gently slowing their falls.

The missile locked on to its intended target and shot across the sky. Some three miles away, its smart warhead hit its mark fair and true. The explosion caught Doomsday unawares, flinging him far from the bay.

In the Kirby County village of Griffith, Chief Ray Newton shook his head as he hung up the phone. "Turn on the TV, Rusty," he called out to his deputy. "CNN. Lowell said a bunch of folk, including some of the Justice League, are being rushed to the hospital over in Ohio. Way he put it, sounded as though some kinda monster tore up a chunk of the Midwest and headed east."

"Should I crank up the civil defense siren, Chief?"

Ray sighed. Rusty meant well, but he'd seen too many Saturday matinees in his youth. "I'm sure we'll get a warning, if this whatever-it-is gets anywheres close—"

"Say, you hear that?"

Ray usually hated to have Rusty interrupt him, but there was something in the air. "What is that? Some sort of . . . whistle?"

"Yeah. Kind of a cartoony sound. You know, like a falling bomb makes just before it goes kerblooey!"

The building was suddenly rocked by a thundering crash.

"Mother of pearl! We *are* bein' bombed!" Rusty grabbed at his holster, fumbling to pull out his side arm on the run.

Ray jumped up from his desk, bolting after his eager deputy. "Rusty, don't go running off half-cocked." *Durn fool's likely to shoot himself if he isn't careful.* But the next moment, Ray came to a halt on the doorstep of the village police station, just half a step behind his deputy.

Not more than five feet away, Doomsday arose from the ruin of their police cruiser.

"Uh, Chief?" Rusty's voice had become a squeak. "I think I'm gonna need a bigger gun."

A low growl came from the monster before them. Ray and Rusty each took a step backward. Then there came another whistling rush of wind. Three heads turned upward to see Superman dropping toward Doomsday feetfirst.

The pavement cracked and buckled as Superman drove Doomsday beneath the village street. Superman looked up at the two policemen.

"Get back! He's too—"

Before Superman could finish his warning, Doomsday's fist shot up from underground. The Man of Steel was thrown half a block away and landed hard, plowing up several yards of Main Street on impact.

And then Doomsday was on top of him, one huge hand encircling his throat.

Ray Newton was already back inside his office, cursing into his telephone. "Look, Mr. Vice–Lieutenant Governor, I'm telling you this is going to be more than 'just' a local emergency, if'n you don't get the blasted National Guard down here ASAP!"

There was a loud thud outside, and the building shook anew. A huge crack appeared in the far wall of the station. "Oh, sweet Jesus!" Ray grabbed the phone and pulled it under his desk as Superman and Doomsday came tumbling through the station in a shower of plaster lath and masonry.

"Mother o' mercy! You hear that, you tin-horn bureaucrat? This county's in the process of losin' its one and only police station!"

Aware of the chief's danger, Superman feinted back and then drove into Doomsday with a double uppercut which knocked him back out of the building.

Out on the village streets, sirens were sounding and people were running for their lives. Overhead, the familiar whir of rotor blades heralded the arrival of another army helicopter.

"This is Blue Leader. Target sighted and we're ready for a run. Over."

"Blue Leader, approach with extreme caution. We've already lost one chopper to this thing. Over."

"We hear ya, Control."

The Apache cut loose with its guns, peppering Doomsday with high-caliber shells. Annoyed, the creature tore a lamppost from the pavement and rammed one end of it into the fuselage of the hovering copter.

"We've been hit!"

"No . . . we've been speared!"

Doomsday swung the Apache around wildly, using his end of the lamppost as a huge handle. Then he let go, and the craft veered drunkenly toward Griffith's town hall.

"Backup systems are down! No time to bail! Mayday! Mayday!"

Moments from impact, two powerful hands suddenly ripped through the cockpit, grabbing the airmen and pulling them from the helicopter.

"Wha—? Who?"

"Relax, soldier. You and your copilot are going to be okay . . . though I'm afraid the town hall won't be open for business anytime soon." Superman set them down on the outskirts of town. "Now you'll have to excuse me. I can see a dozen people trapped inside that building who need my help, and I don't have much time! If anyone comes by, warn them to stay off the streets!"

. . .

In his chambers within the Cadmus Project, Jim Harper pulled off his radio headset and frowned. For much of the morning, the special bands set aside for federal and defense department transmissions had been humming with scrambled emergency messages. A whole chain of incidents—some verified, others not—had been reported, starting in the Midwest and snaking their way east. If the reports were to be believed, there was some sort of monster on the loose in the northern part of Kirby County, less than fifty miles from the Project. And according to the latest communiqués, Superman himself was being hard-pressed to stop the creature from leveling the village of Griffith.

Harper punched up a code on his comlink. "Fitzsimmons? I'm going out. You're in charge until I return. If the directors need to know where I've gone, it's all on the board."

Jim Harper fitted his golden helmet and headed for the motor pool. If Superman needed help, the Guardian would be there.

Maxima had been flying for over an hour, searching for the monster who had injured and humiliated her teammates, when she saw the smoke rising from the horizon. As she descended from the skies over Griffith, she saw Doomsday stride through the burning rubble, roaring his awful laugh to the heavens.

Revel in the destruction while you can, warrior. She could not be certain of his motives, but if it was battle that he craved, Maxima would be pleased to oblige! Silently, she landed behind the seven-foot-tall behemoth and arrogantly tapped him on the shoulder. When Doomsday turned at her touch, Maxima struck him with all the physical might at her command, knocking the creature half the length of the town's deserted Main Street.

The security guard at Metropolis's Galaxy Communications Building was giving Lois Lane a hard time. "You can't just barge in there like that, lady!" Specifically, he was blocking her entrance into Studio B.

"You don't understand, this is an emergency!"

The guard crossed his arms. "Look, lady, that red light over the door means they're taping. The mikes are live and the cameras are rolling, *capice*? You can't go in."

Lois silently counted to ten. "Can you at least tell me how I can get a message to someone in there?"

"Lois? What are you doing here?"

She turned. "Cat Grant! Thank God, a familiar face. Look, Jimmy Olsen's somewhere behind that door, and I need to get to him. He has an assignment."

Cat stared soulfully at the guard, and he shifted uneasily from one foot to another.

He coughed, and his voice grew plaintive. "They're taping that Turtle Boy show in there, Ms. Grant. I got my orders."

"Cat, Jimmy could lose his job at the *Planet*." Lois was pulling out all the stops.

Cat gave the guard a sweet smile. "I'll take the responsibility, Gus. Everything will be fine." His resolve gone, the guard stepped aside, and Cat gestured for Lois to follow her.

"Just keep your voice down, Lois." Cat dropped her own cheery tone to the barest whisper. "This has to do with Superman, doesn't it? And all that destruction upstate?"

"How do you know about that?"

"This is television, darling! We know about everything—as it happens! Oh, good, it looks like they're between takes. Good heavens, is that really Jimmy under all that makeup?"

At the far end of the studio, James Bartholomew Olsen stood atop a riser, his hair moussed into a strange variation of the classic ducktail. Two bulging prosthetic appliances were spirit-gummed over his eyes. He was wearing a green scaled skinsuit with red trunks and an ersatz tortoise-shell strapped to his back.

Lois gaped, her emergency momentarily forgotten. "How can he see through those things?"

It was all Cat could do to keep from cracking up. "Yoo-hoo!" She waved, wiggling her fingers in the air to get his attention. "Oh, Turtle Boy!"

Jim looked up past the camera, shielding his "eyes" to see past the lights. "Cat? Lois?"

"Jimmy Olsen, the Chief will have your hide! Your lunch hour isn't three hours long, you know!"

Jim looked distinctly uncomfortable. "Sorry, Lois, but the taping ran longer than I thought. This *is* my first TV show. What's up?"

"Perry wants us to cover this 'Doomsday' incident. They're holding a chopper for us at the heliport!"

Jimmy turned to the director. "I'm sorry, but I've really got to go."

All the color drained from the director's face. "But we still have another setup to finish!"

Lois stepped between them. "I'm sorry, too, but he does have other commitments. It's your call, Jimmy, what'll it be? This . . . or your day job?"

"Sorry, Dave." Jimmy handed his false eyes to a makeup man and began loosening the straps of his tortoiseshell costume.

Cat tried unsuccessfully to suppress a giggle. "Come on, you two! I know a shortcut out of here." She led Lois and Jimmy through a maze of zigzagging corridors.

I hope she knows where she's going, thought Lois. *I'm completely turned around.*

As they passed through the network's master control, Cat called out to one of the men seated at the panel. "Hi, Leon, what's happening?"

Leon shrugged. "Just got a call from News. Gotta interrupt *The Brave and the Bold* for an alert." He shuddered. "The soap fans are gonna hate that. Glad I don't have to answer the phones." On one of the monitors a blank-faced man could be seen adjusting his toupee. Leon hit a switch, and the man seemed to come alive.

"This is a GBS Newsbreak. I'm Steve Lombard. The destructive force known as 'Doomsday' has left approximately thirty people dead in its wake, and hundreds more have been injured, including members of the famed Justice League. Doomsday's path of destruction has cut across Ohio and through Pennsylvania, and authorities fear what will happen if it should reach the large urban areas of the Eastern Seaboard."

In a penthouse office atop the LexCorp Tower, Supergirl stared intently at a wall of television screens where multiple Steve Lombards delivered the news in unison. "Reports at this hour place the monster in upstate Kirby County, only a hundred miles from Metropolis. More after this."

Supergirl looked away as the Lombardses were replaced by multiple cherubs touting hamburgers.

"Lex, I should go. Maybe I can lend a hand."

Lex Luthor caressed her hand and kissed it gently. "I don't think that would be wise, love. I need my Supergirl here with me. We need a contingency plan in case this menace does make his way to Metropolis."

"I guess you're right." She bit her lip.

"Of course I am. You'll see."

On the edge of the village of Griffith in the parking lot of a small supermarket, Maxima was breathing heavily. "By the House of Almerac, you still stand?" The beating she had given the monster would have killed a dozen warriors, but Doomsday was not even showing a bruise.

"You *will* bow down before me, creature!"

Just then Doomsday lunged at Maxima, but she ducked beneath him and rose to deliver a powerful blow to his lower abdomen. The low blow lifted the creature up and back through the plate glass window of the tiny local supermarket. Aisles of canned goods went flying as a handful of terrified shoppers scrambled for the exits.

With a rush of wind, Superman touched down beside Maxima. "Maxima? What on Earth are you doing? There're bound to be people in that store."

"There are always innocent victims in battle. I resent your tone." Maxima started to elbow him aside, but Superman caught hold of her arm and held it.

"Just think before you swing, okay, princess? We don't have time to argue."

Doomsday had already regained his footing. With a low, feral growl, he charged from the store like an express train, barreling into both of them. Superman flipped about in the air, landing on Doomsday's back and getting him in a throat lock.

"Hurry, Maxima, hit him with everything you've got! I can't hold him long!"

But as Maxima threw her punch, Doomsday suddenly dropped into a crouch, so that her blow struck Superman instead, sending him flying.

How could he move so fast? He didn't before—! Maxima was scarcely more surprised when Doomsday turned and flung her onto the lot of a gas station half a block away. *Was he just toying with me before?* As Maxima lurched to her feet, he charged toward her, scooping up a small panel truck and dumping it down upon her.

Maxima ripped her way through the van, glass and metal flying before her. "Your onslaught does little but stimulate me, creature. Maxima welcomes this. For only when a warrior faces death can a conflict be deemed truly worthy!"

Superman again dove toward Doomsday feetfirst, driving the monster back against a row of gas pumps. *How can Maxima still revel in this? Doesn't she see the danger? Doomsday doesn't seem to be slowing down much.* He grappled with the beast as gasoline began gushing up around them. *We have to do some damage to him soon. I don't know how much longer I can keep this up.*

"Hold him tight, Kryptonian—Maxima will not miss again!"

Superman stole a glance her way. Maxima was ripping out the gas station's signpost by the roots, trailing ripped electrical cables.

"Maxima, no! That pole's sparking—!"

A mile away, the Guardian saw a flash of light a split second before he heard the thunderclap boom of the explosion. *Looks like I won't need the tracking gear.* A plume of thick black smoke arose down the road. He turned his motorcycle in that direction, reaching the devastated village in a matter of moments.

It looked as though a hurricane had battered the area. Just ahead of him, Superman and Maxima lay sprawled in the village street.

"Superman? Friend, can you hear me?"

"Guardian?" Superman accepted the offered hand and struggled to his feet.

"Sorry I didn't get here sooner." Harper turned and knelt over Maxima.

"How is she?" asked Superman.

"She's coming around. I think she'll be okay . . . probably suffered a pretty serious concussion, though." He watched as Superman took an uncertain step forward. "You don't look so hot yourself."

"We've never faced anything like Doomsday before, Guardian . . . never. Where is he?"

"I don't know. You two were the only living things I've seen in this town. Looks like most everyone else managed to get out. Maybe that explosion did him in . . . whatever he was."

"No, we couldn't be that lucky." Superman looked around, scanning the area with his super-vision. He could see signs of destruction heading south out of town. "He must've come to before I did . . . if he lost consciousness at all."

A monster . . . tougher than Superman? The Guardian couldn't believe it. "What sort of creature is he?"

"Hate . . . he is hate." Maxima groggily began to stir. "We must stop Doomsday . . . we must."

"She's right. Doomsday must be stopped! He's a threat to every living thing!"

The Guardian looked up at his friend. He'd never before heard such worry in the big man's voice. Maxima braced herself against the Guardian's knee and tried to rise. "Please, ma'am, take it slow and easy. You took quite a hit."

"She's in no condition to go on, Guardian . . . better get her to a hospital." Superman looked again to the south, and his fists clenched involuntarily. "I'll stop Doomsday—if it's the last thing I do!"

Superman took three great strides and sprang into the air, soaring high above the countryside. Below, a trail of splintered trees and tortured soil meandered southeastward. It was like following the path of a tornado. There was utter destruction wherever Doomsday touched down.

I wish I knew where that monster came from. In all his life, Superman had never seen anything—on Earth or off it—to equal Doomsday either for brute strength or sheer irrational rage.

There was no discernible pattern to the creature's movements. He seemed just to wander from place to place, attacking whatever caught his eye. Sometimes he merely disabled what he attacked, while other times he smashed things to dust. It was a frightening realization.

There were a half-dozen major urban centers in this region. A chill gripped Superman's heart. *Well over twenty-five million human lives could be in jeopardy.*

Miles ahead, Doomsday smashed his way through the gigantic concrete support post of an interstate highway overpass. The huge tanker truck that toppled down on top of him did not appear to concern him one bit. He simply pounded the truck apart. As Doomsday stepped from the wreckage, a late-model sedan came around a bend toward him.

From behind the wheel, Charlie Sussman put on the brakes the moment he saw that the overpass had collapsed. He hit the horn and yanked the wheel hard to the right, but there was little chance of avoiding the monstrous figure that charged right at him.

Doomsday grabbed hold of the swerving car and swung it about, using its own momentum to toss it high into the sky.

Charlie's first thought was that he must be dreaming. *That's it . . . I've dozed off at the wheel. Got to wake up before I have an accident!* "Wake up, Charlie!" *Wow . . . must be nearly a mile up. Everything looks so pretty from up here . . . so real.* "What is the matter with me?" Charlie pinched himself hard and screamed. "Wake up already!" The car reached its apex and began tipping backward. *Omigod, this is no dream— I'm gonna die.*

But then the car jerked slightly to one side, and its fall slowed. It was a strange sensation. For a moment, Charlie wondered again if he was asleep.

A red cape flapped against the side of Charlie's window. "It's okay! I've got you!"

"You've got me?" Charlie was starting to come unraveled. "Heh! Sure." *Somebody caught me. Why not?*

"Sir? Don't be afraid—everything's going to be all right. I'm Superman."

"S-S-Super . . . man? I hope you're real. Otherwise, I know I'm dead!"

"No chance of that, sir. Keep talking, and take long, deep breaths. Don't go into shock on me now. I've been searching for the creature that must have attacked you. Can you remember anything about him—anything at all?"

"Creature? I . . . yeah! He was big . . . came right at me. H-he grabbed hold of my car and just . . . threw it! It happened so fast. Didn't seem real at first. What—what is he, Superman?"

"I wish I knew. He came from out of nowhere—destroying things at random—apparently for the sheer hell of it!"

"Then . . . yeah, it musta been him that collapsed the overpass!"

"Overpass?!" Superman peered down with his telescopic vision. "I don't see any survivors among the wreckage. There're dozens of chain-reaction fender-benders up and down both highways . . . lots of minor injuries there. Ah—there's a state trooper on the scene. And I hear sirens . . . rescue vehicles are on the way." Superman's face fell. "Oh, no!"

"What's wrong?" Charlie could hear the fear in his rescuer's voice. "What do you see?"

"More trouble . . . terrible trouble. I'm needed—! I'll set you down near that state trooper. Tell her to call for more rescue teams. We'll need them at the shopping plaza on the northwest side of Midvale."

At the suburban plaza, the parking lot of a Lex-Mart discount center lay in ruins, as if a bomb had gone off. A line of smashed cars led to a gaping hole where the main entrance had been. Inside, a stammering assistant manager desperately thumbed the public-address system and tried to keep his voice even. "Attention, Lex-Mart shoppers. This is an emergency situation. Repeat, this is an emergency situation. Please exit the store in a calm and orderly fashion." A refrigerator flew past, no more than a foot from the assistant manager's head, and he lost it. "Oh, hell! Just get out! Get out as quickly as you can!"

Doomsday had already smashed his way through garden supplies, sporting goods, and notions and was ripping his way through home appliances when the voice rang out.

"Hey, you!"

Doomsday turned at the challenge, a guttural growl on his lips.

"Yeah, I'm talking to you! Come closer."

Doomsday followed the voice down the aisle into home electronics and found himself standing before a seventy-two-inch video projection screen. Across the screen flashed a series of scenes of half-naked men throwing each other across a cabled-off section of arena. Doomsday moved in on the screen slowly, never taking his eyes off it, but he made not a move to lash out. He seemed spellbound.

". . . you don't want to miss a single moment of the greatest spectacle in the history of professional wrestling! I'm talkin' tag teams! I'm talkin' steel cages! I'm talkin' knock-down, drag-out grudge matches!"

Suddenly, the image on the screen switched to a closeup of a big, beefy man. His flowing blond hair stuck out from under an officer's cap and a bandolier of bullets hung strapped across his bare chest. It seemed to Doomsday that he was pointing right at him.

"I'm talkin' 'bout WAR-BASH 9000! This weekend! At the Metropolis Arena! I'm Major Mayhem, troopers—and I'm out for blood! I'm takin' on the Mighty Gorilla! Ugly Ben Studly! And the Masked Bone-Crusher! And—I—WILL—prevail!" The image of the wrestler screamed out from the screen. "This time . . . IT'S WARRRR!!!"

Abruptly, Major Mayhem disappeared from the screen and was replaced by a supergraphic of the Metropolis Arena logo. An announcer's voice came blasting from the speakers. "Pro-wrestling as you've never seen it before! This weekend at Metropolis Arena . . . Metropolis Arena . . . METROPOLIS ARENA!" With each staccato repetition, the volume shot up and the Metropolis logo flashed bigger. "Now— where ya gonna go?"

Doomsday's huge mouth gaped open, and his lips twisted as he tried to mimic the sound. "Mhh-trr-plss?"

"DOOMSDAY!" The voice of Superman echoed loud and strong throughout the store. The creature turned away from the television as Superman came flying at him. Superman smashed into Doomsday like a lineman sacking a quarterback, driving the creature back through the television screen and the wall behind it. Together they tumbled out across the back loading dock, sending workers scattering to get out of their way.

Bellowing his awful laugh, Doomsday joyously pummeled Superman through the side of a semitrailer truck.

To Superman, it felt as though his entire body hurt. Pain was not unknown to him, but it had been years since he'd felt it this intensely. *I'd swear the harder I fight, the more Doomsday likes it! He's been fighting most of the day, but he still seems as eager—and as strong—as ever! If he has energy reserves as extensive as mine, I may be in trouble!*

From overhead came the sound of rotor blades. As Doomsday shoved him down onto the asphalt, Superman saw two helicopters approaching from the south. One bore the logo of superstation WLEX, the other of the *Daily Planet*.

Oh, Lord, Lois and Jimmy are on board! Superman's blood ran cold. *Those pilots better keep their distance!*

Jimmy Olsen hung halfway out of the open helicopter, camera in hand. "That's Doomsday? Wow, he's a big one!"

Very big, thought Lois. *Be careful, Clark.* She thumbed the switch of the microphone in her hand. "The Midvale Lex-Mart stood in ruins as Superman struggled with the mysterious creature. End of paragraph . . . stand by for more."

Lois released the talk switch and said a silent prayer.

Lex Luthor returned to the video lounge where Supergirl continued to stare intently at the array of screens. "Well, love, my news director assured me that he'd dispatched a camera crew to get to the bottom of this Doomsday nonsense. . . ."

"It's not nonsense, Lex! They're on the air now, and Doomsday just wrecked one of your shopping marts."

"What?!" Luthor turned to the screens. Superman was grappling with a monster in front of what had been the Midvale Lex-Mart. "Bloody hell!"

"Superman's trying to stop the creature, but he's not having much luck. Anything that can give Superman that hard a fight must be incredibly powerful!" Supergirl rose from her chair. "I'd better go help!"

Lex put a hand on Supergirl's shoulder. "We've been all through that, love! The last thing we need now is for you to go flying off! Whenever Superman's away, the local citizenry start getting . . . edgy." It pained him to admit that, but he couldn't deny it. "And with the ol' boy off havin' a go-round with some ugly drongo, the city needs its Supergirl to fill the void."

"Are you sure, Lex?" Supergirl looked at him uncertainly. "Doomsday's already caused so much destruction. Your newsman placed the latest death toll at over a hundred!"

"Superman can handle him, and I can weather the loss of a Lex-Mart! Trust me, pet, the good people of Metropolis will feel better knowing that you and Team Luthor are home."

"All right, I'll stay put for now." She looked back at the screens. One of them showed Superman closing in on Doomsday, but the monster was lifting what appeared to be an empty tour bus.

As if Superman ever really needs help, thought Lex. *He's always survived —despite my best-laid plans!* He pulled Supergirl closer and gave her his most sincere smile. "You'll see, love. Superman will be just fine!"

With a mighty heave, Doomsday hurled the tour bus directly at Superman. Unable to avoid the collision, Superman was driven backward by the impact.

Inside an adjacent Big Belly Burger restaurant, a customer shoved his son to the floor as the Man of Steel came tumbling out of control through the big glass window. Superman had only a moment to shout out a warning before he disappeared out the other side of the building. He landed hard on the shoulder of the highway outside in a shower of glass, steel, and plaster. *At least the bus was empty. But all those people in the restaurant—!* He had to hope, to pray that they were all right. He rolled over onto His chest and pushed himself up to his knees. He had to pull himself together. He had to end this fight before more people were hurt.

A shadow loomed over Superman as he tried to catch his breath. As that horrible laugh again echoed in his ears, he steeled himself for the expected blow, but it didn't come. The laughter abruptly stopped, replaced by a lower, more guttural sound.

"Mhh-trr-plss?"

Superman looked up. Doomsday was starting to turn away. *What's drawn his attention away from me?*

Doomsday stood on the shoulder of the highway, looking intently at a huge information sign. There, emblazoned in letters a foot high, were the words: METROPOLIS 60 MILES.

"Mhh-trr-plss!!"

Oh, no, he remembers that stupid commercial! He's made the connection—! Superman bounded to his feet and launched himself at the distracted beast, pounding away at him with fists that could shatter solid steel. *Sixty miles might as well be sixty paces to this monster! I can't let him get any closer! I can't!!*

Overhead, Olsen let out a low whistle as he snapped off shots of the battle. "Geez! Superman must've gotten a second wind or something! I've never seen him fight so hard!"

"N-neither have I, Jimmy!" Lois fought to keep her voice under control. She had to have faith that her lover would be able to stop this creature. And she had a job to do; maybe if she concentrated on that . . .

"Next paragraph . . . Taking advantage of Doomsday's momentary distraction, Superman redoubled his efforts . . ."

Superman had indeed caught his opponent off guard. Evading the monster's reach, he grabbed Doomsday by the ankle and began to swing him around and around, as though he were a hammer thrower. *He must weigh nearly half a ton. Got to use that weight . . . build up enough momentum.*

On his fifth rotation, Superman let go of Doomsday, sending the monster flying high and away to the northwest, away from Metropolis.

Superman bounded into the sky, streaking after the vanishing form of

Doomsday. *He's taken everything I've dished out so far. Maybe crashing into the hills at a few hundred miles per hour will soften him up. I hope so!* As he flashed past the WLEX helicopter, Superman found himself suddenly surprised by the absence of any "hands-on" LexCorp response. *By now young Lex Luthor must be aware of what happened to his company's store. I'd have expected him to send in Supergirl, maybe with a squadron of his Team Luthor security force. And this is one time I could really use some help.* Superman shook his head. He was never sure what to expect of the Luthor heir. *Of course, if his father were still alive, I'd have half-expected the old man to have* engineered *this Doomsday monster.*

The *Daily Planet's* chopper pilot scratched his head. "I don't know if I can catch up with them, Ms. Lane, not as fast as they're going!"

"Just do your best, Garret. Metropolis isn't that far . . . I'll bet Superman's trying to keep Doomsday away from the city."

"Well, he's got him headed in the right direction. Not much to worry about out where they are. No one's allowed much up into the hills around Mount Curtiss. Even a lot of the airspace is restricted. I think some sort of federal preserve is tucked away up there." Garret glanced at his instruments. "We're getting low on gas. Sorry, but we'll have to set down and refuel while we can."

Lois looked back helplessly as the helicopter turned about, skirting well clear of the restricted area which sheltered the Cadmus Project.

In an underground chamber hundreds of feet beneath Mount Curtiss, Drs. Walter Johnson and Anthony Rodrigues were in the midst of arguing with their Project administrator over research budgets for the upcoming year.

"Paul, with Dr. Augustine still on the mend, we desperately need another research geneticist to take up the slack."

"I'm sorry, Walter, but we can't take on any more personnel at this point. We don't have the wallet for it, and Congress isn't about to increase our appropriation any time soon." Paul Westfield stood and leaned back against his desk, arms folded. Despite his words, he didn't seem very sorry.

Suddenly there was a deep rumble, and the entire complex shuddered. Westfield's feet went out from under him, and he cut loose with a curse he hadn't used since his army days.

"What's going on?!" Johnson ducked, narrowly avoiding a falling chunk of ceiling tile. "Is this an earthquake?!"

"Inconceivable! This is one of the most geophysically stable regions on the continent!" Rodrigues steadied himself against a filing cabinet as the shaking subsided. "The Project must be under some manner of bombardment!"

Johnson turned to help the adminstrator to his feet. "Take it easy, Paul, we'll get to the bottom of this."

"The Guardian would have to be away! This is inordinately inopportune." It had been years since anyone had called Dr. Rodrigues "Big Words," but the origins of his nickname were still clear. "You don't suppose—? No, the level of coincidence is far too great. And yet I cannot help but wonder if this seismic disruption is somehow related to that nearby monster scare which Harper went off to investigate."

Johnson answered with only a shrug. Westfield was still fuming.

Rodrigues himself shrugged and picked up the phone. "This is Dr. Rodrigues. What is the situation?" He listened patiently as the security officer ticked off the damage reports. "I see. Well, then, go to code red and patch me through to the Guardian."

High up on Mount Curtiss was a huge new crater, formed by Doomsday's impact with the mountain. As Superman dove down over the crater, the shattered rock and debris in the center of the depression began to shift. Then Doomsday slowly arose, a raspy growl on his lips.

He's still conscious, thought Superman. *Another second and he'll be back on his feet. I can't allow him that second.* Superman rammed into the rising monster with the speed of an express train, sending him barreling down the mountainside. *Got to pound him—and keep pounding him!*

Superman dove after Doomsday, striking him again and again as they slid below the timberline. Gigantic tree trunks began to crack and splinter as they grappled their way to the base of Mount Curtiss. Gradually, Superman became aware that the great wooden trunks around them weren't just trees. They had tumbled into the middle of Habitat.

Superman recognized the tree city from previous visits to the area. He thanked God that the place stood abandoned. *I must be getting punchy! I was so worried about keeping Doomsday out of the city, I forgot all about Cadmus's research zone extending into this wild area.*

Research . . . Now there was a troubling thought. *All manner of beings have been created in the Project's genetics labs. Could Cadmus be responsible for creating Doomsday?*

Outside the emergency entrance of Midvale General Hospital, the Guardian had dropped off Maxima and was striding toward his motorcycle when it suddenly began to beep. He immediately dashed to the big bike and flipped a switch. A miniature LED screen lit up just behind the handlebars, showing the concerned face of Dr. Rodrigues. "Guardian, return to base at once!"

"What is it, Rodrigues? What's wrong?"

"Unknown. But the mountain seems to be under attack by forces of incredible power!"

In the middle of the deserted Habitat, Superman ducked in under Doomsday's great reach, turning the monster's head halfway around with a devastating right uppercut. Incredibly, Doomsday laughed.

It wasn't getting any easier for Superman. The mere act of hitting Doomsday was starting to hurt, and the big monster didn't seem to have weakened one iota. *This is just wearing me down. Got to change my tactics. Maybe if I hit him with something big.* Above them, a giant wooden column came toppling down, shattered by the pounding. Straining, Superman caught the column and used it like a battering ram, smashing Doomsday back through the heart of Habitat. The whole settlement began to sway.

Half a mile away, the Guardian came riding over the foothills just in time to see Habitat start to topple. There was an ominous crunching sound, as if God Himself were cracking His knuckles. And then the center of the deserted settlement collapsed in on itself, more like a house of cards than a stand of trees.

"Guardian to base! Habitat . . . my God, Habitat is in ruins! And I think that Superman and the Doomsday monster were smack in the middle of it! It's bad . . . I'm going in for a closer look! I'll keep this channel open."

The Guardian zigzagged his bike down the hillside, finally skidding to a halt by a shattered wooden column that had once been as big around as a sequoia. A hand reached up from behind the column, and Superman came crawling out from beneath the wreckage. The Guardian quickly dismounted and ran to help his friend.

"Guardian? Where'd you come from? Where's Doomsday?"

"Buried under what's left of Habitat. You barely got out of it yourself. You took some terrible hits in the collapse. Why didn't you fly out of it?"

"Too wasted. Need to rest . . . soon as I make sure . . . Doomsday's stopped."

The Guardian's breath caught in his throat as he got a good look at his friend. One whole side of Superman's face was bruised and swollen. The eye behind the blackened lid was red and inflamed. He had never seen Superman look so mortal.

The Guardian was so shaken by the sight that it took him a moment to find his voice. "Relax, you got him that time!"

"Hope so . . . but I have to be certain." Superman shuddered. "Hard to see . . . through the ruins. Eyes don't want to focus. I . . . Oh, no!"

Before Superman could utter a single word of warning, Doomsday kicked his way out from beneath the wreckage, sending it flying in a shower of wood and stone. The monster emerged from the remnants of Habitat and surveyed the splintered debris around him. There was no sign of a single living thing. With a snort, Doomsday turned and leapt away. Behind him, buried out of sight beneath several tons of debris, lay the unconscious forms of Superman and the Guardian.

An electronic squawk arose from the buried motorcycle. "Guardian? We were cut off for a moment . . . can you read me?"

In the Cadmus Communications Center, Dr. Anthony Rodrigues paused, waiting for a response. An assistant thrust a seismograph printout into his hand.

"We detected another shock, Doctor."

"What's going on out there? Guardian? Guardian!"

The speaker buzzed and clicked, and a voice other than the Guardian's came on-line. "Dr. Rodrigues, this is Fitzsimmons in Security. Select-scan radar has just confirmed the apparent launch of an object— somewhat larger than man-sized—from the Wild Area. It's headed south-southeast at approximately half the speed of sound!"

"Good Lord!" Rodrigues turned to the radio officer on duty. "Patch me through to Metropolis Civil Defense Command—now! We have to warn those poor people—Doomsday is coming!"

10

The two news helicopters had set down at a small regional airport for refueling when Doomsday flashed by overhead. Lois turned to their pilot in a panic. "How much longer will it take?"

Garret shook his head. "Five, maybe ten minutes."

Jimmy scowled. "That's too long! We'll lose him!"

"Maybe not!" Lois pointed across the field where another *Planet* copter was setting down. "Come on!"

Lois and Jimmy raced across the tarmac to where Bud Sheldon of the *Planet*'s sports desk was deplaning.

"Bud, we need your chopper. It's an emergency."

"Okay by me, Lois—if it's okay by Joe!" Bud hooked a thumb back toward his pilot.

Lois and Jimmy piled on board the idling copter, much to the surprise of Joe Jacobi. "Where did you two come from?"

"Long story," said Lois. "How're you fixed for fuel?"

"Got three-quarters of a tank."

"Good. Get this eggbeater into the air. Jimmy will explain as we go."

As Jacobi took off, a second figure flashed by overhead.

"Superman!" Jimmy let out a whoop. "All right!"

Lois felt her spirits rise. She'd tried not to worry when Doomsday had bounded past alone. Knowing that her lover was still in pursuit didn't alleviate all her worries, but it helped. "Follow him, Joe. Where he goes, we go!" Lois grabbed up a headset and reestablished contact with reporter Fran Thurston in the *Planet*'s City Room.

"Lois? That was fast!"

"We got a new ride. Ready to continue?"

"Whenever you are. Feed me."

"As the monster called Doomsday abandoned the furrow of destruction, he plowed through the northern part of the state and headed, in ten-mile leaps, toward the East Coast and Metropolis. End of paragraph."

At her end of the line, Fran paused at the keyboard. "Metropolis?! Oh, dear God. Lois, you're sure of that?"

" 'Fraid so, Fran. But Superman is on the creature's tail. We're airborne over the beltway now . . . hope to catch up to them soon."

"We're getting company, Lois!" Jimmy pointed to the south where a helicopter showing the WGBS logo was closing in on them.

Lois nodded. "Probably Cat Grant, hoping to finish her interview." She looked ahead, scanning the horizon. The city was coming up fast. "Keep your head down, Fran. If our calculations are right, that monster must be reaching Metropolis right about now."

The ground suddenly shook with a muffled thud at an office park under construction on the far edge of suburban Park Ridge. The foreman looked around, expecting to see that a load of steel had fallen.

"Sounded as though it came from the other side of that dump truck," said a backhoe operator. The dump truck's driver was craning his head in puzzlement.

The dump truck suddenly lurched crazily to one side. The driver tumbled from the cab, screaming, as a huge, hulking figure lifted the truck up over its head.

A hod carrier dropped his load of bricks and jumped back. "What the devil is that?"

"I dunno." The foreman was already looking around, waving away his men. "Just run!"

The dump truck went flying, landing in a tangled heap beside a big diesel crane. Roaring his defiance, Doomsday strode into the midst of the site, grabbing two construction workers by their heads. One worker barely had time to scream before the monster snapped his neck like a matchstick. The other was speechless, still gasping for breath, as Doomsday hurled him against a steel support column.

Superman was just a few hundred feet away when he saw the second man slump lifeless to the ground. He could feel his blood pressure spiking. Doomsday had knocked at the door of the city—his city—and already two men were dead. Superman dove at the monster. There was a sharp crack as his fists found their target in Doomsday's kidneys . . . *If he has kidneys,* thought Superman. Filling his lungs with air, the Man of

Steel then grabbed hold of his enemy's bony back and rocketed straight up. *We'll see who can hold his breath longer on the moon!*

As they closed in on the construction site, Lois nearly shouted into the microphone. "We've got him, Fran! New paragraph . . . Doomsday's rampage in Park Ridge was cut short when Superman grabbed the monster . . . comma . . . rocketing him away from Metropolis toward the vacuum of space . . . period."

Jimmy reached the end of a roll of film and grabbed up a second camera. "Man, that has to be the ugliest cuss Superman's ever fought! Did you get a really good look at him, Lois? He's got a hide like an elephant and a face like five miles of bad road!" Out of the corner of his eye, Jimmy noticed the worry on his friend's face. "Hey, don't sweat it, Lois. Superman . . . he'll be okay!"

"Guardian!"

Jim Harper stirred, roused to consciousness by a voice in his head.

"Guardian, are you all right?"

Harper blinked. He was alone, but he could feel a presence with him. And when he closed his eyes, it seemed that he could almost see a face staring back at him, a gray-skinned, horn-headed face.

"Dubbilex?"

"Yes." From deep within the Project, the DNAlien reached out to Harper telepathically.

He could feel Dubbilex's relief wash over him. "What happened?"

The responding thought was instantaneous: *"As near as I can tell, that Doomsday creature left you and Superman for dead, buried in the rubble of Habitat. When you failed to respond to a radio summons, I . . . came 'looking' for you."*

"Superman . . ." The Guardian sat up and looked around him. The rubble had been scooped out and massive chunks of wood stacked protectively around him. "Where's Superman?"

"Already revived and gone in pursuit of Doomsday. He was digging you out even as I found you. He was quite concerned about you, but I assured him that I could see to your well-being." The air shimmered, and Dubbilex's visage appeared clearer, stronger. *"He is a good man, Jim . . . a good friend. I felt in him a great sense of duty. He is determined to stop the creature."*

The Guardian rose painfully to his feet. "I'm afraid Doomsday may be too big for even Superman to handle alone."

Was the mental image frowning? It was sometimes hard to tell with

Dubbilex. *"I fear that Doomsday might be one of ours, Guardian . . . a DNAlien. Perhaps another Dabney Donovan creation."*

That thought had already crossed the Guardian's mind. He looked around at the ruins of Habitat and prayed that their fear was unfounded, that Cadmus wasn't responsible. "We have to find out. Can you get a mind-fix on Doomsday?"

"It will not be easy at this distance, but I shall try." The image of Dubbilex flickered out, and the Guardian set out to find his motorcycle. He located it, back up on its kickstand at the edge of the space that Superman had cleared around him.

Suddenly Dubbilex's visage reappeared. *"I have found him."* The telepath seemed very alarmed. *"There is nothing in his mind but anger . . . no thought but destruction. I cannot tell from where he came."*

"It's all right, Dub." The Guardian kick-started his bike. "We'll have to work hard to stop him, in any case—if anyone *can* stop him."

Three miles up over Metropolis, Doomsday fought to break Superman's grip. Twisting free, the creature drove the air from his captor's lungs with a savage kick and leapt toward the heart of the city. Aboard the *Planet* helicopter, Lois's heart caught in her throat as she saw the stunned Superman hurtle Earthward. He tumbled out of control, crashing down through the steel skeleton of the building under construction at the Park Ridge office park.

Just a few hundred yards away, the WGBS copter wheeled around in Cat Grant's direction. "Superman's down!" She could hardly believe it. "Get closer! We can't miss this shot."

One time zone away, Martha Kent had been in the middle of cleaning the parlor when the news first broke into her soap opera. She had dropped her Aunt Gracie's milk-glass vase and run to the barn to call in her husband. The vase still lay in pieces where it had fallen beside the old Hoosier cabinet, forgotten as Martha and Jonathan sat on the old parlor sofa, their eyes glued to the images on the television. With a start, Martha realized that Clark had given them the set two anniversaries ago.

The station cut to a dizzying shot of the wrecked steel skeleton of a building. ". . . Here, live at the scene, is WGBS's Catherine Grant."

"Roland, in a battle that has raged across nearly a third of the nation, Superman has so far been unable to stop the Doomsday monster. In fact, as you can see, he's not having an easy time of things at all!"

Martha winced, clamping her eyes tightly shut, and felt Jonathan's arm immediately slip gently over her shoulders.

"That's our son, Jonathan! He's being beaten to a pulp, and those TV reporters are treating it as . . . as entertainment!"

"I know . . . I know." Jonathan Kent drew in a deep breath, searching for the right words. Sometimes he thought his whole life had been a search for those words. "Clark may be our boy, Martha, but to the world he's Superman. It's not that they're callous. Least, they don't mean to be. It's just that they don't think anything bad can really happen to him."

Civil defense and emergency sirens wailed all over Metropolis. Radio and television stations shifted over to the Emergency Broadcast System, and on the streets, police loudspeakers began warning people to take shelter.

At the counter of the Hob's Bay Grille, Professor Emil Hamilton looked up from his pie and coffee. He had been composing a compliment to Mildred's appearance—*Must be careful, can't appear too forward* —when a high-pitched hum suddenly blared from the little diner's radio, most rudely interrupting "Begin the Beguine."

"Attention! This is not a test! Local, state, and federal authorities have declared a state of emergency to exist in the greater Metropolis area. Citizens are urged to seek shelter immediately. If you are within the sound of my voice, tune your radio to 860 kilohertz AM or 93.1 megahertz FM for more information over your designated local Emergency Broadcast Station. Repeat, this is not a test! WUMT must now sign off for the duration of the emergency . . ."

Emil looked at Mildred and blinked. The waitress's face had gone white, and she was frantically pounding on the old radio's dial.

"I told 'im! I told 'im, but would he listen?"

"Whatever is the trouble, Mildred?"

"I don't know! We may never know! The tuner on this thing's been busted for nearly a year! I told the owner, but he said one station was enough! Now what do we do?"

"Well, we can't stay here, my dear! I haven't a clue as to what sort of emergency this is, but the Grille, for all its virtues, is hardly a fortified shelter. Get your coat! I'll help you lock up and we can repair to my building. I've plenty of provisions, and the lab has sufficient stores to hold off a small army, I daresay."

Mildred forced a brave smile. She didn't know what was happening, but if the world might be coming to an end, she could think of few people she'd rather see it out with. "Just let me lock up the register."

Arm in arm, Emil and Mildred sprinted down the rapidly emptying streets. A block away, a police cruiser was warning people to stay inside. "Whatever could be going on?" muttered Emil.

From behind them came a low growl. "Doomsday's comin'!"

They nearly jumped out of their shoes. Emil was about to grab Mildred and run when he realized that they were in front of the Ace o' Clubs, and that the growl had come from the man standing in the shadows of the doorway.

"Bibbowski!" There were few people in the neighborhood who had not encountered the tavern's proprietor. "What are you talking about?"

"Doomsday," repeated Bibbo. "He's some big monster, see? My fav'rit's been chasin' him cross country—an' gettin' nowheres!"

"Your favorite?" Mildred was quickly regaining her composure.

Emil knew there was one man whom Bibbo regarded over all others. "You mean Superman, of course! This Doomsday monster has been giving Superman trouble?"

Bibbo looked troubled. "Yeah—it's been on the TV all afternoon. Can't understand it. Sooperman's the toughest guy I ever met, tougher even'n me! But he can't seem to stop the ugly so-an'-so!" Bibbo's countenance suddenly brightened. "Perfesser, yer smart! Can you think of any ways to help 'im?"

Emil's mind was racing. "Perhaps. But I have to know more about this creature. There may be something in my lab—!"

"Hey, I'm comin' wit' youse!" Bibbo straightened his cap.

"Really, that's not necessary—!" Emil began to protest.

"Hey, if I can do anything to help youse help my fav'rit, I'm gonna do it!" He turned to shout back into the bar. "Lamarr, I got stuff to do. Stay put an' look after things for me while I'm gone, okay?"

"No problem, Bibbo."

"An' don't let me catch you an' Highpockets downing too many free beers this time!"

A cheery belch echoed from within the tavern. Satisfied, Bibbo turned and threw a protective arm around both Emil and Mildred. "Okay, now let's go help Sooperman!"

Back at the Park Ridge construction site, a huge pile of scattered girders shifted. And then, from the bottom of the pile, Superman emerged, shouldering aside several tons of steel, a trickle of blood oozing from the corner of his mouth. *Blood? When was the last time I was hurt badly enough to bleed? If I've become that vulnerable, my reserves must really be depleted. Better finish this quick, if I'm going to finish it at all.* He emerged from the wreckage, aching with every move, his cape in tatters. *Shouldn't be hard to find him . . . just have to follow the path of destruction.*

With a running stride, Superman leapt uncertainly into the air. The coppery taste in his mouth was turning his stomach. All he could think of was that time when he was four, before his powers began to develop. He'd fallen from his folks' old walnut tree, breaking his arm. It'd hurt so bad, he'd bitten his lip, and the taste . . . *Careful, Clark! This's uncomfortably like having your life flash before your eyes.* He tried not to think of the danger. He could not stop now, could not waver. The lives of too many people depended on him. In the distance, across the river, a cloud of smoke rose where a high-rise apartment had once stood. To his ears, it seemed that every siren in the city was sounding. As he flew deeper into the heart of Metropolis, Superman concentrated, screening out the sirens, listening for the squawk of police radios.

"Attention, all units! Doomsday has been sighted—repeat, Doomsday has been sighted—on the four-hundred block of Shayne Boulevard."

The four-hundred block of Shayne . . . that's where the Newtown Plaza is being built. Superman poured on the speed. *Doomsday's found another construction site to attack.*

As he approached the half-completed complex, Superman saw a huge hole near the foundation of the main tower. *Oh, great. He's gone underground!* The Man of Steel plunged down through the hole, a maze of ancient pipes stretching all around him. The lead pipes inhibited his vision, but following the trail of debris, he finally found his quarry. Doomsday was ripping his way into the Metropolis sewer system.

Leaping onto the monster's back, Superman reached under Doomsday's arms and around the back of his neck, gripping him in a full nelson.

"Stop squirming, damn you! You're not kicking free of me this time!" Then Superman caught the telltale scent of leaking gas.

With Doomsday in tow, he shot toward the surface. As they emerged into the light of day, construction workers were still being evacuated from the Newtown Plaza complex.

"Come on, move it! Move it!" The job foreman desperately herded his workers away from the towers.

Amidst all the chaos and confusion, ironworker Henry Johnson saw the monster flailing away at Superman. "What is that thing?"

"Ain'tcha heard? That's Doomsday. He's a demon or something—and he's been kickin' Superman's butt all over town."

"No way, man. No way!" Henry bolted away from the others, grabbing up a sledgehammer on the run. Sledge in hand, he vaulted over a small stack of girders, determined to help Superman stop the monster.

Deep underground, the leaking gas flowed over a sparking power line. There was a sudden, violent, foundation-rattling explosion, and the largest of the complex's buildings split wide open. Henry Johnson fell to his knees, and the floors above fell on top of him as the entire central borough shook from the force of the blast.

.   .   .

In the media suite of LexCorp Tower, Lex Luthor II was in the middle of a news conference.

"In answer to your question, Ms. Anderson—no, I don't know what Doomsday is or where he came from, but it has become increasingly obvious why he is here. The creature has some manner of grudge against Superman!"

Lex could feel Supergirl tensing by his side. He knew that such talk disturbed her, but he couldn't pass up the opportunity to tear a strip off his old foe. WLEX might be blacked out locally during the emergency, but he could still feed his message to the rest of the world via his superstation's satellite and cable connections.

"I'm loath to ask, but does Metropolis need a champion who draws such negative attention? Does Superman's presence here cause more harm than good?"

At that point the shock wave from the Newtown Plaza blast hit them. The tower noticeably swayed, and the cameraman struggled to hold his Minicam steady. Supergirl kept Luthor on a steady footing, but she was clearly alarmed.

"I think Doomsday may be more than Superman can handle alone. Don't be annoyed, Lex, but I have to help him!"

"Annoyed? Not at all!" Lex played to the cameras for all he was worth. "Very generous, love. Indeed, I agree with you, Metropolis must be preserved!"

As the cameraman turned to follow Supergirl down the corridor, Lex smiled. *I couldn't have timed that better if I'd planned it!*

Buffeted by the shock wave, Superman bore Doomsday up toward the vacuum of space. The monster struggled in his grasp, lashing out with the bony spur of an elbow. So hard was the spur, and so weakened had Superman become from the prolonged struggle, that Doomsday drove it deep into his captor's side.

Superman cried out in shock and pain. He could feel an initial gush of blood wash down his side. This was far worse than any cut, this was a ragged puncture wound. *No one . . . has ever cut me like that before!* His head grew foggy and his limbs went numb as Doomsday hurled him away. Unconscious, the Man of Steel fell to Earth.

Doomsday roared with laughter as he stretched out into a free-fall. But before he dropped more than a hundred feet, a red and blue blur streaked up from the city below, slamming into him with unexpected force. Doomsday reached out to grab his foe and found himself gripping only air.

"I don't know what you've done to Superman, but I'll make you sorry you were ever born!"

Doomsday was confused. The voice was much higher-pitched than the one he'd expected to hear. The caped figure that pulled his arm behind him was smaller, slimmer, and topped with long, flowing blond hair. Doomsday turned to shake off the grip, and Supergirl kicked him square in the gut.

On a rooftop far below, Professor Hamilton and Bibbo rushed to assemble a series of huge components. Mildred kept glancing uneasily from their labors to the skies above. She lifted the electronic field glasses Emil had given her—*That man, doesn't he have anything low-tech?*—and looked up, watching Supergirl struggle with Doomsday.

"My lord in heaven! What . . . what *is* that creature?"

Emil tightened one final connection. "I suspect it's a living weapon, Mildred, perhaps sent by some would-be alien invader to decimate the Earth."

Bibbo wiped his brow. "We finally got dis laser cannon put together, Perfesser Ham—so let's use it!"

Emil checked the skies. "As soon as Supergirl gets out of the way, Bibbo." The Girl of Steel's battle with the monster was drawing closer as she strained to carry him away from downtown. They could be seen quite clearly now with the naked eye.

Doomsday hammered away at Supergirl as she fought to subdue him. But her punches seemed to have little effect on the monster, and his were beginning to make her eyes cross. *Can't give up—can't fail Superman.*

With a bellow of rage, Doomsday hit Supergirl so hard that the young shape-shifter's face deformed with the force of his blow. All the color drained from her. Supergirl went limp and fell spinning toward the Earth below.

Bibbo let out a howl. "Doomsday's dropped Supergirl, Perfesser! Hit him now!"

Emil hit a switch, and a mighty beam of coherent energy blasted skyward. For a moment, Doomsday's free-fall seemed to stop as he was transfixed in the cannon's awful energies. A bellow of pain echoed across the sky.

"We did it!" cheered Emil. "We got him! He's falling, but . . . Oh, dear."

"Emil, he's coming straight at us!"

Bibbo squinted. "If he's tryin' ta fall on top o' us, he's gonna make it! Run for it!"

Emil grabbed Mildred and scrambled for the fire escape with Bibbo hot on their heels. As they reached the third floor, Doomsday slammed into the building with the force of a twenty-ton bomb. The metal staircase began to collapse, shaking them loose, and they fell into the building's dumpster.

They landed with little grace among the trash bags but were otherwise unharmed. "Mildred! Mildred, where are you?"

"Over here, Emil." She emerged from beneath a green plastic bag, her glasses slightly askew. Everything had happened so fast, she'd had little time to be frightened by the fall.

"Thank God. Bibbowski? Are you still with us?"

Bibbo rose up at the far end of the dumpster, covered with packing material. "I'm okay, Perfesser. That din't hurt no worse'n fallin' off a stool. Ouch! Hey, what gives?"

Bricks, dislodged by Doomsday's impact with the building, started raining down from above. As they ducked for cover, Emil looked back up at the building and shook his head. It'd be a while before he dared to go back inside.

Superman came to in what had once been an abandoned tenement building, now boarded up and waiting for demolition. His fall had already begun that process. All around him the old structure lay in ruins. A wave of heat washed over him, and the acrid smell of smoke hit him in the face. He could hear a series of explosions rumbling not too far off.

Another gas main must have been ruptured. The thought came to him slowly, as if he were still trying to shed the fog of a deep sleep. Just sitting up was a struggle for this man who had once changed the course of mighty rivers. His side burned as though it were on fire. He felt for the spot where Doomsday had cut him. The wound was already starting to close, but his hand still came away wet with blood. *My blood.* The realization was very matter-of-fact, as though he had become numbed to the shock of finding himself wounded. He grabbed hold of a slab of masonry to pull himself up. His arms felt like lead and his legs like jelly. Every move was agony, but still he forced himself to his feet.

Around him, the neighborhood looked like a war zone. He grimaced at that thought as he staggered from the ruins. Suicide Slum had sometimes been compared unfavorably to New York's South Bronx and Chicago's Cabrini Green. Now this section of it looked more like Beirut.

"Help! Superman—help!"

The cry cut through the fog in his head like a searchlight. It was the high, earnest cry of a small, terrified boy. Superman became instantly alert. Who needed his help? Where—? He strained to peer through the smoke and dust. There . . . just a few blocks away. A fire at the Coates Children's Center . . . the orphanage maintained by the Metropolis Children's Aid Society! The building was being evacuated, but a caseworker and two young children were trapped inside.

Reflexively Superman leapt skyward and almost came crashing down again, so great was the pain in his right side. *Keep going . . . got to keep going . . . they're depending on you! They may die unless you do something!* Gritting his teeth, he dove into the midst of the burning orphanage. The careworker gave out a shriek at the sight of him.

"Don't be afraid!"

The boy in her protective grasp let out a whoop. "It's Superman! I knew he'd come!"

"You just hush, Keith!" The woman looked uncertainly at the bloodstained letter S emblazoned across the front of the man's tattered shirt. His face was bruised and swollen. A raw and bloody wound oozed at his side. This man looked more like someone in need of rescuing than a rescuer.

"I guess I must really look like a mess, don't I?" He tried to grin, but it came out more like a grimace. "Even Superman has a rough day now and then. Come on . . . I'll get you out of here . . . just stay close."

Not good for much, he thought, *but I still make a pretty good shield.*

Fire trucks were arriving as Superman led the woman and children to safety. A fire fighter on the scene was aghast. Superman looked in much worse shape than those he had just saved.

"Sit down for a moment, over here. Let me take a look at you."

Numbly, Superman did as he was told, and a paramedic pressed an oxygen mask gently to his face. The fire fighter shook his head in dismay. *What is the monster,* he wondered, *that it could do such a thing to Superman?!*

The metal back door to the building Emil Hamilton had called home exploded outward, sending shrapnel flying for half a block. The exploding door was followed a split second later by Doomsday.

Doomsday was a hellish sight to behold. The last few tatters of his outer restraining garment had been burnt away by Emil's laser. All that clothed him now was a pair of dark olive trunks, which ended in metal bands encircling his thighs, and a pair of massive boots. He was covered all over in a gray, leathery hide wherever stark white bone did not protrude, and it seemed to protrude in sharp spikes or spurs at every major joint. Doomsday's hideous face was a catcher's mask of chiseled bone, its high forehead topped by an unruly shock of white hair, now singed and smoking at its ends.

From around the corner of the alley, Emil Hamilton watched furtively as the monster angrily flung the huge metal dumpster out of his way. *No wonder the beast has been able to take such a pounding . . . he has a partial exoskeleton, as well as an endoskeleton.* The professor prudently slunk back into the shadows, hugging the wall, as Doomsday looked around. This was clearly not the time to inspect the creature's anatomy too closely. Emil glanced back to warn Mildred and Bibbo to silence. He could hear his own heart thundering in his chest. Should Doomsday turn down this cul-de-sac, they would be finished. But when Emil looked back, Doomsday was already leaping away.

The oxygen smelled sweet to Superman. It was having a revitalizing effect. His thoughts were coming faster now, more coherently. *Is this how boxers feel? Is this what it's like to be hit so hard that your brains rattle? What sort of damage has been done to me?* He considered that thought for a moment. *How dangerous would a brain-damaged Superman be?*

Someone let out a shout. Superman looked up just in time to see Doomsday bounding high into the sky, and his blood ran cold. The monster was headed toward the central business district. Taking one last hit of oxygen, Superman gathered himself together and launched himself skyward.

"Superman!" The little boy whom he'd saved turned to the case-worker. "Ms. Myra, what is that Doomsday thing? Did somebody build him? Like a giant Frankenstein monster?"

"I don't know, baby." Myra held the boy tight. "From the way he's behavin', I'd say he's the devil incarnate . . . usherin' in the end of the world!"

From where she lay, Supergirl could see Doomsday passing by overhead. Painfully, she rolled over onto her stomach and pressed her hands to the pavement. Inch by inch, she worked to raise herself to her knees. Unable to grit her teeth, Supergirl squeezed her eyes shut tight, and concentrated. Her face throbbed, and her breath burned against the inside of her mouth as she tried to reshape and heal her injuries by force of will. But the pain was too great, the effort more than she could bear. Supergirl fell back down into the street. All was silent, save for the wail of distant sirens.

As police helicopters spread out over the city, radioing in Doomsday's ever-changing location, the department's Special Crimes Unit was tightening its dragnet. A line of police cars and vans roaring up Bessolo Boulevard suddenly braked to a halt at Thirty-second Street.

"He's headed this way! Fall out and get ready!" The unit commander, Captain Margaret Sawyer, pulled taut the last strap of her flak vest. This was looking to be their toughest mission ever. Despite the situation, Sawyer allowed herself a quick grin as she watched her second-in-command, Inspector Dan Turpin, slam an oversized ammo clip into his custom assault gun. She'd grown quite fond of the old cop, and she knew the feeling was mutual. "Ready, Dan?"

"Uh-huh. And just in time!" Turpin pointed skyward. "Those sky jockeys were right on the money, Maggie. Here he comes! Ugly sucker, too!"

"You're a master of understatement, Turp. Come on, nail him—now!"

A hail of ten-millimeter armor-piercing shells greeted Doomsday as he touched ground. But if the monster was done any harm, he didn't show it.

"He's not stopping!" a cop yelled.

Like a maddened bull, Doomsday charged the police line, upending cruisers as he went. Answering the challenge, Turpin ran ahead to meet the monster, emptying his weapon in Doomsday at point-blank range. With a hideous laugh, Doomsday grabbed Turpin and flung him away. The old cop flew backward down the boulevard, the storefronts a blur to his eyes. But as he crossed Thirty-first Street, another figure shot past Turpin, and an arm slipped around his midsection. An instant later, he was jerked to a stop, the wind momentarily going out of him.

"Suh . . . suh . . . Superman!" Turpin was having a hard time catching his breath.

Superman's breathing was a little ragged as well. "Get Maggie and the unit out of the way, Turpin—on the double!"

In a flash, the beleaguered hero bounded over the heads of the police line and again faced Doomsday. A look of recognition burned in the monster's eyes.

Superman returned the monster's stare. *Have to hit him with everything I've got. Have to hope that he has his limits . . . like I do.*

Doomsday eagerly lunged forward, and Superman answered with a right to the throat that echoed like the crack of a rifle. Part of the bony escarpment that was Doomsday's chin broke away, and the monster staggered back a step. Doomsday shook his head, and his eyes widened in wonderment. Truly, here was a challenge. Here was an enemy whose power rivaled his own, one who would no more give up than he would.

With a bellow of unholy glee, Doomsday waded into Superman, reopening the Man of Steel's wound with one swipe of his huge fist.

"Closer! Move in closer!"

"Look, Ms. Grant, are you sure you want to—?"

"I said closer! This is going out live."

The pilot crossed himself—something he hadn't done with this much feeling since the third grade—and slowly eased the helicopter in closer. He'd flown in nearly a half-dozen brushfire wars over the past quarter century, but he'd never seen anything like this. Skyscrapers had been ripped down by the monster below them. And the tide of battle looked to be going against Superman. From the WGBS copter, the scene was going out live via satellite to a worldwide audience. And around the globe, a common thought came to billions of people: *If Superman can't stop that monster . . . perhaps this is* our *Doomsday!*

Supergirl crawled painfully down a deserted side street until she reached the corner of a building. Her fingers oozed as she gripped the rough brick and pulled herself up until, finally, she had regained her footing. There, she paused and listened, long and hard. The noise of the battle reverberated through the canyons of the city. One didn't need superhearing to know where it was coming from. Steadying herself with one hand, Supergirl began to hobble in that direction.

Teeth gritted against the pain, Superman came in close, ducking and weaving to avoid Doomsday's greater reach as he fired punch after punch at the creature's midsection. It was one of the few large areas on the beast's body not protected by a bony exoskeleton. Was it his imagination, Superman wondered, or was his assault starting to have an effect on the big monster?

With a roar of rage, Doomsday grabbed the winded Superman and threw him to the street, shattering the pavement. As the Man of Steel struggled to stay conscious, the creature lifted him high overhead and chucked him into the side of the hovering *Daily Planet* helicopter.

Lois screamed as the copter pitched to one side, slamming the pilot hard against the windscreen. The screen spiderwebbed wildly from the impact, and the pilot sagged back in his seat, unconscious.

The WGBS pilot choked as he saw the *Planet* copter drop. "It's getting nasty here, Ms. Grant! That could've been us. We better back off!"

"No way!" Cat grabbed the pilot hard by his collar. "We are not going to miss the story of the century!"

Lois felt her heart pounding as they fell. *Omigod, this is it!*

But four stories above the ground, they abruptly lurched to a stop.

"Superman!" Jimmy excitedly gave a tug on the side door. It fell away. Wrapping a safety strap around one wrist, he leaned out onto the landing skid and looked down. From his precarious vantage, he could see a tattered crimson cape whipping up against the fuselage. Despite his injuries, Superman had managed to get under the falling helicopter and was lowering it to the street. Jimmy surveyed the scene through his lens-finder. "Man, I don't believe this! These are the greatest pictures I've ever gotten—and the most awful."

Once the copter touched down, Lois and Jimmy eased Joe Jacobi from his seat and gently laid him on the ground. Reflexively, Superman removed the pilot's glasses and quickly scanned through the layers of his skin and skull.

"It's a minor concussion. He'll survive . . . assuming that any of us do."

"Superman, are you all right?" Lois wanted to take him in her arms but was all too aware of Jimmy's proximity.

Superman brushed aside her concern. "I'd like to get you two as far from danger as possible, but I just don't have time! No telling how many lives Doomsday could take while I'm gone."

No more than half a block away, Doomsday was lifting a bus, preparing to throw it at the Special Crimes Unit, which was now bombarding him with explosive shell fire from an armored assault wagon.

Jimmy's shutter clicked. "He's shrugging it off like it was nothing! He's unstoppable!"

Superman rose from where he'd been tending to the unconscious pilot. Lois took his arm and felt his blood on her fingers. "Maybe you should fall back and get help."

Superman shook his head. "Too late for that, Lois. The Justice League has already fallen. There are too many innocent lives in jeopardy. It's all up to me."

Jimmy was already cautiously moving away from them to get a closer shot of Doomsday. As the photographer turned away from them, Lois looked into her lover's eyes and her voice dropped to the merest whisper. "Clark—!"

"Shhh!" He took her in his arms and silenced her with a kiss.

Superman looked at her longingly. In that moment, he wanted to pick her up and fly away to the ends of the Earth. But he knew he couldn't. "Just remember, Lois . . . no matter what happens . . . I will always love you." And then he leapt into the sky, a tattered piece of his sleeve coming loose in her hand.

As he sped by, Jimmy caught a fleeting look at the rage on his friend's face. "Wow, I don't think I've ever seen the big guy so fired up."

So hard and fast did Superman collide with Doomsday that the momentum carried them both through the deserted lobby of an office high rise and onto the street beyond.

"Can you believe that?" Overhead, the WGBS pilot spun his copter around to follow the action. "If this keeps up, we won't have a city left!"

"Just stay close and try to hold us steady," Cat ordered. "The whole country will want to see Superman kick that creep's backside!" Then the breath caught in her throat as she suddenly recognized the avenue below. "Oh, my God, look where they've landed!"

There, in front of the *Daily Planet* Building, Doomsday seized Superman and drove him headfirst into the pavement. The tattered remnant of his cape came loose and tumbled away on a gust of wind.

"NO!" Lois ran forward.

"Stay back, Ms. Lane!"

"Superman is in trouble, Jimmy! We have to help him!"

Doomsday was momentarily confused. Who were these yammering little people? No matter. He would just kill them. A low, satisfied growl built deep within his chest.

"Uh, I don't think we're going to get a chance to help. Grizzly is coming this way!"

"Run, Jimmy! I'll try to distract him—!"

Painfully, Superman clawed his way up from the beneath the street, only to see Doomsday menacing Lois and Jimmy. In that instant, the Man of Steel felt no pain, no weariness. The fog in Superman's brain was burnt away by a rage rivaling that of Doomsday himself, and he dove at the monster.

Energy poured from Superman's eyes in a torrent, as if he'd thrown the throttle of his heat vision wide open. Lois flinched as though she'd suddenly found herself standing next to a blast furnace. The monster reeled before the sheer rush of heat. His hide began to sear and blister.

Bellowing in pain, Doomsday lashed out and kneed Superman in the chin. Superman stumbled, and the monster pressed on, delivering a slashing left that laid open Superman's cheek. The Man of Steel could feel the blood flowing again, but even more he felt the energy surging through him. If he had held back earlier that day, he now reached down into reserves of power that he'd never tapped before.

Superman grabbed hold of Doomsday's fists, forcing him back. He lashed out hard with the heel of his boot, catching the bone spur of Doomsday's left knee and snapping it off. The monster bellowed louder, staggering back, but Superman did not let up. He pressed on, using blows he'd never before dared use on any living being. Doomsday returned the attack, but the power of his blows seemed to be waning.

He's weakening. He's finally weakening!

Both warriors were swaying on their feet. Doomsday's eyes appeared dull, cloudy. Superman's face was so swollen that his eyes were barely visible, but they were clear. The throttle, the tap to his deepest energy reserves, was still wide open, and the power was building within him, demanding to be let out. He knew that once he released that power he would be spent . . . that it would all be gone in a flash. But he knew he could do it—he knew he could take the monster down. He had to—for Lois, for his parents, for the world. Everything depended on him. *This is it, Doomsday. We check out together!*

Heart pounding, Superman threw himself at the monster one last time. The echoes of their blows were heard as far as fifty miles away. Windows shattered, and observers on the scene were shaken to the very bone. Then, before the unblinking gaze of the television cameras, both fighters collapsed. Superman toppled over onto his back, his chest heaving. Doomsday fell facefirst to the pavement and did not move again.

Lois and Jimmy were the first to reach Superman's side. Jimmy numbly clicked off pictures, unable to believe what he had just witnessed. Lois tenderly reached out to cradle her lover in her arms.

Superman's face was so bruised and swollen that he could barely see. It was a struggle for him to speak. "Doomsday . . . is he . . . is he . . . ?"

Lois held him to her. "Down. You stopped him. You saved us all!"

Superman nodded. Then his head fell back against Lois's shoulder, and he slid limply to the pavement. Lois saw all their hopes and dreams slide with him. She began to weep uncontrollably. For a moment the whole world seemed still, save for the sound of her crying.

"He's . . . dead." Cat Grant looked down in shock, the microphone falling slack in her hand.

"He can't be." Her cameraman gripped his Minicam all the tighter. "I mean . . . he's Superman."

"I don't know . . ." The pilot shook his head. "Every man has his limits."

Cat bit her lip. The pain seemed to galvanize her. She reached down and pulled the plug on her mike. "Cut the feed."

"What—?"

"You heard me, cut it! Tell the network there's a technical difficulty. We'll keep taping the video, but there's no need to stay live with this— not until we know what's really going on." She turned to the pilot. "Set us down—but not too close."

As if in slow motion, people began to gather around Superman. Police of the Special Crimes Unit began to fan out, securing the immediate area. From uptown came the roar of a powerful turbine engine, and the Guardian came riding in, a heavily cloaked figure seated behind him on the motorcycle. They both hopped from the bike and strode quickly to where Lois knelt over the fallen hero.

"Damn. We can't be too late!" The Guardian's curse hissed out under his breath. He looked at his companion. *Dub?*

The disguised Dubbilex slowly shook his head. "I've been scanning Superman's mind and there's nothing there . . . no brain-wave activity . . . nothing."

"No—aw, no!" Dan Turpin came running up alongside the Guardian, Maggie Sawyer close on his heels.

"He's alive, Turpin," said Sawyer. "He's got to be." But her voice sounded neither convinced nor convincing.

"Why are you all just standing around?!" Lois rose to her feet, gripping the tattered remnant of Superman's cape. "We've got to do something! We can't just give up—we owe him more than that!"

"Of course we're not giving up!" The Guardian knelt down by Superman. "Captain Sawyer, call the paramedics in here!" He carefully tilted Superman's head back and checked to make certain that the airway was clear. Then, pinching the nose shut, the Guardian took a deep breath and, placing his mouth over Superman's, began to breathe for his friend. It was not easy going. *His lungs must be like steel tanks . . . all the wind I've got barely gets a rise out of his chest.*

In between breaths, the Guardian searched in vain for a pulse. "Turpin! Come here—quick!"

The big, beefy police inspector was at his side in a flash. "What do you need? I'll do anything!"

The Guardian came up for another breath. "Do you know CPR?"

"Yeah, but I'm a little rusty. Sixty compressions a minute, right?"

"More like eighty to a hundred. Let's do it!"

Turpin laid his big hands on Superman's sternum and pushed down hard with all the force his two hundred pounds could muster, again and again and again. And all the while the Guardian continued with the breath of life.

Just a few feet away, SCU police gathered around Doomsday's body. The creature lay sprawled, motionless, across the shattered pavement.

"Oh, man!" One of the cops looked up and down the length of the monstrous gray body. "If Superman's really dead, we'd better pray to God that he put this Doomsday thing down for keeps. Doesn't look like it's breathing—but maybe it didn't need to."

"Stand back!" another cried out. "I—I thought I saw it move!"

"No." Dubbilex stepped closer. "It was only the broken pavement settling beneath him."

"I'm telling you, it moved!"

"Put a lid on it, Champley." Maggie stepped between her officer and the cloaked man. "We don't need any more excitement here."

"Captain Sawyer, please order your unit to back away from the creature. I believe I can determine whether there is any further reason for concern."

Sawyer looked at the cloaked figure skeptically. "Uh-huh. And just who are you supposed to be?"

"You may call me Dubbilex."

Sawyer blinked and took a step back. The answer she'd received was decidedly not vocal.

"I believe you once had occasion to visit the Cadmus Project? I am of that facility. You could call me the resident telepath." Then, aloud, "Guardian can vouch for me, if you have any further questions?"

"N-no. Go ahead . . . check things out."

Dubbilex knelt over Doomsday's body and reached one hand out to touch the upper cranium. The color of the monster's rough hide, he noted, was disturbingly similar to that of his own skin. Several minutes passed.

"Well?" Sawyer was becoming impatient. She began to regret her decision to stop smoking.

Dubbilex did not need any powers of the mind to sense her anxiety. He decided against any further nonaudible communication and chose his words carefully. "Before . . . this creature was filled with rage . . . anger. Now . . . there is nothing."

"Good." The captain turned to one of her officers. "Russell, throw something over that monster and get it out of my sight."

"Any response?"

The Guardian looked up to see a team of paramedics setting up around him. "He's still not breathing on his own. Beyond that it's hard to tell."

One paramedic broke out an oxygen canister while another felt along Superman's throat. "No discernible pulse."

The Guardian paused between breaths. "I couldn't find one, either. But I wasn't sure if I was looking in the right place . . . his origins *are* of another planet."

The paramedic with the oxygen moved in quickly, inserting an endotracheal tube through Superman's mouth and down his throat. One of her partners slipped in to take over the chest compression from the exhausted Inspector Turpin. Another pulled away what was left of the tattered blue and red shirt and attached two round adhesive-backed electrodes to Superman's chest.

Lois and Jimmy stood close by, helplessly watching with quiet horror as an ominous flat line appeared on the screen of the rescue team's heart monitor equipment.

Paramedic Mark Spadolini's voice broke slightly as he radioed their findings to the trauma center at Metropolis General Hospital. "Victim is asystolic. We're administering epinephrine via the breathing tube. No, we can't get an IV into him. No, we've already wrecked three needles trying. There's a puncture wound, partially closed, on his lower right side, just below the ribs. Uh-huh. Okay . . . try to find a vein in the wound."

The monitor was still showing a flat line. Mark shook his head. "We'll have to try shocking him."

There was a discernible crackle as voltage was applied to the Man of Steel's broad chest. But he didn't even twitch.

Dan Turpin stepped away, a tear welling up in the corner of one eye. He'd seen too many fellow officers cut down in the line of duty. He'd had to deliver the bad news to too many young widows. He'd never gotten used to it. As the big cop turned, he saw a brightly clad figure stumble from an alley and collapse amid the rubble. Turpin rushed up to render assistance. "Hey, are you okay?"

Supergirl rolled onto her back. Her jaw was slack and misshapen, her skin discolored to a sickening lavender. "Superman . . ." Her voice was a thin, reedy whisper. "Where is he? Am I near him?"

"Mother o' mercy!" From the looks of her, Turpin could hardly believe that she was still alive, let alone able to talk. "Hold on, little lady, I'll get a medic—!"

"They wouldn't know where to begin with my Supergirl, Inspector."

Turpin turned to find himself nearly face-to-face with Lex Luthor II. The LexCorp heir brushed past the old cop, pulling off his jacket and gently wrapping it around the battered young woman. Turpin looked back over his shoulder and saw a limousine with LexCorp vanity plates waiting less than half a block away. The fact that it had gotten through the police lines was proof positive that the name Luthor still carried a lot of power in Metropolis.

Supergirl looked up into her lover's eyes. "I . . . tried to help Superman . . . but . . . hurt so much . . ."

"Shhh. It's all right, love." Luthor gingerly picked her up and headed for the limo. "He's beyond help now—beyond our reach. But we can help you."

As the paramedics continued to work on Superman, Lois stood clutching his cape. Her hands had nearly wadded one end of the cloth into a knot. Jimmy watched her worriedly, uncertain of what to do next.

"Lois?"

She turned with a start at the sound of her name. Cat Grant stood less than a yard away. She hadn't even heard her approach.

Cat reached out to Lois, taking her by the arm and steering her away from Superman's body. "Lois, are you going to be all right?"

"I don't know if any of us will ever be all right . . . ever again."

Cat caught Jimmy's eye. "Where's Clark? He should be with her at a time like this."

"Geez, I don't know. He was gone all morning, chasing down some story, but I'm surprised he hasn't shown up here. He must have heard by now. The news has been all over radio and TV."

Cat nodded. "I can guarantee that!"

"Maybe he couldn't get through the police lines."

"I doubt that. Nothing's ever kept Clark Kent from getting where he wanted to go!" Cat looked around as if expecting to see Kent suddenly materialize. She shook her head. "He must have gotten tied up somewhere."

"Lois?" Jimmy took her by the arm. "Let's go inside the *Planet*."

"No . . . we can't leave him now . . . not like this . . ."

"Lois, listen to me!" Cat grabbed her by the shoulders. "You've got to snap out of it. We can't do Superman any good by getting in the way of the paramedics. Look, I know he meant a lot to you . . . He meant a lot to all of us. But you're a reporter—and a darn good one. This story needs to be told . . . by you." She stared hard at Lois until the other woman blinked.

Lois brought up a hand and kneaded the bridge of her nose. "You— you're right."

Cat heaved a sigh of relief. She could see her cameraman waving to her from down the block. "Look, I have to run. Take good care of her, Jimmy."

"Sure, Cat." Olsen managed a weak thumbs-up. "We'll get by . . . somehow."

"No go." The weary paramedic shook his head. "We've run the voltage off the scale, and we're still getting no response. I'm beginning to think we'd need to hit him with a bolt of lightning to get a rise out of him."

"We can't give up!" The Guardian gripped the man's shoulder so hard that he flinched. "We mustn't!"

"H-hey, don't worry! We never do. Once a resuscitation's started, we don't stop until an MD takes over." Mark waved over one of his partners. "Back that ambulance over here. Metro General's standing by for us. We'll pack him and work on him en route."

Mark looked back at the line on the monitor. It was still flat. "I just wish we could get *some* response. Anything!"

Halfway across the country, Jonathan and Martha Kent held one another as the horrible sights and sounds were played out and replayed on their television. A somber news anchor stared back at them from the screen. "This just handed me . . . Superman has been loaded into an ambulance and is at this moment being moved to Metropolis General Hospital, where GBS correspondent Martin Phelps is standing by. Martin, what's the situation there at Metro General? Can you tell us what preparations are being made?"

"David, it's still not clear what measures, if any, can be taken to revive Superman. We're told that the alien nature of his body precludes normal revival techniques. We do know that Dr. Jorge Sanchez has been called to the hospital and is expected to arrive momentarily. Dr. Sanchez, it should be noted, has treated Superman in the past, the first time over two years ago, when the Man of Steel was shot with a kryptonite bullet by the sociopath Bloodsport. We'll try to speak with Dr. Sanchez when he arrives."

"Thank you, Martin. Again, for those of you just joining us, Superman has been loaded into an ambulance and is being moved to Metropolis General Hospital. His condition is unknown. We know that paramedics have been making attempts, heroic attempts, to revive him. There has been one report from the site of Superman's battle with Doomsday—and again, this is unconfirmed—a report that no brain activity could be detected."

"Please turn it off, Jonathan." Martha clamped her eyes shut and hid her face in her hands.

Jonathan angrily snapped the set off, almost wrenching away the switch. "Damned fool doesn't know what he's talking about."

They stood for several minutes before Martha broke the silence. "What if they're right? What if it's true?"

Jonathan hugged his wife to him. "We keep on praying to the good Lord for our boy, Martha."

"If only . . . I could . . . have helped him, Lex."

As his limousine rushed through the darkening city streets, Lex Luthor cradled the battered Supergirl in his arms.

"Love, if I could turn back time, I would have sent you and Team Luthor in to help as soon as we heard about that monster. But who knew—who knew?" Lex stared numbly out the window. *I certainly didn't—Not until the very end did I have the slightest inkling this could happen.* He had long looked forward to the day when he would successfully engineer the death of Superman. But now that moment had been forever stolen from him. *Unless they manage to revive him . . .*

Supergirl began to sob, and Luthor clutched her to him tightly. "I know . . . I know . . . it's a tragedy. We can't ever forget what was, but we all must carry on. Show me some spirit, love. We need you—good and whole—now more than ever!" He kissed her mottled cheek. "You must try to pull yourself together now. Take it one step at a time. Use those wondrous shape-shifting powers of yours and mend yourself. You can do it, love! I know you can!"

"It . . . will be . . . painful, Lex . . . but for you, I would move mountains." Her brow furrowed and her fists tightened. She shook, as if in the throes of a seizure, but the swelling of her face began to subside. Her color noticeably improved, and her jaw appeared to flow back into its normal position.

"Amazing. Simply amazing." Lex stared at her, enraptured.

"How do I look, Lex?" Her breathing was labored, but she was clearly finding it easier to speak. "Am I . . . presentable?"

Lex ran his fingers through her hair. Once again, it glistened like spun gold. "You're far more than presentable, love. You're beautiful . . . my precious, precious gem. Together, you and I are going to make a new future for this city!"

Jimmy Olsen threw a stack of pictures down on Perry White's desk in disgust. "Here they are, Chief. The photo editor's still out sick, so I guess it's up to you to pick the shots that'll earn me my thirty pieces of silver."

Perry got up from behind his desk. His hand went reflexively to his vest pocket. It was empty—had been so since he'd given up smoking three months before, but old habits died hard. "Jim, I understand why you're upset . . ."

"Do you, Chief?" Jimmy looked back out through the managing editor's open door. The City Room was unnaturally quiet, despite the fact that most of the day staff was still around. Every eye in the room was glued to the television monitors. "Superman—was the greatest. And look at the way the media reacts! The television crowd's crawling all over themselves, trying to be the first to officially pronounce him dead. You'd think they were happy he died—he probably saved them all from a slow news day."

Jimmy slumped back against Perry's filing cabinet. "And they call it 'journalism.' It makes me want to puke! We lost a friend today, Mr. White . . . a good friend."

"That we did, Jimmy. We owe it to him to honor his memory."

"You know these pictures I took of Superman? When I saw them coming out of the developer, I couldn't believe that I'd taken them. I wanted to rip them up, destroy the negatives. Using them to sell papers . . . I don't know . . . it seems like a violation of my friendship with him."

Perry sorted through the stack of pictures. There was no denying their power. "Olsen, one of these photos will serve to remind this city—no, the world—of the tremendous sacrifice one man made." He placed a hand on the young man's shoulder. "Superman's passing has left a great void in all of us. But we are still journalists. And we've still got a paper to publish. Think of what Lois is going through."

They both looked across the City Room to where Lois Lane sat alone at her desk. She was staring a hole into her desktop monitor, tears sporadically beading up in the corners of her eyes. But her hands moved ceaselessly back and forth across her keyboard, as if trying to purge her system of some unbearable knowledge.

Perry shook his head. "She may have lost more than any of us. There's been no word from Kent, and the area of town he'd gone to was hit pretty hard by Doomsday. Latest reports have at least a hundred buildings down. Thousands of people are missing, presumably trapped in the rubble. Kent could be one of them."

Jimmy's face fell. "Oh, no. He's got to turn up, Chief. It's bad enough that Superman died in her arms. What'll it do to her if she's lost Mr. Kent, too?"

SECTION TWO

FUNERAL FOR A FRIEND

11

Ruby Mayer stood behind the large front window of her store, staring off down the street. For nearly forty years, she had been running Mayer's Newsstand & Sundries, at first with her husband and then, after he'd passed on, by herself. Every day, year in and year out, in all kinds of weather, a parade of customers trooped through her door seeking the latest magazines and newspapers, and Ruby always did her best to see that they found what they were looking for. Often, in the evening, they'd linger over a cola or an egg cream at the old soda fountain and talk with her about what sort of day they'd had.

But not tonight.

Tonight, the store was empty, and Ruby felt more alone than she'd felt since the Mister had died.

Down the street, a lone pair of headlights came around the corner, and a big panel truck whizzed by the store, dumping its bundle of newspapers without even slowing down. That in itself was nothing new; it happened at least twice a day. It was, in fact, the subject of a long-standing joke between Ruby and her customers. "They always drop the papers and run," she'd say. "I think they're afraid we're going to blame them for the news!"

Tonight, however, she wasn't laughing. Tonight everyone had reason to be afraid. Ruby had had her radio on all afternoon, listening to the news, and she had dreaded this delivery. She pulled her sweater tight against the wind and trundled out to the curb to retrieve the bundle. Back inside, Ruby pulled out a pair of snips and cut the wire that held the bundle together. The wire snapped, and six dozen copies of the *Daily Planet*'s late-evening extra spilled across the counter. The front-page headline consisted of just two words: SUPERMAN—DEAD.

Ruby shivered when she saw it. *A headline that big you'd expect for nothing less than a notice of the end of the world*. She dabbed at her eyes with the kerchief she kept up her sleeve. *And maybe it is . . . maybe it is.*

Miles away, in WLEX's Studio Seven, anchorman Wallace Bailey felt his throat tighten as the floor manager held up a hand and began the five-second count to air. He'd been at the news desk most of the day without a break, and the strain was beginning to take its toll. The tally light atop camera one suddenly glowed red, and he swallowed hard.

"For those of you just joining us, much of Metropolis remains under a dusk-to-dawn curfew, following the—" Bailey took a deep breath. "—the death of Superman."

The death of Superman. There, he'd said it.

Bailey took a second deep breath and opened his mouth, but no more words came out. He glanced nervously at his written notes, then at the lines on the TelePrompTer, but they might as well have been written in Sanskrit. In a panic, he tried to think of something—anything—to say, but all that came to his mind was an old videotape he'd once seen in journalism school. Among other things, the tape showed one of those rare moments when Walter Cronkite fumbled on-screen, an unsteady few seconds the afternoon that JFK was shot. It was another terrible day, not unlike this one, but he found the memory strangely reassuring. *See,* it seemed to say, *this can happen to the best of us. It's no sin to get flustered. Somehow, we all manage to go on.* Miraculously, Bailey discovered that he could read his notes again, even as the silent, traitorous voice in his head reminded him that he was still a long way from being a Walter Cronkite.

"The world-renowned hero laid down his life today to stop a berserk monster called Doomsday, who threatened to level the city. The origins of the monster remain unknown at this hour. The final battle followed a several-state rampage that resulted in over five hundred deaths and left the Justice League in disarray."

The camera cut from Bailey to taped footage of Superman and Doomsday punching each other across the parking lot of a suburban shopping plaza. No longer on-screen, the anchorman felt his voice steady a bit further as he began the voice-over. "Superman joined the battle at midmorning, but though he fought valiantly, he seemed unable to stop Doomsday's odyssey of death and destruction. It was, tragically, a fight to the finish . . . that claimed the lives of both combatants."

The on-screen images changed again, this time to clips of hustling paramedic teams working over Superman's body. "Despite prolonged heroic efforts, the Man of Steel could not be revived at the scene. Resuscitation efforts continued as Metropolis's paramedics rushed the Man of Steel to Metro General Hospital, where a trauma team headed by Dr. Jorge Sanchez labored for hours in an attempt to save his life."

Bailey paused in his narration, tears coming to his eyes. "The final pronouncement came just ninety minutes ago." On the studio monitors, he could see a slim, mustached man approach a makeshift podium outside the Metro General emergency entrance. Across the bottom of the screen, a superimposed caption identified the man as Dr. Sanchez. The clicking of camera shutters sounded like crickets chirping as the doctor stepped up to the microphones.

Dr. Sanchez cleared his throat. "It is my sad duty to inform you that Superman was declared dead at approximately 6:23 PM, eastern daylight time." On the pretaped segment, the doctor blinked, apparently dazzled by all the television lighting.

In the studio, Bailey was cued to continue his narration. "For more on this story, we go now live to Scott Harris." The cameras abruptly cut to a rugged-looking, dark-haired man with a microphone standing outside a nondescript municipal building.

"Wallace, Superman's body was brought here to the city morgue just minutes ago. As Superman has no known relatives, there is apparently some controversy brewing over who has rights to the—" Suddenly there was a loud electronic squawk, and the picture broke apart to snow.

"Scott, can you hear me?" The screen cut back to the anchor desk and a noticeably surprised Wallace Bailey. "Well, we seem to be experiencing some technical difficulties."

Back outside the morgue building, Harris turned, startled by the sound of gunfire. "Wallace, are you there? Someone is shooting—" He looked up and knew it was pointless to say another word; armed soldiers were being deployed from a troop carrier just a few yards away, and one of them had just shot apart the microwave uplink dish atop the WLEX broadcast van.

Harris had spent time overseas covering a number of brushfire wars, and he could tell at a glance that there was something odd about these troops; they weren't dressed in standard army-issue uniforms. He located a soldier who was wearing officer's bars and started screaming at him. "What's the big idea of shooting out our dish? You can't get away with this! What's going on here?"

The officer gave Harris and his news crew a cursory glance and turned to an aide. "Arrest that man . . . arrest them all!"

.   .   .

Police Captain Maggie Sawyer and Inspector Dan Turpin stood at the head of a squad of heavily armed Special Crimes Unit police, blocking the path of Paul Westfield and an equally armed squad of soldiers wearing the shoulder patch of the Cadmus Project. Turpin was fit to be tied. "Westfield, I advise you an' yer pack of ghouls to turn 'round and goosestep outta here!"

"I'd listen to Inspector Turpin if I were you!" Maggie slipped the safety switch of her automatic.

"You and your Special Crimes Unit don't impress me, Captain Sawyer." Westfield coolly pulled a folded set of papers from his coat. "I direct a *federal* project. And under section twelve of the Executive Emergency Act, I am authorized to collect for study the bodies of any alien decedents, which includes Superman and that monster he fought!"

"Yeah." A soldier at Westfield's side had his rifle pointed directly at the police line. "So you and your boys better step aside, or things could get real messy!"

"You can't be serious!" The Guardian emerged from a doorway behind the police, astounded at finding troops of his command involved in an act of force outside the Project. "What do you think this is, the Old West? There'll be no shoot-out with local authorities! Lower your weapons!"

"Ignore that order!" Westfield scowled. He hadn't expected the Guardian to still be here.

"B-but, Mr. Westfield," one soldier wavered, "the Guardian *is* our security chief."

"And I'm Project administrator!"

"Pulling rank, Westfield?" The Guardian defiantly folded his arms. "I'd say you've already exceeded your authority."

"That was out of line, Guardian! You of all people must realize how important this is to us. There's no telling what we could learn from Superman's body!"

"You're exposing the Project to further public scrutiny!"

"Not at all." Westfield's face twisted into a nasty smirk. "My troops have the entire area secured. Only one television crew was set up when we arrived, and they've already been dealt with. The good people of Metropolis won't learn anything about the Project that I don't want them to."

"What do you mean, there's a news blackout?" In his quarters atop the LexCorp Tower, Lex Luthor had phoned his news director the moment that WLEX's remote crew was knocked off the air. "A blackout by whose authority? A federal agency? What federal agency? Well, find out! We are not going to stand for this!" Lex slammed down the phone. *We are most definitely going to do something about this.*

Luthor stalked into the next room, where Supergirl sat staring blankly off into space. The bruises she'd sustained in her battle with Doomsday had already faded, but she'd been deeply emotionally affected by her failure to help Superman. *A little mission now might do her a world of good.* "Supergirl . . . love?"

"Yes, Lex?" She sounded hollow.

Lex gently laid his hand on her shoulder. "Time to call out the dogs, love. There's work to be done."

The Guardian drew himself up, standing tall and blocking Westfield's path with his own body. "Have you lost all decency? Show some respect for the dead!"

"There'll be time for that later!" Westfield was becoming impatient. "We have to act quickly before the bodies start to decompose! Now, are you going to do your duty and help or—"

"No, Westfield." The Guardian looked him square in the eye. "If you want Superman, you'll have to go through me!"

Westfield's face and lips paled visibly.

Uh-oh. Maggie Sawyer could feel her stomach clenching. From hard experience, she knew that when the blood drained from the face, the bluster was over and the body was committed to action. *It's fight or flight, and I doubt that Westfield has the grace, the brains, or the guts to back down now.* She also knew without needing to spare a glance in their direction that Turpin and her men had read the situation the same way.

Suddenly, before anyone in that corridor could make another move, two armored figures crashed through the walls on both sides of them. A highly amplified voice bellowed, "SURPRISE!"

"Holy Geez! It's a couple o' Team Luthor's armor boys!" Dan Turpin sounded a lot less annoyed than he ordinarily would have been at a civilian commando raid. Maggie was far from displeased herself. Luthor's men had broken the impasse nicely.

As one, the Guardian and the SCU dove for cover as Westfield's troops opened fire on Team Luthor. The Cadmus soldiers were heavily armed, but for all the effect their assault rifles had on the intruders' glistening body armor, they might as well have been throwing popcorn.

"Nuts!" Turpin's pleased surprise was swiftly giving way to embarrassment. "That's *our* fight they're fighting!"

Sawyer grabbed the inspector by the arm and held him back. "All things considered, Dan, I don't really mind."

The Guardian brought his shield up as a seven-millimeter bullet whizzed by his head. "Keep your forces down, Captain. Team Luthor seems mainly to be drawing fire. They must have something up their sleeves." He peered at the nearer wall, through one of the gaping holes left by Team Luthor. "And I think I see what it is!"

The first Cadmus trooper who saw the blue-and-red-caped figure come through the opening was so shocked that he felt his heart skip a couple of beats. He looked again and elbowed his superior officer. "Uh, Sarge—?"

"Keep firing, McIntyre! Don't stop for anything!"

"Anything? What about *her*?"

Supergirl landed among them, and the fire fight stopped as abruptly as if someone had thrown a switch. "Good start." Supergirl looked them over sternly. "A very good start. Now put down your weapons or I'll take them away from you."

Westfield dashed toward her, nearly tripping in his haste. "Supergirl, no! You're making a big mistake. We're an authorized federal agency!"

"Don't trust 'im for one minute, li'l lady!" Turpin's voice boomed as if he still needed to shout above gunfire. "He an' his goon squad are tryin' to take Superman's body!"

"They're *what*?" Supergirl's eyes went wide, and she thrust her hands out at Westfield and his troops.

They never knew what hit them.

Paul Westfield was the last to regain consciousness. As he came to, he thought he could hear someone calling his name. When his eyes finally focused, he saw the Guardian crouched over him, offering a helping hand. If a sudden wave of nausea hadn't hit him, he would have been sorely tempted to slap the hand away, or maybe bite it.

"Is he going to be all right?"

Westfield turned his head—slowly—to look for the source of the second voice. He gaped. *It's Supergirl, and she has the consummate gall to look concerned.*

"I think so. He'll be sore for a few days, though." The Guardian also looked concerned, Westfield noted. *Charming. If only these people showed half the regard for my authority that they did for my health.*

"Paul? Can you hear me?"

"Yes." *What hit me?* Westfield had to force himself to listen to the Guardian.

"Good. Do you remember your full name? Do you know where you are?"

"Yes, dammit! I'm Paul Westfield, and we're in Metropolis . . ." There was a slight chill in the air, and Westfield looked around, suddenly realizing that he was lying on a stretcher on the sidewalk. ". . . outside the city morgue building! And don't worry, I don't have a concussion! I'm just—just—" *I'm just mad as hell! I'll have your shield, you self-righteous fool, as well as Superman's body, before this is over.* "Never mind!"

The Guardian smiled wryly. *I wish Dubbilex hadn't already left for the Project. I can guess what you're thinking, Paul, but I'd love to get confirmation.* "Do you feel like sitting up?"

Westfield dearly wished to say no, but he decided that he'd already shown enough weakness for one day. He nodded carefully and grudgingly accepted the Guardian's hand. He started to look around, saw Supergirl again, and drew back involuntarily.

"What did she do to me?"

Much to Westfield's distress, Maggie Sawyer stepped forward. "It's called a psychokinetic blast. And you're lucky that all she did was sweep you and your toy soldiers out the door."

Lucky? "You can't talk to me that way, Sawyer!"

"Paul . . ." The Guardian's hand tightened on his. "You *were* lucky. Don't press it."

Westfield shuffled uncertainly to his feet. He nearly fell over when he saw Inspector Turpin supervising the roundup of his Cadmus forces. They were filing back into their troop carrier, walking a gauntlet of heavily armed SCU cops. One last Cadmus soldier was glumly dropping his weapon atop a pile of captured assault rifles.

"Hey!" Turpin shoved his derby forward. "Come back here and stack that neat!"

The soldier looked up at the big bear of a man. Turpin glowered down at him, ominously cracking his knuckles. The soldier swallowed hard and rushed to comply.

This was too much. Later, Westfield would wonder where all the adrenaline was coming from, but for now he was simply grateful for the energy rush. He pulled himself up as tall and straight as he knew how and peppered the air with every profane and pungent comment he could think of.

Maggie Sawyer stood patiently with her hands on her hips until his verbal barrage had died down to a sputter. Then she poked a finger into his chest. "I'd light a *candle* if I were you, Westfield." Her voice was a brittle whisper. "You could have gotten your boys killed in there . . . and we've had enough killing around here today."

Westfield glared at her, furious and frustrated almost to the point of apoplexy. A glance across the street brought added insult: The WLEX news technicians were mounting a new microwave dish to the top of their van.

"You won't get away with this, Sawyer! I'm holding you all responsible! When Washington hears about this fiasco—!"

"Washington has already heard, Mister . . . Westfield, is it?" Westfield jerked around, but he'd already recognized the voice; the Australian accent was a dead giveaway.

Lex Luthor II sauntered toward him; a shorter man huffed alongside. Luthor gave Westfield his most sharklike smile. "Yes, Mr. Westfield, Washington knows all about this fiasco, as you so accurately put it. And what's more, they hold you responsible. They're none too happy with you for ordering the destruction of equipment belonging to my television station, not to mention your interference with the local constabulary." Lex glanced down at the man who accompanied him. "Isn't that right, Mayor Berkowitz?"

"You can take that to the bank, Luthor." Berkowitz stepped forward, his face red with fury and wounded civic pride. "I have a little something for you, *Mr.* Westfield—faxes from the *White House!*" The mayor brandished a curling sheaf of pages like a protective talisman, waving them under Westfield's nose.

Westfield almost laughed in Berkowitz's face. *The man's seen too many old movies.* But then he caught a glimpse of the seal of the President on the top page of the faxes. Suddenly there was nothing at all funny about the little mayor.

"The President himself has rescinded your authority in this matter." Berkowitz continued to shake the faxes as he spoke. "Superman's genetic heritage may be alien, but as far as we're concerned—and the President agrees—he's an American! And by God, we intend to see that he's given a decent burial. *In Metropolis!*"

"But, Mayor Berkowitz . . ." Westfield swallowed his pride. "Sir, please, if only you'd let me explain—"

"Don't bother, mate." Lex looked at Berkowitz, ready to step aside in case the mayor wanted to do his own interrupting. Berkowitz just smiled tightly and gestured for Luthor to continue.

"I'd say you've already blathered on quite enough. You put your foot right in this one, Westfield. You've made a priceless ass of yourself and your entire organization. Oh, and don't bother trying to claim that Doomsday beastie, either. We've convinced the president to let S.T.A.R. Labs dispose of him."

Westfield felt numb. *How could everything fall apart on me like this? What did I do wrong?*

"Now, as a patriotic citizen, I'm willing to overlook the extensive damage done to my property." Lex took the Cadmus boss by the arm and steered him toward the captured troop carrier. "I'll even agree to keep mention o' your little project out of the news, *if* you get in your truck and return to your base—*now*. Do we understand each other?"

Westfield nodded weakly.

"Good. Team Luthor will help the Guardian *escort* you to the county line. Good-bye to you, Mr. Westfield."

In a matter of minutes, the Guardian kick-started his big motorcycle to life and pulled out, leading the caravan up a deserted Metropolis boulevard. The Cadmus troop carrier followed close behind, and the two Team Luthor men flew alongside, the eerie whine of their armor's miniature jets echoing down the empty streets. For the sake of Project security, the Guardian had decided that they'd take the long way home. Once they were out of the county and free of Luthor's men, they could proceed over the back roads to Mount Curtiss undetected. It wasn't that he had any reason to distrust the LexCorp team, but Westfield had already made far too public a display of Project resources, and Harper was determined to see that some of Cadmus's secrets remained secret.

I knew that Westfield had it in for Superman—he could never trust anyone with that much power, especially someone not under his control—but I never thought he'd stoop so low as to pick a fight over the man's body. The Guardian couldn't deny that Cadmus had harbored more than its fair share of loose cannons over the years, Dabney Donovan being the prime example, but he'd been caught unprepared for this kind of reckless behavior from the administrator's office. *Hijacking Superman's body was the sort of high-handed stunt I'd have expected from Donovan. There had better be some changes made at Cadmus after this!*

Scott Harris had just about convinced himself that the interests of national security would be best served by suppressing the story of Westfield's aborted mission when Wallace Bailey's voice crackled over his earphone. "I'm told that our remote crew has corrected their technical problems. Scott, are you there?"

"Yes, Wallace." Harris firmly silenced any last qualms of conscience. "Everything is . . . under control now." *Except for my nerves. As soon as we're off the air, I think that I just might go behind the van and throw up.* He paused for a moment, thinking of all those millions of viewers tuned in to WLEX, totally unaware that a paramilitary operation had just been squelched at the city morgue. *And they'll never know. They'll never have the slightest idea.* The surrealism of the situation hit him and he had to grit his teeth to repress a sudden hysterical urge to giggle. *Hello, Mr. and Ms. America and all the ships at sea! Guess what? I've got a secret!*

Scott hurriedly cleared his throat and launched into the introduction he had already prepared. "LexCorp CEO Lex Luthor II has just arrived, accompanied by Supergirl. I believe that Mr. Luthor is about to make a statement."

The cameras cut to a medium close-up of Luthor and Supergirl standing on the steps of the morgue building, just in front of the main doors. No one would ever have guessed that, just minutes before, both of these glamorous people had taken sudden, ruthless action. Harris *had* been there, as his queasy stomach kept reminding him, and he himself could hardly believe it, even now.

Luthor stared into the cameras as if he were making eye contact with each viewer individually. "Ladies and gentlemen, the . . . death of Superman . . . has affected us all very deeply. A legend has been cruelly taken from us.

"It is fitting and proper that we mourn his passing . . . especially those of us in Metropolis, who knew him so well. To that end, Mayor Berkowitz has informed me that a section of Centennial Park will be set aside as a final resting place for our fallen champion.

"And I pledge to you now that the full resources of LexCorp International shall be put to work at that site, to erect a monument worthy of a Superman!"

Among the millions following Luthor's broadcast were three people in the office of Perry White, managing editor of the *Daily Planet*. Lois Lane sat on an old swaybacked couch, blank faced and blank eyed, still clutching the torn remnant of Superman's cape. Jimmy Olsen stood across the room, nominally listening to Luthor but keeping a worried eye on Lois. Perry himself stood next to the television, his hands jammed into his pockets. In times of stress, his old nicotine cravings were still acutely strong, and listening to the Luthor boy was most stressful. If Perry closed his eyes and ignored the accent, he swore he could hear Lex the First speaking. When young Lex pledged his company's help in erecting a monument to the Man of Steel, the editor swore softly but fervently under his breath. *Slimy, opportunistic bastard. He's setting himself up as chief mourner!*

Jimmy kept glancing anxiously from the TV to Lois, increasingly concerned by her lack of reaction. *She's hardly said a word since she turned in her story.* He started to take a step toward her, hesitated, and uneasily leaned back against White's desk. *I guess I shouldn't be surprised. She's had two awful shocks, what with Mr. Kent missing and Superman dying in her arms. Why, she was even responsible for giving Superman his name, for gosh sakes.* Jimmy stared forlornly past Lois, looking out unseemingly through one of the big windows in the corner office. *I wish Superman were still alive. I wish Mr. Kent would show up. And I wish Lois would say something. Anything!*

Jimmy was so lost in thought that he jumped when Perry White abruptly snapped off the television set. "It's been a long, hard day. Why don't you kids go on home?"

"Home. Sure." Lois spoke as if using the words for the first time.

Jimmy walked over to her. "Need a lift, Lois?"

"Thanks, Jimmy . . . but no. I'm . . . well, I'm *not* all right, but I can find my way." She paused at the office door. "Thanks again, though."

Lois was halfway across the City Room before she was noticed by Allie Fitzgerald. "Ms. Lane? L-Lois?" The copygirl had a round, cheerful face, a cherub's face, but tonight she looked drawn, and her eyes were red from crying. "Has there been any word yet from Mr. Kent?"

"F-from Clark?! Clark is . . . is—!" *Oh, God!* "No, Allie. No word."

"Well, don't give up hope. There are thousands of folks still missing— and the phones are such a mess! Mr. Kent will turn up all right. I just know he will!"

"Sure. G'night, Allie."

From the doorway to White's office, Jimmy watched Lois pass through the double doors of the City Room and turn down the hall toward the elevators. "I hope Allie's right."

"Amen to that, Olsen. But, great Caesar's ghost, you were there. You know as well as anyone—scores of buildings were toppled during Doomsday's attack. Most of the people still missing—Kent included— are trapped in all that wreckage. Even if Clark is alive out there some- where, he might not be by the time rescuers find him. If ever there was a time when we needed Superman and his X-ray vision, it's right now! But he's gone . . . and I doubt we'll ever see another like him."

"It's so unfair, Chief. Ms. Lane and Mr. Kent had been engaged just a few months."

"You don't have to remind me, Jim. She's taking it pretty hard." White paused absently. "I've known Lois since she was little more than a girl, and I've never seen her so absolutely shattered. Lord, I don't even want to think about how this must be affecting Clark's parents! Jon and Martha Kent are damned good people—salt of the Earth! And Clark was—dammit, *is*—their only child. I should have called them earlier, but I keep waiting, hoping there'll be some good news to give them. But with things still up in the air . . ." Perry sadly shook his head. "I tell you, Olsen, I'd almost rather face a firing squad than place that call!"

．　　　．　　　．

Lana Lang stood in a phone booth on the perimeter of a little self-service gas station outside Cloverdale, Indiana. She glanced nervously through the streaked glass, watching Peter Ross fill the tank of their car with unleaded gas. Their car . . . it was still strange to think of things as being theirs, to think of Peter as her fiancé. She loved him—loved him dearly—but it would never be like it was with Clark.

Clark—! Tears began to stream down Lana's cheeks. She was one of the few people on Earth who knew that the boy from her hometown, the boy that she'd loved so very much, had gone out into the world to become Superman.

Lana had met both Clark Kent and Peter Ross at old Eisenhower Elementary School in Smallville, she remembered. She was infatuated with Clark from the day she started first grade, much to the young boy's dismay.

Like many other six-year-old boys, Clark thought that all girls were cooties. He gradually came to revise his opinion—of girls in general and Lana in particular. By the time they entered their teens, Clark had come to regard Lana as one of his closest friends.

By the time they reached high school, Lana's infatuation with Clark had grown into something much stronger. She was perceptive enough to realize that her feelings for him were deeper than his for her, but she lived in hope that he would come around. As for Peter . . . well, she was always fond of Peter, and she knew that he liked her. He was always there for her if she needed him. But there was no one quite like Clark for Lana. She always thought he was someone very special.

It wasn't until their senior year that she discovered just how special he truly was.

Clark had shown up on her doorstep one moonlit evening and asked Lana to come for a walk. As they strolled along an old country road, part of her was hoping that he'd come to propose. But instead, Clark started to talk about world events, about war and crime and so many other things.

"One man *can* make a difference, Lana, if he's the right man. And I think, maybe, I was meant to be that man."

"You, Clark?" She smiled up at him. If any other boy had said such a thing, she would have giggled. "Well, you're a terrific athlete—and smart as a whip! But what can you do that a thousand other people can't?"

"Lots of things, Lana. Things maybe nobody else on Earth can do. I've been learning things about myself. Let me show you."

And with that, Clark scooped Lana up in his arms and flew off into the night sky.

Lana was astonished to see the land zooming by beneath them. The rush of the wind nearly took her breath away. Oddly, she was not afraid, and certainly not repulsed, to be borne along in Clark's strong embrace. Even so, when they finally touched down on the outskirts of San Diego, the first thing she asked was whether Clark had considered that this stunt might scare her out of her wits.

Clark seemed genuinely surprised. "Gosh, no, Lana. I . . . I guess I was just so sure that you'd understand."

And so she had.

They flew around the world that night. In Hong Kong, Clark bought several small packets of firecrackers and lit them for Lana from yards away with his heat vision. Atop the cliffs of Dover, he used his thumbnail to carve her initials on a flat white stone. Her initials only, she noticed, not theirs. Clark asked her to throw the stone out into the English Channel. Then he dove in and recovered it for her, all within seconds.

Throughout that magical night, Lana came to realize that Clark wasn't showing off. He wasn't even really trying to impress her; rather he was sharing a secret, showing her why he felt a responsibility to help as many people as he could. With every incredible power and ability he displayed, Lana became more and more certain that Clark wasn't going to propose to her. Not then, and not ever. He was looking for a confidant, not a mate, and he'd chosen her.

When they finally landed back in Kansas, Clark escorted Lana home and kissed her good-bye. The kiss was short and sweet . . . and on her forehead. It was the sort of kiss a brother would give his sister.

And then he'd flown away—away from Lana, away from Smallville, away from any life they might have shared—as she knew he must.

Years after graduation, when Lana read about the mysterious flying man who had saved the space plane, she knew immediately that it had to be Clark. And when an in-depth article on Superman saw print days later under Clark Kent's byline, she'd laughed out loud. *Talk about hiding in plain sight!*

Her laughter was a reassurance that she'd finally gotten over the pain of Clark's leaving. She and Clark had kept in touch, and with every year, she felt more honored that he'd taken her into his confidence. She had been the first person outside of his parents who'd known about his powers, the first he himself had told. That had to count for something. Lana Lang knew that she would never be Mrs. Clark Kent, but in a way she had become Superman's sister. That, she told herself, ought to be enough for anyone. And eventually it was.

She'd faithfully kept his secret all those years, even from Peter.

. . .

Dear, sweet Peter. I could never tell him. Not even now.

Lana's hands shook as she shoved quarters into the slot of the pay phone and punched in the area code and number. There was a buzz and a click, and then an old familiar voice answered. It was all Lana could do to keep her voice from breaking.

"H-hello, Jonathan? It's Lana. Pete and I were on the road when the news came over the radio. I told him I wanted to call . . . to see if you'd heard from . . . from Clark—!" She lost control and sank against the side of the booth, sobbing. "Oh, Jonathan, I still can't believe it! He *can't* be gone . . . he just can't be! It has to be some horrible mistake!"

"I wish it were, Lana, but Martha and I—we saw the whole thing on the television." Jonathan Kent paused to listen and dabbed at his eyes with a corner of his bandanna. "Martha? She's holding up as well as could be expected. Neither of us . . . ever really expected we'd have to mourn a child. Guess we were just foolin' ourselves. There's not a one of us who isn't mortal. Not even Superman. I expect that this's made just about everybody stop and think a little."

At her end of the line, Lana could see Peter replacing the pump handle. Now, at least, she could tell him that she'd talked to Clark's parents. She could tell him that their old friend was among Metropolis's missing.

Now she would have an excuse for her tears.

Word of Superman's death spread quickly across the country and throughout the world. In years to come, all who were alive that day and old enough to realize the significance of the event would recall where they were and what they were doing when they heard the news.

The streets of Fayerville, South Carolina, were dark and quiet. Aside from three functioning streetlamps, the only real source of illumination on Main Street was the light that came from Gasper's Diner. Other than the sheriff's office and the little county hospital on the edge of town, Gasper's was the only establishment in Fayerville that you could count on to be open around the clock. Tonight the diner was all but deserted. The only customer in the place was Sheriff James Frye, who'd wandered in at around half past nine for a late dinner and stayed on to keep Daisy and Clovis Gasper company. *Not a good night for anybody to be alone,* thought Frye. He drained the last few drops of coffee from his mug, and Daisy reflexively reached over to refill it. *Not a good night at all.*

None of them had exchanged more than a few words for over an hour. They just sat watching the shifting images on the tiny portable TV that Daisy had plugged in at the end of the counter. The old Soder Cola clock on the far wall was grinding its way to eleven when the big stylized letter G filled the screen.

"Our continuing coverage of the death of Superman will resume in one half hour. This is the Galaxy Broadcasting System. We return you now to your local affiliates."

The network logo abruptly disappeared, replaced by an earnest-looking gray-haired man who looked up mournfully from a stack of papers piled before him. "Good evening, this is *News-Five at Eleven*. Tonight's top story: The city of Metropolis begins to dig out of the rubble as the world mourns the passing of a great man."

"Lordy. " The lanky short-order cook slapped his hands down onto the counter. "Didn't anything *else* happen in the world today?"

Sheriff Frye looked up from his coffee. "If it did, Clovis, it doesn't matter."

"Yeah . . . reckon yer right, Sheriff."

"Course he is!" Tears began welling up in Daisy's eyes, and she gave her brother that hurt expression that their mother had used so many times before to put him in his place. "We all owe our lives to Superman, an' you know it!"

Sheriff Frye handed the waitress his napkin, motioning for her to dry her eyes. "A lotta folks're beholden to that man, Daisy, the whole world over!"

In a rough-and-tumble pub at a settlement in the Australian outback, the usually rowdy patrons grew still, as news of Superman's death came over the satellite dish. At one end of the bar, a station manager turned to a tall, broad-shouldered man in the uniform of the Australian Special Forces. "You met 'im once, didn't you, Jack?"

Lieutenant Jack Higbee threw back his drink. "Yeah. It was back during the bloody alien invasion. He saved my men and me from getting blown sky-high!" The lieutenant set a wad of bills down on the bar and nodded to the bartender. In minutes, everyone's glass was filled, and the teary eyed bartender was filling a pint for himself. Jack raised his own glass high, and the whole pub followed suit.

"To the finest bloke who ever drew air! To Superman . . . God bless 'im!"

.   .   .

In downtown Tokyo, people stood shoulder to shoulder, filling the streets, as giant display screens carried a worldwide address by Lex Luthor II.

"There is reason to mourn, but not to panic." Luthor's mouth moved slightly out of sync as translators filled in. "Superman may be gone, but Supergirl and Team Luthor are still on the job."

In Jidda, a Saudi sheik watched Luthor's address with interest. He knew of Luthor as a corporate leader with extensive oil holdings, and he respected the young CEO's ability to take charge. But the sheik felt trepidation when a close-up of Supergirl appeared on his wide-screen television. If an emergency in his country should require her assistance, how would his people react to this unveiled young woman?

In a small African village, a young couple sat before a battered, old shortwave radio, listening.

"Superman, it will be remembered, personally flew tons of grain and medical supplies to remote areas during last year's drought. Many of our people are alive today, thanks to Superman."

The woman ran a hand down over her swollen belly. She and her husband were two of those many people. Now she was pregnant, and she again knew what it was like to be fearful. Whatever world they were bringing their child into, it would be a world without a Superman.

In Moscow, crowds gathered around sound trucks broadcasting the news in front of the Kremlin. Yes, it was true. Superman—the famous Superman, who had saved a city of half a million people in the Urals—was dead.

In Paris, pedestrians clustered around a taxi to listen to the news from its radio. Many wept openly.

In London, Rome, and Berlin . . . in Cairo, Jerusalem, and Mecca . . . in Beijing, New Delhi, and Islamabad . . . in thousands of cities, towns, and villages, people around the globe mourned in public and in private.

Superman was dead.

The world would never be the same.

12

Jorge Sanchez sat at the cramped little desk in the morgue, filling out what seemed to be an endless stream of forms and affidavits. *I know that there are good, legal reasons why this must be done, but I wish that I was not the one who had to do it.* The doctor put down his pen and gently massaged his writing hand. Normally, this would have been the job of the city coroner or her assistant, but through his involvement in the resuscitation efforts, the duty had fallen to Sanchez. He pulled his jacket tighter around him. *Wish I'd brought a sweater with me. They always keep it so damned cold in here.* He shivered—*what was the old expression?—"as cold as the grave"? Whoever came up with that one must've worked in a place like this!*

A knock came at the door, and before Sanchez could answer, a derby sitting atop a massive pair of shoulders pushed it slightly ajar.

"Ah, Doc, you're still here. Good. Got a moment to gab with a VIP?"

Sanchez looked at the pile of forms. *Given the alternative . . .* "Of course, Inspector Turpin. Be glad to."

Turpin nodded and swung the door wide. "Mr. Luthor, this is Dr. Jorge Sanchez. Doc, say hello to—!"

"Mr. Luthor!" Jorge was already on his feet, taking the hand offered by the red-haired visitor. "This is an honor, sir!"

"An honor, Doctor? What, to shake hands with me?" The hint of a smile flickered at the corners of the young man's mouth. "Why, the inspector here could tell you, I'm just a lucky young bastard who inherited too much money from an absent father."

"From what I've seen, you spend it as well as he did, sir. The funds you've given my hospital have helped save many lives."

"Well, we all do what we can. I understand that you signed Superman's death certificate, Doctor."

"Yes, Mr. Luthor. As I'm sure you're aware, due to his body's virtual invulnerability, a standard autopsy was impossible. And as I'd had occasion to examine Superman during his life—"

"You had? Really?"

"Yes, sir. Just a couple of years ago, I treated Superman when he was shot with kryptonite bullets by a deranged killer who called himself Bloodsport."

"Ah, yes . . ." *Bloodsport botched the job badly; I never should have employed such a sociopathic fool.* "I—ah—believe I read about that, Doctor."

"Because of my familiarity with Superman, I was called in to assist with the resuscitation efforts. After those proved unsuccessful, this—" he gestured around the room "—became my duty."

Luthor looked over at an examination table where a still form reposed. It was covered by a stark white sheet. "Is that—?"

Sanchez nodded. "Yes."

"May we—?"

Sanchez nodded again and solemnly pulled back the sheet, revealing Superman's battered face. Turpin removed his hat, holding it respectfully over his heart, while Luthor silently stared long and hard at the fallen hero. It was as if, thought Sanchez, Luthor was trying to commit every contour of Superman's face, every bruise and contusion, to memory.

"I never thought I'd live to see the big guy in here." Turpin's voice cracked and snuffled. "I still can't believe that he's gone. There'll never be another like 'im. Never."

"No." Luthor finally turned away. "No, there never shall." He stopped and speared Sanchez with his eyes. "The murderer—Doomsday—where is his body?"

The doctor wilted slightly in Luthor's gaze. "O-over there."

Across the room, behind a curtain, Doomsday had been laid out across two examination tables shoved together. Luthor pulled back the sheet. "So this is the beast." He glowered at the ugly creature. "It isn't right. It's just not right!"

Luthor's hand brushed against an old straight-backed wooden chair. Before either Sanchez or Turpin could react, Luthor swung the chair up over his head, smashing it down on Doomsday again and again.

"Hey!" Turpin came charging across the room. "What do ya think you're doing?"

"Not right! Not right at all!" Lex was screaming as the chair broke apart. "Miserable, stinking—!"

Turpin grabbed Lex by the shoulders and hauled him back. "Take it easy, Luthor! I know how ya feel, but smashin' furniture over Mr. Ugly here won't do you any good."

No, Inspector, you do not *know how I feel.* Lex stood shaking with anger. *Superman was mine to kill. Mine! And this bloody monster has robbed me of my revenge.*

The elevator of the Clinton Apartments stopped at the third floor, and Lois Lane stepped out. Like a sleepwalker, she shuffled down the hall to apartment 3-D, her head bowed as if in prayer. *Please, God, don't let anyone come along. I couldn't bear to talk with any of Clark's neighbors . . . not now.*

Lois fished a key from her purse, fitted it into the lock, and went in. Clark's apartment was just the way they'd left it that morning. *Maybe I shouldn't have come here, but all I have of Clark's . . . all that's left me . . . is in this place.* She felt suddenly light-headed and had to lean back against the door for support. After several minutes of slow, deep breaths, she regained enough of her equilibrium to make it to the bathroom, where she lost what little was in her stomach. After washing her mouth out under the tap and splashing her face with water, she felt more capable of facing the empty apartment again.

Lois looked around. It wasn't a very big apartment, but it seemed monstrously large and empty without Clark. *I can't believe I've lost him. Just this morning, we were having breakfast here. Just last night—!* She ran her hand along the edge of a table, collecting no dust. Clark always kept the place so tidy. Lois's fingers brushed against two framed photographs. One picture was of her and Clark, taken just a few weeks after they'd become engaged, just days after he'd told her that he was Superman. The other picture was of his parents.

Jonathan and Martha . . . by now they must know what happened. The whole world knows by now. The room seemed to sway, and Lois gripped the desk to steady herself. *By tomorrow morning, the Kents will be getting the same sort of reassurances from their friends as I got from Allie at the* Planet. Lois shuddered, remembering her earlier encounter with the newspaper's copygirl. *Allie meant well, but it just about killed me when she said that Clark would turn up. I almost slipped . . . almost told her that Clark was Superman.*

Lois reached under her coat and pulled out the tattered piece of Superman's cape. She held it out in front of her, trying to smooth the wrinkled S-shield. *I mustn't tell anyone. Superman had so many enemies . . . some of them wouldn't think twice about taking their revenge on his family.* Lois looked again at the picture of the Kents. *His family . . . I was almost a part of it.*

I . . . I must call them. They loved Clark so much. Lois turned and managed to take two steps toward the telephone before she felt all the strength go out of her legs.

Clutching the cape, Lois sank to her knees. *We all loved him . . . so very, very much.* She knelt there on the floor for several minutes, sobbing until there were simply no tears left in her. Completely drained, Lois then slid the rest of the way to the floor and fell into a mercifully dreamless sleep.

In a dark alley in the Metropolis borough of Bakerline, George Rogan sat behind the wheel of a late-model Plymouth. He nervously drummed his fingers against the steering wheel and kept glancing from his watch to the service entrance of the jewelry exchange, waiting for his friends. *What're they doing in there?* George didn't care if Superman *was* dead, this was no time to dawdle. *Why can't I ever pick smart guys to work with?* George shook his head. *Because* I'm *not smart, that's why.* There they were, risking their necks on a heist that might net them a few thousand bucks—if they were lucky—when every day, guys in suits sat in their offices and scammed millions from suckers who never knew they were being taken. *Yeah, white-collar crime . . . that's where the real dough is.*

Inside the jewelry exchange building, Danny Wilson and Richard Drucker had finally forced open the door of an old vault and were merrily scooping precious gems into a couple of canvas bags. Danny felt something rustle under his touch, and broke into a broad grin. "Oh, mama! I believe we've hit the mother lode!"

"Keep your voice down!" Drucker's warning was a harsh, hissing whisper.

"Okay, okay! But dig it, Richie, there's a huge wad of bills back underneath these gem cases . . . twenties, fifties, hundreds!"

"And you're excited about that? Danny, that's petty cash compared to what we got here in stones . . . even after the fence takes his cut." Richard pulled tight the drawstrings on the bags. "You want that chump change? Fine. But don't take time to count it here. We gotta run!"

The two men grabbed up their booty and dashed down a back hall, kicking open the rear door of the exchange. Danny laughed like a kid on the last day of school.

" 'S about time!" George Rogan turned in his seat as they scrambled into the idling car. "Did you have to make so much noise? What took you so long?"

Richard jerked a thumb at his partner. "Ask Danny-boy."

"Hey, I was just pickin' up a little tip, that's all! Talk to me nice, and I might give you some."

"You there—this is the *police!*" The cry echoed down the alley.

George spun back around in his seat and felt the bile rise into his throat. A patrolman was standing in the mouth of the alleyway, his service revolver drawn, and he was walking their way.

"Get out of that car and put your hands on top of your heads!"

"No—aw, no!" George could feel his sweat start to flow. He swiftly slipped the car into gear and hit the gas.

"Stop! Stop or I'll shoot!"

George wasn't going to give him the chance. The big Plymouth side-swiped the cop as it peeled out of the alley, knocking him back against a stack of crates piled by a dumpster.

"Look what you doofs have gotten me into now!" George yanked hard on the wheel and turned onto Dunmore Avenue, heading uptown.

"Hey, watch those corners, Georgie! You'll make me lose count!" Danny fanned himself with the stolen cash, laughing wickedly.

"Oh, you're a funny man, Danny. Real funny! Both you guys are just hilarious! 'It's a simple, easy job,' you said. Lordy, I may have just killed a cop!"

"Relax, George! Even if you did, they'll never be able to pin any of this on us. We didn't trip any alarms. By the time anybody finds that cop, we'll be halfway across the state."

"Oh, yeah. That's real easy for you to say, Richard—your sheet's clean. I'm lookin' at hard time if I'm caught!"

"Will you lighten up?! The blue boys are way too busy digging people outta rubble and enforcing the curfew downtown. They won't be looking for us."

"Danny's right. It was just a fluke that cop came by when he did! We got nothing to worry about!"

George had stopped listening to Richard and Danny. He glanced at his side mirror, half-expecting to see a flashing red light. But all George could see in the tiny mirror was a swirl of red and yellow curves. It took him a few seconds, but George finally realized what he was looking at. It was a reversed letter S . . . Superman's emblem!

George made a choking sound as a red and blue blur shot past the Plymouth.

"Hey!" Danny slid across the backseat as the car was buffeted by backwash. "What was that?"

George gripped the wheel so tightly that his knuckles turned white. "Superman . . . it's Superman. You said he was dead!"

"He's supposed to be—" Danny stared down the street to where the flying figure was landing. "Wait a minute, that's not Superman!"

The figure was now framed in the Plymouth's headlights. They could clearly see the trim, tapering legs . . . the long, flowing blond hair.

Richard gave an appreciative whistle. "Definitely not Superman!"

"It's that Supergirl bimbo! Damn—" Danny let out a long string of curses.

"Who?"

"You know—that flying chippie that LexCorp's been promoting! From what I heard, she ain't nowhere near as tough as Superman! Floor it!"

George's foot reflexively went to the floor, and the Plymouth shot straight at the Girl of Steel. At the last possible moment, Supergirl dove for the pavement. There was a loud thump from beneath the car, and then nothing.

"Did you see that?" Danny roared. "Tripped over her own feet and fell flat on her face! I told you she wasn't so tough!"

"Shut up! Just shut up!" George's shirt was wringing wet with sweat. "Two of 'em. I never killed anyone before, and now I've killed two in one night!"

Richard patted the driver on the back. "It's okay, George. It's over. No more trouble now."

The next instant, the Plymouth lurched six feet into the air. Danny and Richard fell to the floorboards and slid to the right. George lost his grip on the wheel and was flung, screaming, across the right front passenger's seat. He hung there, helplessly searching for the seat-belt release, as the car shook like a loose shutter in a windstorm.

Out on the street, Supergirl had risen from the underside of the car. She held it by its frame high overhead, shaking the vehicle as hard as she could. The doors on the right side finally swung open, and the felons and their loot tumbled roughly to the pavement. Satisfied that the car was empty, Supergirl hurled it into a vacant lot and turned to face the three men.

"S-she . . . she's alive!" George was practically gibbering.

Richard grabbed him by the arm and gave a shove. "Run!"

Supergirl stalked after them. "I hate reckless drivers."

Danny reached under his jacket and pulled a scored and battered .38 automatic from his waistband. "How about lead, huh? Ya like hot lead?!" He squeezed the trigger, and three sharp retorts rattled the air.

Danny was never quite sure what happened next. From what he could see, the air started to ripple around Supergirl, and the bullets stopped just inches from her face.

For a moment, the Girl of Steel seemed to study the bullets. Then she frowned. "I don't think I like hot lead at all."

The bullets suddenly veered away from Supergirl and flew back toward the fleeing men, striking the pavement all around them. George and Richard froze in their tracks and Danny hit the ground, still clinging to his automatic.

"Drop that gun and stay where you are—all of you!"

Danny looked at Supergirl, then looked back at the others. George and Richard were already standing with their hands behind their heads. All the fight drained out of Danny, and he let the gun drop.

Within minutes, police were on the scene, handcuffing the men and reading them their rights.

A police sergeant tipped his hat to the Girl of Steel. "We can't thank you enough, Supergirl. We're pretty shorthanded right now. Most of my men were shifted downtown to help out in the precincts under the curfew, and . . . well . . . it hasn't been a good day."

"No, Sergeant, it hasn't. How's the officer who was hit?"

"He's pretty banged up, but he got off lucky . . . just a few cracked ribs and some bruises."

"I'm glad to hear that. Now, if you'll excuse me." With a sudden spring, Supergirl lifted off into the air.

"Hey, you take care!" the sergeant shouted after her. "We need you more than ever now!"

A patrolman stepped up to the sergeant and followed his gaze as Supergirl disappeared over the rooftops. "You know, Sarge, I never really worried about any of those supertypes before. They always seemed sort of . . . immortal, I guess. But they're not, are they?"

"No, they're not. They're harder to kill maybe, but they put their lives on the line the same as we do."

Supergirl soared across Bakerline and headed back toward downtown Metropolis. She was glad she'd happened across that crime in progress, but now there was other work that demanded her attention. Buildings were down all over the city, and people—most of them, she hoped, still alive—were buried in the rubble. She prayed that those still living could be found while there was time to save them. As Supergirl flew over Hob's River, tears came to her eyes. With Superman gone, she had some very big shoes to fill.

Bibbo left the Bayside Clinic and stalked down the still-deserted side streets of Suicide Slum. The doctors had checked him, the professor, and

Mildred over and given them a clean bill of health but suggested that they spend the night at the clinic for their own safety. Bibbo wasn't having any of that. "Keep them beds open fer people what really need 'em," he'd told them, and headed for his bar.

As Bibbo turned onto Simon Street, a shadow flickered across the sidewalk in front of him. He looked up in time to catch a fleeting glimpse of a caped figure flying by overhead. For a split second, he thought it was actually Superman, but then he realized *Naw, it ain't my fav'rit. It's just that Supergirl. We'll never see Sooperman again. When he needed help the most, there was nothin' I could do.*

His head bowed, Bibbo crossed the street to the Ace o' Clubs, lost in thought. *Why'd I think I could do any good anyways? Perfesser Ham, he's the smart one, an' even he couldn't do any good. I was just dumb muscle, gettin' in the way.*

The tavern was uncommonly quiet as Bibbo entered, empty except for Lamarr, who leaned back against the bar, polishing a glass, and Highpockets Hannigan, who sat on his usual stool listening to the soft drone of the TV. Lamarr looked up as the door swung shut. "Hey, Bibbo —where ya been, man?"

"Walkin'. Walkin' an' thinkin'."

"Guess it's not easy gettin' around tonight, huh? Half of Metropolis must be under curfew."

"Izzit? I di'n't notice. Course, it wuzn't like I had anyplace to go . . . or anythin' important to do."

Highpockets swiveled around on his stool. "Lamarr an' me heard about what you did, Bib—how you an' the perfesser tried to help Superman. It was on the TV. That wuz a real good thing ya tried to do."

Lamarr put a hand on Bibbo's shoulder. "Yeah, we're proud o' ya, man. Howzabout *we* buy *you* a drink for a change?"

"Don't wanna drink." Bibbo stared down at his shoes. "You guys go on home. Bar's closed for this evenin'."

"Closed?" Lamarr stopped with a clean mug, already halfway to the beer tap. "You sure, man?"

Bibbo swung out one huge mitt, angrily clearing the mugs from the bar with one swipe. "This is *my* bar! When I say it closes, it *closes!* Now go on home!"

Lamarr shrugged and reached for his jacket. "Okay, Bibbo, whatever you say. You're the boss."

Lamarr and Highpockets filed out of the tavern, closing the door behind them. Highpockets scratched his head. "Chee, I ain't never known Bibbo to turn down a drink. I ain't never seen him like this before!"

"Me neither, man. Then again, I've never seen a day like this one before . . . and I tell ya now, I hope I never see another."

Inside the Ace o' Clubs, Bibbo turned over the CLOSED sign on the door and flipped a switch, shutting off the lights. The only illumination left was the streetlight filtering in through the tinted windows. Bibbo stood alone in the middle of his tavern, hands thrust deeply into his pockets, waiting for his eyes to adjust to the darkness. Then he cleared his throat and addressed the air around him.

"God? 'S me . . . Bibbo . . . been a while since we talked. I know my pal Sooperman is with ya now, so I guess he don't really need my prayers. But the rest o' us sure do."

Bibbo removed his hat and, with head bowed, knelt on the barroom floor. "Hail Mary, fulla grace, the Lord is with you. Blessed art thou amongst women an' blessed is the fruit o' thy womb Jesus. Holy Mary, Mother o' God, pray fer us sinners now an' at the hour of our death. Amen."

A tear formed at the corner of Bibbo's right eye and began to make its way down the stubble of his cheek.

"Take good care o' Sooperman . . . okay, God? I miss 'im . . . I 'spect just about ever'body misses 'im." The tavern owner paused for a moment before continuing. "God? I gotta ask ya—why? I mean, I know ya got yer reasons, but why should Sooperman die, when a washed-up ol' roughneck like me goes on livin'? It ain't right, God . . . it just ain't right."

13

Franklin Hastings took one look at the rush of activity within the LexCorp Executive Suite and slipped back out the door before he could be noticed. Alone for a moment in the outer corridor, he reached for the bottle of antacid his wife had tucked into his jacket pocket yesterday morning and took a deep swig. There were, at his best guess, at least a dozen people inside the office, most of them waving papers and all of them vying for the boss's attention. In the two days since the official pronouncement of Superman's death, Hastings had had little sleep and less peace. His entire department had been called in to coordinate arrangements for the funeral.

Hastings was impressed by all that Luthor had set in motion. The boss had mobilized LexCorp resources within the state, across the country, and even around the world to bring everything together for tomorrow's memorial service. From what Franklin had seen, Luthor worked the phones as expertly as his father had ever done, cutting through more red tape in half a day than the CEOs of most companies usually dealt with in a year. An incredible amount of work had already been accomplished, but so much remained to be done. Security for the various heads of state and foreign dignitaries had to be coordinated, the worldwide satellite feed had to be set up, the foundations for the tomb had to be completed, and the memorial statue—! Hastings heaved a weary sigh. He didn't want to think about the statue, but he had to.

Months ago, two students at the Cleveland Institute of Art had started work on a twenty-five-foot statue of Superman for an upcoming exhibition. Learning of the statue after the Man of Steel's death, Luthor had hastily designed the planned tomb and memorial around it and offered the budding sculptors an extravagant fee to rush completion of their work. He wanted the statue in place for the interment, and Franklin Hastings had been handed the task of arranging for its delivery and installation. In the last few hours, it had become his most pressing assignment.

The demands that Hastings was being asked to meet on such short notice were beginning to take their toll. He hadn't gotten any sleep in the past thirty-six hours, and his mind was starting to get a little fuzzy around the edges. To be fair, the boss hadn't so much as napped since this ordeal began, but Luthor was barely twenty-one years old. *That long-haired kid could probably go a week without sleep and still be sharp enough to buy and sell half of the Fortune 500,* thought Franklin. He ran a hand through his own thinning hair. The days when he himself could blithely shrug off the effects of an all-nighter were long gone.

Hastings was starting to close the antacid bottle when Supergirl brushed past him and headed into the suite. He paused and took another quick gulp of the chalky liquid. Then he took a deep breath, squared his shoulders, and pushed open the door. *Okay, once more into the breach.*

Supergirl had already moved through a sea of writhing arms and swirling papers and reached Luthor's side. She crouched beside him, whispering in one ear, while he took a series of calls. *Progress report on the rescue efforts?* wondered Hastings. Six of Hastings's most ardent rivals were jockeying for position around the boss, but they had to compete both with Supergirl and with Mr. Roy, Luthor's personal barber. Incredibly, Mr. Roy ignored the chaos around him and continued to trim the boss's hair as calmly and nonchalantly as if he had the LexCorp CEO seated in his private salon.

Hastings began to weave his way through the crowd as Luthor took yet another call.

"Yes? No, that's out of the question. Look, we have room for national and international leaders *only!*" Luthor listened impatiently for a moment, then let out a long, exasperated breath. His reply was almost a hiss. "Okay, include Perry White, but no one else! And make sure you contact the Justice League about providing pallbearers!"

As Luthor hung up, a junior aide handed him a series of requisition forms to sign. He hurriedly scrawled his name across them and was about to shove them back when he stopped himself. "Sorry, lass." He half-smiled, a sudden gesture of extraordinary charm. "It isn't you I'm upset with."

The aide, an astonishingly buxom young lady with green eyes, nodded sweetly and gave the boss a warm, sympathetic smile of her own before withdrawing. While others were momentarily distracted by the aide's departure, Hastings managed to slip into the space she'd occupied.

"Mr. Luthor? Sir?"

Luthor whipped around. "What is it, Hastings?"

Hastings opened his mouth and absently shut it again, fascinated by how Mr. Roy had compensated so smoothly for Luthor's sudden movement and gone on trimming.

"I *said,* what *is* it, Hastings?"

Franklin snapped out of his momentary reverie and gripped his report more tightly. "It's about the memorial statue you commissioned, sir. The sculptors say that they'll be finished in time, but we're going to have trouble getting it to the crypt site in Centennial Park. Rubble is still blocking the main access routes."

"So bring it in by helicopter, Hastings. Do I have to think of everything?"

Hastings bit his tongue. He'd already thought of using one of their heavy-duty construction helicopters, but they were all tied up at the moment, helping to lift the wreckage of collapsed buildings. He nervously shifted his weight from one foot to another. *We can't divert the choppers from the rescue efforts, but how do I tell the boss that without having him jump down my throat?*

Supergirl suddenly spoke up. "Let me bring it in, Lex."

"You, love?"

For a moment, all the furious activity surrounding Luthor ground to a halt. The aides grew silent and the papers stopped swirling. Even Mr. Roy paused and put down his scissors. Without moving his head so much as a single degree, Hastings glanced from Luthor to Supergirl and back again.

Supergirl put a hand on Luthor's shoulder and tilted her head to look deeply into his eyes. It was, Hastings thought, almost a caricature of earnest intent, but he could swear that the young woman was completely sincere.

"I want to bring the statue in, Lex. I want to do it for Superman."

Lex reached up and laid his hand over hers. "You do that, love. I can see it's important to you."

Still holding Supergirl's hand, Luthor glanced at Hastings. "I believe that solves your little problem, Hastings. Do you have any others?"

"No, sir." *Maybe just a question or two . . . like how did you manage to gain such a hold on this stunning young woman? She's clearly worried enough about your welfare that she willingly took time out from her own rescue efforts.* For one giddy instant, Hastings actually considered asking the question. *That'd be rich, but it'd probably be safer to cut myself shaving and go swim with the sharks.* "No other problems at all."

"Fine." Luthor turned his whole attention back to Supergirl. He raised her hand to his lips and lightly kissed her curled fingers. "You bring that statue in, love. I know you'll do us proud."

Supergirl blushed. *She blushed! All that power,* marveled Hastings, *and she actually blushed.* "Thanks, Lex. I won't let you down."

As Hastings followed Supergirl from the room, the phones began to ring again and the flurry of activity resumed. In all the confusion, no one noticed the fury in Luthor's eyes. *Try as I might,* he thought, *I couldn't kill Superman—but I'm sure as hell going to bury him.*

The television had become a constant presence in the Kent household. Jonathan and Martha would watch until they couldn't stand to see or hear another word. Then one or the other would turn it off . . . only to turn it back on after a few minutes, when the silence in between became just as unbearable.

Jonathan sat staring into his coffee as a somber network commentator outlined plans for the public ceremonies. "The funeral cortege will roll past the spot where Superman fell defending the city he loved, then continue to Centennial Park, where world leaders will witness the interment."

Martha nervously picked at the hem of her apron. "They're gonna put our boy in the ground, Jonathan. They're gonna put him in the ground, and we'll never see him again. We should be there in Metropolis."

"Now, you know that we couldn't get anywhere near him, Martha. We lost a son, but the world lost a hero . . . and they're gonna bury that hero with full honors. You heard what they said, only the big shots'll be allowed in close."

A silent nod was the only acknowledgment Martha gave her husband. She turned and looked back at the television, a vacant, faraway look in her eyes.

"Martha?" Jonathan slowly got up from his chair and laid his big farmer's hands on her shoulders. She hardly seemed aware of him. "Martha, you're staring at that damn set like it's gonna bring our Clark back. You can't go on like this. Neither of us can."

In the silence of the room, the volume of the television seemed to blare. "Live coverage of the funeral will begin tomorrow at eleven o'clock eastern, ten o'clock central time."

"I can't take another minute of this." Fuming, Jonathan strode across the room and, for the fifth time that day, turned off the set. "I just can't stand it."

.   .   .

The sun did not come out the next morning in Metropolis. A dense cloud cover had rolled in over the Eastern Seaboard during the night, and the skies outside looked threatening as Jimmy Olsen walked into the *Daily Planet* City Room.

"Hey, Jimbo, great photo!"

Jimmy looked up with a start as Danny Jawarski clapped him on the back. "What? Which photo—?"

" 'Which photo?' he asks! *The* photo, my man!" Jawarski unfolded the memorial edition of the *Planet* and smacked his hand across the picture that covered nearly a third of the front page. It was one of the last shots Jimmy had taken of Superman. "Incredible composition, Olsen. I love the way the shot is framed with Superman sprawled out like that, and the cracked pavement sort of radiating out from his body. It's like . . . it's like a Michelangelo, you know? It's as though you got him just as he was breathing his last."

"I did." Jimmy's voice was so low that the other photographer could barely hear him.

"Yeah? Well, I tell you, Jimbo, you really captured the spirit of the old boy's death. Man, I wish I'd snapped this one!"

"I wish you had, too. I'm sorry I ever took it."

Jawarski looked genuinely puzzled. Was Olsen pulling his leg? "Hey, lighten up, guy. That picture's gonna make you famous. The wire service picked it up—it's appearing in papers all over the world! After this, you can write your own ticket."

Jimmy shook his head. "Dan, I'd give it all up—I'd take that ticket and tear it into confetti—if it would bring Superman back."

"Uh, well, sure. But it couldn't." Jawarski coughed nervously into his hand. "Bring him back, I mean. So, you might as well enjoy the glory, right?"

"There's nothing to enjoy." Jimmy fixed the other photographer with his most penetrating stare. "You just don't get it, do you, Dan? The man was my friend. He was everybody's friend."

A few feet away, Perry White caught the tail end of the exchange as he paused to straighten his tie. The managing editor just shook his head. *Danny will never get it. He has no heart, and it comes through in his work. That's why he'll never be more than a good photographer. But Olsen . . . Olsen has the makings of a great one.* Perry squared his shoulders and walked on; he doubted that Jawarski even knew the meaning of real friendship.

Across the room, Lois stared at the telephone on her desk with something akin to dread. The phone had always been one of the main tools of her trade, but now it seemed like a miniature gargoyle crouched on the corner of the desk, daring her to pick it up. It had been over two days since she'd lost Clark, and she still hadn't called his parents. *What's the matter with me? Why can't I call them?* In addition to all the shock and horror she had endured, Lois now felt overwhelmed with guilt. The more she fretted, the guiltier she felt, and the harder it became to reach for the phone.

"Lois?" Perry leaned across her desk, gently breaking into her thoughts. "You know, I always thought of you as one of Superman's real friends. You're the one who should be marching in the funeral procession—the one to be present at the burial, not me. Want to go in my stead?"

"Thanks, Perry, but . . . no."

"You're sure?"

Lois shook her head. "I don't think I could bear it."

Perry came around the desk and crouched down beside her. "Are you going to be all right? I can send someone else—"

"No." Lois gave him a halfhearted smile. "You go ahead. I'll be fine."

Perry saw that she was hurting; she'd lost a close friend and, as far as he knew, perhaps her fiancé as well. He started to say something, then thought better of it. Before he became managing editor, he'd had a good, long career as a reporter, and in that time he'd seen hundreds, maybe thousands, of people in mourning. Sooner or later, he knew, everyone needed to weep and wail in the company of friends. But some folks just wished to be alone, at least at first. If that's what Lois wanted, Perry would respect it. He patted her gently on the shoulder and eased off down the hall.

Lois glanced back at the phone. The superstitious part of her could swear it had moved closer. *Ridiculous. It's just a trick of the light. Or maybe Perry brushed against it.* Tentatively, she reached out one hand toward the phone. Her fingers were just about to make contact when it rang. Lois nearly jumped out of her chair. In the stillness of the half-deserted City Room, the phone seemed to ring as loud as any fire bell. Heart pounding, she snatched up the handset. "H-hello?"

"Mary?" The voice at the other end sounded confused.

"Excuse me?"

"Is this the *Daily Planet*? I'm looking for Mary Powers."

"Oh. Yes, this is the *Planet,* but you have the wrong extension. Mary's number is 0320. I can try to transfer you—"

"Naw, that's okay. Sorry if I bothered you." There was a click, and the dial tone began humming in her ear.

Lois set the phone back down and turned away. *I can't stand to look at that hateful thing anymore.* She pushed away from her desk and headed for the door, grabbing her coat on the way. She paused briefly by the elevators, then shoved open the stairwell door. Almost without realizing what she was doing, Lois started up the stairs, her brisk pace turning into a run. Minutes later, she stood on the metal catwalk within the building's rooftop globe.

Lois pushed open the cleaning port and stepped out onto the globe's outer deck. The wind hit her full in the face as she looked out between the giant metal letters—DAILY PLANET—that encircled the globe. A light rain began to fall as she tried to collect her thoughts. A gust suddenly swirled her coat around her, making it flap . . . *just like a cape.* The image startled her, and she suddenly recalled the first time she'd come up there with Clark. Until he'd showed her the way, she'd never even realized the globe had an interior access. Ever since he'd shared his dual identity with her, she'd considered this as their secret place. She had often come to this spot to see him off on missions . . . or to wait for him to return.

Is that why I came up here? To wait for him? Sure, why not? Superman's gone missing before, but he always comes back, doesn't he? Doesn't he?!

Lois gripped the side of the big metal D and fought off the feeling of hysteria. *But he's never been dead before.*

From far below came a slow, rhythmic rumble. It took Lois a moment to recognize the sound as the echoing beat of drums. Superman's funeral cortege was approaching the building. It would be passing by soon on its way uptown.

He won't be flying back to me this time. I . . . I have to go to him. Lois shivered and stepped back inside the globe. She bolted down the stairs to the top floor and leaned on the button for the express elevator. *Wait for me, Clark. I'm coming.*

The crowds lining the street in front of the *Planet* Building were ten deep by the time Lois made it to the lobby. Pushing her way out through the revolving doors, she began to squeeze through the crush of people on the sidewalk. She was making slow, steady progress until the toe of her boot caught on something and she stumbled into a space along the curb that was clear of people. Though there were no barricades, the crowd was standing back from this area, almost reverentially. In the center of that clearing, freshly set into new pavement stones, was a big brass plaque bearing the pentagonal S-symbol and the words: IN MEMORY OF SUPERMAN. KILLED ON THIS SPOT WHILE DEFENDING METROPOLIS. All around the plaque, people had left flowers.

Lois knelt silently in the drizzle before the plaque. It seemed impossible to her that this was where her lover had died in her arms barely three days before. She looked at the garlands of lilies and dozens of roses piled neatly all around. *So many flowers,* she thought. Many had little notes attached to them; some were formally printed, but most, she noticed, appeared handwritten. One little dandelion had been laid carefully beside the brass S, accompanied by a taped-on scrap of paper. Lois touched the rain-soaked paper gingerly. The childish printing on the paper read simply, *I miss you.*

"Lois?"

She looked up, tears in her eyes, into Jimmy Olsen's worried young face. "They loved him too, Jimmy."

"Yeah . . ." Jimmy was trying hard to choke back his own tears. "Guess we all did." He reached down, helping Lois to her feet. "I've been looking all over for you. Some of the guys from the sports desk are saving us a place down front. Come on, we have to hurry . . . he's almost here."

Jimmy wrapped one arm around Lois's shoulder as they gently elbowed their way through the crowd. They reached curbside just as the four drummers—one each representing the army, navy, air force, and marines—passed by, beating their mournful rhythm. Slightly out of tempo with the drums came the clip-clop of hoofbeats. And while Lois and Jimmy held one another, two chocolate-brown stallions came abreast, pulling the funeral carriage.

The carriage itself was quite simple in design, its only distinguishing factors being the burnished metal S-medallions affixed to either side. Upon the carriage, covered with the flag of the United States of America, the coffin bearing the Last Son of Krypton was borne through the streets of Metropolis.

Directly behind the carriage came a procession of the most powerful beings who had ever walked the Earth. There were members of the Justice League, past and present, and veteran mystery-men of the Second World War. There were heroes from around the world and beyond the stars. There was Wonder Woman and the Flash, Green Lantern and Captain Marvel, and so many more. There were dozens of them, resplendent in their colorful uniforms, marching along to the slow, staccato drumbeat. Each of them wore a black armband emblazoned with a scarlet S-shield in tribute to the fallen Superman.

As they passed by, those heroes with especially acute senses could not help but catch snatches of conversation from mourners lining the route.

"Mommy, is it true that Superman was from another planet?" A little boy looked up at his mother for the answer.

"I don't know, honey." The woman held her son close. "But he was the greatest hero this poor old world has ever seen."

A tall black man stood with his head bowed as if in prayer. His hair was closely cropped, with a Superman S shaved into one side. As the coffin passed by, he turned to an older Middle Eastern couple who stood nearby. "Dude pulled me out of the wreck when my cab was hit. If he hadn't been there then, I wouldn't be here now."

The old man nodded, brushing tears from his eyes. "Many of us have such stories, my friend. Superman once stopped a thug who had robbed our deli." He shook his head in sorrow and turned to his wife. "Remember, Mara?"

"I remember, Bashir. When we have been dust a hundred years, I still will remember. He would take no reward. He protected us as if we were his own family—it was plain he cared so much for everyone."

A little girl squirmed in her mother's arms, straining to see better. "But, Mommy, Superman saved us from that bad fire! Why did he have to die? It's not fair."

No, child, thought Wonder Woman as she passed by, *it is not fair. But there is much in life that is not fair. All we can do is strive to make things better.*

The procession of super-heroes was followed by units of police and fire fighters, with Mayor Berkowitz and members of the city council close behind. And then, flanked by a special Secret Service detail, the President of the United States walked down the street, leading a long line of international dignitaries. Virtually every nation in the world had sent a delegation. Never in all of history had so many heads of state been in one place at one time.

When the cortege had passed the *Daily Planet* Building, Jimmy started to steer Lois away from the curb. "It's over, Lois. Come on, let's go inside."

"No, Jim." Lois pointed down the street. "It's not over yet. Look, the whole crowd is following."

People were indeed filtering out into the street and falling in behind the procession. It looked as if most of Metropolis had decided to walk to the burial site.

"Uh, Lois, wait. I'm not sure that's such a good idea with a mob that size, things could get out of hand."

"I want to go, Jimmy." Lois gave him a tug. "I—I need to be with him at the end . . . the way he was always there for . . . for all of us."

Unable to dissuade her, Jimmy let Lois lead him along.

As the funeral procession moved further uptown, one furtive little man slipped through the crowd, darting back and forth as he searched for the delegation from the Republic of Kanad. When he found them at last, his eyes fixed on a gray-haired man in the lead. *Kanad's president struts in this funeral parade as if he had every right—as if his people did not labor under the yoke of ethnic oppression!* The little man reached into his coat pocket, his hand fingering a crude bomb of plastique explosive. *Before the day is over, the world will know of the Kanad Liberation Front and its heroic struggle.* As soon as an opportunity presented itself, he would hurl his bomb at the president and disappear into the crowd before anyone was the wiser.

The opening never came. Instead, a loop of high-test nylon cord suddenly dropped down over the little man's shoulders, tightened, and yanked him skyward. Several stories above the ground, the man found himself dangling in the grasp of a dark, brooding figure. The figure was cloaked in a black cape that flared out around him like ebon wings, and his face lay hidden behind a black, horned mask. The would-be bomber knew that this could be but one man.

"B-Batman!" The little man swallowed hard. He'd thought nothing of the fact that the Dark Knight was missing from the procession. *I didn't think he came out in the daylight.*

The Batman crouched on the cornice of a building, the cord that held the terrorist aloft looped around one powerful hand. His eyes narrowed behind his mask, and his voice thundered. "Explain the bomb in your coat pocket."

"B-bomb? What bomb? I don't—"

The Batman shook the cord, and the terrorist felt his shoulders start to slip through the loop. The little man desperately clutched at the cord. The pavement seemed miles below.

"A-all right," he confessed, "I *do* have a bomb. I'm a patriot—fighting oppression! I—"

The Batman hoisted the little man up until they were face-to-face. "Innocent people would be hurt in a bombing."

The little man screwed up his courage. "None who harbor that monster, that so-called president, are innocent!"

The Batman started letting the cord slide.

"No! Don't drop me!" The little man closed his eyes tight and pleaded for his life. "I'll turn myself in! Anything! Just don't drop me."

"If this were Gotham, I'd almost be tempted . . ." The Batman let his threat trail off. "But Metropolis is Superman's town. And for today, I'll play it his way. Today, I'll be merciful."

When Lois and Jimmy passed by, moments later, they saw the police setting up a ladder to rescue a little man who dangled precariously from a rope attached to a third-story flagpole. And what was more amazing, the man was begging to be arrested: "Hurry, please. He might be back!"

.   .   .

Several blocks away, Professor Hamilton and Mildred Fillmore stood watching the growing procession.

"Look at that crowd, Mildred. There must be over a million people."

"They don't want to let Superman go, Emil. He helped them—he helped all of us!—so many times. Oh, Emil, if only we could've done more. Your laser machine was brilliant!"

"Not brilliant enough, my dear. Literally. Not nearly enough to save him."

In silence, Mildred watched the crowd pass by for a few minutes more. Then she turned to Hamilton. "Come on, Emil. Let's follow them to the park."

The professor frowned. "I don't think that would be wise, Mildred. A crowd this large can so easily turn into a mob."

As the cortege skirted the edge of Suicide Slum, a huckster started working the crowd. "Getcha T-shirts! I got Superman T-shirts right here! I got *Daily Planet* memorial editions—custom bagged with a commemorative armband! Getcha T-shirts!"

"Hey, you!" A big arm shot out of the crowd, grabbing the man by the lapels of his jacket. "You tryin' to cash in on Sooperman's death? In *my* neighborhood?!" Bibbo tightened his grip on the huckster and shook him like an old mop. "Ain'tcha got no respect?"

The man's merchandise slid from his hands as he hung in Bibbo's grip, gasping for breath. "H-hey, l-look, man. You think I *like* doing this? Superman saved my family from a burning building. B-but now we're on the streets—and I'm out of work. I gotta feed my family somehow!"

Bibbo gave the man a fishy eye. "Ya wouldn't be lyin' to me, would ya?"

"N-no, man. I swear." The huckster looked close to tears.

Bibbo considered that for a moment. The man did seem too afraid to be lying. And from the looks of him, he hadn't been eating regularly for some time. Bibbo didn't like the idea of anybody making money off his favorite, but he liked even less the idea of people going hungry. Slowly, the old roughneck lowered the huckster to his feet.

"Okay, tell ya what. I'll take 'em."

"Excuse me?"

"I'll take 'em all," repeated Bibbo. He spoke more slowly this time, trying to make himself as clear as he knew how. "Every T-shirt. Every paper."

"All?! But there must be nearly three hundred—!"

"I tol' ya, you've sold yer stuff! Now shuddup an' lissen." He poked a big beefy finger into the man's chest. "You want honest work, you come see me tomorrow. M'name's Bibbo. I own the Ace o' Clubs on Simon Street. You got that?"

The huckster barely had time to nod before the tavern owner threw a huge arm around his shoulders.

"C'mon. Everybody's headin' ta the park ta pay their last respects. You can come along with me. I wanna be there when they buries him."

Bibbo's voice ordinarily boomed even when he whispered, but now it softened and thickened to little more than a croak. And when the former huckster looked up, he was startled to see tears running freely down Bibbo's face.

The nearer people got to Centennial Park, the higher emotions ran. All around the ceremonial grounds, police barricades were in danger of being overwhelmed by sheer numbers. As people caught sight of the massive new stone statue of Superman towering over the treetops, they began pushing, trying to get closer to the tomb. Caught up in this giant shoving match, Lois and Jimmy suddenly found themselves being separated.

"Lois, grab my hand—quick!"

Lois strained to reach her young friend, but it was no use. "Jimmy, I can't—!"

"Lois?!" Jimmy couldn't see her, couldn't even hear her anymore over the noise of the milling crowd. The press of human bodies was carrying them farther and farther apart. The increasingly restless throng was on the verge of becoming a full-blown mob.

Fortunately, those in charge seemed alert to the potential danger. Several large stadium-size video screens, which had been placed at regular intervals around the perimeter of the park to show televised coverage of the funeral, were suddenly filled with the image of Lex Luthor II.

"People of Metropolis!" Luthor's voice boomed out over the park. "The eyes of the world are on us. I ask you . . . please remain calm."

While Luthor got the people's attention, the super-heroes in attendance fanned out through the crowd, bolstering the police lines and gently separating those spectators who were on the verge of becoming violent.

The situation was defused in a matter of minutes, although for those caught up in the crowd—and those watching at home on TV—the tension seemed to go on for an eternity.

.   .   .

Jonathan Kent came in from the barn to find his wife sitting mesmerized in the parlor. "Martha, you haven't got that TV on *again*?"

"They're making a circus of his funeral, Jonathan. Doesn't anyone have a sense of dignity?"

Jonathan looked at the screen. Lex Luthor stood on a dais at the base of the tomb appealing for calm. Peace was slowly being restored, though the compression of the television lens still made it appear as if people were pushing and shoving up to the edge of the tomb.

"Some of those folks have surely lost their heads," said Jonathan. "But they mean well. They loved him, Martha. Everybody loved him."

"You're being too charitable, Jon. Remember what happened that time when Clark rescued the space plane? Remember how they mobbed him? He said it was like they all wanted a piece of him. Things haven't changed a bit." Martha shook her head, tears streaming down her cheeks. "Jon, he was our son. I can't stand what they're doing to his funeral."

"Martha . . . honey . . . turn the thing off."

Martha closed her eyes and switched off the set. Jonathan knelt beside his wife and hugged her to him, gently stroking her hair. "Let all those people say good-bye to Superman their way. We'll go say good-bye to Clark in ours."

As order was restored at the Metropolis funeral site, Lois Lane found herself standing less than fifty yards from the base of the tomb. The carriage that had borne the Man of Steel through the city sat virtually in front of her. As Lois watched, the six surviving members of the current Justice League lifted the coffin onto their shoulders and began to slowly carry it to the waiting crypt. Unable to move any closer, Lois craned her neck to follow the pallbearers' slow progress and then gave up and turned to watch the rest of the ceremony on one of the giant screens.

As the coffin was placed onto its bier, a group of clergymen and women gathered on the dais for a series of invocations. It was a most ecumenical gathering. There were ministers and priests, rabbis and mullahs, and bishops and monks. Virtually every religion had sent a representative to invoke the deity on behalf of Superman.

Finally, a stocky black man whom Lois recognized as the pastor of the Hob's Bay Mission approached the microphones.

"Brothers and sisters," he began, "we, the family of humankind, have gathered here to celebrate the life and mourn the passing of a great and kind man. We do not know his name. We knew him only as Superman.

"He was different from us, possessing powers and abilities almost beyond imagining, but he did not use those powers to set himself above us. No, Superman used his powers to bring comfort to those in need and hope to those mired in the depths of despair.

"And he could fly. Oh, how he could fly! He soared through our skies —some say like a great bird, but I say like an angel.

"I once saw him tear apart the walls of a burning building—rip them apart with his bare hands!—and pluck a young baby from certain death, cradling that child in his mighty arms as gently and as tenderly as would that child's own mother.

"It is said that Superman had enemies. Well, there were among us men who made of him their enemy; that cannot be denied. But his real enemies were the enemies that bedevil us all: greed . . . fear . . . hate . . . ignorance! He fought those enemies and inspired others to fight them as well!

"Superman came to us, a stranger from another planet. He was many things to many people. Some saw him as a champion of life, others as a protector of the oppressed, and still others as a mighty warrior in the battle for truth and justice. And, yes, he was all those things and more. But mainly, he was our friend.

"He did not care about our religious beliefs or our politics. He did not care about our nationalities or our gender or the color of our skins. He cared about people. He cared about us. We are, all of us, richer for having known him, and poorer for having lost him.

"Superman was, as I said, from another planet—and I do not know what God, if any, he worshiped. But I pray to my God to comfort and protect him, as he comforted and protected us all."

Lois had heard so many prayers that day—dozens, it seemed—but few had been as personal, or as direct, as the pastor's. The image of Superman as an angel was strangely comforting, and she let the pastor's words repeat over and over in her head. She became so caught up in his final prayer that she barely heard the next speaker.

The next thing Lois knew, the President of the United States was walking onto the dais, accompanied by the First Lady. Hand in hand they approached the microphones. His face lined with sorrow, the President began to speak.

"Undoubtedly, Superman himself would remind us to care for the many victims of Doomsday's attack, and so we do. But how could we not especially honor the man who gave his life to save so many more?

"His powers and abilities were amazing, but how much more amazing was the way he chose to use those powers! If there is a lesson in this, it is that the greatest power of all is our own ability to care about each other, to help each other."

The President nodded to the first lady, and she stepped forward to complete their brief eulogy.

"As we extend our help, our care and concern, to the families of Doomsday's other victims, we also send our thoughts and our prayers to Superman's loved ones . . . whoever they may be."

Upon hearing those words, Lois felt a great barrier breaking apart inside her. It was as if the first lady were speaking directly to her, as if the hundreds of thousands of people around her simply weren't there. She turned and slipped back through the crowd. Incredibly, the people let her pass.

On the edge of the park, Lois saw a pay phone, and before she was conscious of it, her telephone credit card was in her hand.

". . . *we also send our thoughts and prayers to Superman's loved ones . . .*"

Lois punched in the code for directory assistance. She saw now that she didn't have to make sense of Clark's death; no one could do that. She didn't have to resolve her own grief; only time could do that—time and sharing.

"Directory assistance for what city, please?"

"Smallville—Smallville, Kansas. The number of Jonathan and Martha Kent."

Lois still wasn't certain what she was going to say, but she knew that she had to call—that she had to reach out to Clark's parents—that only by trying to speak could she ever hope to find the right words.

In Kansas, Jonathan and Martha Kent stood side by side in an untilled section of field at the far south end of their property. It was here that they'd first found the vessel that had brought them their son over thirty years before.

Jonathan had pried away the half-rotted planks that covered the eroded old impact crater. Now he leaned on his shovel and stared down into the Earth as if he could see to its core the way his late son could.

"Here's where it all began, Clark . . . where the rocket that brought you to us came crashing down. I'll never forget how amazed we were when we found it. It didn't seem possible that anything could have lived through that crash, but there you were."

Martha inched nearer the crater, cradling an old strongbox in her arms. "I remember, Clark. I reached right in and lifted you up in my arms. We didn't know where you'd come from, but we didn't care. From that moment forward, you were ours . . . the sweetest little baby in the universe. You were our gift from heaven, and right from the start, we loved you with all our hearts."

Martha opened the strongbox, and together they looked once more inside, as if to pay their last respects. Within the box was an old threadbare blanket that Martha had wrapped her baby in when they'd first taken him back to the house. There was also a battered old teddy bear that Aunt Sal had sent the boy for his first birthday and a worn baseball and mitt that Jon had bought Clark when their son had turned ten.

Jonathan closed the box and latched it. "Doesn't seem like much."

"These were just a few of the things Clark loved. There were others in the house, but I couldn't bear to part with any more." Slowly, Martha stepped down into the depression, setting the box into the ground as gently as if it held the body of her son. "Good-bye, Clark. Good-bye."

Jonathan gave his wife a hand up out of the crater and then tossed in the first shovelful of dirt. The dirt hit the old strongbox with a thump that seemed to echo forever. Jonathan hurried to finish the burial. He was just tamping down the last bit of soil when he felt a painful pressure building in center of his chest. He stiffened, gripping the shovel for support.

"Jonathan, what is it?"

"Nothing." He caught his breath. "Just my stomach acting up."

"Are you sure?"

"Course I'm sure." He wasn't really, but the last thing he wanted was for Martha to worry about him. "I'd hoped that this little service would help some, but . . . it just wasn't enough, was it?"

"No. No, it wasn't." Martha covered her face with her hands. "I feel like nothing can plug the hole in my heart."

Jonathan leaned against his shovel, trying to rub the ache out of his left arm. He felt just as empty. *I'm just a useless old man. If it wasn't for Martha, I don't think there'd be any reason to go on living.* He put his arm around his wife and they headed for home.

As they got closer to the house, they could hear the phone ringing. Though they had no way of knowing, it had been ringing off and on for nearly ten minutes. Martha hurriedly unlocked the back door and rushed across the kitchen to answer it.

"Hello? Kent residence—"

"Martha, thank heavens. I was so worried!"

The voice that cracked over the receiver sounded so frantic that it took Martha a moment to recognize it. "Lois? Lois, is that you, dear?"

"Yes. Oh, Martha, I'm so sorry I haven't called sooner. I—I just couldn't. I couldn't believe it was true . . ."

While Lois had been trying to call, she'd imagined the worst, that the Kents were ill or had suffered some terrible accident. Now that she'd gotten through, all her grief and guilt came gushing out.

". . . just couldn't believe he was really gone. I kept asking myself, what could I say to you? And I just didn't know, so I didn't call, but the longer I waited, the worse it was."

Lois began to cry softly, and Martha put her hand over the phone's mouthpiece, gesturing for her husband. "Jonathan, it's Lois! The poor child needs us."

Jonathan came near, as Martha cradled the receiver between them. They both did their best to reassure Lois, but when she could speak again, she kept on apologizing.

"I was there . . . all the time Clark was fighting that monster . . . and all I could do was report on the battle . . . a-and watch him die. I couldn't do anything but watch him die. Clark died in my arms and I didn't even call you. How can you ever forgive me?"

Jonathan spoke up firmly. "Now you listen to me, Lois. It was *not* your fault. You did all that you could. Everyone did what they could. You're talking with us now. That's all that matters."

"Jonathan is absolutely right. We've all had a—a terrible loss. And I think we need to be together." Martha looked over at her husband, and he nodded his agreement. "You hold on a while longer, honey. We're coming to Metropolis."

Jonathan pulled out his bandanna and dried his eyes. If he could do anything to help that young woman through her pain—well, maybe he wouldn't be so useless after all.

14

As night fell on Metropolis, the gangs came out to reclaim Avenue M.

Avenue M skirted the edge of Suicide Slum and for almost a decade had been teetering between renewal and squalor. The Newtown Plaza project had been designed to save a five-square-block area and perhaps even bring the possibility of rebirth to all of Hob's Bay. Doomsday had put an end to that. All that remained of Newtown Plaza now were several blocks of rubble and twisted girders. The project had been left in such a hopeless mess that the construction company hadn't even bothered to post guards.

The police were busy elsewhere. Superman was dead. And so, the gangs filtered out of Suicide Slum, out of the shadows, and down Avenue M.

On a vacant lot that had been planned as a green space for the plaza complex, the Dragons met the Sharks, and words were exchanged. Both gangs were armed and dangerous, but the Sharks were packing what amounted to one-man portable artillery pieces. They called their weapons Toastmasters, and the big guns lived up to the name. Within minutes, their incendiary shellfire had reduced a half dozen young men to toast and sent the surviving Dragons running for their lives.

The Sharks had little time to savor their victory. Their ammunition spent, they were forced to fall back as police sirens wailed up the avenue.

The first patrol car onto the lot had to brake sharply to avoid hitting the smoldering remains of what had been a fifteen-year-old boy.

"My God, what happened here?" Patrolwoman Jean Coyle was suddenly thankful for the head cold that had blocked her sense of smell.

"Looks like a freakin' war zone, Jeanie." Fred Moore, her partner, had served a hitch in the army and seen action in the Middle East, but this was beyond his experience. He fought to keep the contents of his stomach down. *What kind of weapons do this? What kind of people would use them?*

A second cruiser was just pulling up to join Coyle and Moore when there came a sharp, cracking noise from not more than twenty feet away. The officers had their automatics out and were bringing them up to the ready position when the headlights of the backup car silhouetted what appeared at first to be a huge figure crouching behind the rubble.

"Police!" There was just the slightest hint of an edge in Fred's voice. "Get those hands up where we can see 'em! Now!"

"Hold your fire!" Jean rushed forward, bringing up her flashlight. "He's not hiding back there. He's—oh, Lordy. He's trying to dig his way out!"

"Huh?" Fred couldn't believe it. "I thought this place had been evacuated. Who—?"

"Who doesn't matter." She turned and barked at their backup, "Call for an ambulance."

In the glare of flashing lights, ironworker Henry Johnson rose up out of the rubble, his sledgehammer still in his hand. His shoulders were cut and bruised, and his overalls hung in tatters. The big construction worker's every pore was caked with dust and dirt, but he was alive!

"Take it easy, mister." Jean was cautiously solicitous. "You can put that hammer down now. Why don't you sit down and let us help you? Is there anything we can get you?"

"Doomsday . . ." Henry's voice was a parched croak.

"What?"

"Gotta . . . stop . . . Doomsday." Henry took one step forward, and then all the strength drained out of him. His hammer slipped to the ground, and he toppled forward, unconscious.

It was pouring rain the day that Mitch Andersen arrived in Metropolis. For several minutes, he stood in the doorway of the old midtown bus terminal, hoping that the rain would let up. He was alone in this big city, hundreds of miles from home—from where home had been, anyway—and he didn't have enough cash in his pocket even for bus fare back. Hailing a cab, even if he could find one, was out of the question. Still, Mitch knew where he had to go, and the man at the information desk had told him it was only twelve blocks away. He turned up the collar of his jacket and stepped out into the deluge.

By the time Mitch had gone two blocks, he'd discovered two things: Metropolis city blocks were a lot longer than Ohio city blocks, and his jacket wasn't as waterproof as he'd thought. Looking back, Mitch found that the bus station had already disappeared from view. *No sense in turning back now,* he thought. *It's not like I have a ride back or anything. Mom is probably gonna freak when she finds my note anyway.* Head down, he trudged ahead, convinced that the lousy weather was probably just what he deserved. At one point he took refuge under a storefront awning, only to be drenched from the splash of a passing truck. Mitch cursed under his breath. As far as he was concerned, this was just more evidence that his life sucked.

Still, Mitch pressed on, plodding his way downtown with a determination he rarely displayed except, perhaps, when he was trying to advance to the next level of the latest video game. As he progressed against the downpour, his thoughts kept going back to his mother and how she had changed, how everything had changed, since things had fallen apart. She somehow seemed tougher and stronger to him now. *Maybe she* wouldn't *freak over my blowing town and coming to Metropolis. Maybe she'd understand that it was something I* had *to do.* Mitch hoped that he'd made that clear enough in his note. His note—if he'd done something like this a couple of weeks ago, he wouldn't have bothered to even leave a note. Maybe he had changed, too.

Mitch tried to put his family out of his head, concentrating instead on his destination. According to what he'd heard on the radio, some relative of Superman's was supposed to be speaking here in Metropolis at three o'clock. Mitch checked his watch; it was already 2:50, almost 2:55, and he had six blocks to go yet. *Better step on it!*

The rain was finally starting to slack off as Mitch crossed his twelfth block. For one awful moment, he was afraid he'd made a wrong turn. But then he saw a crowd gathered under the awning of what looked like a big hotel and a cluster of microphones set up by the building's entrance. As Mitch got closer, a bank of lights switched on, and he could see several cameramen jockeying for position under the awning. A thin brown-haired woman came out of the hotel and slowly inched her way to the microphones.

"Hello. I want to thank all of you for coming to hear my announcement."

Mitch was surprised by the woman's appearance. She reminded him a little of his mother, only his mother was prettier. This woman wore so much makeup that she looked almost cheap. The only really distinctive thing about her was a star-shaped birthmark on her right cheek, and Mitch could swear that it was fake. He wasn't sure what he'd expected, but this woman wasn't it.

The woman coughed into her hand, clearing her throat. "There have been a lot of rumors floating around, a lot of malicious gossip, and I felt that I had to come forward and tell my story . . . the story of Superman and me. Though we kept our love a secret all these years, I was—I am— Mrs. Superman."

She paused, and for a moment all that could be heard was the click of camera shutters and the soft patter of the rain on the canvas awning. Mitch started to notice smirks on the faces of people in the crowd, and a lot of those smirks belonged to reporters and cameramen. They clearly didn't believe her, and Mitch wasn't sure what to believe himself. The woman seemed sincere, but there was something strange about the way she stared into the cameras.

"Yes, it's true. For years, Superman and I lived secretly in a Park Avenue penthouse in New York. He kept our relationship secret from the world to protect me from his enemies." She clutched the microphone stands and leaned forward, her eyes very wide. "But ours was a life of vacations in Vegas and Paris. It was an endless adventure!"

Mitch was starting to feel uneasy about all this when a voice rang out just a few feet away from him.

"Oh, please! Give me a break!" The skeptic was a tall, attractive woman—much more attractive, noted Mitch, than the woman who claimed to be Mrs. Superman—and appeared to be a reporter. She had a miniature cassette recorder in her hand, but she was switching it off and starting to stick it in her coat pocket. The photographer next to her seemed as surprised as Mitch by her outburst.

"Lois! Why don't you let the woman finish?"

Lois looked totally exasperated with the young photographer. "Jimmy Olsen, don't tell me you're actually buying this line of baloney?! That charlatan is no more Mrs. Superman than . . . than I am!"

Jimmy shrugged. "Well, yeah . . . sure. Anybody can see that she's lying, but I say we cover the story and pin her to the wall—her and all the other pretenders."

"No, Jim." Lois pulled a small, collapsible umbrella from within her coat and began to unfold it. "People are already flocking to Metropolis in droves to visit Superman's tomb. Most of them are good, earnest souls, but too many of them are morbid leeches like her. Any publicity, even negative publicity, just encourages more of them, and I don't want to have any part of that." She put her umbrella up against the rain. "I'll see you later, Jim. I have some friends to meet."

"Sure, Lois. Later." Jimmy stood there for a moment, rubbing the back of his neck and staring after Lois.

"Uh, 'scuse me? Mr. . . . Olsen?"

Jimmy turned, startled at hearing a younger voice call him "Mr." *No wonder Lois always seemed so weirded out when I called her Ms. Lane . . . or Clark, when I called him Mr. Kent.* He found himself looking down into the face of a rain-soaked teenager. *Geez, I can't be that much older than he is.* "Yeah?"

"That lady you were talking with? The one who just left? Did I hear her say that the other lady"—Mitch pointed toward the microphones—"wasn't really Mrs. Superman? Is that true? I mean, that the other lady isn't Superman's wife?"

"I'm afraid so, pal. 'Mrs. Superman' there is just the latest in a long line of frauds to surface in the past week. One con man claimed that he was Superman's business manager, and another even tried to pass himself off as Superman's tailor." Jimmy stopped. There was something oddly familiar about this boy. "Uh—why do you ask?"

Jimmy glanced back toward the mike, but "Mrs. Superman" had virtually disappeared behind a wall of photographers. *She's probably posing for cheesecake shots by this point.* He looked back at Mitch. "You don't know her—?"

"Oh . . . no." Mitch stared down at his feet. "I was just hopin' to talk to somebody who knew Superman is all. I rode buses all night to get here. I guess I came all this way for nothing." He looked as though he'd lost his last friend in the world.

"Well, hey, *I* knew Superman." Jimmy saw the doubting look all too clearly in Mitch's face. *I can't blame the kid.* "No, really! I work for the *Daily Planet* . . . I met Superman through working for the paper." He offered the boy his hand. "The name's Jimmy Olsen."

"I'm Mitch Andersen."

Jimmy studied the boy closely. "I have the darndest feeling I know you, Mitch. Have you been in the news recently?"

"No. Well . . . yeah, sorta. I mean, the house I lived in—in Ohio—was trashed by that big Doomsday monster. Afterwards, the TV guys were all over us. It was a pretty big deal, I guess."

"That's it! I must've seen your picture on the *Planet*'s photowire. I knew you looked familiar."

"I do, huh?" Mitch went back to staring at his instep.

Nice going, Olsen. You've gone and embarrassed the kid. "Well, Mitch, I know what it's like . . . to have been that close to Doomsday. Your family's okay, I hope?"

"Oh, yeah. I mean, the house was wrecked, but Mom and my sister

Becky are in great shape. We've been staying with friends. They're fine
. . . just fine. But Superman—Superman's dead. He's dead, and it's all
my fault."

"Whoa, hold the phone, Mitch!" The boy's shoulders were shaking,
and Jimmy thought he might be crying. The rain had picked up again,
and it was hard to tell. *Better change the subject.* "Hey, you look hungry."
That's true enough. "When was the last time you ate?"

"I dunno. Yesterday."

"What do you say we catch an early dinner? Then we can talk."

Mitch shrugged. "I'm kinda broke."

"It's on me. Come on, I know a place where the food can't be beat!"
Jimmy led Mitch down the block to the nearest subway entrance. He'd
paid the boy's fare and they were well on their way when he realized that
he'd never taken a good photo of "Mrs. Superman." *Oh, well, Lois was
probably right. Lois . . . geez, I hope that whoever she was meeting will be
able to offer some emotional support. She could use it. We all could.* Jimmy
shook his head. *The chances of Clark turning up alive get slimmer every
day.*

Lois turned onto Clinton Street, retracing the path she had taken so
many times to Clark's apartment building. They'd shared so many happy
moments there, but now it stood only as a reminder of her loss. She
hadn't been back since that awful night. She didn't want to go there now,
but she had to. Walking the last block had taken longer than the whole
rest of the trip; each step took more and more effort.

Lois nodded slightly to the doorman, trying hard not to cry. *Daddy
always said, "Don't cry."* It felt odd to be invoking Sam Lane's advice, but
she was grasping at anything that might help her get through this. There
was still so much she was keeping bottled up inside, so much the world
must never know.

In the elevator, Lois fumbled for the keys Clark had given her after
they were engaged. It was only three floors to his apartment, but the
elevator ride seemed to be taking even longer than that last block. The
doors finally whisked open, and she somehow made her way back down
the hall and into his apartment. Lois closed her eyes, trying hard to hold
back the tears, but they were flowing anyway. *Dear God*, she prayed, *he's
yours now. He's never coming back to me. I'm all alone.*

"Lois?"

Lois opened her eyes. Martha and Jonathan were emerging from
Clark's kitchen. She rushed into Martha's embrace, and Jonathan
stretched his big arms out around them both. Lois held tight and cried in
the way she hadn't dared cry before her own parents. "Oh, thank God

. . . at last . . . I can talk to someone about all this." They stood there together, just holding on and crying for several minutes.

Lois finally pulled back a little to look at the Kents, as if she couldn't quite believe they were really there. "I wasn't expecting you so soon. I was going to try straightening things up a bit before you arrived."

"We lucked into an earlier flight." Jonathan looked a trifle alarmed. "I left a message on your machine. Didn't you get it?"

"Sorry, I . . . I haven't been very good about my messages lately." Mentally, Lois kicked herself. *I had no right to give them one more thing to worry about. Lord, they look so much older than they did the last time I saw them. A total stranger could see the strain in their faces.* "Oh, Martha . . . Jonathan . . . I'm so sorry."

Martha gently patted Lois's back. "There, there. Let it all out, dear. We're here for you."

"You're here for me?" Lois wiped away her tears with the back of her hand. "What about you? You . . . you couldn't even attend—!"

Martha stroked Lois's cheek. "Now, don't you worry about Jonathan and me. We're here to help out. And to get Clark's things . . . in order."

Jonathan nodded. "Amen to that. My pa always said, 'Sharing multiplies joy and divides grief.' It was true in his day, it's true now, and it always will be true."

To Lois's surprise, a young strawberry-blond woman came out of the kitchen. "You're so right, Jonathan. My Aunt Helen used to say much the same thing."

"Lana? Lana Lang?"

"Hello, Lois. I came along with Jonathan and Martha—sort of to lend moral support. I hope you'll let me help."

"Of course, Lana. Thank you, I . . . I . . . ." Lois literally didn't know what else to say.

A moment's awkward silence was suddenly broken by the whistle of a teakettle.

"I'll get that," said Lana. "We'll all be able to cope a little better after a cup of tea."

Lois was genuinely, deeply touched. She'd first met Lana before she and Clark were engaged. And after a slightly strained introduction, they'd gotten along quite well. Lois liked Lana Lang and was sure that the feeling was mutual, but this visit was totally unexpected. *I've always thought that in her own way, Lana still loved Clark every bit as much as I did. For her to have made this trip must have been incredibly painful. Could I have done the same, if I were in her shoes?*

"Let me help you, Lana." Lois followed the other woman into the kitchen. "We have a lot to talk about."

. . .

"Hiya, Red. How ya doin'?"

Jimmy looked up from a corner booth as Bibbo shouldered his way into the Hob's Bay Grille. "Hello, Bibbo. I'm getting by. Care to join us?"

" 'Ey, don' mind if I do." Bibbo slid into the booth next to Jimmy and across from a teenage boy who was polishing off a double cheeseburger deluxe and a jumbo order of fries. "Who's yer li'l buddy there?"

"This is Mitch Andersen, Bib. Mitch, say hello to Bibbo."

"Hullo." Mitch already looked considerably less peaked than he'd been an hour before.

Mildred came by, bearing a cup of coffee and a big slab of raspberry pie. "Your usual, Mr. Bibbowski?"

"Yeah, thanks much, Miz Fillmore."

Mitch looked longingly at the pie Mildred set down before Bibbo, and his stomach gave an impatient growl.

" 'Ey, Mitch, you hidin' an animal in yer shirt?"

Mitch's face turned a bright catsup red, and Bibbo roared. "Aw-haw-haw! Don' let it bother ya none, kid." He shoved the pie across the table. "Here, you look like you need this more'n I do. 'S on me!"

Mitch grabbed up a fork and tore into the pie. "Thanks, Mr. Bibbo."

"It's just plain Bibbo to you, kid. Any pal o' Red's is a pal o' mine."

The pie disappeared so quickly that Bibbo ordered another slab for the boy and one more for himself. Jimmy just looked on in amusement, remembering the days not that long ago when he too possessed such a bottomless stomach. Midway through the second slab of pie, Mitch started to slow down, and Jimmy got the boy to talk about himself and Doomsday.

"It was kinda unreal," said Mitch around bites of pie. "Doomsday just seemed to come outta nowhere. He was tearing through the neighborhood when Superman and the Justice League showed up to save our skins."

Bibbo felt his throat tightening. "That was Sooperman for ya. Tough as nails, but always helping folks. That's why he wuz my fav'rit."

"Yeah, well, our house got totally trashed in the process. I'm still not sure what all happened—everything happened so fast. All I know for sure is that the Justice League got knocked out, and Superman took off to chase after Doomsday. Maybe he'd have caught him and stopped him right then and there, if it hadn't been for me."

Jimmy shifted forward on the vinyl-covered bench. "What do you mean, Mitch?"

"There . . . there was an explosion, see? Our house was on fire, and my mom and baby sister were trapped." Mitch nervously played with his empty plate, and his voice grew faint. "All I could think of was how crummy I'd been to my mom, and now she was maybe gonna die right before my eyes. I started screaming for Superman to come back. I screamed and screamed, and he did—he came back. He came back and saved them, and Doomsday got away. That's why it's my fault." He looked up at Jimmy and Bibbo. "If I hadn't made Superman come back, he might've been able to beat Doomsday then and there. He might still be alive if not for me."

Jimmy shook his head. "Superman wouldn't have wanted your mother and sister to be hurt, Mitch. It's not your fault."

"Yeah, don't go saying things like dat, kid." Bibbo reached a huge hand across the table to pat Mitch's shoulder. "Savin' folks wuz Sooperman's job. You couldn'ta done nothin' to save him. There wuz nothin' nobody coulda done. I know."

"Maybe not. But I keep thinking of how he was there for us when we needed him. And after all I used to say. . . ." Mitch slumped back in the booth. "See, I used to think Superman was some goody-goody—you know, a real dork. I was even joking about it with my friends earlier that day. I mean, it was like I jinxed him or something. Anyway, that's why I came to Metropolis. I heard on the radio that one of Superman's relatives was going to make a speech or something. I didn't know it was part of some scam. I wish that woman *had* been his wife—I just wanted to apologize."

"Mitch, as far as I know, Superman didn't have any family. I know how you feel, but you don't have anything to apologize for." Jimmy searched for the right words. *How would Mr. Kent put it?* "Just because Superman died after you ragged on him doesn't mean that you *caused* him to die. The world doesn't work that way."

"Wait a minute!" Bibbo squinted over the rim of his coffee cup at Jimmy and Mitch. "Somebody wuz claimin' to be Sooperman's wife? No way! My pal was a bachelor! No way wuz he ready to settle down."

Mitch scowled. "That's another thing. My own old man walked out on us months ago, like he didn't care about us anymore. He said he never shoulda settled down—never shoulda married. But then a complete stranger came along and stood up for us!" Mitch hit the table with the side of his fist, hard enough to rattle the glasses. "Superman fought for us, saved us and most of the world, while my own father was nowhere to be seen!"

Jimmy put a hand on the boy's shoulder. "I'm sure it's more complicated than that, Mitch."

"Yeah, you've got that right." Mitch stared out the window at the pelting rain. He'd never told this to any of his friends before, much less a couple of strangers. But now that it was coming out, he couldn't stop it. "Ya know, I still love my dad. I love him so much that I used to blame my mom for everything. But she wasn't the one who left us—he was. My mom . . . my mom's surprised me lately." Mitch shifted uncomfortably in his seat. "I mean, she's still sweet enough to give you diabetes, but . . . I never realized how strong she is, ya know? Ever since our house got wrecked, Mom's been more—more—I dunno, assertive? I can't believe how she's changed." Mitch shrugged. "Maybe she hasn't. Maybe she always was that way, and I just never noticed."

"Mothers can fool you, Mitch." Jimmy smiled, remembering how his own mother had kept their family going after his father had been declared missing in action. "Look, I can tell that you're still upset over everything that's happened."

"Yeah," Mitch nodded. "You guys have been great. But I guess what I really need to do is unload to Superman. And it's too late for that now."

"Maybe not. There is a place we can go, if you want to pay your respects."

Bibbo nodded. "I know what yer thinkin' about, Red, and it's a good idear."

Mildred brought the bill to the table, and Bibbo laid his hand down over it. "Dis is on me. You two go on about yer bizness."

Jimmy smiled as they slid out of the booth. "Thanks, Bib, that's another I owe you."

"My pleasure. 'Ey, hold on a minute." Bibbo pulled out a wad of cash and pressed several big bills into Mitch's hand. "Yer maw's prob'ly worried about ya, kid. Give her a call an' tell her ya'll be on yer way home soon."

"Well, thanks, Bibbo, but I can't take bus fare from you. I'll just hitch a ride home."

"Like hell you will, kid! That's all yer maw needs to worry about! I gave ya enuff for *air fare,* an' that's what ya damn well better spend it on!"

"No, really, I can't take—"

Bibbo waved off Mitch's protest. "Lissen, if my buddy Sooperman was still around, he'd fly ya home hisself, so you just shut up an' let me stand in fer him, y'hear?"

Mitch nodded mutely and shook Bibbo's hand. A sheen of moisture clouded the tavern owner's eyes as he watched the two young men head out of the diner and down the block to the subway. "Watch out fer 'im, Red."

"Did you say something, Mr. Bibbowski?" Mildred looked up from behind the counter. "Is there anything more you want?"

"Uh, yeah, Miz Fillmore. Bring me anudder slab o' that pie. Watchin' that kid eat has given me an appetite."

Lana finished pouring Martha a second cup of tea and slowly gazed around the apartment. One of Clark's old high school football trophies sat in a place of honor on a shelf. *I can still remember the day he was awarded that. We were both so proud.* Lana choked back a tear and found her voice. "We have a big decision before us, don't we? Sooner or later, we have to decide whether or not to tell the world that Clark and Superman were one and the same."

Jonathan looked startled. "Why ever do we have to decide any such thing? Why can't we just keep our mouths shut like we always have?"

"I wish it were that simple, but the question may become academic." Lana bent down to refill Jonathan's cup. "I've already seen magazine excerpts from a couple of those instant books that publishers cobble together from news reports. And it won't stop there. Researchers will spend years digging into Superman's life."

"Oh, no!" Martha nearly upset her teacup. "Do you really think that someone might uncover the truth? Clark was always so careful! He changed his voice, his manner, his whole bearing when he was Superman! And it's not as if he ever wore a mask, so why would anyone wonder if Superman was ever anyone else? They might wonder *where* he was whenever he wasn't in public sight, but surely not *who* he was!" Martha looked from her husband to Lana to Lois, hoping for unequivocal agreement.

Lois nodded slowly. "Those are all good points, Martha. Clark *did* cover his tracks well, and—as you say—he took care never to get people wondering about a 'secret identity' in the first place. Not like, say, the Batman, who clearly has something to hide; . . . a famous face, or a terrible scar, or whatever." She stared for a while into her tea. "Even so, Lana also has a point. Never underestimate a dogged researcher."

Jonathan let out a snort. "Well, if anyone ever did get that lucky, it would be plain awful. I couldn't stand to have a bunch of media vultures swarming over us, looking for personal angles to hot Superman stories." He glanced at Lois. "No offense meant to our present journalist, dear."

"None taken, Jonathan." Lois smiled at him and squeezed his hand for extra reassurance. Then her smile faded. "Yes, I'm afraid that Lana might be right. We can all trust each other to be silent, but there might be some loose end that none of us knows about—some slip that Clark made without knowing. Someone might uncover the secret that way."

Jonathan snorted once more. "Well, if that happens, so be it—but I see no reason to hurry it along! Clark always worked to keep a decent measure of privacy so he could have a normal life away from being Superman. We respected that throughout his career, and I say we go on respecting it now. Maybe the world thinks it deserves to know everything about Superman, but I say the world can just go fish! It's up to us to keep some things quiet."

"Amen to that." Martha nodded, her voice a little quavery, and Jonathan put his arms around her shoulders and hugged her tightly. He kissed her hair and laid his cheek against her head for a long moment, then looked up at the two young women. "Far as we're concerned, you two are both like daughters to us. I hope you agree with what Martha and I plan to do. Or rather"—he grinned humorlessly—"what we plan *not* to do."

Lois stepped close, putting one hand on Martha's shoulder and the other on Jonathan's. She began to tear up again, but her voice was firm. "Absolutely."

Lana moved close on the other side of the Kents and laid her hands atop Lois's, her voice just as firm. "One hundred percent."

The rain had petered out to a light drizzle by the time Jimmy and Mitch reached Centennial Park. Despite the day's weather, a long line stretched along the newly planted memorial garden leading to the wide plaza that was Superman's final resting place. Ahead of them sat the tomb, a massive cube of stone, unadorned save for the pentagonal S-shield carved into one side. The tomb was topped by an eternal flame and the twenty-five-foot granite statue of Superman standing boldly with his left arm outstretched as a perch for a great, majestic stone eagle.

The line moved slowly, and Mitch stared reverently at the statue for most of the twenty minutes it took to approach the tomb. "You were right, Olsen. This is awesome."

Jimmy nodded, his eyes on the rough-hewn statue. "You're not alone in thinking that, Mitch. Folks have been coming from all over to visit Superman's tomb."

Around them, people were expressing similar feelings. A hushed murmuring filled the plaza. But for a moment, under it all, Jimmy thought that he could hear something else. *What is that noise? It sounds muffled . . . or far away . . . but it's almost like—what?—a drill?* He shook his head. *Probably just a trick of acoustics. All this stone paving . . . maybe it was picking up vibrations from the rescue efforts in town.* There were, Jimmy knew, massive machines at work just a few blocks away, sifting through the rubble left by Doomsday. The noise seemed to fade, and he put it out of his mind.

As Mitch and Jimmy came up to the tomb, they saw flowers and little notes placed lovingly around its base. It reminded Mitch of what he had learned in school about the Vietnam Veterans Memorial Wall, about how people left letters and other mementos there for their loved ones. He knelt beneath the granite S and looked above him at the statue that, up close, seemed to loom even taller.

"Superman?" Mitch cleared his throat. "Uh . . . hi. I feel kinda stupid talking to a statue but, hey, who knows? My grandma says my grandpa—he died a couple years ago she says he can hear us when we talk to him, so maybe you can, too. I owe you a lot, Superman, but first off, I owe you an apology. Y'see, I used to figure you for a real loser. Shows what a zero *I* was. I'm gonna try to do better—try not to judge people without, you know, really knowing 'em. I know a lot more now . . . about you, anyway. You laid it on the line for us. My old man had cut out, but not you."

Mitch reached into his pocket and pulled out a wallet-sized photo of his family. "This is my family from before my father split. You'd remember my mother and my sister Becky. They're okay today, thanks to you. If you'd ignored us, *you* might be alive today. But you came back and saved them. That took guts." He gently tucked the photo into a seam in the stones at the base of the tomb, between a small book of poetry and an old athletic medal someone had left.

"Thanks, Superman. That probably sounds really lame, just saying thanks, but I really mean it." Mitch took a deep breath. "And when I get home, I'll try to get along better with my mom. I guess it's about the only thing I can do to pay you back. With Dad gone, Mom really needs the help."

Mitch rose to his feet, never taking his eyes off the statue. "Thanks again, Superman. For everything."

Jimmy stood just a few yards behind Mitch, marveling at how the boy had bared his soul. *I don't know if I could have done that when I was his age. I think I'd have died of embarrassment.* Remembering that awkward, adolescent feeling, Jimmy was careful not to look directly at Mitch until the boy joined him and they turned to leave.

"Jimmy? I want to thank you for bringing me here. I don't think I'd have had the guts to do it alone."

"Don't mention it. I hope you're feeling a little better now."

"Yeah. Yeah, I am. A little." Mitch stopped and looked back at the statue. "But the whole world still feels a lot more empty now, doesn't it? I mean, what's gonna happen to us without him around?"

Jimmy shrugged. "It's hard to tell. We just have to have hope."

Mitch blew a short raspberry, a glimmer of his old cynicism shining through. "Easy for you to say!" Then the boy's expression softened. "I just wonder if Superman really did have a family somewhere. If he did, I sure hope they're holding up okay. They'd have lost more than any of us."

"Yeah." Jimmy was impressed all over again with Mitch. *This kid has really been through some wars, but I think he's going to be okay. I'd tell him so, but he'd just say I was being sappy.* "Come on, we'll take a cab to the airport."

They silently walked away from the plaza, lost in their thoughts. As they left the park, neither of them heard the distant whir of the drills.

Henry Johnson had been out of the hospital less than ten hours, and he did not like what he saw.

A week before, when a building had come falling down on top of him, he'd had no time to fear for himself. His only thought then was, *Superman needs help. I owe him my life . . . I can't die now.* Henry still couldn't remember much of the ordeal that had followed. He recalled voices—old half-forgotten memories he'd done his best to forget—and he remembered digging. He'd been out of his head, scraping his way out of the rubble, trying to get to Superman and help him stop Doomsday.

When Henry finally came to in the hospital, he'd found out how drastically the world had changed. Superman was killed trying to stop Doomsday, and Metropolis was in a mess. The city was experiencing its first major increase in street crime in nearly a decade, and according to the news, the police commissioner's job was on the line.

The hospital nurses had told Henry to ignore the news and concentrate on getting well; not that he'd had to concentrate that hard. The doctors were so impressed with his speedy recovery that they'd called him their miracle patient. He'd had to plead to keep them from giving his name to the papers and argue to have them release him as soon as he had a clean bill of health.

Now Henry was home in the apartment that had been his for over a year. And while the neighborhood had never been the best or the safest, things had clearly changed for the worse. Sirens echoed down the street from Avenue M, and the radio was full of reports of gang activity. Superman, Henry knew, would never have allowed this to happen.

The gangs were running wild all around Suicide Slum, and word on the street was that they even had the police outgunned. That was bad enough, but it was the talk about the gangs' weaponry that especially bothered Henry.

And so Henry went down into the basement of his apartment building and checked the locks on an old storage locker near the furnace room.

They seemed intact, and he knew they were impossible to pick without showing some signs of tampering. He knew, because he'd designed them himself. Henry unlocked the door and went in, flicking on the sputtering old fluorescent light. Inside, stacked neatly along one wall, were the remnants of his past, back when he was still the topflight engineer John Henry Irons, back before he'd assumed another name.

As Dr. John Henry Irons, he'd designed armament and ballistics systems for Westin Technologies. He was their rising star—number one with a bullet—until the day he discovered that his new design for a one-man artillery piece had been copied. Bootleg knockoffs of Dr. Irons's new gun had been produced and sold in the Middle East, and there was some indication that higher-ups at Westin, in collusion with someone in Washington, were responsible. He'd heard that such things happened in the software trade, and he knew how difficult it was to trace such acts of piracy. Tracking down the culprits proved no easier in John Henry's case; all he knew for sure was that a lot of innocent civilians had been killed by his guns.

That had been too much for John. He'd dropped out, gone underground, and changed his name. But his past was still down here, sealed away in crates and footlockers. The equipment he'd designed had been put to terrible use, but it was still his work. He could not deny it or bring himself to throw it away. Instead, he had tried to bury it here in this basement, where no one would think to look.

Was I wrong? Similar weapons are showing up on the streets. Did someone find my gear?

A moment's inspection reassured him that it was all there. Nothing had been disturbed, but John Henry still couldn't shake that sickening feeling in the pit of his stomach. The description of the "Toastmaster" guns that some of the gangs were using sounded very close to his BG–60s. If the guns were in fact based on his designs, the police would never stand a chance against them. If the gangs weren't stopped and the flow of guns cut off, the city could conceivably become a war zone. He couldn't let that happen.

John Henry rummaged through the crates. *Superman said to make my life count.* His prototype body armor was still there, along with the experimental rocket boots. An idea began to take form. *I owe him a life. There's no way I can bring Superman back, but maybe I can build Metropolis a Man of Steel.*

For days and nights, volunteers had been working alongside LexCorp construction crews, searching for signs of life amid the urban ruin left in the wake of Doomsday. At some sites, sophisticated listening devices were employed to ferret out those who might be buried beneath the shattered buildings. At other sites, rescue teams picked their way through the rubble, using specially trained dogs to sniff out survivors and casualties. As the days passed, they turned up more and more of the latter.

At one midtown disaster site, on the afternoon of the eighth day, a large black German shepherd let out a yelp and began pawing the edge of a patch of crumbled masonry. His human rescue partner came stumbling after him.

"What is it, Akila? What is it, boy?"

The dog barked once and kept on digging. The rescue worker put his ear to the masonry. He could hear a moan. It was very faint, but it was definitely a human voice.

"We've found another one over here. A live one!"

"Step aside!" The order came in a high, clear alto, and both dog and workman scrambled to get out of the way as Supergirl dropped down from the sky beside them.

The Girl of Steel ran a hand along the edge of the masonry. It was a section of steel-reinforced concrete, twelve inches thick and roughly ten by thirteen feet.

"There's a crack running about halfway through this thing, but if I'm careful, it should hold together." She favored the rescue worker and Akila with a polite smile. "I'll need room."

The man nodded and hooked a leash onto the dog's collar. "Akila, come!"

Once man and dog were a safe distance away, Supergirl knelt beside the fallen concrete. Cautiously, she thrust one arm under the edge of the slab and gripped a piece of thick steel rebar that protruded from the side. Setting her feet, Supergirl slowly began to ease the slab off the ground. When she had it about five feet up, the edge started to crumble and crack. Moving quickly, she ducked under the slab, shifting the crushing weight onto her shoulders.

Looking down, she could see a man wedged into a tiny space between two fallen girders. A cracked water pipe ran near his head. The rubble still looked fairly damp around him. Supergirl paused a moment to center herself; then, every muscle straining, she stood bolt upright, hurling the concrete slab into the middle of a cleared area some fifty feet away.

Supergirl immediately dropped down beside the man, gingerly shoving aside the girders that still pinned him. She felt for a pulse. It was there, but it was very weak. The man's eyes fluttered, and he tried to talk.

"Help . . . me . . ."

Supergirl was astounded that the man was still able to breathe, let alone speak. "Please . . . don't try to talk."

Paramedics quickly slipped in around Supergirl and the injured man, checking the victim's vital signs and administering emergency first aid. Within moments, they had the man strapped to a backboard. Supergirl helped them carry him to a waiting ambulance.

"Roof fell in . . . jus' fell in on me." The man rambled on, as if trying to cxplain his way back to life. "Couldn't move. Yelled an' yelled but nobody camc."

"We're here now." Supergirl held the man's hand.

"I didn' give up . . . 'cause I knew *you* wouldn' give up. Knew you'd save me—Superman?" The man's eyes finally seemed to focus on the figure beneath the bright red cape. "You—you're not Superman."

"No. No, I'm Super*girl*. But it's all right. You're in good hands now!"

Supergirl smiled brightly for the man as he was loaded into the ambulance. But once it had pulled away, her face fell, and she heaved a weary sigh.

One of the paramedics on the scene walked up, holding out a steaming paper cup in offering. "Coffee? It's not very good, but at least it's hot."

"Thanks." She cradled the cup in her hands. "What do you think his chances are?"

"Hard to say, Supergirl. A lot dcpends on how much water he was able to get from that pipe. A human being can't go more than a few days without water. And he was down there for a long time." The paramedic glanced off to his right. "At least he's still alive. That puts him one up on these poor souls."

Supergirl followed the paramedic's gaze. Nearly two dozen bodies had been laid out, side by side, covered with sheets and awaiting identification. Some of the lumps beneath the sheets were heartbreakingly small.

"Kids." The paramedic shook his head. "They never had a chance."

Supergirl slumped back against a pile of girders. "How many more are still out there? How many are still alive?"

"Not many. It was a miracle that fellow hung on like he did. He must've had an amazing constitution. No, at this point, I wouldn't think there'd be any more that we'll find alive."

Supergirl stared numbly at her steaming cup. She'd yet to take a drink.

The paramedic looked at her more closely. "How long has it been since you had a night's sleep?"

"Hmmm?" It took her a moment to realize he'd put the question to her. "Oh . . . I don't know. What's today? Monday?"

"Try Wednesday. You don't need coffee, you need rest."

"No time. There are so many places left to search, so much work to be done."

"Make time." He snatched the cup away from her hands.

Supergirl stared blankly at her empty hands for a moment and then gazed, bewildered, into the man's face. He'd caught her totally off guard.

The paramedic raised an eyebrow. "See what I mean? Would I have been able to do that if you were on top of things? Go home; get some sleep. Or the next time you go to lift a chunk of concrete, you're liable to drop it on yourself—or on someone else!"

"All right. But if you need help—"

"We know where to call. Now go home!"

Supergirl sprang unsteadily into the air, feeling as wrung out as an old washcloth. The rush of air helped a little, but in her heart she knew that the paramedic was right—she did need sleep. As the city swept by beneath her, she could see the rescue efforts continuing at other sites. *If only I had Superman's X-ray vision. Maybe I would have been able to find more of those people before it was too late. If only—*

Supergirl shook her head. Life was full of "if onlys." Maybe she would be better able to face them tomorrow.

Midnight passed, and Wednesday night gave way to Thursday morning. Paul Westfield paced impatiently at the far end of a long tunnel that connected Metropolis with the Cadmus Project. It had taken him days of maneuvering and subterfuge to get this new operation up and running. Westfield's handpicked field team had, of necessity, been working incommunicado for over twenty-four hours while he was forced to placate both the Washington bureaucrats and his own department heads. But if all went well, he would soon have what he wanted. *If only they'd report in. What's keeping them?*

A walkie-talkie hooked to Westfield's belt emitted a soft buzz. He pulled the unit loose from its clip and thumbed the scramble switch. "Report."

"Snatcher here. Sorry for the delay. It was touch and go there for a while. With so many people visiting the tomb, we were afraid that some of the mourners might hear our drills."

Westfield's breath caught in his throat. "They didn't, I hope."

A dry chuckle came over the walkie-talkie. "If they did, they didn't do anything about it."

"That is not an acceptable answer."

"Uh, no, sir. There were no problems, sir. According to our spotters on the surface, no one took any notice that would compromise our operation. Phase one of the mission is complete. The body is ours. Repeat, the body is ours."

"Well done." Westfield allowed himself a smile. "Return to base on the double. We will meet for initial inspection in Lab Seven. You are to maintain strictest security at all times."

"Understood. Snatcher out."

Westfield switched his walkie-talkie back to standby and exited the tunnel. *Now, all we need is a cell—just one, single viable cell—and I'll give this poor misbegotten world a hero it'll never forget.* Despite the late hour, there was new energy in his step. Westfield could feel destiny calling him, and hc had his answers all prepared.

15

An alarm sounded on the ninetieth floor, awaking Lex Luthor II from a sound sleep.

"Bloody hell!" Muttering under his breath, Luthor threw on a dressing robe and pushed open the double doors to his private office. "Alarm off!" he ordered. "Identify the problem."

The alarm instantly shut off, and a soft computer-synthesized voice responded in answer to Luthor's command. "Infrared sensors registering movement in outsector ten."

"Damn and blast! Show me."

"Impossible to comply. Surveillance cameras have been disabled, Mr. Luthor." The computer voice sounded almost regretful.

"What is it, Lex?" Supergirl shuffled out of the bedroom, stifling a yawn. "What's going on?"

"That's what I'd like to know. Computer, give me a full-range schematic."

"Projecting outsector ten . . ." A holographic grid immediately lit up in the air over Luthor's desk, a glowing X moving slowly across it, like the cursor of a computer screen. "Heat source now moving away from vector point zero."

Luthor began to curse, softly but steadily, in a way that, Supergirl knew, he did only when he was greatly distressed.

"Lex? Where is outsector ten?"

"In Superman's tomb, love." Luthor stuck his finger into the glowing schematic. "Or, to be more precise, some ten meters beneath it."

"What?!" Supergirl's eyes popped open wide. "Oh, Lex! Could he be—? I mean, is it possible that he's alive?!" Even as she spoke, Supergirl gave the molecules of her sleeping gown a mental shove. Then, just that easily, she stood clothed in her blue and red costume.

Ordinarily her transformations delighted Luthor, but the last thing he wanted to see her wearing—considering what his security systems were telling him—was that pentagonal S-emblem. *Superman . . . alive?* Too late, he tried to repress a shudder. Fortunately, Supergirl seemed too excited to notice his discomfort. Luthor took a deep breath and made a calming gesture.

"Well, my dear, I suppose that with a man from another world anything is possible, but I frankly doubt that he's actually alive." *At least, I hope he isn't.* "At the very least, though, someone is tampering with his crypt, perhaps even to the point of desecration. I hope you feel up to investigating."

"Of course I do. Just try to stop me!" Supergirl reached for the portable transceiver headset even as Luthor started to hand it to her. "Don't worry, Lex, I'll search the area from top to bottom. And I'll keep in close touch."

"You do that, love." Luthor forced a smile, hoping it would cover his lingering unease. "And be careful. Remember, we don't know what's going on down there. Let's not give the public any reason to panic. Use the secret access we built into the tomb's foundations."

"Oh, you're so smart." Supergirl kissed Luthor twice—first, slowly on his lips, and then lightly on his nose. "Don't you worry. I'll get to the bottom of this."

"I know you will, love. Godspeed."

Luthor had always loved to watch Supergirl fly, taking a frankly proprietary pride in watching her soar above the city skyline. But tonight he hardly saw her leave. His attention kept being drawn back to the wandering X on the schematic projection.

"Lord, he couldn't have cheated death. Could he?" As Luthor watched, the X began to move off the grid and fade out.

"Heat source is moving north-northeast." The synthetic voice suddenly went up half a decibel in volume. "Warning! Heat source will be out of surveillance range in five seconds . . . four . . . three . . . two . . ."

"Oh, shut up!"

The voice instantly complied.

Supergirl shot away from the lofty L-shaped tower, making a beeline for Centennial Park.

Lex seemed awfully quick to discount the possibility that Superman might be alive. I guess he doesn't want me to get my hopes up. She smiled at the thought. *That's awfully sweet of him, the big silly, but he might as well try to hold back the tide! How could I not hope for the best?*

Luthor's mention of tomb desecration did bother her, though. *I can't fault Lex for being concerned. Superman* did *have a lot enemies, and I suppose one of them might stoop to grave robbing.*

Reaching the park, Supergirl flew in a slow, silent loop high over the tomb. The rain had been intermittent since dusk, and there was an unseasonable chill in the air. At this late hour, she could see only two people in the memorial plaza—a derelict who appeared to be dozing on a park bench, and a young man who had paused briefly, head bowed, by the tomb.

Supergirl knew from previous flyovers that hordes of mourners had been haunting the tomb, day and night, since the funeral. The sheer emptiness of the plaza made her realize how truly nasty the weather had become. *And it is late—dawn is still a few hours off. More people will turn out by morning. In the meantime, the lack of a crowd should make my investigation easier.* Below, the young man slowly walked away from the tomb, and the derelict slumped deeper down into his coat for warmth. Neither man, she noted, looked up.

Making a wide circuit of the grounds, Supergirl could see no signs of tampering from the outside of the tomb. *Then again, Lex's computer system did say the disturbance was below. Time to take a look inside.*

Banking sharply, Supergirl dove down toward a large subway ventilator grating set into the side of a retaining wall on the east side of the plaza. The circular grating was nearly six feet in diameter and made of heavy-gauge steel, but she slid it sideways into its mountings with a single quick yank. Slipping through the opening, she gave the grating a shove back into place. When she was several yards down the inner utility tunnel, she suddenly stopped and smacked her forehead with the heel of her palm. *Why didn't I turn invisible before I approached the grating? I must still be a little out of it.* She shook her head ruefully. *Oh, well, as fast as I was moving, anyone watching wouldn't have seen much more than a blur. Besides, the only one around was that old derelict. Who would believe him anyway?*

Back out in the plaza, the derelict peered from under the edge of his old woolen hat, staring intently at the grating. Despite his overall seedy appearance, the man's eyes were very clear. He reached into the folds of his shabby overcoat and pulled out a tiny cellular phone. A chorus of muted beeps sounded in his ear as he hit an autodial button. A sleepy growl answered at the other end of the line.

The "derelict" spoke softly but distinctly into the phone. "This is Rusty. Sorry to interrupt your beauty sleep, but I think I just saw something go into that ventilation shaft on the east retaining wall. I'm not sure what it was, but we'd better check it out."

A loud yawn came across the line. "Whaddaya talkin' about? Can't ya be more specific?"

Rusty pondered the request. "Depends on what you mean by specific." The movement at the grate had been very fast and not very distinct, but he knew that he'd seen flashes of red and blue and a sudden billowing, like that of a cape. "For all I know, it might have been a ghost!"

Supergirl flew down the slowly descending utility tunnel until she came to another recessed grate blocking a corridor that veered off sharply to the left. As she swung open the second grating, concealed lighting switched on automatically, illuminating the corridor. She proceeded on down the corridor for nearly a hundred yards to where it ended in a small chamber.

The chamber was dominated by a huge circular metal hatch that looked like nothing so much as the door to a bank vault. From the schematics that Luthor had shared with her, she knew that she was directly beneath the tomb. Behind that access hatch was the crypt into which Superman's coffin had been lowered.

Okay, girl, this is it. So, what are you waiting for? Afraid of what you might find?

"Supergirl?" Lex suddenly broke in, the circuitry buried in the surrounding walls transmitting his encoded signal strongly and clearly into her headset. It was as if he'd come up behind her; she almost jumped. "Are you in the tomb yet?"

Not yet, lover, but I suppose that it's now or never. "Lex, I'm opening the hatchway, and I'm about to step inside." Supergirl hesitated a moment. "And I know you think I'm being foolish, but I can't help but hope he's alive."

"Let's not get our hopes up too high, love." There was a slight edge to the voice that came over the headset.

Supergirl stepped through the hatchway, light flooding in from the outer chamber. In the center of the crypt was nothing but a bare marble slab.

"Lex! Oh, my God!"

"Well, what is it? What have you found? Don't leave me hanging, girl!"

"The crypt is empty! Even the coffin is gone! And there's a big hole leading down a steep shaft from the wall to my left. Superman is gone!" She felt giddy at the discovery. "Did you hear me, Lex? Now do you think I'm being foolish?"

"No, dear, but I'm afraid you sound much too optimistic. Listen to me, love. If Superman *were* alive, if he'd dug his way out of there, why would he have taken the coffin with him?"

The question gave Supergirl pause.

"Okay, Lex, I admit that it doesn't look as if he just got up and walked home, but . . . maybe he arranged this breakout beforehand. I mean, there're probably a lot of things we don't know about Superman." *A lot that even I don't know!* "Maybe he had people standing by in case he ever died, or appeared to die—a team that would take him somewhere to be revived!" Supergirl was grasping at straws, and she knew it, but she wasn't about to give up hope yet.

Back in his offices, Luthor was gripping the arms of his chair so tightly that his hands were turning white. *Damn her optimism.* He could well imagine the look on her face, that vital glow in her eyes. He loved it when she looked at him that way. But now, he knew, that look was for Superman. *Superman!* It was all he could do to choke back his rising bile.

"Lex? Did you hear me? Are you still there?"

"I'm here." Luthor took a deep breath and let it out slowly. "All right, love. I myself admit that anything is possible. See where the shaft leads, but make sure you keep me posted. Over and out." It was a rather graceless directive, he knew, but it was all he could trust himself to say.

Halfway across Metropolis, Jonathan Kent tossed and turned in an unfamiliar bed.

"Jon?" Martha switched on the light. "Are you all right?"

"Can't sleep."

"Me neither, not well anyway. I keep seeing that statue. It was so beautiful. And so awful." Martha plucked a tissue from the box beside her pillow. "Still, I'm glad that Lois took us to see the tomb. It was a lot bigger than it looked on TV, wasn't it?"

"Yeah, Martha. That Luthor woods colt did all right by our boy. Almost makes up for the hell his father put Clark through." Jonathan fumbled for his glasses on the nightstand. "I wish Lois had let *us* take the couch. It was enough that she put us up in her apartment. We should've insisted on staying in a hotel, like Lana did. I hate to put anybody out of their bed."

"Poor Lois. Jonathan, how in the world can we go back to Smallville in the morning? The thought of her having to face all this—"

"I know, Martha, I know. But when she looks at us, all she sees is Clark. I'm afraid we've done all we can for now, and it's best we leave on schedule."

"I suppose you're right, Jon. Lois has tried to put on such a brave front for the world, but I've caught that look in her eyes . . . that horrible, haunted look."

"Uh-huh. I've seen it too, especially when she's looking at you or me and doesn't notice that we're looking back." Jonathan patted his wife's hand. "Try not to worry, Martha. It isn't as if we're abandoning her. Lois has a family of her own to lean on."

"But there are things she can't confide in them."

"I know, and that can be awful. But we'll keep in touch, never you fear."

Jonathan swung his feet down to the floor. "I've got to get some water —maybe take an aspirin."

"Headache, dear?"

"Sore muscles. Nothing to fret about." He leaned across the bed and kissed Martha lovingly on the forehead. "I'll be back. You try to get some sleep."

As Jonathan slipped from the bedroom and padded down the hall, he thought he saw something move in the living room. *Sounds like someone else can't sleep.*

Lois stood by her apartment's big sliding glass doors, holding her cat Elroy in her arms and staring out past the balcony into the night. Her back was to Jonathan, but he could see a partial reflection of her face in the glass. Lois's expression wasn't so much sad, he thought, as it was bleak. The bleakness was echoed in every line of her body.

Jonathan hung back in the hallway, wondering if he should disturb Lois. She seemed deep in thought. His own thoughts were bitter and wistful all at once. *Her and Clark's best years were ahead of them . . . marriage, children—well, probably not children, not of their own, anyway. For all that Clark looked like an ordinary Earthman, he was anything but!* As a farmer, Jonathan had learned enough practical genetics to know that the chances of cross-fertilization between native and Kryptonian stock were virtually zero. *Still, if they'd wanted kids badly enough, they could have always adopted. That's more or less what Martha and I did.*

It suddenly hit Jonathan all over again that Clark was gone. The pain of that realization struck like a sledgehammer. *I still can't hardly believe it. It's all so unfair . . . so unfair to us all.* He tried to choke back a sob, only to have it escape as a sneeze.

Lois heard him and turned. "J-Jonathan? What—?"

"I'm sorry, Lois. I didn't mean to startle you, but—" The words caught in his throat. Suddenly, all the reassurances he'd given Martha, all the platitudes about leaving on schedule, struck him as the stupidest things he'd ever said. "Lois, Martha and I are worried about leaving you."

"You're worried about *me*?" Lois's eyes widened. "I've been worried about you two. I was just thinking how terribly hard this must be for you and Martha. I couldn't have been much comfort to you."

Jonathan opened his mouth to protest, but Lois continued on. "And being in Metropolis must only make it worse for you. This city is the heart of a media fire storm over Superman's death, and you should get as far away from it as you can. It's not likely to get better anytime soon." She gestured to the coffee table, where she'd angrily tossed a copy of the *Metropolis Daily Star*.

Jonathan glanced down at the paper and then quickly looked away, but he knew that he'd never forget the lead story. Next to a lurid photo of a blond woman who might charitably be called a floozy was the banner headline: SUPERMAN'S SECRET WIFE?

Lois slowly stroked her cat behind the ears. "Yes, it's hard to look at, isn't it? And that's one of the more tasteful stories. You and Martha have to get away from this." She looked once more at the newspaper, and her face grew drawn. "This trash makes me so ashamed to be a journalist."

"You're not to blame for any of this, Lois. You shouldn't be so hard on yourself."

Hard on myself, am I? Jonathan's assessment almost struck Lois as funny. *That's not what my father would say. "Kids today are too soft. You've got to be tough!"—that was Sam Lane's philosophy.*

"Lois?"

"Sorry, Jonathan. I was just lost in thought for a moment." She glanced at her wristwatch. "Hey, look at the time. We should both try to get some sleep while we can. Your flight leaves pretty early in the morning."

"Well, all right. If you're sure. . . ."

"Very sure, Jonathan. I'll be fine."

Lois shook her head as she watched him shuffle back down the hall. *How different Clark's childhood must have been from mine! How lucky he was to have been raised by the Kents!*

In his office, Lex Luthor was doing his best to remain calm. In an attempt to relieve his tension, he had rung for a young masseuse named Lori. That had proven to be a mistake. He was simply too keyed up to unwind, even with the enticement of Lori's ample endowments. After several uncomfortable moments, he had gotten up from the massage table and stalked back to his desk to sit staring at his computer displays.

Lori slipped through the door, a bottle and two glasses in her hand. "Oh, you're so tense!" She gave Luthor her best little-girl pout. He turned away.

"I mean," she cooed, "why don't you try relaxing with this nice cabernet sauvignon, and let Lori relax all those nasty old neck muscles for you?" She poured him a glass and held it temptingly near.

Lex barely acknowledged her. "Go away, Lori."

Lori stared, uncomprehending, for a moment. Then a cautious, almost guilty look came to her eyes. "We *are* alone, right? I mean, *she's* not here . . . is she?" Lori knew that Luthor and Supergirl were an item and had guessed that was why he hadn't requested her services lately. His call tonight had surprised her, actually, but if there was any chance of Supergirl showing up and causing a scene—!

Without looking at Lori, Luthor reached for the glass of wine. "She is not. We are quite alone." Lori smiled, reassured but still just a little uncertain. She handed him the glass, letting her fingers brush intimately against his.

"But I said—go away!" Luthor snatched the glass away from her hand and flung it—not quite at her, but close enough that she screamed.

"I—I—I'm sorry, Mr. L! I only wanted to—"

"You only wanted to leave, isn't that right, Lori?"

"Yes, Mr. L." Lori nodded, near tears, and scrambled for the door.

"Bloody cow." Luthor slouched back into his chair, his face burning with irritation. *Shouldn't have let her get under my skin like that. But no real matter . . . her kind always responds to a quick apology. Bloody nuisance, though.*

A buzz came from the desk console, and he lunged for the speaker switch.

"Hi, Lex. Did you miss me?" Supergirl's voice was a happy chirp.

Luthor was about to lash out again when he caught himself. *Don't forget who this is and what she is capable of. She's young and still very naive, and that's precisely what makes her so valuable.* "I've . . . been waiting with bated breath, love. Have you found anything?"

"Yes and no. That hole in the wall does look as though it was made by someone breaking into the crypt, rather than breaking out. But the shaft itself is really very strange."

"Just tell me what you see, love, and we'll go from there."

"Well, the shaft appears to have been drilled right through the bedrock under the crypt's foundations. There are no signs of concrete, steel, or any other reinforcing materials. The walls of the shaft look as though they've been heat-glazed or something. They're very smooth, even glassy. I'd imagine the glazing was done to seal the walls and help provide structural support, but I couldn't begin to guess how it was done. Want me to keep looking? I might lose radio contact if I get too far underground."

"I'll take that chance. Just find the body!" Luthor switched off his microphone and purpled the air with a string of curses. He sat fuming for a few seconds and then pulled a special telephone from his bottom desk drawer. There were no buttons on this phone; the simple act of picking up the receiver initiated the call over the private line.

At the other end of the line, the receiver was picked up between the first and second rings. "Yes, Mr. Luthor?"

"We have a situation, Happersen. Meet me in the garage in five minutes."

Rusty jumped up in surprise as Dan Turpin came stalking toward him through the underbrush.

"I didn't expect you so soon, Inspector. The roads are pretty slippery out there tonight."

" 'S no problem if you know what you're doin'. This just better be good, to roust me outta a warm bed."

"It's good, all right." He pointed along the wall. "There's where I saw our ghost."

"Shhh! Keep it down." Turpin looked around, making sure they were alone. "The last thing we need is for the tabloids to write about cops chasing shadows."

"I hear you." Rusty stamped his feet in a futile attempt to keep warm. He was wearing two layers of good wool socks, but his shoes had been authentically tattered to maintain his cover. "Meaning no disrespect, sir, but can we keep moving? I'm freezing my badge off out here."

Turpin grinned. "Just think warm thoughts, kid. Show me what you've found."

Rusty led Turpin along the wall to the ventilation shaft. The grating was still slightly ajar. The opening left between the grate and the edge of the wall was almost—but not quite—big enough for a grown man to slip through. "This is the way I found it, Inspector."

Turpin ran his hand along the rim of the metal grate. "Pretty crafty. Nobody ever gives these things a second look. Lotsa folks never notice 'em at all. You could hide all sorts of things in there." He gave the grating a little tug; it just barely moved. "Hmmph. Heavy sucker."

Rusty tucked his hands up under his arms and shifted his weight from leg to leg, dancing to keep his blood flowing. "Yeah, I tried sliding the grate the rest of the way open, but I couldn't budge it."

"That's 'cause ya never eat a good breakfast, kid." Turpin gave Rusty a cockeyed grin and squared his shoulders. "But I bet if ya let an ol' hand like me help ya out, we can move it just fine."

After a few minutes of pushing and heaving, Rusty and the inspector managed to slide the grating open a few more feet. "Well, it ain't perfect," groused Turpin, "but it's close enough." He stuck his head in the opening. "Warm in there."

"Yeah?" Rusty leaned closer to the opening. "Oh, yeah!" He stood there warming himself while Turpin fished a flashlight out of the lining of his coat. "Hey, you know, Inspector, LexCorp financed a lot of the work to this part of the park, even before they had Superman's tomb built. You think they might have something to do with this?"

"Maybe." Turpin shrugged out of his coat and switched on the flashlight. "Could be the answer's inside. If it is, I'll find it."

"You want any backup?" Rusty glanced back at the empty plaza. "Technically, I'm still on duty out there, but—"

"Don't sweat it, kid. I ain't afraid of ghosts."

Rusty smacked his hand against the grate. "Hey, no 'ghost' could've moved this mother."

"You're learnin', kid. You hold the fort up here, but give Cap'n Sawyer a call and tell her I said to get her skinny butt over here, okay?" The old cop slipped past the grate, then stuck his head back out and treated Rusty to a grin that was halfway on the road to becoming a scowl. "If I'm not back in an hour, send in the marines and tell my daughter Maisie that I love her!"

Rusty watched Turpin disappear into the darkness of the shaft and just shook his head. *What's that old saying? "There are old cops, and there are bold cops, but there are no old bold cops." Whoever came up with that one surely never met "Terrible" Turpin.* Rusty pulled out his phone. "Sorry, Captain Sawyer, but orders are orders!"

Some sixty blocks downtown, a late-model van shot out of an untended parking lot and roared onto 114th Street.

"Hey, watch it, will ya?" In the back of the van, three men crouched in the empty cargo bay, straining to keep their balance.

"Sorry." The driver didn't sound sorry; there was a nervous edge to his voice. "I thought I heard something. I think we may have been spotted."

As if in answer to the driver's worries, the glare of a single headlight filled his side mirror. The three men in the back of the van looked at each other and began pulling machine pistols from beneath their coats as the whine of a high-performance engine grew louder. One of them called up to the driver. "What's that?"

"Cycle cop, I think." The driver's voice had gone hollow. "He's gaining on us. I can't shake him in this heap."

"Don't sweat it. Let him get closer." The men in the back waited tensely, guns at the ready, as the motorcycle pulled up alongside the speeding van.

A commanding voice suddenly boomed out over an amplifier: "You in the van—pull over!"

The gunmen threw open the van's sliding side door and opened fire. To their surprise, the man on the motorcycle deflected every one of their bullets with a gleaming golden shield strapped to his left arm. One slug even ricocheted back into the van, narrowly missing one of the gunmen.

"That's no cop!" The driver was white as chalk. "That's . . . that's the Guardian!"

"The Guardian?!" One of the gunmen went wide-eyed. "It can't be! He busted my grandfather once—an' Gramps was younger'n me back then! The Guardian'd be older'n dirt by now!"

"Who *cares*? Waste 'im!"

But the only thing they wasted was their ammunition. The Guardian suddenly leapt from his speeding motorcycle into the open van, his shield held out before him, and slammed into the gunmen like a battering ram. Guns went flying in all directions.

"What're you doin' back there?" screamed the driver. "He ain't bulletproof, is he? Shoot 'im!"

A big hand reached out and grabbed the driver by the collar, and a cool, even voice whispered in his ear, "As lousy shots as your friends were, I don't need to be bulletproof! Now, once more, pull this van over!"

Moments later, the Guardian was sitting back astride his motorcycle, giving his statement to the police as they loaded the dazed gunmen into a paddy wagon. ". . . that's the story, Officer. I don't know why that crew went to the trouble of stealing a delivery van. Maybe you can get them to tell you."

"Well, Guardian, even if we can't, we have plenty to hold 'em on. In addition to grand theft auto and the weapons charges, there're warrants out on the whole lot of 'em. Still and all, we may have a problem—at least, you may, Guardian." The cop shook his head. "Those creeps are making a lot of wild accusations about use of unnecessary force. If they can make their stories jibe, they could file charges against you."

"Let them try. My bike recorded everything."

"Your bike—?"

"That's right. There's a camera built into the windscreen on this motorcycle." The Guardian pressed a button on the handlebars, and a silvery disc popped out of a slot on the console just over the engine. "The entire chase was recorded on this laser disc."

The cop slipped the disc into an evidence folder and broke into a wide grin. "The DA's office will love you for this."

"My pleasure. Tell them I'll be in touch!"

With a single kick, the Guardian started up his big bike and peeled off down the avenue. *That didn't go too badly,* he thought. It had been years since he'd covered the streets of the city with any regularity, and being back on patrol brought back bittersweet memories. *I'm glad I was able to get leave from the Project to come back and lend a hand. Metropolis has been hurting since Superman died.*

As the Guardian turned east onto Bessolo Boulevard, he felt a mild pressure at his temples. The face of Dubbilex seemed to shimmer before his eyes.

"Guardian!"

"Dubbilex? What's up?"

"Trouble. We need you at the Project—hurry! I must gather the others." The mental projection faded as quickly as it had appeared.

The Guardian made a quick U-turn and headed uptown toward Suicide Slum. He didn't know what was going on, but it had to be serious for Dubbilex to send a telepathic message all the way from the Project. *It's a drain for him to cast his mind across so many miles. I'd better take the rail back.*

At the Hob's Bay exit, the Guardian made a sharp right and motored down Kurtzberg Lane to a squat brown building. The sight of the place brought a momentary smile to his face. *The good old Red Horse Garage! It seems like only yesterday that my boys were hanging out here, tuning up old jalopies and getting into mischief.* He flipped a switch on his bike, and the garage's overhead door began ratcheting open. *In a way, they're still causing mischief behind these doors . . . far behind and below.*

As the Guardian rode into the darkened garage, the door automatically closed behind him. A soft, diffuse light came on around him as the garage floor began to sink rapidly down a deep shaft. The Guardian dismounted, marveling once again at the automated systems that Cadmus's engineers had been able to hide beneath the streets of the old neighborhood. *I must remember to commend the maintenance division. I know this hydraulic lift hasn't been used in months, but it still runs as smoothly as the day it was installed.*

The lift came to a cushioned halt nearly five hundred feet below street level, and the Guardian walked his bike toward a bullet-shaped monorail car that sat waiting. A warning bell chimed as he approached, and he was challenged by a prerecorded message.

"This is a high-security zone. Please state your clearance code now."

"Priority code seven-A. This is Agent Harper! Repeat, this is Agent Harper!"

There was a click and a ding from a wall-mounted speaker, and the door to the railcar began to slide open. "Voiceprint check confirmed. Agent Harper cleared for transport access."

As the railcar got under way, the Guardian began to ponder Dubbilex's summons. He had felt the anxiety in the DNAlien's thought-cast. *It usually takes a pretty heavy crisis to get Dubbilex that disturbed. I wonder what could be going on? Not more trouble with Paul Westfield, I hope!* The Guardian thumbed a switch on the railcar's console. "Estimated time of arrival at Cadmus?"

The recorded voice responded with a click. "This car will dock in five minutes, three seconds."

The Guardian drummed his fingers impatiently against his shield. Arrival couldn't come fast enough for him.

Far below the surface of Centennial Park, Supergirl carefully picked her way through a maze of caverns, wishing that she'd brought a flashlight.

The steep walk down the shaft had been no problem; the shaft's glossy sides had diffused remarkably well the lighting from the crypt and its antechamber. But the lower end of the shaft had opened into the caves, and the caves rapidly swallowed up most of the light. *A flashlight? I wish I had a miner's helmet!*

She expanded her eyes to four times their normal size to collect as much as possible of the dim light that still remained. "Are you still reading me, Lex?" In the still of the caverns, Supergirl kept her commentary to a hushed whisper without even being aware that she'd lowered her voice. "I can't hear you, but I guess that doesn't necessarily mean that you can't hear me. The shaft that led down from the crypt was about a hundred yards long, but what's really surprising is that it was started down here in these caves. I never knew there was anything like this under Metropolis. Wait a minute. I think I hear something." Supergirl stopped and listened intently. She could definitely hear footsteps behind her not far away, and there was a pale glow coming from just around the bend. Slowly, silently, she glided down the cave, heading toward the sound.

Suddenly a bright light washed over Supergirl, momentarily dazzling her in its brilliance. She whipped up her cape to shield her eyes as they shrank back to their normal dimensions.

From farther down in the cave came a string of colorful expletives, and the voice that gave them breath sounded vaguely familiar.

"Inspector Turpin?"

"What the hell are you?! How do you know me?"

"It's me—Supergirl." She lowered her cape and gave the old cop her sweetest smile.

Turpin approached slowly with his pistol drawn and flashlight just slightly lowered now. "Jesus, Mary, and Joseph—it *is* you! You gave me quite a scare, li'l lady. For a minute there, I coulda sworn your eyes were as big as dinner plates."

"Uh, yes, well . . ."

"What're you doin' down here?"

"I might ask you the same, Inspector."

"I came to check out something fishy that happened in the park, and it led me down a hole under Superman's crypt—which was empty, I might add! I don't suppose you could tell me anything about that?"

"Not much, Inspector. Sounds like we both answered alarms in the night, but I'm about as much in the dark as you are. I discovered Superman's body was missing and followed a shaft down to—to wherever it is we are now. Did you know there were caves like this under the city?"

Turpin scratched his chin. "Seems to me I remember hearing something about caves when I was a boy. Something to do with how they screwed up some aqueducts the city was trying to build."

Turpin's flashlight began to flicker. "No-good cheap batteries!" He shook the lamp angrily, and it blinked out. "Oh, this is just dandy! Now we're really in the dark!"

"Not to worry!" Supergirl took him by the hand. "I think I remember the way back."

From midtown, a black stretch limousine sped northwest across Metropolis, as if racing the dawn. In the back of the limo, Luthor sat silently fuming as Sydney Happersen did his best to reassure his employer.

"Really, Mister L, there's probably nothing to worry about!"

"Nothing, Happersen? Superman's body is missing from its tomb!"

Happersen flinched and glanced at the privacy window. It was sealed, of course; their driver hadn't heard a word. Happersen had checked the window himself, twice, before they'd set out, but he couldn't stop himself from checking again. *I'll be checking under my own bed next.*

He cleared his throat. "Grave robbers, sir. Some nut cases have stolen the body—that's the answer, pure and simple! After all, Superman had a lot of enemies. You weren't the only one who wanted him dead."

Happersen reached up under his glasses to rub the sleep from his eyes. "You saw the news footage of Superman's battle with that Doomsday creature. He couldn't possibly have faked his death!"

"No, Happersen? I faked mine!" Luthor stared out at the city, his city, as it flashed by. "Could Superman have found that out? Could he have set all this up to catch me off guard?"

"Mr. L, that's highly unlikely—!"

"But not impossible, Happersen! Nothing is impossible for men of power."

The car phone buzzed, and Luthor switched on the speaker. "Yes?"

"Lex! At last!" The relief in Supergirl's voice came across loud and clear. "I was afraid my headset had gone completely on the fritz. How much of my report got back to you?"

"Your signal faded out as you descended the tunnel, love. What did you find?"

"Not much. Mainly a series of caves—and Police Inspector Turpin."

"Turpin?!" Luthor's face flashed red as he struggled to maintain his calm. "Then the police know of Superman's disappearance?"

"Yes. In fact, more of them are arriving now. Do you want me to return to the tower?"

"No! No, I'm en route to the tomb now with Doctor Happersen. He has some equipment that should aid in the investigation. Just stay put. We should be there soon."

Luthor turned to his aide. "Well, the fat's in the fire now, Sydney."

Minutes later, at Luthor's direction, the limousine pulled up to the curb on the edge of the park. Happersen spoke not a word as he pulled a backpack of electronic gear from the trunk, and the two men set off on foot for the tomb. At the east retaining wall, they found two uniformed officers of the Special Crimes Unit standing guard.

One of the officers recognized Luthor and gestured toward the grate. "We were told to expect you, gentlemen. Go on in. You *do* know the way, don't you?"

Luthor answered the sarcasm with a wry chuckle and his best corporate smile. "I believe the officer's having a bit of sport with us, Sydney." As he led the way down the incline, he lowered his voice to a bare whisper. "Did you get his badge number?"

"Yes, sir."

"Good; we'll deal with him later."

When Luthor and Happersen finally reached the antechamber, they found Supergirl waiting patiently for them, along with Inspector Turpin, another SCU uniformed officer, and Captain Margaret Sawyer.

Supergirl looked up as they approached. "Lex, there you are!"

"Hello, love . . . Captain Sawyer . . . Inspector Turpin. I believe you all know my senior science advisor, Dr. Sydney Happersen. Beastly night for such a thing, eh?"

"Is there ever a good time to investigate a grave robbery?" Sawyer fixed him with an icy stare. "Mister Luthor, in all my many years in police work, I'd never before seen a tomb with access vents and secret tunnels. I'd like to hear your explanation for this setup!"

Give 'im hell, Maggie! Turpin tipped his derby forward, trying hard not to show how much he enjoyed hearing her read Luthor the riot act. *I got me a feeling this slippery cuss has been playin' fast and loose way too long!*

Luthor was the picture of humility. "I assure you, Captain Sawyer, I never meant for anything to disturb the integrity of Superman's final resting place." He gestured to the walls around them. "This section of Centennial Park, you see, was recently refurbished under a LexCorp grant. Originally, a time capsule was to be buried here, hence this 'setup,' as you called it. After Superman's untimely death, the foundations proved the ideal structural support for his crypt. True, this access corridor wasn't public knowledge, but there was absolutely no intention of subterfuge! And from what I've gathered, this access was not involved in the removal of Superman's body." Luthor turned to Supergirl. "That *is* the case, is it not?"

"As far as I can tell, Lex."

"Well, then, let's have a closer look, shall we?" He gestured to the open hatchway. "Dr. Happersen, if you would do the honors—?"

Moments later, Happersen looked up from the edge of the hole in the wall. "You were right, Supergirl. From the scoring and the rubble, it's obvious that this crypt was broken *into,* not out of! Given the amount of rock they had to go through, whoever did this had access to some pretty high-tech gear. You say that the other end of the shaft is an underground cave?"

Supergirl nodded. "More like a series of caves, Doctor. In fact, there are two major branches, splitting off from each other. Between the two of us, the Inspector and I pretty much checked out one fork, and all we found was a dead end."

Luthor stroked his beard thoughtfully. "Then I'd say it's incumbent upon us to search the remaining fork at once! Superman's body must be found. You do agree, Captain?"

"I certainly do." *I don't trust you or your flunky any farther than I can throw you, but I'm not about to turn down your help—or Supergirl's.* Sawyer turned to her uniformed officer. "Break out some more flashlights, Ramirez. We're going back down."

The Guardian left the monorail dock and sprinted down the Cadmus Project's huge central corridor. He could feel something tugging at him, as if leading him to where he was most needed. *Dubbilex's doing, no doubt.* Within minutes he came upon the telepath and the five department heads crowded around a huge security door.

The sight gave him pause. *Yes, they're all here.* Anthony Rodrigues and Pat MacGuire had the lock panel off the door and were fiddling with its internal circuits, while John Gabrielli focused a pocket flash on their work. Tom Tompkins and Walter Johnson stood on the periphery; both men were visibly agitated. The Guardian was so used to being around the young clones of these men that seeing "his boys" all grown up was momentarily disorienting.

"Dubbilex! What in blazes is going on?"

"Our Mr. Westfield has sealed himself off in Lab Seven with an advanced study team in violation of all known protocols!" Dubbilex nervously chewed at the end of one fingernail. The Guardian had never seen the DNAlien in such a lather before.

Tompkins was more forceful in his accusations. "Westfield's pulling some kind of fast one, Jim! He has to be! He's even set up psionic buffers around the lab so Dubbilex couldn't probe it!"

Walt Johnson nervously flipped the button of a ballpoint pen. "It doesn't look good, Guardian. Pat and Anthony are trying to override the security locks, but—!"

"Success!" Anthony Rodrigues stepped back as the security door began cycling open. "Gentlemen, we have ingress!"

The seven men crowded through the door, Dubbilex at the forefront. Three feet into the lab, they all came to a dead halt. Before them, Paul Westfield and a group of geneticists in surgical greens were clustered around an examination table—upon which lay the body of Superman!

The Guardian exploded. "Westfield, you damned ghoul! No wonder my leave was granted so quickly—you *wanted* me away from the Project, didn't you? You wanted me out of here, to make sure that I wouldn't catch on to your infernal scheme!"

Westfield stepped in front of Harper, blocking his path into the lab. "The research under way here is not your concern, Guardian. I suggest that you refrain from any thoughts of interference."

"Not my concern?! You steal the body of the world's greatest hero—you commandeer Project facilities and enlist Project personnel for—for God only knows what you plan to do!—and you have the unmitigated gall to tell me it's not my concern?!"

"Spare me the histrionics, Guardian!" Westfield crossed his arms defiantly. "This is a sensitive scientific operation of the highest possible priority. I have no desire to stand here and listen to a lot of insubordinate moralizing!"

"You don't want to listen? Fine! I'll make my point another way!" The Guardian leapt at Westfield, grabbing the Project administrator by his tie and shirt collar, and hoisted him up off the floor with one hand. The security chief balled his other hand up into a fist and was about to let it fly when the others finally grabbed hold of him.

"Guardian, no!" It was all Dubbilex could do to hold back his friend's arm. "Jim, this isn't the way—!"

"Maybe not the best way, Dub, but our esteemed administrator here just made it the only way!" The Guardian locked eyes with Westfield. "So I'm insubordinate, am I? The President himself ordered you to cease all attempts to claim Superman's body—"

"N-n-no. N-not exactly." Westfield was starting to turn red. "My orders said to allow Metropolis to hold their funeral. I—I interpreted that to mean . . . once the services were over . . . my original authorization to collect and study alien decedents w-would resume."

Westfield made a strained choking noise as the Guardian tightened his grip.

"So you just took it upon yourself to do a little grave robbing, is that it? You are really some piece of work, Westfield! Just what did you have in mind for Superman? Were you afraid you'd miss your chance to preside over the dissection of the last Kryptonian?"

"No, you fool! Think. We could re-create Superman! Bring him back to life—as you were brought back!"

"Clone a new Superman?!" John Gabrielli's eyebrows seemed about to leap off his forehead. "You can't be serious!"

"Hold it, John." Tom put a hand on his old buddy's arm. "Maybe he's on to something!"

That was too much for Pat MacGuire. "Tompkins, you're as nutty as he is! The procedures you used to save the Guardian were experimental, and we had a living template to work from! Superman is dead—and an alien! Who knows what we'd wind up with if we tried to replicate him?!"

"Who knows, indeed." Walt Johnson started tapping his chin with his pen. "Still, if there's a chance, even a slight chance of success . . ."

The Guardian was so shocked that he lost his grip and let Westfield fall, stumbling, to the floor. "I can't believe I'm hearing this!" He turned to Dr. Rodrigues, looking for a voice of reason. "All questions of ethics aside, you've told me how touch and go my rebirth was. My body might just as easily have wound up as twisted and misshapen as—as some of those poor creatures Dabney Donovan created. And Pat's right! Even if you succeeded in cloning Superman, he wouldn't *be* Superman. You don't have his mind to plug into a new body."

"Valid objections to be sure." Rodrigues stopped and pushed his glasses back up the bridge of his long nose. "The odds against success would be monumental—but not necessarily insurmountable! A facsimile of Superman's psyche could conceivably be simulated by recording the mental impressions that Dubbilex absorbed from him in previous encounters."

Dubbilex stepped back, at first startled by the suggestion. He frowned and then began to look distant, as if searching through his mind for a misplaced memory. "He . . . he has a point, Jim. I'm a walking example of Project science gone awry, but I consider my life a most precious gift. I do carry certain psychic impressions in my subconscious. There *is* a possibility of success here, however slim."

The Guardian threw up his hands. "All right. I still think you all ought to have your heads examined, but I guess maybe we do owe it to Superman—and to the world—to at least try."

"You'll see." Westfield rubbed his neck as he attempted to regain his composure. "I have the greatest confidence that we'll succeed—!"

"Not so fast, Westfield!" The Guardian glowered down at the administrator. "If there's to be an 'Operation Superman,' *you* are not going to be in charge of it! I want this run strictly by the book from here on—under the direct supervision of Drs. Tompkins, Johnson, and Rodrigues!" He nodded to the three men who, of the five department heads, were the most directly involved with research.

"Very well, if that's the way it must be." Westfield bristled at the thought of caving in under such humiliating circumstances, but at this point he was willing to make just about any compromises necessary to get the operation under way. *There'll be plenty of time to regain control, once things are up and running.*

Westfield turned to the man closest to the examination table. "Well, Dr. Packard, you heard the Guardian; it's in their hands now!"

Carl Packard stepped away from the body, pulling down his surgical mask. "I wish you luck, gentlemen. You'll need it, if you're hoping to obtain significant tissue samples."

"Oh?" Dr. Tompkins was already moving forward to inspect what had been done. "And why is that, Carl?"

"It appears that, even in death, Superman's body is still quite thoroughly invulnerable!" Packard held up a scalpel for all to see. The instrument's blade was bent nearly double.

Several hundred feet under Metropolis, Captain Sawyer and Inspector Turpin stuck close to Dr. Happersen and Lex Luthor as they all followed Supergirl down the unexplored branch of the cave system. The cavern was beginning to narrow when they came to an abrupt dead end.

"Are you sure this is the right way, love?"

"Well, it's the only branch we haven't explored, Lex." Supergirl grasped a huge fallen stalactite and heaved it out of her way. "I have to admit, I didn't expect this much rubble, but it all appears to be newly fallen!"

"I agree, Supergirl." Happersen moved ahead to join her, pausing every few feet to wave a probe device through the musty air. "My equipment's detecting minute airborne traces of explosive residue. Someone was trying to cover the trail, and they succeeded admirably, I'm afraid. We're so far underground, I doubt that anyone would have heard the blasts from outside in the park."

Supergirl sank her hands deep into the wall of rubble and yanked aside another huge section of rock. Happersen stopped in midcalculation, a horrified look on his face.

"Supergirl, stop! Just a moment, please!" The doctor punched up a series of numbers on his hand-held apparatus. "Yes—according to my readings, we're actually below the northwest fork of the Hob's River at this point. We must proceed with all due caution."

"Oh, don't be such a worrywart, Dr. Happersen! I'll be careful!"

"Just the same, love, it wouldn't hurt to exercise a bit of restraint." Luthor stepped ahead of Supergirl to peer down the hole she had opened. The light of his flash caught the glimmer of a small metal disc with stenciled markings just a few yards away. "Happersen, what do you make of this?"

"Good Lord. That . . . that looks like some kind of unexploded charge!"

"What?!" Supergirl grabbed Luthor and Happersen by their coats and flung them backward, nearly bowling over Sawyer and Turpin in the process. The next moment, the chamber was rocked by a bone-rattling explosion. Massive sections of rock and showers of dirt poured down upon Supergirl, but almost magically, the debris traveled no further up the cave. After a few seconds, the Girl of Steel backed out of the rubble. There wasn't so much as a speck of dust on her.

"Is everyone all right? I extended my energy shield as quickly as I could, but I've never tried to protect so many people before."

Luthor took Supergirl by the arm. "You did just fine, love. Happersen—?"

"F-fine, sir. Just a little shaken."

"Dangdest thing I ever saw." Turpin tipped his hat back and scratched his head. "What's wrong, Maggie? You've got that funny look on your kisser."

"Wrong?" Sawyer frowned. "I don't know, Dan. I just got this sudden feeling . . . does anyone else hear something?"

Everyone grew still. There it was—a faraway sound, but building. It was a rushing noise.

"Omigod," gasped Happersen. "The river—!"

Somehow, Supergirl scooped up all four of them—grabbing Luthor and Happersen bodily and lifting the other two along with her psychokinesis. She rocketed them back up the branch of the cave as a wall of water came surging through the rubble. Rock and debris were washed aside as the torrent swept after them.

Not until they reached the shaft leading to the crypt did Supergirl pause or look back. "Go! Up—quickly! The flood seems to have slowed, but let's not take any chances!"

Onward they ran, the sound of lapping water echoing after them. The flood crested a third of the way up the shaft, but they didn't stop until they'd reached the crypt.

Officer Ramirez, still on guard, came instantly alert as the five explorers ran stumbling into the crypt. "What's going on? Why the rush?"

"Just tryin' to keep from gettin' waterlogged, Rami." Turpin leaned back against the wall, gasping for breath. Improbably, he'd managed to hang onto his hat, and now he tipped it to Supergirl. "You do good work, li'l lady. That's a fact." *An' if I ever hear that this young pup Luthor ain't treatin' her right, I'll personally kick his behind till his nose bleeds!*

"Thanks, Inspector. I just wish things had turned out better." Supergirl ran a hand, comblike, through her hair. "We're back to square one now. It's all so frustrating!"

"Buck up, love. We'll untangle this mystery yet. Superman's body will be recovered—I promise you that!"

"I wish I had your confidence, Lex. We still don't know who robbed the tomb, and that flood probably washed away any clues we might have found."

"I'm afraid Supergirl's right, Luthor." Sawyer jotted down notes in her report book. "I'm not looking forward to breaking this news to the public."

"What?!" Luthor's jaw dropped. "Captain, surely any disclosure must wait until we know more! Can you imagine the outcry if we revealed that Superman's body had disappeared?"

Turpin wore an awful frown. "I gotta admit, Maggie, he's got a point. If this got out, it could start a riot."

"It could, indeed, Inspector." Luthor clapped the old cop on the back and pressed on. "Superman's death left so many people bereft. If word should leak that his crypt was empty . . . well, our more distraught citizens might jump to all manner of conclusions!"

Ramirez cocked his head toward Sawyer. "Some of them have already, Cap'n, if we can believe the reports I've gotten from the guys out by the grave site! You'd better take a look."

Moments later, they were all back at the east wall grating. Spread out before them in the dawn's light was a small sea of people milling about before the tomb. Over half of them were wearing royal blue robes that bore the red and yellow pentagonal S-shield of Superman.

Sawyer raised an eyebrow. "Early-rising bunch. Where'd they come from?"

"California," reported one of the outer guards. "From what one of 'em told Rusty, that's where their cult got started."

"Cult?"

"That's right, Inspector. Those people actually *worship* Superman— and I don't mean hero worship!"

At the base of the tomb, one of the cultists was already preaching to his flock. ". . . and I say to you, sisters and brothers, do not despair! Be not afraid! In our hour of greatest need, Superman shall return to us from beyond the grave! Yea, he will return and save us all! Say the name now. Say the name and be free!"

The plaza began to echo with their chant: "Superman! SUPERMAN! *SUPERMAN!*"

"Oh, great! Of all the times for this to happen!" Sawyer smacked her hand against the grating in disgust. "It looks like we have no choice but to keep a lid on this for now. We'll expect your full cooperation in our investigations, Luthor."

"Of course, Captain. For now, though, I think it would be best if we sealed this access and slipped away as quietly as possible. Don't you agree, Doctor?"

Happersen nodded, his head nervously bobbing as though it were mounted on a spring.

Minutes later, as a Special Crimes Unit van drove away from the park, Maggie Sawyer finally gave voice to her suspicions. "I didn't want to say anything in front of Luthor and the others, Dan, but I'd bet a year's pay that Paul Westfield and the Cadmus Project are behind this!"

"Well, their last attempt at tryin' to grab Superman sure makes 'em prime suspects, Maggie." Turpin shook his head. "I hate to think of the Guardian bein' mixed up with that bunch. He struck me as a straight-arrow kinda guy."

"And maybe he is, Dan, but he doesn't run the show. And from what I've seen, Cadmus has the kind of technology to carry off something like this." Sawyer grew silent for a minute. "You know, I think I'll call Ben Friendly at the FBI and see if he can add some federal muscle to our investigation."

"We'll need it if Westfield is involved." Turpin sounded angry enough to bite nails. "That weasel wouldn't come clean if you ran him through a car wash! Speakin' of weasels, do you think we'll get any real help from Luthor?"

Sawyer shook her head. "No, Dan, I don't. Luthor didn't rob Superman's grave, but he does have some personal agenda in this mess. I can almost smell it!"

Several blocks away, Luthor's limousine pulled away from the curb and turned back downtown. Supergirl flew high overhead, keeping a protective eye on the car.

Below, Luthor sealed off the back of the limousine and began to grill his science advisor. "How good a look did you get at that charge before it went off, Happersen?"

"Well, I noticed some markings, but I couldn't see it clearly enough to make out any serial numbers."

"What about those markings? Think, man, what did they look like to you?"

"It all happened so quickly." Happersen closed his eyes and tried to recall. "There was a large design of some kind—some sort of crossed out X or something."

"No, Happersen, not an X . . . more like a stylized DNA helix!"

"Excuse me, sir?"

"That was a Cadmus imprint on that charge, I'd swear it. The men that Westfield used in his stand at the morgue wore a similar insignia."

"Sir, do you seriously think that Westfield would defy a direct presidential order?"

"Oh, don't be an idiot, Sydney! Westfield would circumvent an order from God Almighty if it suited his purposes! So would I. I could almost admire the man's tenacity. If only I knew what he was up to—!"

"It's a pity you had to terminate Dr. Teng after he assisted Dabney Donovan in your—ah—'resurrection,' Mr. L. Teng did a masterful job of infiltrating Cadmus for us, and no one there was ever the wiser. He would be the perfect mole, if he were still alive."

"No matter, Happersen. If we planted one mole in the Project, we can plant another! I want you to get on that immediately. I must know what Westfield is up to. I must!"

"Your attention, please! LexAir Flight 2710, nonstop service to Kansas City, is now ready for boarding at gate five."

"Well, that's us." Jonathan Kent shifted slightly under the weight of his carry-on bag. "Good-bye, Lois. You take care of yourself now!"

"I will, Jonathan. You take good care, too." Lois tried to hold back the tears as she hugged him and Martha and then Lana. "Safe traveling, all! I promise that I'll keep in touch!"

As the hugs broke off, Lana gave a shy little wave and began shepherding the Kents down the jetway.

Lois waved back from just outside the gate. "Give my best to Peter, Lana. Let me know if you need any help with—with your wedding."

Lana paused in the jetway and looked back. All those years with Clark

—and then without him—came flooding back to her. *And I thought that I'd lost him, just because he didn't love me the way I loved him. My loss can't begin to compare to hers.*

"Lois!" Lana ran back up the jetway and threw her arms around the reporter. "Oh, Lois, if it would bring him back, I'd gladly give up twenty years of my own life."

"So would I, Lana. S-so would I. I—I know how much you loved him. Please, keep an eye on the Kents. They're going to need you."

"I will. And you take care of yourself. I know how hard it will be. If you ever need a shoulder—"

"Sure."

Lana reached out and brushed a tear from Lois's cheek. "I promise— whenever you need me, I'll be there for you. Always."

16

When the Kents returned home to Smallville, everything in Kansas seemed gray, but nothing was grayer than Jonathan's mood. The afternoon sky was overcast from Salina to the Rockies, but even a bright, sunny day would have done little to raise his spirits. Everything Jonathan saw made him think of Clark. Just staring out the truck window at the plains, stretching out to a gray horizon, had reminded him of the drab little Kansas farm in *The Wizard of Oz,* and the many times he and Martha had read that book to their son.

For Martha's sake, Jonathan had tried not to brood, but neither of them had said more than three or four words since they'd left the airport parking lot at Great Bend. Silence seemed to suit them both at the moment, but Jonathan had seen a lot of grief in his life and knew too well the difference between the quiet that heals and the silence that festers. He was very much afraid that he was slipping into a dangerous silence, but at the same time he felt wholly unequal to the task of resisting it.

It wasn't until they turned down the gravel road to their farm that Jonathan finally forced himself to speak. "Old farm looks the same as it did when we left, don't it, Martha? Funny . . . feels like we were away in Metropolis a million years."

Martha nodded slowly. *For a while there, it felt like two million.* "It's good to be back, Jon. Home is a good place to heal. Leastways, I hope it will be."

As they pulled up to the farmhouse, Ed and Juanita Coleman came out to welcome them back. *We're so lucky to have them for neighbors,* thought Jonathan. *They're such good folks.* It had been a load off his mind, knowing that the Colemans were looking after the house and livestock while they were away.

No sooner had Martha stepped from the truck than Juanita swept her up in a big hug. Ed started to shake Jonathan's hand, then changed his mind and gave his old friend a hug as well.

"Good to have ya back, Jon."

"Thanks, Ed." Jonathan reflected that there weren't many men in these parts—of their generation, at least—who felt secure and comfortable enough to give so physical a greeting. He felt honored that Ed thought that much of their friendship.

Jonathan reached over to pull their suitcases from the back of the pickup truck, but without seeming to hurry, Ed somehow got there first. "I've got these, Jonathan. You take it easy."

"Sure, Ed, sure." *Me take it easy? He's five years older than me, if he's a day. Then again, Ed never has looked his age—"black don't crack," isn't that what he always said?—and me, I probably look a hundred years old.* "Thanks again. And thanks for seeing to the chores while we were gone. Both of you."

There were tears in Juanita's big dark eyes. "Supper's all ready and in the oven keepin' warm for you. But listen, if'n you folks don't feel like eating alone tonight, why, you just pop that casserole into your fridge and come over to our place. That meal won't suffer any for it. It'll even be better the next day."

Martha's eyes glistened with tears as well, but she smiled bravely and hugged her neighbor again. "You didn't have to go to all that trouble, Juanita."

"Wasn't any trouble. You'd do the same for us." Juanita's face was lined with sorrow. "I can't tell you how sorry we are 'bout what happened to Clark. I never would've thought . . ." She shook her head. "I mean, he reported from so many dangerous places over the years, and then right there in Metropolis . . ."

" 'We never know the place or the hour,' " Martha quoted softly.

Juanita bit her lip. "Have they found . . . any sign of him yet?"

"No, not yet. That Doomsday creature caused so much destruction. They may never find him."

"Now don't you talk like that, Martha Kent. If'n there's no bad news, there might yet be good news. I don't want to hold out false hope, but they could find him alive, you know! Big, strong boy like Clark—if anyone could beat the odds and survive, it'd be him."

Ed returned from stowing the suitcases inside and put his arm around Juanita's shoulder. He smiled gently, encouragingly at Martha. "So, you an' Jon gonna be join' us?"

"No—no, not tonight, Ed. It's awfully kind of you, but I think we need a little time to ourselves just now."

The Colemans nodded and headed over to their own pickup. As Ed started up the truck, Juanita rolled down her window. "Remember now, anytime you feel the need to talk, you just give us a call. And if we don't hear from you soon, we'll call you!"

The Kents stood by the back porch, watching as Ed and Juanita's truck disappeared down the road. Jonathan zipped his jacket shut against the wind. "You go on in, Martha. Ed said that he'd tended to the milking, but I want to look in on old Bessie."

As Jonathan entered the barn, Bessie mooed her hello. "Hello, old girl, how're you doing?" He looked around. Bessie's stall—the entire barn for that matter—was tidy as it could be. "I knew I could trust Ed and Juanita to do right by you, Bess."

On the wall beside Bessie's stall, a few faded bits of ribbon fluttered in the breeze from the open door. *Clark's old 4-H ribbons—the ones he won with Bessie's mother—they've been tacked up there so long, I'd almost come to overlook them.* Jonathan shook his head. *How can everything look the same, when everything is so different?*

"Hey, Pa, look! I got Bessie all cleaned up! What d'you think?"

Jonathan jumped. "C-Clark?" His memory was so vivid, the voice had sounded as clear as if his young son were actually there. He looked from the ribbons to Bessie and back again. *Clark must have been about twelve when he won that blue ribbon. . . .*

"Bessie is really the best, isn't she, Pa?"

Jonathan beamed at his son. "I never saw a prettier little calf in my whole life, Clark!"

"Really? Do you think maybe she might take a ribbon at the 4-H fair?"

"If hard work and care can make a calf a winner, son, that little gal's got more than a chance—she's got a *good* chance!" Jonathan knelt down beside his son, scratching the calf behind the ears. "Just don't go getting cocky, son, and counting your ribbons before you win 'em."

"I won't, Pa. Thanks!" Young Clark gave his father a big hug. "If she does win, it'll be because of you!"

"Because of me, Clark? How so?"

"Because of what you taught me—you and Ma both!" Clark rolled his eyes in exasperation. "I wasn't *born* knowing this stuff! You taught me how to care!"

.　　　.　　　.

"Well, we surely tried, son. We tried our best."

"Jonathan?" Martha stood in the doorway of the barn, trying not to look too worried. "Jonathan, did I hear you talking to somebody out here?"

Jonathan looked around. The twelve-year-old boy had vanished long ago. "Nobody's here, Martha. How could I be talking to anybody?" His voice sounded dead, even to himself. Jonathan managed no more than a weak smile for his wife; lifting those muscles in his face seemed to take more effort than hefting a fifty-pound bale of hay.

Jonathan gave Bessie one last pat and headed back to the house with Martha. And though they walked arm in arm, she found herself thinking that her husband had never seemed so far away.

Behind the doors of Lab Seven in the Cadmus Project, Dubbilex stood like a statue, contemplating the faintly green, Plexiglas-walled cold storage unit that held the body of Superman. The DNAlien did not even look up as the chamber door cycled open. "Come in, Jim."

The Guardian crossed the room in three great strides. "I'm not surprised to find you still here, Dub."

"Nor I you. We harbor many of the same reservations."

"No doubt." The Guardian rested a hand lightly on the storage chamber. "Well, I've sent a report to Washington, listing my reservations about all this. If nothing else, I guess we'll find out how many friends Westfield has left in high places." He stared down at Superman's body as if trying to will the Man of Steel back to life. "You know, I still don't really feel right about this. That probably sounds hypocritical, and maybe it is, but it's the truth."

"Indeed. I'm also concerned about Westfield's proposal to clone Superman. The Project's only truly unqualified cloning successes—yourself and the young Newsboys—involved the replication of purely human stock. We understand so little of Kryptonian physiology, Guardian; we could easily create a monster." A dour smile tugged at the corners of Dubbilex's mouth. "A prime example of which stands before you."

"Don't ever say that, Dub." The Guardian looked up at his friend. "You're no monster."

"Not intellectually, perhaps. You must admit, though, that I have a face only the tabloids could love. It is not easy being the only one of your kind, Jim. But I have made my peace with my situation. I am reasonably happy in my work and enjoy life as much as I can, within my self-imposed restrictions. But what if we were to create a being that possessed all of

Superman's power and none of his humanity? That would be a true monster." Dubbilex leaned over the Plexiglas surface, peering at Superman through his own reflection. "A superpowered monster might not be so easily restricted—or restrained. Wouldn't it be the ultimate irony if, in trying to re-create the Man of Steel, we instead gave the world another Doomsday?"

The Guardian shuddered at the thought. "That's why I wanted Tommy, Anthony, and Walt to supervise this. I trust them to pull the plug if things should get out of hand."

"Yes, to the best of their abilities, they would." Dubbilex stroked his long chin. "But there is another question that we should be asking ourselves. What if, somehow, Superman is still alive?"

"Alive? You mean, you've detected a mind—?"

"No. Not a trace. But look at him, Jim. This is not the result of any mortician's art. The body has been thoroughly cleaned and there are no signs of any contusions. The terrible wounds that Doomsday inflicted upon him have closed!"

The Guardian bent close over the body. "Yes, you're right. But surely that must have happened before he died. You've spent days searching for signs of life—ever since we discovered what Westfield had done."

"Even longer than that, Jim." Dubbilex gently shook his head. "I examined Superman at the battle site. Consider this: Even before you began CPR, when the Man of Steel's wounds were still open and oozing blood, I could sense nothing of his spirit. Your valiant efforts, and those of the paramedics and of Dr. Sanchez, were all unsuccessful. *At no time* —and believe me, my friend, I kept close watch—did I ever sense the faintest stirrings of life."

The Guardian sucked in a sharp breath and turned back to the DNAlien. "I see what you mean. Then, to the best of your knowledge, Superman was already dead, yet his wounds still closed."

"Not merely closed. They apparently *healed*."

The Guardian's eyes widened. "Do you have any idea how? Or why?"

"I can think of two possibilities. Perhaps the healing of Superman's wounds was a last reflex of an extraordinarily vital body; the separate tissues trying to heal themselves even after the individual life-force as a whole was gone. Certainly, cells expire at different rates in all multicellular organisms. Some tissues live on for minutes, even hours, after brain death has occurred."

Wearily, Dubbilex rubbed his eyes. "Or possibly, his spirit *was* still present, but I did not look closely enough, or in exactly the right 'place.' Perhaps it is present even now, and I simply do not know how to find it."

The chamber grew quiet as both men silently pondered what, if anything, they should do next. For several minutes neither said a word.

Then, quite suddenly, the stillness of the lab was broken by a thumping sound. A utility panel set into the far wall suddenly swung open, and five young clones came tumbling out.

"I told ya to quit shovin', Scrapper! Didn't I tell ya to quit shovin'? Now look what ya made me do!"

"Gabby, if ya don't button yer trap, I'm gonna button it for ya!"

Tommy and Flip each grabbed one of the smaller boys and pulled them apart.

"Leggo a'me, Johnson! Lemme moiderlize the little motormouth!"

"Hey, chill out, Scrap." It was all Flip could do to hang on to the squirming boy.

"That goes for you, too, Gabby." Tommy held his captive's mouth shut. "Keep the volume down, or the whole Project'll hear us."

"Uh, gentlemen?" Big Words gave an audible gulp. "I fear that our compatriots' altercation has already betrayed us."

Five pairs of eyes stared up into the face of the Guardian.

"Guardian! Hi!" Tommy mustered up the most innocent-looking grin he could manage. "We were looking all over for you! Weren't we, Flip?"

"Yeah, that's right. We heard one of the techs say you were inspecting the utility tunnels and—"

The Guardian held up a hand. "I don't want to hear another word. I want you boys straight out that door and back to your quarters on the double. Got that?"

The Newsboys made not a sound. They didn't nod, run, or otherwise acknowledge the Guardian's orders. Their eyes had snapped open wide, and Tommy lost his grip on Gabby's jaw.

"Holy jumping jeez! It's . . . it's . . . it's Superman! They got Superman all laid out like this was Donnehy's Funeral Parlor or somethin'!"

Scrapper broke free from Flip and shot past the Guardian, just narrowly avoiding the big man's grasp. The other Newsboys swiftly followed suit, scrambling to within a few feet of where Dubbilex stood by the cold storage unit.

"You boys should not be here." The DNAlien looked deeply troubled.

Probably annoyed with himself for not having sensed the boys earlier, thought the Guardian. *He hates to be caught unawares like this.*

Jim Harper ostentatiously cleared his throat. At the sound, Big Words jerked his head around to stare with disbelief at the Guardian. "With all due respect, sir . . ." He paused and nodded back to Dubbilex. "*Sirs,* I request an explanation for the presence of the late Superman in this chamber."

"Yeah!" Scrapper belligerently pushed his cap down onto his forehead. "What's Cadmus doin' wit' Superman's body?!"

"We'll discuss this later, boys."

"No!" Tommy defiantly stepped up to the Guardian. "No, 'later' isn't good enough. A week ago, you made a big deal out of stopping Mr. Westfield from claiming Superman's body. Now, we turn around and here it is. Big Words is right; I think you owe us an explanation."

"Yeah!"

"I'll say!"

"You tell 'im, Tom."

"We all concur, sir."

One by one, the other Newsboys lined up beside Tommy.

Just like his father. Tommy Tompkins always was the leader. Well, the cat's out of the bag now. And maybe that's a blessing in disguise. Harper squared his shoulders. "All right, you deserve to hear the truth. Perhaps, if we all talk about this, even Dubbilex and I will start to make sense of it."

The Guardian smiled; it was the first time these young clones had ever stood up to him on a matter of principle. He was proud of them for that, but there was a trace of melancholy in his smile, just the same. Through them, he could see his boys growing up . . . all over again.

Early the next morning, Lois Lane stepped up to the curb outside her apartment building and flagged down a passing cab. As she pulled open the door, she made a mental note to stop at Dooley's for coffee and bagels on her way in to work. With all the interviews she'd scheduled for herself, she was certain that she'd be expending a lot of calories today.

"Where to, ma'am?" The cabbie was a pleasant-faced African-American in his late twenties. He had a nice deep voice, the sort of voice you could listen to for hours, but Lois scarcely noticed. Her attention was drawn to the small Superman emblem sculpted into the right side of the man's hair and his black armband with a matching scarlet S.

"Ma'am?" He half-turned toward her.

Lois started slightly, suddenly aware that she was staring. "*Daily Planet* Building, please. And hurry."

"I'll do what I can, lady, but the streets are gettin' seriously messy." He adjusted his rearview mirror before pulling back into the street. A twisted piece of metal hung from the mirror. For Lois, it was as if the other shoe had finally dropped. She looked at the cabbie's license; Marlon Brown, the card said. Clark had told her of this man.

That hunk of metal was a "souvenir" from what had been left of Marlon's old cab after a drunk in a pickup truck had plowed into him. Superman had pried the wreck open with his bare hands and eased

Marlon out. They'd crossed paths sometime later, after the cabbie's ribs had healed, and Superman had been very touched by the man's profound gratitude. *No wonder he still wears his black armband. And the hair . . .* Lois felt her throat tighten. *Clark said that when they met that second time, Marlon had already had the Superman emblem cut into his hair. I hope he doesn't want to talk about Superman, because if he does, I might just break down and cry.*

As if on cue, Marlon glanced at her in the rearview mirror, and his face brightened in recognition. "Say, you're that reporter, aren't you? Lois Lane?"

Lois admitted that she was, and the cabbie beamed at her in the mirror. "I thought so! Listen, you're a *real* good writer. I read your stuff all the time." His face clouded suddenly, and Lois had an awful suspicion she knew what he was going to say next.

"That story you wrote after Superman died. That was—that was—" Marlon shook his head. "Sorry. Whoever heard of a cabbie at a loss for words, right? I cried like a baby when I read it. I even *framed* my copy of that story." He shook his head again and looked back sympathetically into the mirror. "Must've hurt like hell to write that. I dunno how you did it."

Lois managed to return a sad smile. "Neither do I."

Marlon glanced at the twist of metal hanging from the mirror, and Lois felt her hands clench into fists. *Please, don't talk about how you got that. I already know, and if you say anything more about Superman, you'll have to pull over because we'll* both *be crying.*

Marlon seemed to sense her silent plea. He took a deep breath and fell silent, leaving Lois alone with her thoughts. *I wrote the story, and Clark died. And now, here I am, trotting off to cover another story. Why do I even bother?*

All those words, what good do they really do? Lois stared out the window and tried to lose herself in the noise of the city.

Jonathan Kent slowly shuffled into the kitchen, planting a weary kiss on his wife's cheek. "Morning, love."

"Morning, dear!" Martha brought the kettle over and filled his mug. "I'm trying something new today. I mixed a little regular coffee in with your decaf. See how you like it."

Jonathan took a big sip. "Tastes all right. Why the change? I thought we were supposed to be cutting back on caffeine an' fat an' such."

"Well, we are, but I thought it wouldn't hurt to put just a little more zip in our day." *At this point I'd try just about anything to brighten you up.*

Jonathan was sleeping later and later every day, but he seemed less rested each morning. "You know, I wish you'd talk to Doc Lanning about your sleep."

"Oh, I probably just need a nap in the afternoon is all. Gettin' old, y'know."

"Well, here's some nice hot oatmeal." She set a steaming bowl down before him. "Lois calls it comfort food, and Lord knows we could use some comfort. I made it with raisins—just the way—the way *he* always liked it."

"That's nice, Martha."

Martha looked at Jonathan as he numbly swirled his spoon through the oatmeal. She had the distinct feeling that she could have set a boiled gum boot in front of her husband and he still would have said, "That's nice, Martha." *Did he hear me at all? The way Jon's acting, it's as if I wasn't even here.*

In fact, it was Jonathan who wasn't quite there. As he sat at the table, he was reliving a breakfast from over thirty years ago.

Clark was four and was interested in getting the maximum enjoyment out of his breakfast. "Here comes the oatmeal plane, Pa." Little Clark swung his spoon through the air. "It's comin' in for a landin'! Power-dive! Rrrrr-zooomp! Open the hangar door!"

Into his mouth went the spoon.

"Yum! I love airplanes with raisins! But I wish I had a real airplane!"

Jonathan reached down into a bag by his feet. "Well, I was saving this for later, but if you think you can spend more of your flight time *away* from the table . . ."

Out came a long, slender balsa wood glider.

"Wow! Hey, Ma! Pa made me an airplane! Thanks, Pa!" Clark jumped up from the table and ran around the room, waving his new toy through the air. "Up, up an' away! 'Bye, Pa. I gotta fly now!"

Jonathan sat playing with his oatmeal, chuckling under his breath. "Gotta fly. Someday, son . . . someday!"

Martha looked up from the refrigerator; she couldn't believe her ears. *Jonathan was never one to talk to himself.* Her great-uncle Conrad had started doing that one day, she knew, and he was never the same again. Martha shook her head. If anything like that happened to Jonathan, she just didn't know what she'd do.

.　　　.　　　.

In Cadmus Lab Seven, Drs. Tompkins and Johnson rolled Superman's body out of the cold storage unit as Dr. Rodrigues checked the calibrations on a sophisticated electron microscope. With a soft plastic probe, the doctors gently held open their subject's eye as a fine beam of coherent light was directed through the pupil and into the retina.

Sitting down at his computer keyboard, Rodrigues logged into a genetic analysis program and began entering the special entry codes:

DIR H: \\OPERATION KRYPTON

INITIATE ELECTRON-CAPILLARY SCAN.27/READ

TRIAL.012

The monitor suddenly came alive with color, as twisting, interlocking helixes swirled across the screen. Walter Johnson nearly dropped his pen. "My God, is that—?"

Rodrigues nodded. "The Kryptonian genome, gentlemen—or rather, a minute fragment of same. After cross-correlating a dozen scans, we're finally starting to see some results."

"I've never seen anything like it." Tompkins was frankly spellbound. "It's—big . . ."

"Yes, truly remarkable, really, that given such different genomes, the Kryptonian phenotype was so similar to that of *Homo sapiens*." Rodrigues's fingers danced across the keyboard, calling up additional screens of mathematical calculations and analyses of chemical compounds. "The program has already found ninety-eight chromosomes, and this is just the beginning. I believe we may need more memory before this is all mapped out."

"*If* it's ever all mapped out." Walt began flipping the button on his pen. "And even if we do succeed in mapping the whole thing, are we really going to be able to do anything with it?"

Several corridors away, Paul Westfield and Carl Packard sat in the administrator's office watching as Rodrigues's figures and computations played over a tapped-in monitor system.

"Remarkable. Absolutely remarkable." Packard marveled at the growing data. "We could spend years studying this information."

"The world can't wait years, Doctor, and neither can I." Westfield got up from his desk and started pacing. "We need a Superman now."

"But—but this . . ." Packard ran his hands around the edge of the screen as he groped for the right words. "It's revolutionary! It's all so complicated. Ninety-eight chromosomes! And there may be more. It would be different if we could obtain a tissue sample, but you're talking about trying to simulate an alien genome in terrestrial cells! How are we to determine which chromosomes hold the triggers to which powers?" Packard tugged at one corner of his mustache. "I mean, I suppose we could test theoretical models on the supercomputer array, but—"

"Then do so." Westfield picked up his phone. "I'll arrange authorization immediately. I'll provide whatever support is necessary to ensure our success."

As the Project administrator got on the line to the computer wing, Dr. Packard turned back to the monitor, mesmerized by the figures on the screen. Neither man was aware that their preparations were being observed from a ventilation duct in the wall behind Westfield's desk.

The observer was dressed all in black, from the goggled ski mask that covered his face to the two layers of wool socks on his feet. He listened silently as the logistics of Packard's work were mapped out, occasionally jotting down key words in a small pocket notepad. And then, with infinite care, he slowly slid away, taking care to make not a sound. For nearly five minutes, the masked observer worked his way through a maze of ductwork until finally he came to an open ventilator. He then swung down into a dimly lit bunkroom and was greeted with a chorus of questions.

"How'd it go? Did ya find it? Were ya able to see anything? Geez, I don't know why the rest of us couldn't go with ya. We could've been witnesses and everything and—"

Scrapper slapped a piece of duct tape over Gabby's mouth and around his head, effectively silencing the boy. "Yeah, an' Westfield woulda heard us comin' from a mile away. So pipe down already, an' give Words a chance to catch 'is breath."

Flip and Tommy climbed up on chairs to replace the ventilator wall grille as Big Words divested himself of his ski mask and heavy socks.

"How did it go, Words?" Tommy hopped down from his chair and turned it around to face the taller boy.

"Yeah, what's goin' down?"

"Plenty, Flip." Big Words adjusted his glasses. "To answer Gabby's queries—yes, I was most successful in locating the administrator's office. It appears that Mr. Westfield is conspiring with Dr. Packard to utilize the fruits of our fathers' studies, though whether with or without their knowledge, I was unable to determine."

"Then the bum is goin' ahead wit' plans to make his own Superman."

"So it would seem, Scrapper. And the longer the *corpus Kryptonus* resides at Cadmus, the greater the chances are that our esteemed administrator will see his Frankensteinian scheme to fruition."

Tommy smacked his hands together. "Then we have to get it out of here."

"Yeah, right." Flip just rolled his eyes. "I can just see the five of us trying to sneak a body out of the Project."

"Nrrr whrm ghrr frr drr crr!" Gabby gestured wildly with his elbows as he tried to ease the tape off his mouth.

"Jus' relax, Gabby." Scrapper grinned wickedly at his little pal. "You got an idea ya wanna share wit' us?"

Gabby nodded eagerly.

"Well, why din't ya say so?" Scrapper grabbed the end of the tape and gave a quick yank.

"Yeow! Geez, Scrapper, what're ya tryin' to do, take my lips off with that stuff?!"

"The way those things flap? Never happen. Now, if ya got an idea, spit it out—before I change my mind!" Scrapper playfully tossed the roll of tape from one hand to the other.

"Okay, okay!" Gabby gingerly pursed his lips. "The way I see it, maybe we can't get Superman out on our own, but we can get the word to someone on the outside."

"I believe our talkative little chum may have something there. After all, the Guardian did promise us some free time in Metropolis, and he seemed exceedingly eager to placate us after we discovered the contents of Laboratory Seven."

"Now yer talkin'! We get an afternoon in the city, an' the world finds out about what happened to Superman." Scrapper clapped Gabby across the back. "Yer finally startin' to use that bony head fer somethin' besides a hat rack!"

"I don't know." Flip looked skeptical. "Who's gonna believe us? After all, we're just kids! And besides, you know that the Guardian will be watching us like a hawk when we get to the city—*if* we get to go!"

"Aw, Guardian-shmardian! There's just one o' him an' five o' us! I can get by him—it'll be a piece o' cake!"

"Scrapper's assessment is perhaps overly confident, but we do have the advantage of numbers. As for your point, Flip, there is no need for us to physically approach an outside contact. We have but to prepare the proper presentation and enlist the services of a bonded courier, or barring that, a postal service employee."

Tommy rubbed his chin. "It could work. But we'll have to make sure we get enough evidence to be convincing."

"Shucks, that'll be easy, fellers." Gabby started rummaging through the old footlocker at the end of his bunk. "I got a camera and plenty of film. We can take pictures and draw diagrams and everything."

"That's good, Gabby, but we'll also have to find somebody outside the Project who we can trust with the info—somebody who'd want to do right by Superman."

"That ain't a problem, Tommy."

"You have an idea, Scrap?"

"Are you kiddin'? Gents, I got the answer right under my hat!" And with that, Scrapper doffed his cap and pulled out a battered newspaper article clipped from the pages of the *Daily Planet*.

17

Lex Luthor stood stripped to the waist, his upper torso coated with a thin sheen of sweat, as three athletic young women wearing karate *gi*s bowed toward him. He paused for a moment before returning the bow, reducing the act of respect to a mere formality. The women departed, and Luthor grabbed up a towel.

Luthor scowled as he dried off. He had taken up karate months ago, as a way of keeping his fine new body trim, but lately he found less and less satisfaction in his workouts. Neither the exercises, the kata, nor even the actual fighting brought him any pleasure. *There's no challenge anymore,* he thought, *no challenge in anything with Superman gone.*

For years, Superman had been Luthor's obsession, his one true rival in power. He had reveled in the Man of Steel's inability to bring him down and had come to look upon their competition as a game to be savored. But now the game was over, and while the industrialist had not lost, neither had he truly won.

Someone else killed him. Luthor threw the towel across the room. *And another crew of bastards stole his body!*

"Lex, is something wrong?" Supergirl pushed open the door of the little gym. "You look so angry!"

"Do I?" Luthor forced a smile. "Well, I'm just a bit peeved is all. Not a very good workout today, my timing was off. I was just about to hit the showers. Care to join me?"

"Lex!" Supergirl blushed and looked back toward the door. "Ms. Lane is waiting outside. I know you hate to be disturbed here, but she insists on speaking with you right away."

"Does she now? Well, then, love, show her right in."

Supergirl flashed him her wonderful smile, and Luthor felt the sharper edge of his irritation pass. *Things could be worse. Superman may be dead, but Supergirl most definitely* isn't.

He shrugged into a dressing robe as the reporter entered the gym. "G'day, Lois. How good to see you again. Has there been any word on Kent?"

"I'm afraid not." Lois briefly—but tightly, Lex noted—closed her eyes. "Thank you for asking. No, I'm here because I want you to read an article of mine before it goes to press."

Luthor raised an eyebrow. "A grand gesture to be sure, Lois. But why? If it involves LexCorp—"

Lois shook her head. "Once you read it, I think you'll understand." She glanced at Supergirl as she handed Luthor a file folder. "You both should read it."

Lois stepped back a pace or two, watching unobtrusively as the two most powerful people in Metropolis read her story together. She tried her best not to notice as Supergirl snuggled an arm around Luthor's waist.

Luthor skimmed over the pages, his face starting to turn a fiery red. Supergirl's fair skin did not flush, but her entire body seemed to tense.

At the back of the folder, Luthor came to a series of photographs, and he went bone white. Even his lips turned pale. "This—this is an outrage. The Cadmus Project has stolen Superman's body?!"

"Then you've heard of Cadmus?"

Luthor could tell Supergirl was about to say something, so he squeezed her hand tight, giving her their private look. She nodded her understanding, and he answered for them both. "I'm afraid we have, Lois. It seems to be some manner of clandestine federal agency, involved in all manner of mysterious goings-on. That Guardian fellow is mixed up with them somehow."

Luthor looked again at the series of photos. Though a bit amateurish in composition, they clearly showed Superman's body on an examination table. In some shots, the Cadmus insignia could be seen on the lab coats of surgically masked doctors and technicians. "Where did you get these?"

Lois shrugged her shoulders. "They arrived in a package from an anonymous source, along with a long letter. I would probably have discounted the whole thing if not for the pictures—and the response I got from the police."

"The police? What did they have to say?"

"It's what they *didn't* say that bothers me, Lex. I went directly to Maggie Sawyer over at the Special Crimes Unit and told her I'd gotten a tip that someone had tried to steal Superman's body. She stonewalled me, Lex. And from her reaction, I could tell she knew something. The information I received . . ." Lois shook her head. "I know it reads like science fiction, but I believe it, Lex. These federal spooks want to cut Superman up for cloning."

"A frightening thought, indeed." Lex carefully closed the folder but did not hand it back. "Does anyone else know?"

"No, not even my editor. Once I put the story together, I realized that if we ran it, the government would just deny everything and hide Superman's body somewhere else. That's why I came to you—to both of you." Lois looked from Luthor to Supergirl. "You're the only ones I know with enough power to ensure that Superman gets the treatment he deserves."

"I'm glad you came to me with this, Lois. I promise you that we'll get Superman back where he belongs and put Cadmus in its place for good!"

"You have our word on that, Lois." There was a determination in Supergirl's voice that Luthor found vaguely disquieting.

Luthor tapped the folder against his hand. "Do you mind if I hang on to this? We'll need the information in here to nail down the exact location of this 'Lab Seven.' "

"You can keep it, Lex. I have copies . . . of everything." Lois paused to make sure he understood. "Because if you *can't* do anything about this—I will."

At about two-thirty in the afternoon, Jonathan Kent had gone upstairs to take a nap. He hadn't meant to enter Clark's old room, but for some reason, he couldn't bring himself to walk past the door without looking inside.

It was dark in the room. The shades had been drawn to keep the sun from fading the spartan furnishings. Without clearly remembering how he'd gotten there, Jonathan sat down on the end of the bed. The memory of his son was very strong here.

In the shadows of the room, Jonathan could see Clark sitting there in the old armchair by the bed. *What a fine young man he's grown up to be.* "What's the matter, Clark? What's wrong?"

Clark slumped back into the chair. "I saw the plane fall, Pa. I saw it fall and I just leapt into the sky and saved it. And then, the mob arrived. They were like animals . . . clawing and screaming at me. Everybody had something they wanted me to do, Pa. *Everybody!* People wanted me to heal them. They wanted me to heal their children, their parents. They wanted the impossible and they all wanted it right away."

Clark raised his eyes to his father. "It felt wonderful to rescue the astronauts and that reporter. It felt . . . I can't begin to tell you how great it felt to carry a plane—a *plane,* Pa!—in my bare hands, and fly it to a safe landing."

He leaned forward, resting his big arms on his knees. "I know I have to use my powers to help people. I *want* to! But that was my first public appearance, and now they're going to be looking for me." Clark shook his head. "They wanted a piece of me, Pa. They all wanted a piece of me. And I . . . I don't know how to deal with that."

Jonathan felt tears coming to his eyes. "I think I do, son." He reached out to pat Clark on the shoulder, but his son was no longer there.

"Jonathan?" Martha walked into the room. "Who are you talking to? What are you doing, sitting in Clark's room here in the dark?"

"I had the idea, Martha." Jonathan just sat there, staring at the empty chair. "The costume . . . the dual identity. I loved him. I thought I was helping, but I wasn't. It's all my fault, Martha. I keep telling myself that I just didn't know how things would turn out, but that doesn't help."

Martha knelt in front of her husband and took his face in her hands. "Jonathan, dear, no! It's no more your fault than it was Lois's. You *know* that."

Jonathan said not a word. In desperation, Martha sat down beside him on the bed and put her arms around his shoulders. "Knowing isn't the same as feeling, but it's where we've got to start. It wasn't your fault, Jon. You *do* know that, don't you, honey?"

When he still didn't respond, Martha tightened her grip and leaned her head against his. "Jon, please. Say something."

Slowly, Jonathan reached up and stroked her hair. "I didn't know, Martha. I had such hopes. . . ."

Ten thousand feet above Mount Curtiss, Supergirl turned invisible and dove Earthward at a quarter of the speed of sound. Following the information supplied by Lois Lane, she braked sharply over the ruins of the Habitat tree city and sped into a camouflaged cave access at the base of the mountain. She flew on, unchallenged as she rocketed past three security checkpoints and into the central corridors of the Cadmus Project. The psychokinetic shields that rendered Supergirl invisible to the naked eye also made it impossible to detect her by radar or infrared sensors. The only noticeable sign of her passing was the inexplicable wind that rushed through the Project, ruffling hair and sending papers flying.

It wasn't until Supergirl reached Lab Seven that she truly made her presence known. Still invisible, she sank her hands into the six-inch-thick stainless steel doors of the secured laboratory and ripped them out of the wall. Within the lab, a surprised technician suddenly found himself grabbed up by his collar and thrown into a wall storage locker.

As bells and Klaxons began sounding all over the complex, Paul Westfield stormed into the Project's security command center. "What the hell is going on here? The alarms are going crazy!"

"I'm well aware of that." The Guardian acknowledged the administrator's presence with little more than a cursory glance. "There's been a major security breach, and we're in the process of tracking it down right now."

"What do you mean, 'tracking it down'? If there's been a break-in, which of the sentry posts detected it?"

"None of them." The Guardian leaned over the security master console and began zapping through a rapid succession of security camera images. "Apparently, some person or persons unknown have managed to enter the Project without being seen and are tearing up the central lab core."

"What?!" Westfield was aghast. "How is that possible?"

"It isn't, or at least it shouldn't be, but—my God!" The Guardian's finger froze on the touchpad as the security monitor showed Lab Seven —or rather, what was left of it. Virtually every piece of equipment in the lab had been torn apart. The only thing left untouched was a single storage locker; a plaintive knocking could be heard coming from within it. Most disturbing of all was the wreckage of the cold storage unit that had, until moments before, held the body of Superman. It was completely shattered, as if it had been battered apart with hammers. And Superman's body was missing!

The Guardian's jaw dropped. "Lord, did he come back to life?"

"Impossible!" Westfield snatched up a microphone. "Attention all posts, commence lockdown! Seal the Project!"

The Guardian grabbed the mike away from the hyperventilating administrator. "I already gave that order before you got here."

"Oh."

A speaker began to crackle, and the face of an uneasy security guard appeared on the monitor. "Guardian, this is post ten."

"Guardian here. What's your situation?"

"I don't know exactly. We were lowering the blast doors when they suddenly stopped, as if something was jamming them. But there's nothing there, and—hey!"

The guard suddenly went flying off-screen. There were a few more off-camera shouts, and then silence.

"Post ten, report!" The Guardian thumbed up the volume on the speaker. "Post ten! Is anyone there?"

There was an odd movement in the center of the screen, like heat rippling the air above a hot pavement. And then Supergirl shimmered into view.

She spoke but ten words: "Superman is coming with me. Don't *ever* touch him again!"

And then the monitor went blank.

Lois headed for Centennial Park the moment she got the call. When she arrived at the memorial plaza, it was just before two o'clock in the morning. It was a crisp, clear night and a small group of the Superman cultists were holding a vigil at the base of the tomb. As per the instructions she had been given, Lois skirted the edge of the plaza and surreptitiously crept along the east retaining wall to a spot where a maintenance van sat parked in front of a partially opened ventilator grating. Suddenly the door in the back of the van swung open and a light was shone in Lois's face.

"Hey!"

The light winked out and a big burly figure hopped out of the van. "Sorry, Miz Lane, I had to make sure it was you."

Lois blinked. "Inspector . . . Turpin, isn't it?"

"That's right, ma'am." Turpin tipped his derby. "Cap'n Sawyer's busy tonight on another detail, or she'd've been here herself. She said to give ya her apologies for not being able to level with ya before."

Lois looked around the side of the truck, watching the cultists. "How are we going to do this without drawing their attention?"

"Easy. We use the back door. The others are already down there, waitin' for us. Just follow me."

Moments later, Turpin ushered Lois through the underground access corridor and into the anteroom outside the crypt. Luthor and Supergirl looked up as they entered.

"Hello, Lois . . . Inspector." Supergirl went over and gave Lois a supportive hug. Of the others there, only she shared with Lois the secret of Superman's dual identity. And she could only imagine the agonies the reporter had endured.

The Girl of Steel took Lois by the arm and led her into the crypt for one last viewing. There, atop the marble slab, rested a new coffin, its lid open. In the half-light of the crypt, Lois saw the body of Superman in final repose. The sight of this man whom she had loved so much was almost too much for her. Lois gripped the edge of the coffin for support and bit her lip, using the pain to help her keep her composure.

"Are you all right?" Supergirl's concern was a hushed whisper in

Lois's ear. She wrapped her cape around them both, lending support to the reporter, as Luthor and Turpin entered the crypt.

"Yes." Lois raised her voice just enough that the two men would be able to hear. "Yes, I'm convinced that it's him. It couldn't be anyone else."

Supergirl nodded, and they both stepped outside.

Turpin ran his hand along one wall, inspecting the new masonry. Luthor patted it almost affectionately. "Granite facing over steel-reinforced concrete—with a new electronic sensor grid embedded in there. If anyone tries to break through this wall again, we'll have plenty of advance warning."

Turpin nodded and, hat in hand, filed by the coffin to verify the identity of its occupant one last time. Then Luthor helped lower the lid into place and followed the inspector out. No one noticed the half-smile on his face as Supergirl resealed the crypt.

Paul Westfield was up all night assessing the damage that had been done. The only thing that had survived Supergirl's rampage through Lab Seven had been the storage locker and the bewildered technician the security team had found inside. The computer files of Dr. Rodrigues's electron-capillary scans had been broken into and wiped. All they had left were the copies he had pirated for Dr. Packard's experimentation, and those were woefully incomplete.

Westfield was nodding off at his desk when the phone woke him. "Whoever this is, it had better be good!"

"Carl Packard here, Paul—and yes, it is very good!"

"You've found the key?"

"Well, not *the* key, perhaps, but certainly *a* key. It's on the sixty-third strand—"

"Save the details for later, Doctor. The question is, can you give me results?"

"Why, yes, of course. We can begin implementation immediately. Lab Thirteen is all set up and ready to go. All we need is your approval."

"My approv—?" Westfield choked off his laughter. "Did you think you had to ask?"

"Well, considering the circumstances . . ."

"Experiment Thirteen is green for go, Doctor. Give it all you've got— top priority!" Westfield started laughing hysterically as he hung up the phone. *Let Metropolis keep its dead hero. Within a month, I'll have myself a champion who'll make the entire Justice League look second-rate!* Westfield swung his feet up onto his desk. He could finally see his career on the rise again.

.　　　.　　　.

When Martha Kent woke up, Jonathan was nowhere to be seen. She'd been all through the house twice looking for him when she finally discovered him out behind the barn, staring off at the far field where they'd first found their son. The morning was cold, and the wind was bitter, but Jonathan's windbreaker dangled from one hand as though he wasn't aware he'd brought it along.

"Jonathan David Kent! What in heaven's name are you doing way out here in your shirtsleeves?! It's freezing!" Martha yanked the windbreaker from his hand and flung it over his shoulders. "Land sakes alive, put on this coat before you catch your death of cold, and come on back to the house! I swear, the past few days, you've shown less sense than a day-old turkey!"

"The *world* doesn't make any sense, Martha. Don't you see?" Jonathan gestured out toward the back field. "That's where the rocket brought Clark to Earth. He seemed so helpless then. I swore I'd protect him. I swore I'd keep him safe."

"And we did our best, Jon. That's all we can ever do. No, it isn't fair when parents have to bury their children, but we're not the first couple that that's happened to, and we won't be the last. We've got to go on, Jon. Do you think he'd want you to give up?"

When her husband didn't reply, Martha's anger flared, and she roughly shook his shoulder. "Answer me, Jonathan! Do you think he'd want you to give up? There are other people who need us. *I* need you!"

"Martha, I failed him. I keep thinking how he said, 'They all wanted a piece of me!'" Jonathan shook his head. "And now he's lost to us. He's lost to us all! He's gone, Martha! He's—"

Jon's eyes seemed to go out of focus. He clutched at his chest and crumpled to the ground. Martha tried to catch him, falling to her knees as his breath wheezed out.

"Jonathan? Oh, Jonathan! Not you, too!"

18

Martha was never sure what happened next. She knew that she must have gotten to the phone and called for help, and she had a vague memory of riding alongside her husband in an ambulance. The next thing she knew, she was standing in the emergency entrance of the Lowell County Hospital, and Eugene Lanning, their family physician, was running up to her.

"Martha, I just got a call that Jon has been brought in. What happened?"

"Oh, Gene, I don't know." She hugged the doctor's arm as if it were a lifeline. "The paramedics said it was his heart."

"Well, don't you worry, Martha. I've been doctoring Jonathan for a long time, and if anyone can pull through this it's him! He's healthy as an ox!"

"I hope so, Gene. I dearly hope so. Jonathan hasn't been himself for days! What with Clark gone, and all . . ."

"Yes, yes, I know. You just have a seat there. I'll do everything that I can."

Lanning slipped through the curtains of the emergency OR. The emergency room intern, he saw, had already connected Jonathan to the hospital's oxygen system and was hooking him up to the heart monitor. The farmer's shirt had long since been ripped open; he looked as pale and worn as old linen.

The intern glanced up at the doctor. "Your patient?"

Lanning nodded. "What's his status?"

"EMTs reported a fibrillation when they found him. They bagged him, shocked his heart back to a normal rhythm, and set up an IV." The young woman shook her head. "His pulse is very weak; respiration is shallow."

Jonathan muttered something, his voice all but unintelligible through the breathing tube.

"Now, you listen here, Jonathan Kent!" Lanning grabbed his patient's hand. "You and I have been friends too long a time for you to check out on me like this! I want you to fight with me, Jonathan! Fight!"

Jonathan's eyes fluttered and his lips moved weakly. "C-Clark . . ."

The heart monitor began to show a wild pattern of beats and then a straight, flat line.

"Shoot some epinephrine into him!" Lanning centered his hands on Jonathan's sternum and began to pump. "C'mon, Jon, you old cuss— live!"

From Jonathan's point of view, the world had become a bright but misty place. It was as if he'd stumbled into an iridescent fog. The light was brilliant, almost blinding white straight ahead of him, and he could swear that he saw Clark standing there, as if waiting for him.

"Clark? Is that you, son?" Jonathan grasped the other man's hand tightly, not in a handshake, but in a firm grip, the way you would reach to pull someone away from terrible danger.

"I can't stay long, Pa." Clark stood unmoving in the light.

Jonathan held tight and pulled along the other man's arm, clutching at his shirt. "Clark, it *is* you! I've found you at last." A look of relief filled the old farmer's face. "Hold on, son, we're going home."

Clark shook his head and abruptly pulled away.

"Son, wait! Come back!" Jonathan tightened his grip on Clark's shirt, but the fabric tore and came apart in his hands. The rest of Clark's street clothes swiftly fell away in tatters until he stood revealed in his Superman uniform. He removed his glasses and spoke slowly, patiently, as if Jonathan were the son.

"I have to go, Pa. The light is pulling at me, compelling me to enter."

"No! Don't leave me, Clark!"

"I must. Clark is already gone. These glasses . . . these scraps of cloth . . ." Superman gestured to the shredded clothing drifting around him. "They are all that remain of Clark Kent." His voice changed— becoming lower and deeper, as Clark's voice always did when he spoke as Superman—but now it was different, detached. "From here on, the journey must be made by Kal-El, the Last Son of Krypton. Go back and rejoin the living, Jonathan Kent. The voices whisper to me that your time has not yet come." Superman pressed Clark's glasses into Jonathan's hand and began to drift away.

"Not my time? It isn't your time either, son!"

But Superman had turned his back on Jonathan and was already some distance away. Before the farmer's eyes, two shrouded figures emerged from the mists to escort the Man of Steel on toward the light. "Do not delay, Kal-El. Your destiny awaits."

Jonathan desperately swam through the mists after them. "Clark, listen to me—don't go! Let me go in your place!"

Superman half-turned back toward his father, but one of the figures restrained him and thrust a wraithlike arm toward the farmer. "You cannot exchange places, Jonathan Kent, and you cannot cross over with us."

"That's right, Jon." Superman seemed more distant than ever. "Martha needs you back home. She needs you now more than ever."

The other wraith pulled at Superman's hand. "We must go on."

"Good-bye, Pa. I love you . . ." Superman turned away again and the three of them were engulfed by the brilliant whiteness.

"No! No, I'm not letting you go!" Without hesitation, Jonathan dove after them, into the blinding light.

"We've got a heartbeat!" The intern took a deep breath and slowly let it out. "It's not strong, but it's regular."

"I'll settle for that . . . for now." Dr. Lanning ran the back of his hand across his brow and started scribbling instructions onto a notepad. "Administer lidocaine and call me if there's any change."

Martha scrambled to her feet as the doctor came out into the emergency room's waiting area. "Gene, is he—?"

"He's alive, Martha." Lanning accepted the woman's grateful hug, deciding it was best to give her at least a few moments of relief before he gave her the rest of the news.

"Can I see him?"

"That wouldn't be a good idea just yet, Martha. We did have a bad moment in there. His heart stopped beating and we almost lost him."

"Oh, dear God!" Martha's eyes widened in horror.

"I said *almost*! We got it started again. His heart's beating regularly again, but still very weakly." Lanning put his arm around Martha and led her down the hall. "The best thing we can do for him now is to move him into the intensive care unit and keep watch on his condition."

"Gene . . . what are his chances?"

"Hard to say." The doctor looked worn with frustration. "He's in a light coma right now. Hopefully, that will pass."

"Martha!" Lana Lang came running down the hall toward her. The two women embraced and stood holding each other for several minutes.

"Lana, how—?"

"The Colemans called and told me. I've called Lois. She's catching the first flight out." Lana glanced from Martha to the doctor. "How is he?"

Lanning could only shrug. "Stable, for now. The next few hours will tell us more."

Lana tightened her grip as she felt the older woman sag against her. "It'll be okay, Martha. Why, Jonathan's one of the strongest men I know."

"Oh, Lana." Martha wanted to smile but couldn't. "You're a dear to say that. But . . . in all our years together, with all the ups and downs we've faced, I've never been so scared that Jonathan was going to die."

Jonathan Kent emerged from the light into a jungle he recognized immediately from his army days. He was in full field uniform with helmet and rifle. He wasn't sure why he was there, but he knew he had a mission. Yes—his unit had been assigned to liberate a captured airman.

He eased up a rise and cautiously peered over the edge. The men of his unit were sprawled all over the ground beyond—dead, all of them, from the look of things. Jonathan steeled himself to check every mangled body, just to be sure, but his first assessment was right; he was the only survivor. Near one body, he found a field telephone.

"Mission command, do you read? Over." He tried again and again, using all the passwords he could remember, but it was no use. *Radio's dead. Everyone around here is dead, except for me. I'm the only one who can bring that airman back. It's all up to me.* He started walking. *There's just no way we can abandon one of our own.*

There was a light in the near distance, and smoke. Jonathan found what was left of a tiny hamlet, still on fire. There were more bodies here, civilians this time. He swallowed hard, trying to steady his stomach, and again began to check the bodies. *More death. Enemy's been through here, too. God knows why they burned out these poor villagers; none of them is armed.*

One of the villagers looked strangely different from the others. He was taller than the rest, and as Jonathan drew near, he saw that the man was dressed in bib overalls. *Funny that I didn't notice his clothes before. Dressed like that, he almost puts me in mind of my brother. . . .*

Jonathan gently turned the man over and jumped back in shock. "Harry?!" *Dear God in heaven, it is my brother. But that makes no sense. Harry never went overseas. He died long before he was old enough to join the army.* But the man on the ground was undeniably Harry Kent.

"Harry? Can you hear me?" Jonathan eased an arm under his brother's head, and the man's eyes flickered open. "Harry, what in heaven's name are you doing here in this Godforsaken jungle?"

Harry looked like death warmed over, and his voice echoed as if coming from the bottom of a deep well. "What am I doing here? Don't you *remember,* Jonny? I'm *dead.* I fell under the thresher back on Pa's farm. We're all dead here. Except you. You're not quite gone yet. And that other one ain't either."

Harry coughed, the phlegm rattling in his throat. "As for where this is, you got me. It ain't really a jungle, that's for sure, but the enemy . . . the enemy *has* got your boy. They can't be far away, Jonny. Go get him. Go find him while you can . . ." Harry sighed and closed his eyes.

Jonathan shook him, gently at first, and then frantically. "Harry Kent, don't you go dyin' on me again! Please! I'll find that airman, I swear. Just stay with me, Harry!"

"The boy don't belong here, Jonny." Harry's body sagged, limp and lifeless, to the ground.

From behind, another voice cut into Jonathan's grief. "He is wrong. The airman *does* belong here, but you, Jonathan Kent, do not."

Jonathan whipped around, sweeping the enemy soldier's gun hand away with one fist and knocking him cold with the other. "Damn your lying eyes!" Jonathan glowered down at the fallen enemy. "Damn you straight to hell!" As if to oblige, the enemy's flesh melted away to smoke. In seconds, all that was left was a soiled and tattered uniform.

Jonathan took a hasty step back and then a couple more. He looked around for his brother's body but found nothing. He dragged a hand across his face. *Combat fatigue. First I'm talking to Harry, God rest his soul, and then I start fighting a ghost. And none of this gets me any closer to that airman.*

He turned and pushed deeper into the jungle.

In room 112 of the Lowell County Hospital's intensive care unit, Martha and Lana sat side by side in a couple of straight-backed chairs, watching the slow rise and fall of Jonathan's chest. They'd sat there for over three hours, mostly in silence, listening to the soft hiss of the oxygen feed and the soft, steady beep of the heart monitor. Together, the two sounds had an almost hypnotic effect. After a while, Lana began to think of the beep almost as Jonathan's mantra. *He lives for as long as it sounds. Once it stops . . .* She shuddered and tried to banish that thought from her head.

"Martha, are you sure I can't get you something? Cup of coffee? No? How about some water?" Lana ducked into the bathroom and emerged moments later with two paper cups of water. "Here, you won't do Jonathan any good by letting yourself get dehydrated."

"Thank you, dear." The water was gone in a second, and Lana gave Martha the other cup. "I guess I am a little dry."

Martha sipped her second cup more slowly. "You know, Lana, Gene—Dr. Lanning—had told Jonathan that he should relax more, try to avoid stress." She took another sip. "Jon's way of relieving stress was through hard physical labor. And that worked fairly well when he was younger, but . . . well, he's no spring chicken anymore. Neither one of us is. We've both been through so much in the past weeks." Martha stared down at her reflection in the cup. "I can't help but wonder if Jon somehow brought this attack on himself, to try to get closer to Clark. He loved that boy as much as life itself."

"Don't even think that, Martha. When I was just a little girl, my Aunt Helen told me how Jonathan had been a prisoner of war, and how he'd managed to escape. 'That Jonny Kent's got the persistence of a bulldog,' she used to say. 'Once he sets his sights on something, he doesn't give up till he gets it.' And, you know, I never knew my Aunt Helen to lie."

Lana patted Martha's hand. "He fought his way out of that POW camp, and he'll fight his way back to us. You'll see."

Jonathan emerged from the jungle onto a wide rolling plain, as green as the prairie in spring. He could have sworn he was somewhere in southeastern Kansas, or possibly Missouri, if not for the city in the distance. It was a series of spires, all of them thousands of feet tall, and the tallest seemed to stretch at least a mile into the sky. No such city had ever existed on Earth, yet Jonathan recognized it immediately. It was something that Clark had told him and Martha all about. . . .

Years ago, long after Clark had adopted the identity of Superman, he had finally discovered the secrets of his origin. On a visit back to Kansas, he'd accidentally activated an electro-psionic recording, sent to Earth by his Kryptonian father, Jor-El, along with his birthing matrix. That recording had fed images from the history of Clark's homeworld directly into his mind. He had learned all about the lost world of Krypton, and how it had been destroyed—shattered by a supercritical nuclear reaction within the planet's core. He learned that his mother's name was Lara—that *his* name would have been Kal-El had he been born on that doomed world—and that he was Krypton's sole survivor.

Clark had described those images in detail to his parents many times. And here, now, on this green plain, Jonathan knew without a doubt that he was looking at a city from the Fifth Historic Age of Krypton.

There it is, Clark, just as I visualized it from your stories. The world of Krypton. Jonathan scrambled to the top of a low ridge and slowly scanned the horizon. He'd made no more than a quarter turn when he saw a parade.

It was just a small procession, really, a curious combination of high and low tech. Several men wearing the black bodysuits and long flowing tunics of Krypton's Seventh and Final Historic Age marched along carrying flags and banners embroidered with the Superman S-shield. They were followed by a cluster of servitor robots that hovered in midair, looking like wingless metal wasps. Walking alongside was a white-haired individual in a flowing black robe who had the bearing and manner of a clergyman. And in the middle of it all, four pale men in Kryptonian garb bore up a gleaming metal sedan chair upon which sat a slumped and listless Superman. He appeared to be drugged or sleeping.

The white-haired cleric was keeping pace with Superman, praying loudly and gesturing with great sweeps of his arms. "Oh, Great Rao, accept this Last Son of Krypton into your embrace! Allow him entrance into your realm, that he may be reunited with the family of El."

"Family of El, my foot!" Jonathan came charging down the ridge, bellowing at the top of his lungs. "If you guys are real Kryptonians, how come *I* can understand you?!"

The procession didn't stop, but it slowed, as the Kryptonians turned to stare at the strange, uniformed human who was running toward them. One of the flag bearers moved to stop Jonathan, but he feinted to the man's right and then darted past him on the left.

"Son! You're on the wrong path! You've got to wake up."

"Silence this blasphemer!" The cleric's voice shook with a cold fury. He rose up between Jonathan and his son, throwing out his arms to block the Earthman's path. More flag bearers surrounded Jonathan and began dragging him away from the chair.

"Cleric?" Superman raised his head slightly. "Who disturbs my journey?"

"One who does not belong, Kal-El." The cleric's voice dropped to a more even tone, but he still looked angry.

Jonathan drew a deep breath. "Don't believe that baloney, son! These aren't real Kryptonians, they can't be! And that black-robed creep is about as saintly as a rabid mule!"

"A rabid mule? Pa?" Superman looked up from the chair, faintly puzzled. "Pa, is that you? What are you talking about?"

"Ignore him, Kal-El, and stay with us." The cleric assumed an injured air and put a hand on the Man of Steel's shoulder. "Your legacy beckons. He is but an outsider, with no respect for things Kryptonian."

"Oh, yeah?!" Jonathan shook off a hand that was trying to silence him. "Those litter bearers of yours are dressed like Kryptonians from their last days, but that city back there—that's from Krypton's Fifth Age. The last of those buildings fell over a hundred thousand years before anyone dressed like these phonies!"

The cleric now had both hands on Superman's shoulders. "Ignore his ranting, Kal-El." The cleric glared angrily at the others, who fought to drag Jonathan further away. Jonathan made himself a dead weight to slow their progress as much as he could and drew another deep breath.

"That smooth talker called on the name of Rao—the name of Krypton's sun! Since when were Kryptonians a bunch of sun worshipers?!"

Superman sat bolt upright, his puzzled look turning suspicious.

"That's it, boy—open your eyes! They're taking you the wrong way! They're as genuine as a three-dollar bill!"

Superman quickly scanned the litter bearers and turned fully to the cleric. "Something *is* different about them, Cleric. And about you."

"The heretic confuses you." The cleric's smile was meant to be soothing, but there was desperation on his face. Jonathan was still close enough that he saw the cleric's features appear to momentarily ripple. From the way Superman's fist shot out, Jonathan knew that his son had also seen the partial transformation.

The "cleric" dropped like a stone, transforming into a demonic, shrouded wraith as he fell. Shocked, the others froze, transforming themselves, and Jonathan squirmed to twist free of a tentacled "hand."

"That's it, son—give 'em hell! They'd have tried to take you there. But we'll show 'em now! Let 'em know they're in for a fight when they cross the Kents!"

Outside a United States scientific research station on the Antarctic peninsula, two men stood in the subzero cold as if mesmerized. To the south, lightning snaked back and forth between two banks of roiling clouds, and above that display, the eerie, multicolored bands of the aurora australis flared and swirled in a curtain of light.

One of the men let out a low, mournful whistle, the moisture of his breath instantly freezing on his balaclava. "Some light show! What the devil is going on out there, Steve?"

"Boy, you've got me, Marty. I've spent five of the past ten years down here, and I've never seen the aurora flare up like this." Steve shook his head. "And that lightning—it's unreal!"

Marty shuddered. "Feels like the air around us is carrying a charge. I don't like this, Steve. We'd better get inside."

As the two men turned to reenter the research station, Marty looked back over his shoulder at the aerial display. "Hey, could all this be a side effect of that growing hole in the ozone layer?"

"Possibly." Steve stopped to knock the compacted snow from the soles of his boots. "More charged particles might be streaming in. I don't know, though . . . that lightning storm looks to be centered just beyond the Ellsworth Mountains. A lot of weird electromagnetic phenomena have been reported in that area recently." He stared up into the skies. "Something like this makes you realize how much there is that we still don't know."

The storm *was* centered beyond the Ellsworth Mountains, but the real nucleus of activity lay buried hundreds of feet below the surface in the Kryptonian Fortress. There, wasplike robots, identical to those of Krypton's ancient past, flitted around a spherical containment field as energies rippled within. One robot paused to receive data from another. "Has the intelligence been completely isolated?"

"Negative. The Master's essence dispersed following the dysfunction of the corporeal body." The answering robot completed a complex mathematical calculation and continued. "Retrieval has been limited to 98.073 percent. Despite the loss, there is a 79.237 percent chance for reconstruction. We will continue the process."

Superman tore through the demon wraiths, *mowing them down just like they were weeds,* thought Jonathan. Two robotic shapes swooped down on the Man of Steel, taking on wraithlike qualities as they approached. "You must not resist death's grip," squawked one. "There can be no turning back!"

Superman reached up, catching one robotic wraith in each hand, and smashed them together. Their remains melted away to smoke, and Superman leapt to Jonathan's side in a single bound. "Pa! Are you all right?!"

"Never better, son. Or at least, I will be once we hightail it out of here." Jonathan grabbed Superman by the arm and turned to run, but his son had set his feet. It was like trying to drag a mountain. "Clark, *now* what's got into you?!"

"Pa, I can't go back. You were right about these phony Kryptonians—I won't follow them anymore—but I can't go back to Earth either. I've been gone too long."

"Horseapples! I didn't come all this way to hear you talk like that! You're a Kryptonian, the last of your kind. Son, you can't walk through death's doorway willingly."

"It was hardly 'willingly,' Pa." Superman started to shake his head. Then he abruptly wrapped his arm around his father and leapt into the air.

Jonathan coughed and caught his breath. "Th-that's more like it, son."

"I'm just taking you away from this, Pa. That's all."

"Like hell, 'that's all'! Clark, listen to me. For the first years of your life, you thought you were a human being—stronger than most, but human. You grew up on our farm and you saw things get born, and you watched them live, and you saw them die. You grew up thinking that someday you would die, too . . . but maybe it doesn't have to be that way at all. Don't you understand, son? For once I'm begging you not to think like an Earthling!"

A dark tunnel opened up in the misty skies in front of them. Behind them once more was the dazzling light. Superman hovered before the tunnel but began drifting back toward the light.

"Pa, this is as far as I can take you. I'm telling you, I've been away too long already. Pa, you yourself said it . . . I *am* the last Kryptonian. Billions of my people have died. Why would I be the sole exception?"

"There are no exceptions." The voice came from everywhere and nowhere; it was very deep and very cold. A tall figure dressed in black stepped out of the light. His resemblance to Superman was unmistakable.

"Jor-El!" Superman looked stunned, and Jonathan himself felt badly shaken.

Jor-El inclined his head. "It is good that you recognize me, Kal-El." He turned sternly to the Earthman. "My son must come with me, Jonathan Kent. You must cease your interference."

"Like hell I will! Maybe Clark will die someday, but it doesn't have to be now!"

"I regret that it does. I correctly predicted the destruction of Krypton, and I am correct in this matter as well." Jor-El extended a hand toward Superman. "Come. You know that I have always looked after you. You survived our homeworld's destruction only because I sent your birthing matrix to the Earth."

"Looked after him, my eye!" Jonathan stormed up to Jor-El. "Yeah, you sent him to Earth, where he might have died for all you knew! You blindly hoped that someone would find your son and bring him up—and, by God, someone did. My wife and I raised your boy, and we love him like he was our own. And dammit, I am *not* going back without him!"

Jor-El actually took a step back. His face didn't ripple, as had the false cleric's, but he did look uncertain.

Jonathan whirled around. "You see, son? He *isn't* sure! Now let's get going."

"I still don't know, Pa."

Jonathan grabbed Superman by the wrist and stared squarely down the dark tunnel. "Have a little faith in your old man, son. What have you got to lose? Let's just do it!"

"Martha?" A woman peered in from the doorway.

"Lois! Oh, Lois—" Martha leapt to her feet and hugged the younger woman to her. "You didn't have to come all this way!"

"Shhh! It's okay. I wanted to be here. I don't know how much good I can do, but I'll do everything I can." Lois looked up, tears in her eyes. "Hello, Lana."

"Lois. You made good time."

"The advantages of being an army brat! I called in an old favor and caught a ride on a transport flight. How's Jonathan doing?"

Before either woman could answer, the heart monitor beside Jonathan's bed began beeping louder. Martha stifled a scream, and Lana lunged for a call button, but Dr. Lanning and a staff cardiologist were already charging into the room.

"Is . . . is it bad, Gene?"

"No, Martha." Lanning slipped his stethoscope across his patient's chest. "I think it's good; very good, in fact. Jon's heart is beating good and strong . . . blood pressure's back to normal . . . and his breathing—"

Jonathan suddenly coughed and reached up, pulling out his endotracheal tube before the startled doctors could stop him. He blinked and drew in a long, deep, satisfied breath. "Made it!"

He looked up to see his wife staring down at him, her mouth open wide. "Martha! Martha, honey, we're back."

"Oh, yes!" Martha gently framed his face between her hands. She could hardly see him through her tears. "Yes, thank God, you're back!"

"Not just me, Martha." A tear trickled down Jonathan's cheek. "I found our boy. Clark's come back, too. He's come back . . ."

"Jonathan, you don't know what you're saying."

"Course I do, honey." Jonathan smiled up at Martha and squeezed her hand, startling her with the strength of his grip. A movement caught his eye, and he looked past her at the two young women standing near the foot of his bed.

"Lana? And is that Lois? Hey, don't cry now. Don't you worry . . . everything's going to be all right. You'll see." He gave a huge yawn. "I'll tell you all about it later. Right now, I'm all in."

Within minutes, Jonathan was sound asleep, his vital signs rock steady.

Martha, Lana, and Lois quietly slipped from the room and gathered with Dr. Lanning and the cardiologist for coffee at the nurses' station. The cardiologist stirred creamer into her cup and shook her head with amazement. "You know, I started out as an EMT. I've seen a lot of cardiac cases over the years, but I've never seen a recovery as abrupt and as strong as your husband's, Mrs. Kent."

"Do you really think he'll be all right?" Martha nervously tore at a packet of sweetener.

"Don't you worry now, Martha." Lanning patted her hand reassuringly. "We'll have him back on his feet in no time."

"Doctor . . . what Jonathan said after he woke up—" Lois played absentmindedly with her engagement ring. "About Clark? Was that delirium?"

The cardiologist looked at her colleague. "Your call, Gene. You know the man better than I do."

"He didn't seem delirious, Ms. Lane." Lanning took a long swallow and looked back toward the room. "My guess is that he was recalling some manner of mild hallucination he'd had while his heart had stopped."

"I see." Lois turned away and stared off out the west window at the bright, full moon. *An hallucination . . . just an old man's dream. I wish it were true, but I saw Clark's body in the tomb myself. He won't be coming back.* Her tears again began to flow. Martha and Lana were tearing up, too, and she knew with certain sorrow that they were thinking the same thing. *None of us will ever see Clark again.*

SECTION THREE

REIGN OF THE SUPERMEN

19

In a cold, sterile chamber in the Fortress of Solitude, far beneath the ice of Antarctica, an eerie standing energy wave began to form. The roiling, seething forces trapped within the spherical containment field seemed to coalesce. Over a series of hours, the energy compacted further, outlining a vaguely manlike shape curled up as if in a fetal position. Slowly, this Energy Man unfolded, emerging in a crackling discharge through the containment field.

Several small Kryptonian robots that had been adjusting and maintaining the field wheeled about to observe the emergent Energy Man.

"Where am I? I remember a battle . . ." The Energy Man looked about, confused. "I know this place. This is my Fortress—but how did I get here?"

The robots clustered together, going on-line in silent communication.

"He lives! Our programming has been successful!"

"Interesting. The energy form's vibrations are producing sounds."

"He is still disoriented. He attempts to vocalize in English. We must respond in kind."

One of the robots broke off from the cluster and approached the Energy Man. "Do not fear. You are safe here."

"What is going on?" The Energy Man reached out to the robot, but his faintly glowing "hand" passed through the metal form, causing a disruptive energy discharge at the point of entry. Sparking and sputtering, the robot darted away, swaying drunkenly.

The Energy Man inspected his hand. "I—I'm immaterial. What has happened to me?"

A second robot approached, keeping a cautious distance. "You were rendered discorporate, Master. We had created a mobile field effect to collect and contain your essence."

"Discorporate? Then all that's left of me is a disembodied intelligence?" The concept seemed too much for the Energy Man to bear. He'd begun to curl back up into a ball when he noticed a huge bank of video screens in the chamber beyond. *The monitors! The Professor—Hamilton?—had adjusted them to receive and record satellite transmissions.* A hope grew within his mind. *Perhaps it can show me something that will help me remember.*

The Energy Man half-walked, half-floated toward the monitor bank and reached for the control panel. Sparks flew as his hand passed through the panel. *This will never do.* "Robot, activate the monitor bank. Program it to display any and all recent news dealing with Superman."

The robot rushed to comply, and the screens flashed with a rapid montage of scenes—from grainy telephoto shots of the Doomsday monster battling Superman through the city of Metropolis to sharp close-ups of mourners lining the route of the long funeral procession. Accompanying the images was a chorus of voices.

". . . Justice League was ruthlessly attacked by a creature that is being called Doomsday . . ."

"Following a cross-country chase, Superman has faced off against Doomsday in the very heart of Metropolis . . ."

"Superman has reportedly been seriously injured . . ."

". . . declared dead at approximately 6:23 PM eastern time."

". . . the solemn drumbeat as the world's great heroes march along in tribute, following their gallant leader one last time."

"The world will long remember this great man, who sacrificed his own life to end the threat of Doomsday . . . God bless him."

The Energy Man looked on aghast. "Dead? Discorporate?"

The last of the video screens showed a slow pan down the huge granite statue of Superman to a crowd of people gathered at its base. "Mourners continue to visit his tomb in Metropolis's Centennial Park, leaving tributes to this Last Son of Krypton who grew up to become the most American of heroes."

"No! It can't end this way!" The Energy Man turned away from the screens. "The body! There must still be power in the body!" The Energy Man arose, passing through the ceiling of the Fortress like a ghost.

At 4:27 that morning, there were only three people to be seen around Superman's tomb. A uniformed city policeman rocked back and forth on the balls of his feet near the edge of the plaza; it was his job to be there.

A stoop-shouldered old bag lady who had nowhere else to go came pushing a shopping cart across the paving stones, muttering to herself. And a man stood before the tomb at that late hour; his grief had brought him there. He paused to secure a skullcap to his head and knelt amid the flowers at the base of the tomb and began to pray.

"O God, full of mercy, who dwells on high, grant proper rest on the wings of the divine presence—in the lofty levels of the holy and the pure ones who shine like the glow of the firmament—for the soul of Superman. May his resting place be in the Garden of Eden—therefore may the Master of Mercy shelter him in the shelter of His winds for Eternity. And may He bind his soul in the bond of life. HASHEM is his heritage, and may he repose in peace on his resting place. Amen."

Tears in his eyes, the man rose and walked slowly from the tomb. The policeman watched the man leave, feeling a bit misty-eyed himself. He'd pulled park duty several times over the past two weeks, and in that time he'd heard prayers to every conceivable deity in more languages than he'd ever realized existed. *Everybody misses Superman. Just not as many tonight . . . too cold for 'em, I guess. There've been barely fifty people here since midnight. I hope they're not starting to forget him already.*

The officer was roused from his thoughts by an electronic squawk and a garbled voice from his walkie-talkie: "One-Baker-sixty-three . . . see a man at Bessolo and Park Entrance South . . . stolen car reported."

"One-Baker-sixty-three. On my way!" The policeman turned and sprinted from the plaza.

The old bag lady looked around cautiously and then pushed her cart up to the tomb. "Uuhm. Pretty flowers." She plucked a thornless rose from one of the bouquets that had been left in tribute. "Pretty, pretty. Never miss one."

The bag lady was still sniffing her treasure when the Energy Man dropped down from the sky beside her. She seemed not to pay him any attention, and that gave him pause. *The Fortress robots could perceive me; why doesn't she? Is she that lost within her own mind? Or is it simply that no human being can easily perceive me in this state?* He pondered the question for but a moment before turning and passing through the side of the tomb. So swift was his passage that his energies shut down the tomb's security net before it could send a single alarm.

Dropping down into the crypt, the Energy Man hovered over Superman's coffin; he could sense a raw power stirring within it. *Over thirty years of bioconverted solar energy is stored in the body. If I can't reclaim it, I'll forever remain an immaterial phantom.* He reached through the coffin and into Superman's body.

A brilliant energy discharge crackled about the body, and the Energy Man shook as if in the throes of some seizure, his scream echoing off the walls of the crypt. Outside, the entire tomb began to glow, and this the bag lady noticed immediately. "Oh! I . . . I'm sorry! You can have the flower back!" She tossed the rose back onto the pile as tiny bolts of lightning crackled off the big statue, and scrambled off across the plaza, dragging her cart after her.

Back inside the crypt, the Energy Man was gone. A tall, powerfully built form arose in his place and stepped back from the opened coffin, clutching a long, flowing cape in his hands. *The cape! I can touch it . . . hold it! I'm alive again . . . alive! But I feel so strange . . . light-headed.*

He staggered across the crypt, feeling unsteady on his feet, and set one hand against a wall to brace himself. He could feel a slight tingling in his palm and realized with a start that there was a gridwork of electrical circuitry buried within the walls. *There are control systems here . . . alarms coming on-line . . . I can somehow sense them. And beyond that wall lies some sort of passageway! Who would put such things in a tomb?* The idea disturbed him so that—almost without his thinking—a small surge of energy leapt through his fingertips and into the wall grid, effectively overriding the rebooted security systems.

"The air . . . musty in here. Got to get out."

He shoved open the crypt's vaultlike door, only to recoil as the antechamber's automatic lighting switched on. He threw up his arms and drew the cape around him to shield his eyes from what was to him a blinding glare. *Something is wrong. I have stared into the sun before without ill effect; how could any artificial light source induce such pain? Something has changed within me. I'm not safe here—I must return to the Fortress.*

Henry Johnson was awakened from a deep sleep by the sound of an exploding car. He threw on a pair of pants and ran out into the street just in time to see a teenage boy dancing gleefully around the burning wreck of what had just moments before been a late-model Cadillac. From the smell that drifted up the street, Henry knew that there'd been someone alive inside. He bent over and just managed to keep the contents of his stomach down.

When Henry looked up again, he saw that the boy had in hand a gun about the length and width of a car muffler. The gun looked ludicrously huge in the boy's hands, but the sight of it drove the big man wild with anger. Henry charged forward, grabbing hold of the gun barrel, and yanked the weapon away before the youth knew what hit him. Enraged, the former engineer slammed the gun down hard against the pavement, cracking its plastic and aluminum stock.

"Hey, man, leggo my Toastmaster!" The boy jumped on Henry's back, punching and clawing.

"Toastmaster?" Henry whipped around and grabbed the boy by the front of his baseball jacket. "Toastmaster?! Where did you get this—this piece of filth?!" Henry shook the boy until his teeth rattled. "Answer me!"

"N-no way. I'm a Shark. Sharks don't have to answer to nobody!"

Henry stared hard at the boy under the glare of a streetlight. *My God, he can't be more than fifteen.* He nodded back toward the burning wreck. "Why?"

The boy grinned. " 'Cause I'm a Shark. An' 'cause I could!"

The words were still ringing in Henry's ears long after the police had taken the boy away.

". . . 'cause I could."

Those were the words of someone with nothing to lose; of someone who knew no hope and saw no future.

". . . 'cause I could."

John Henry did not bother returning to his room. He knew he wouldn't get back to sleep.

He went down into the basement and got to work. He had to put an end to this madness. At the very least, he had to get those big guns off the street.

In his second-floor walk-up, Bibbo had risen unusually early and begun rummaging through a battered old chest of drawers. He stopped to sniff various items of clothing, tossing some onto the bed and others onto a growing pile of laundry in the corner. After a few minutes of furious sorting, Bibbo had a clean pair of blue sweatpants, a brilliant crimson pair of satin boxing trunks, and a blue sweatshirt laid out across his bed. He looked at his ensemble for a moment, then nodded his approval and started to get dressed.

Bibbo paused for a moment after pulling on the sweatpants and gazed up reverently toward a grimy skylight in the ceiling.

"Hullo, Sooperman? This's yer ol' pal Bibbo. I hope God don't mind if we talk awhiles. We all miss ya, Sooperman—we miss ya terrible bad. I been thinkin' 'bout ya a lot, pal. It just ain't the same here without ya."

Bibbo picked up the sweatshirt—his official Superman sweatshirt—and stared at the pentagonal emblem. "These shirts . . . ya coulda made a mint from merchandizin', but ya never kept a dime! Ya always gave your part to charity . . . a real share-the-wealth kinda guy . . . jus' like me!"

Atop the chest of drawers, an old clock radio clicked on: "Radio-Nine news time is six-o-two. Violent crime continues to worsen in all parts of the city. And in a related story, doctors report a sharp increase in cases of clinical depression in the wake of Superman's death."

The tavern owner reached over and turned off the radio. "Y'hear that, Superman? Things're fallin' apart down here. Supergirl's been workin' real hard but somehow it just ain't enough."

Bibbo pulled on the sweatshirt. "Now, what I got in mind might strike some folks as disrespeckful—but I sure hope you don't think so, Superman. Ain't nobody in this world I respecks more'n you . . . you were my fav'rit! I know I'm not man enuff to fill yer boots, but I'm still gonna give it my best shot!" He pulled the trunks on over his sweats and pulled a pair of red high-tops out from under the bed.

"The way I sees it, we all gotta pull together—do everythin' we can to help each other out. I know that's the way ya'd've wanted it, and I ain't gonna let ya down. I'm gonna help everybody I can, pal—an' I'm gonna do it all in yer memory!"

Bibbo finished lacing up his sneakers and stood up to survey his appearance in the mirror. He brought his big hands together and cracked his knuckles. "If it's a Sooperman that Metropolis needs, it's a Sooperman they're gonna get!"

Hours later, the newly resurrected Kryptonian stood in an upper chamber of the Antarctic Fortress, freshly clothed from head to toe in a dark blue and black bodysuit. Over his eyes rested a smoky amber-colored visor.

Before him, a huge crystalline egg, some eight feet tall, hung suspended in midair via various electromagnetic fields. Clusters of transmission fibers snaked up through the Fortress and the ice above, channeling solar energy down into the egg, suffusing it with a warm glow.

"Bless Krypton and the House of El." The man gently ran his fingers along the surface of the crystalline egg. "Their legacy—the technology of this Fortress—has given me new life!"

A robot drew near. "Is all well, Master?"

"Yes, Unit Six, all is very well. This glorious Regeneration Matrix has ensured that the heart of Krypton's Last Son will keep beating! It channels life-giving energies to me—now that I can no longer absorb them directly from the sun and stars."

"And your vision, sir? Is the visor satisfactory?"

"It serves its purpose, Unit Six. But . . ." The Kryptonian turned from the Matrix, his hand reaching up to trace the rim of his visor.

". . . once I could see to the ends of the Earth, if I so desired, and now the dimmest light blinds me. I don't know if I'll ever get used to that."

He frowned darkly and raised one clenched fist to his chest. "I must not give in to despair. I may have lost the gift of supernormal sight, but I am alive! My senses, my body may have changed . . . but I am still strong! I still can fly free of gravity's hold. I still possess powers and abilities far beyond those of normal men!" To underscore his point, he thrust out a hand and sent a beam of raw energy blasting into the far wall.

Unit Seven automatically assessed the damage to the Fortress wall. "Sir? Might I suggest caution in the exercise of those powers within these confines?"

"Your suggestion is noted. See that the wall is repaired, and reinforced."

"At once, sir."

As Unit Seven set out to effect the repairs, his master flew from the chamber and headed for the monitor bank. For a solid hour, the Kryptonian stood and absorbed the news of the world. The news was not good.

Metropolis had suffered its fifth bank robbery in as many days, and incidents of violent crime were up dramatically in the city.

A fire in an office tower had claimed thirty-seven lives, while the intense heat of the blaze kept fire fighters at bay.

One commentator cited a growing general malaise in urban centers worldwide in the days since Superman's death and reported that public health officials feared a dramatic rise in the incidence of suicides and suicide attempts.

But the images that kept drawing the Kryptonian's attention were from reports taped on the scene in Centennial Park: "A surprising number of people have joined a cult that gathers daily at Superman's tomb, awaiting his resurrection." A hint of weary sarcasm crept into the reporter's voice. "Members of the cult worship the late hero as a messiah and maintain that he will rise from the grave to carry on what they refer to as his never-ending battle."

The Kryptonian did not notice the reporter's sarcasm. His eyes were on the faces of the hopeful. His ears were filled with their prayerful cry: "Superman! Superman!! Superman!!!"

He turned away from the monitors and called out to his robots. "Unit Four! Unit Nine! Bring me the cape and shield!"

In response, two metallic servitor units came flying in, carrying a bundle of red cloth. "Here they are, sir. Everything has been prepared and ready, as per your orders of this morning."

The robots unfolded the cape from around the thin metal alloy of the pentagonal shield. Amazingly, the cloth had been bonded to the upper corners of the shield so exactingly that not a seam showed. Moving as if they had spent years as personal valets, the robots lowered the cape over the Kryptonian's shoulders, affixing the shield electrostatically to his chest.

One of the robots fussed with the draping of the cape as the other hovered solicitously beside his master. "Sir, you returned to us just sixteen-point-seven hours ago. Wouldn't it be wise for you to recuperate more fully from your ordeal before you again leave the Fortress?"

"No. I cannot rest while the world is in such a desperate state."

The caped man flew up out of the Fortress, carving a new exit out of the ice. "The people cry out for Superman! I must be their champion!"

In Metropolis, Patricia Washburn had just entered her apartment building's laundry room when the door was slammed and locked behind her and she was grabbed by a man wearing a ski mask. Patricia was so tired after a long day's work that her first thought was that this must be one of her friends trying ineptly to be funny. She pulled away in anger. "There's nothing funny about trying to scare people. Who is that? Barry, you creep, is that you?"

Then the man pulled a gun, and she knew he was no friend.

"Who're you—? NO! Stay away from me! HELP!"

"Shut up." The man grabbed her roughly and threw her against one of the washing machines.

"Police—!"

"I said, shut up!" He swung his pistol up against the side of Patricia's head and then grabbed her again, this time in a choke hold. "Ain't nobody here to help you, so you might as well settle down! You an' me . . . we're gonna party."

Suddenly the door was smashed open, ripped right off its hinges by a tall, caped man. "Get away from that woman!" His voice seethed with righteous anger.

The man in the ski mask froze, staring dumbly at the newcomer. "What in the hell—?"

"Hell? I have seen hell, fool." The caped man took a step forward. "Put down that gun or I will send you there."

"Sonovabitch!" The man released his hold on Patricia and gripped his pistol with both hands, emptying it at the caped man.

The caped man didn't even break stride. He grabbed the man in the ski mask by the throat with one gloved hand and yanked away the man's gun with the other. "That was the wrong decision." The pistol made a horrible creaking sound as he crushed it in his hand.

Nose to nose with the caped man, and helpless in his grip, the man in the ski mask gasped for breath. "Who . . . who are you?"

"I'm Superman."

"You can't be Superman. He's dead!"

"No—you are." The Superman turned and hurled the attacker clear through a masonry wall.

"Oh, God." Patricia slid along the side of a dryer. "Oh, my God!" She was desperately trying to get to her feet and run, but her legs didn't want to obey.

The Superman turned toward Patricia, holding out his hands to her. "Do not be afraid. You are safe now." All traces of anger disappeared from his voice as he knelt down to help the bruised and battered woman to her feet. "He can no longer harm you. I have seen to that."

There was little expression on his face, and she could not see his eyes through the visor, but there was a sincerity to his voice. Somehow, Patricia knew she had nothing to fear from this man.

At that moment, farther downtown, Sandra and Daniel Henry and their son Jake left their hotel and started walking up Collyer Boulevard, tour map in hand. Sandy and Dan had been promising Jake this trip to Metropolis for several months, and after Superman's death, they had considered vacationing somewhere else. But young Jake had been adamant, and finally his folks had caved in.

"Over here, Dad, it's right on this next block! See?" Jake pointed up the street to the *Daily Planet* Building. "The story in that magazine said that it was just over there that he died." The boy was about to run on ahead when his mother reached out and took him gently by the arm.

"Just hold your horses, Jake Henry." Sandra glanced around cautiously. It was still supposed to be relatively safe in the downtown area, but neither she nor her husband knew their way around Metropolis all that well, and there were all those stories about the rising crime rate. She was glad that Dan had put away his tour map; she was sure that they looked enough like tourists as it was.

"Mom! We don't want to miss it."

"We won't miss anything, Jake." Dan slipped his hand over his son's. "It's not as if that spot's going to go away."

Arm in arm, the Henrys walked up to the main entrance of the *Planet* Building. There, set flush into the stone of the sidewalk, was a big square of brass marking the spot where Superman had died, making the supreme sacrifice to stop Doomsday.

Jake grew as quiet as his parents had ever seen the boy. They all gathered around the plaque with their heads bowed and just stared at it for the longest time. The noise of the streets seemed to fade away. *It's a little like being in church,* thought Sandra. *And this is the altar.*

It was Jake who first noticed signs of the approach. There was a sudden, flickering movement reflected in the burnished brass, and the boy looked up to see a powerful caped figure drop out of the night sky.

The Henrys scrambled back out of the way as he landed solidly beside the plaque. The caped figure bent down and pried the brass square loose from its moorings with his bare hands. He then straightened up, keeping his back to the Henrys, holding the plaque in his right hand. He appeared to be staring at it.

The Henrys watched in frozen silence, but they were not completely surprised to see the outlines of the plaque begin to soften and run.

"Heat vision—he has heat vision!" Jake's words came tumbling out in a hushed whisper.

Sandra fumbled around in her jacket pocket, trying to get out her camera, while her husband took a tentative step forward. "Why . . . why did you melt that plaque?"

The caped man glanced back over his right shoulder. "It's out-of-date."

"You—are you—?" Dan wasn't sure what the right question to ask was, but the stranger already had an answer.

"Yes. I'm back." And then, with a single bound, he was gone again, disappearing behind the tall buildings of Metropolis.

When Lois Lane came downstairs in the Kent farmhouse the next morning, she found that Martha was already up, had breakfast ready, and was packing a lunch.

"Martha, *now* what are you doing?"

"Making sandwiches, dear. You like turkey on whole wheat, don't you?"

"Yes, that's fine—but why? We can get something on the road, if you don't care that much for the hospital cafeteria."

"No need, Lois . . . no need. We have plenty of food here, and it'll just go to waste if we don't use it. I'm also fixing a little something to take along to Jonathan today. He's been grousing about the hospital food, and Doc Lanning said it would be all right. Oh, there are fresh-baked muffins and marmalade on the side table."

"I knew there had to be . . . the aroma woke me up." Lois claimed two of Martha's bran and raisin delights and poured herself an oversized mug of coffee. "Martha, I don't know where you get your energy." She gave the woman a peck on the cheek.

The phone rang and Lois picked it up. "Good morning, Kent residence."

"Lois?" There was confusion in the voice at the other end.

"Hi, Lana—is something wrong?"

"I'm not sure. Have you been watching the news?"

"No, I just got up. Why?"

"Maybe you'd better turn it on."

Lois hung up the phone, dashed into the parlor, and switched on CNN. The *Daybreak* anchor was accompanied on-screen by a vivid graphic, a question mark superimposed on Superman's pentagonal emblem.

"Repeating our top story . . . authorities in Metropolis this morning are scrambling to investigate numerous evening and overnight sightings of a mysterious costumed figure who witnesses claim was Superman. Here with our first report is CNN's Lucinda Watanabe. . . ."

Lois heard a gasp behind her and turned to see Martha standing in the parlor door. The older woman's eyes were wide and her mouth had opened into a big "O." *She looks like the way I feel,* thought Lois. "Let's not go getting all upset, Martha. It's probably just some sick practical joke or something. When I left Metropolis, the supermarket tabloids already had Superman living on the same South Sea island with Elvis and Marilyn Monroe."

Lois turned back to the set to see a bruised, shell-shocked Patricia Washburn standing in the midst of a rubble-strewn laundry room, describing her ordeal.

"This used to be a safe building. I don't know how he got in, but this man—he was wearing a ski mask—he grabbed me and started hitting me with his gun. I wouldn't have had a chance if Superman hadn't shown up."

The reporter interrupted her. "Then you're convinced that it was Superman?"

"Who else could it have been? He was over six feet tall, red cape, big 'S' on his chest. . . ." Patricia pointed toward the opening where the laundry room door had been. "He broke right through there and kept that sleaze from killing me! I'm not sorry that my attacker's dead, either. He sure won't threaten anyone ever again."

Together, Lois and Martha sat down on the edge of the old parlor sofa. "Lois, that couldn't have been Clark. He wouldn't have killed that man."

"Of course not, Martha. He wouldn't have needed to."

The picture switched to another reporter standing in front of the *Daily Planet* Building. "At virtually the same moment that Patricia Washburn was being rescued from her attacker, the Henry family had a close encounter of a different kind here, some sixty blocks away. A man they claim was Superman landed in front of this landmark building and destroyed a brass plaque marking the spot where Superman *supposedly* died. I say supposedly because someone reduced the plaque to a molten puddle. It has been taken away for study by city officials. But we do have a copy of a photograph taken by Mrs. Henry . . ."

Lois looked on slack-jawed as a close-up of the photo came on-screen. It was dark, grainy, and somewhat out of focus, but it did look like Superman. The figure's face was mainly in shadow, but that familiar lock of hair fell down across his forehead.

There were other reported sightings. A confessed carjacker was in critical condition with burns and fractures that he claimed had been inflicted by Superman. A cat burglar had been left tied to a seventh-story flagpole. And a little girl named Cindy produced a crude drawing of the man who she claimed had rescued her kitten from a tree. In the drawing, her Superman had beard stubble and wore a cap instead of a cape. "He smelled kinda funny, like daddy when he's been drinking beer." Cindy wrinkled her nose but never lost her smile. "He said to call him 'Sooperman,' so I did."

Eventually, the news turned to other stories, and Lois switched off the set. "Martha, I don't know what to say. You heard the one reporter; a couple of those sightings happened at the same time. Clark was never able to be in two places at once. Some of those things had to be hoaxes."

"But not all of them, Lois. Someone broke through that wall. And the photo . . ." Martha shook her head. "I wish we could have seen more of his face. It did put me in mind of Clark."

"Martha—"

"I know, I know. But Jonathan did say he'd brought Clark back. What if it wasn't just an hallucination—what if he did meet Clark in the beyond? Clark was capable of so many amazing things, but—oh, I don't know! This is all so bewildering to me."

To me, too, Martha. "Well, look at the time. We'd better get going if we're going to get to the hospital for early visiting hours. We don't want to keep Jonathan waiting."

"No, of course not, Lois. I—I wonder what he'll make of all this?"

The next day, Lois flew back to Metropolis, her ears still ringing from Jonathan Kent's thoughts on the subject. The old farmer had already seen the TV reports and become so agitated that Dr. Lanning had prescribed a new blood pressure medication and threatened him with a longer hospital stay. Jonathan had calmed himself as best he could. After all, he couldn't very well tell the doctor why he was so upset without spilling the beans about his son's double life. And he wasn't about to do that. "We need to keep that secret for Clark, especially if he's come back." In his heart of hearts, Jonathan remained convinced that he'd met his son on "the other side." "But these fool stories on the news—! None of 'em sound right to me. You've got to check 'em out for us, Lois. The fool doctors here won't let me travel yet!"

From Smallville, Lois had tried to contact Captain Sawyer or Inspector Turpin to see if there'd been any further disturbances at Superman's tomb, but the Special Crimes Unit seemed preoccupied with other business; no one had returned her calls. She had finally put through a person-to-person call to Police Inspector William Henderson. Bill Henderson had been one of Clark's oldest friends on the force, and he'd taken her call immediately.

Over the phone, Lois had made a case for checking the crypt. She'd argued passionately as well as persistently, and Henderson had promised to do what he could. They planned to meet upon her return.

Back in the city, Lois went directly to Centennial Park, where she found Henderson waiting for her by the east wall. Flashlights in hand, they proceeded down the underground access corridor.

"I still think this is a waste of time, Ms. Lane. The department's been plugged into the tomb's security grid ever since the last incident. We haven't detected so much as a cockroach down here."

"Maybe so, Inspector. But I've never heard of a security system that was a hundred percent foolproof, have you?"

"No, I haven't. That's why I got authorization from the mayor's office to check it out." Henderson grew pensive as they entered the crypt's antechamber and stood before the vault door. "Are you sure you're ready for this?"

Lois took a deep breath and let it out. "Not completely, but we have to know. We have to be sure."

Henderson inserted two special keys into a newly installed locking mechanism, electronically opening the bolts that sealed the vault door shut. Then he grabbed hold of the handle and slowly eased the big door open. Both he and Lois let out a gasp as they entered the crypt. The coffin sat empty, its lid open.

The inspector made a quick check of the crypt. Its ceiling, walls, and floor all appeared to be intact. There were absolutely no signs of entry.

Lois stared at the empty coffin. *Maybe Jonathan was right. Maybe Clark is back!*

"Well, this is a fine kettle of fish!" Henderson scratched his head. "Now what do we do?"

"Well, one thing's for certain, Inspector; we can't keep this a secret. Not this time!"

The video monitors in Lex Luthor's executive offices showed a close-up of an empty coffin, as a somber WLEX reporter delivered the bombshell. "Superman's coffin is empty! But the questions remain . . . has he somehow miraculously returned from the dead? Or are these sightings the handiwork of a super-opportunist? Several radical groups have already claimed responsibility for robbing Superman's tomb and reviving him, while Superman-worshiping cultists warn that Judgment Day is at hand. Only one thing is certain—Superman's body *is* missing!"

"Missing!" Luthor pounded his desk. "And we don't know how or why —do we, Happersen?!"

Happersen tugged nervously at his collar. "Well, sir, my people—"

"Your people! 'Don't worry, Mr. Luthor, the new hidden cameras will record anything that happens at the tomb!' Bah! All we have are several hours of blank tape!"

"I assure you, Mister L, it's just a matter of time before—!"

"How long, Happersen? How long?! After we recovered his body from the Cadmus Project, you assured me that security was improved! And now this!" Luthor slouched back in his chair, stroking his beard. "I swear, Superman's as much trouble to me dead as he was alive!"

Luthor sat straight up at the sound of a series of loud thumps and muffled shouts from the outer hall. The office door flew open, and a uniformed security guard came tumbling backward into the executive suite.

The youthful CEO slammed a fist down on his desk. "Bloody hell, now what?! I gave specific orders not to be disturbed!"

"S-sorry, Mr. L." The guard scrambled to his feet and tried to hold the door closed, but he was obviously fighting a losing battle. A sharp cry of pain came through the half-opened door. "We tried to tell her that, but the lady insists on seeing you!"

"Out of my way!" Supergirl came charging into the room, knocking the guard aside and leaving a half dozen others trailing in her wake. She had a rolled-up newspaper in her hand, and her face was flushed with anger. "Lex, we have to talk!"

Luthor wearily rose to his feet as the guards picked themselves up off the floor. "Love, I was in conference with Dr. Happersen. Can't this wait?"

"Wait?! Lex, haven't you seen the news?!"

"Of course I have. As a matter of fact, I was just about to send for you." He turned toward the guards. "You men resume your posts! We'll forget about this . . . little misunderstanding." *This time.*

"Oh—sorry, guys." Supergirl suddenly looked acutely embarrassed by what she'd done. "I know you were just doing your jobs. No hard feelings?"

"No, miss." *Not on our part anyway. I don't know about the boss.*

Once the guards were out the door, the Girl of Steel whirled back around to face Luthor. "I've just come from the tomb. I went over every inch of it and there are absolutely no signs of a break-in. Superman really must be alive this time!" She paused, hurt and frustration plainly showing on her face. "Lex, you must have known earlier. Why didn't you tell me? When I saw this—!"

She threw down a copy of the latest edition of the *Daily Planet.* The front page was dominated by a huge photograph of the open coffin and twin headlines: BACK FROM THE DEAD? SUPERMAN'S BODY MISSING!

Luthor came out from behind his desk, his face a mask of concern. "I didn't want to upset you needlessly, love." He reached out and took her hands in his. "All the reports I've seen so far have varied wildly, as have the descriptions of this supposed Superman. Or perhaps I should say Super*men.* If all the accounts were true, there'd have to be more than one!"

"You're saying that it could all be some sick hoax?"

"Perhaps, love. We still don't know."

Supergirl pulled away from him. "Well, I'm going to find out—one way or another!" She strode from the room, and within moments, Luthor saw her flash past the far glass wall of his office.

"Lord, she's headstrong!" For a moment he stood at the glass, just watching her fly off over the city. *To have all that power at your beck and call.* Luthor smiled. *But then, in a way, I do.* "Happersen, put everyone we can spare on the investigation. Call in all of our sources. I want to know for certain whether Superman is dead or alive. And I want to see proof . . . or heads will roll!"

In his Cadmus Project office, Paul Westfield flicked off the television and furiously punched up a number on his scramble phone. "Packard?! How goes the work in Lab Thirteen? Have you started feeding our subject information yet? Good, very good. But can you accelerate the process? We need to pick up the pace. Yes, Carl, I understand the need for caution, but some other parties are already out there trying to pass themselves off as the new Superman. How long until the maturation process is complete? Two weeks? Well, if that's the best you can do. All right, keep me informed if there are any changes. Right. Good-bye."

Unseen behind the ventilation duct, Big Words silently scribbled down notes, very glad that he had decided to look in periodically on Westfield's office. The boy did not like the sound of this at all. He had to get back and tell the others about it immediately. The Newsboy Legion, he was certain, would want to take a look at Lab Thirteen.

The sun was just beginning to set in Metropolis when Lois Lane heard the plane approach. She looked up in horror as a small twin-engine aircraft passed by overhead, not more than two stories above the ground.

The driver of a cab at curbside hung halfway out his window, his jaw wide with amazement as he watched the plane go by. "Holy Christ! Who's flyin' that thing?"

Lois dove into the back of the cab. "That's what I aim to find out. Follow that plane!"

The cabbie looked at her as if she were from another planet. "Ya want me to follow—? Are you kiddin' me, lady?"

"I've never been more serious in my life. Come on, there's a big tip in it for you if you keep it in sight."

"All right, lady, you're on!" He switched on the meter and shot away from the curb. " 'Follow that plane!' Now I've heard everything."

Inside the small plane, the pilot sat slumped over in his seat. His lone passenger sat in the copilot's chair, desperately trying to remember how to work the radio. "Calling Metropolis Tower—can anyone hear me? I need help! My brother collapsed against the controls—I think it may be his heart!—and I don't know how to fly! Oh, God, we're so low!" Frantically, the passenger wracked her brain, trying to recall the procedures her brother had followed. *We're too low. Got to pull up! Stupid wheel— why won't you pull up?!*

Slowly, the plane started to gain altitude. But as it did, one wing clipped the side of a building and the plane tilted violently.

"We're going to crash! We're going to die!"

No sooner were the words out of the passenger's mouth than the plane seemed to right itself. People on the streets looked up to see a figure clad in black, red, and blue balancing the craft upon his own broad shoulders, the streetlights glimmering off his amber visor. As the plane's engines sputtered and stalled out, he brought it down over the narrow stretch of green that was Simon Kirby Riverside Park.

A policeman came running up as the Superman emerged from beneath the craft. "Officer! Please radio for assistance."

It took the policeman a moment to find his voice. "I . . . already have, sir." He looked up and down at the tall man with the cape. *The Captain's never gonna believe this. I don't believe it!* "You are . . . Superman?"

"Who else would I be?" The Superman turned and pulled the door off the side of the plane.

Yeah, thought the cop, *who else could he be? His outfit's a little different, but I don't wear the same thing every day, so why should he?*

The Superman helped the sobbing passenger down into the policeman's arms and turned to check on the pilot.

The cop put an arm around the woman and did his best to console her. "It's okay, ma'am. You're down safe and sound. Do you know where you are?"

"It's . . . it's Metropolis, isn't it? We took off from O'Hara Field. My brother . . ." She took the policeman's proffered handkerchief and tried to dry her eyes. "One minute, Johnny was laughing and smiling, and the next—he's . . . he's dead, isn't he?"

"Yes." The Superman emerged from the plane. "His heart failed. Too much time has elapsed; he cannot be revived."

The policeman stared at the caped man in disbelief. *Jesus, buddy, did you have to be so blunt?*

Not fifty feet away, Lois's cab braked to a halt just inside the park entrance. "I can't get you any closer, lady. I'm breakin' the law just by pullin' in here."

"It's okay, this is close enough." Lois saw a crowd starting to form; she tossed the driver double what was on the meter and sprinted toward the plane. When she'd spotted the rescue several blocks back, she hadn't been sure whether she believed her eyes. But now that she was within hailing distance, she was determined to get some answers. "Hey! You with the cape! Hold it right there, buster!"

As Lois reached the Superman, the cheering crowd began to close in around them.

"See? It's him! It's really him!"

"Superman!"

"He's back! Oh, thank the Lord Almighty, he's come back!"

"Let me touch you!"

"Please, heal my child!"

Lois could see that the situation was fast getting out of hand. She grabbed the caped man by the arm. "We need to talk. Get us out of here."

The Superman scooped Lois up in his arms and leapt up into the sky, leaving the mob far behind. So swiftly did they soar up over the rooftops that Lois's head began to spin. It had been over a month since she had flown in Superman's arms, and she had thought that she would never fly like that again. She drew in a deep breath and pointed to the roof of a tall office tower. "I think this is far enough. Set us down over there."

The Superman nodded. "As you wish."

"As you wish"?! He resembles Clark, but he sounds so cold, so . . . hollow. Lois looked him over closely. "You know, I've been trying to find you since I first heard about you. Who *are* you? What's your game?"

"I am Superman. I don't understand your second question. I am not playing any game."

"Oh, really? Superman never hid his face, he didn't wear a metal shield on his chest, and he didn't wear black like some executioner!"

"No. Not before. But I have been through much. I have changed."

"If you're really Superman, tell me who I am. Or don't you know me?"

"You?" Superman studied Lois as if seeing her for the first time. "Yes . . . I know you. You're Lois Lane . . . a reporter. Before my passing . . . you were an important part of my life. You were the first to write about me."

Lois felt her throat constrict. *His voice—it's softening. He's starting to sound more like Clark. Not like Superman—like Clark! Don't you cry, Lois Lane. Don't you* dare *start to cry! And don't give anything away—demand proof!*

"That I'm a reporter is a matter of public record. Tell me something that only Superman could know!"

The Superman reached out his hand, gently touching her cheek. "I know . . . that we were more than friends. You were engaged to marry Clark Kent." His voice came haltingly. "Kent loved you very much. He trusted you completely—even with the secret of his double life."

"Then you *are*—!"

"I am." He suddenly pulled back his hand, as if he could no longer bear to touch her. "I am sorry. I grieve for your loss, Ms. Lane."

The Superman turned and began to walk away from her.

"What're you saying? If it's really you—" The words were catching in her throat. "Clark—?"

"No! We must not speak of this again." He looked back over his shoulder at her. "As I told you, things have changed. *I* have changed. Kent is gone. There is only Superman now."

And then the Superman rocketed away into the sky.

"Wait! Don't go!" Lois looked skyward, her face a mixture of fear, sorrow, and confusion. *Dear God in heaven. If he's lying, someone's learned that Clark was Superman. And if he's telling the truth, then I've lost Clark all over again.*

20

Hidden away in the basement of his apartment building, Henry Johnson finished soldering one last contact and stepped back to survey his work. Here, in his makeshift workshop, it had taken him over a week to integrate all the components of his prototype equipment into a functional battle suit, but he was finally done. All that remained was the field testing. *Might as well get started. The problems on the streets aren't going to clear up by themselves.*

The streets in and around Suicide Slum had never been really safe. For over a century, one neighborhood or another had been written off, their people told that they were unneeded, unwanted, expendable.

The telling used to be quite blatant. John Henry had seen pictures of earlier days, when employers posted help wanted notices telling certain groups not to even bother to apply. As the years had passed, the discrimination had become much less obvious but not necessarily less pervasive; the underclass hadn't gone away, it had simply changed color somewhat.

No, human nature hadn't changed, but the weaponry had. Knife fights had given way to gunfights, and handguns had given way to automatic weapons. The addition of drug money had resulted in increasingly deadly turf wars. In some neighborhoods, the murder rate was nearly as high as it had been during Prohibition.

Henry knew that it would take something on the order of a Superman to stop the killing. He prayed that his work could make a difference. He began to suit up.

The reinforced body armor went on first, with its miniature servomotors designed to amplify his strength tenfold. Next, he stepped into the rocket boots, feeling the satisfying click as they locked into place around his feet, ankles, and calves. Then he slipped the power gauntlets on over his hands and secured them at his wrists. The larger of the two, fitted over his left wrist, was equipped to fire steel spikes with fearful accuracy.

Henry took a few tentative steps across the room, hearing the hard pounding sound of metal on concrete. *Well, I won't have an easy time sneaking up on people, but then I didn't design this suit with stealth in mind.*

He reached down into a newly opened parcel and pulled out a thick red cape made of tightly woven Kevlar. The cape had cost him plenty to have made to order, but he felt it was necessary. He fastened the cape to special mountings set into the collar of his armor, letting it drape back over his shoulders. He then tightened a pentagonal shield of burnished steel to his chest. Machine-tooled into the shield was the familiar stylized letter S. *If I'm going to dedicate myself to keeping the spirit of the real Superman alive, I have to wear his colors and his insignia.* He inspected his reflection in an old mirror that had been propped in the corner and forgotten years ago. *It looks all right. Now all I need is a helmet.*

As Henry strode back across the room, a stolen car motored slowly past the back of the building, driven by two members of the Sharks.

"That's the place, brother." The Shark behind the wheel sneered. "That's where that Johnson mother lives."

"Well, I hope the man's home." The other Shark reached into a bag at his feet. " 'Cause I got a few little presents for 'im." He pulled out a liter bottle filled with gasoline, a rag wick stuffed down its neck. He lit the wick and hurled his homemade bomb through a basement window. He lit and hurled a second one, then a third, and then he snarled at his driver. "Go!"

As the car streaked away, the incendiaries erupted in the apartment building's furnace room. On the other side of a cinder block wall from the furnace room, Henry heard the whoosh of the firebombs and swiftly locked his masked metal helmet into place, switching on its emergency air supply. John Henry grabbed up his long-handled sledgehammer, but before he could take another step, the bomb blaze ignited the furnace's fuel oil reservoir.

In seconds, fire swept up through the old building. As he walked unharmed through the burning basement, John Henry heard a wail come from Rosie Jakowitz's apartment one floor above. He charged up the smoke-filled stairwell to the first floor, only to find the door to Rosie's quarters and most of the lobby engulfed in flame. He could still hear Rosie inside, screaming hysterically. She was unable to get out through that door, and he suspected that she'd lost the key to the security bars over her windows.

280

His tongue tripped a microswitch inside his helmet and his amplified voice boomed above the roar of the fire. "Stand back from the door!"

One mighty swing of his hammer reduced the door to burning embers. He stalked into Rosie's apartment and swept the tiny woman up in one arm, wrapping his cape around her. Then he flew through the fire, setting her safely down on the sidewalk across the street.

Rosie looked up in wonder at her steel-clad rescuer. She was a self-taught theosophist who spent her nights studying the cabala and her days supporting herself by reading tea leaves and advising people on their horoscopes. She had never foreseen anything like this armor-plated man. "Who are you?"

"You can call me the Man of Steel." His voice was like thunder.

"But who are you"—she put a hand out to his metal chest plate—"inside?"

"You're the fortune-teller. You tell me!" He then turned and dashed back into the building to help others escape the blaze. By the time fire fighters arrived on the scene, everyone had been rescued, and the Man of Steel had vanished.

The next morning was dark and murky. Rain poured down on Metropolis, turning the city's potholes into water hazards and further eroding the streets. Lois had been up half the night, unable to sleep and—worse still —unable to write. Her encounter with the visored Superman had left her so rattled that she hadn't trusted herself to write it up for the paper. *What do I say? That he's Superman returned from the dead? Do I really believe that?* She'd finally given up in despair and phoned in a greatly abbreviated eyewitness account of the airplane rescue to the *Planet*'s night news desk.

At seven-thirty in the morning, Lois was sitting in an all-night diner, staring blankly at her fourth cup of coffee, when the cellular phone in her purse rang.

"Hello?"

"Morning, Lois. It's Jimmy. I didn't wake you up, did I?"

"No, Jim." She stifled a yawn. "Actually, I've been awake for some time. What's up?"

"We just got a hot tip on a new Superman sighting—at S.T.A.R. Labs, no less! The caller told me that he saw Superman fly into the main lab complex just a few minutes ago, and then all sorts of alarms started sounding. We haven't been able to raise anyone at S.T.A.R. for confirmation, but the Chief thought you'd want to know."

"Thank Perry for me, Jimmy. I'll call in if I learn anything!"

When Lois arrived at the west side facility of Scientific and Techno-logical Advanced Research Laboratories, the entire complex was still in an uproar. The security guards refused her admittance until she managed to catch the eye of a technician she knew who was willing to vouch for her. Grudgingly passed through, Lois found the main laboratory corridor full of confused people, most of them wearing lab coats. Everyone she buttonholed had seen something, but no one could quite agree on what they'd seen. Eyewitness accounts varied wildly, *and these are experienced scientists and technicians,* thought Lois, *people who are trained to observe.*

Slowly, a halfway coherent story began to emerge. Apparently some-one presenting himself as Superman had arrived just ahead of the morn-ing support staff and demanded Doomsday's body, which S.T.A.R. xenobiologists had been attempting—without much success—to study. When technicians attempted to bar him from entering the xenobiology lab, he'd tossed them aside and located the body on his own. He then left with the body, and that was about all that anyone knew.

Most disturbing of all was their description of Superman. No one made any mention of his wearing a visor, but most seemed to agree that this Superman looked hard, as if partially made of metal.

"Metal?" Lois found that puzzling. The only metal she had noticed on the Superman she'd met the night before was in the insignia he wore on his chest. "You mean like a shield or helmet or something?"

Her witness was apologetic. "He moved so quickly, it was hard to tell. But, no. I got the distinct impression that he was wearing some manner of prosthesis."

Three-quarters of a million miles from Earth, a caped figure landed upon a meteor nearly ten feet across. Slung across one of his shoulders were great lengths of heavy chains and thick cables; slung over his other shoulder was the body of the monster Doomsday. Neither the mass of his burdens nor the vacuum of space seemed to cause the caped figure any trouble.

He tamped Doomsday into the meteor, taking care to bury the crea-ture's bone spurs as deeply as he could. With the chains and cables, he then secured Doomsday tightly to the rock in a virtual cocoon of metal. Beams of radiant heat shot from his eyes, fusing the bonds into the metallic core of the meteor. And to the creature itself, he attached a sophisticated sensor device designed to transmit a warning signal to its maker, should the bonds be disturbed in any way.

The caped figure then stared off into the vastness of space, calculating a safe trajectory. Once those calculations were complete, he swung about and hurled the meteor bearing the body of Doomsday off into the void.

On a hillside overlooking S.T.A.R. Labs, Lois walked through the drizzling rain, trying to make some sense of what she had learned. At least two men were trying very hard to pass themselves off as Superman; of that she was certain. Both men could fly, both were very strong. Both wore red capes and pentagonal insignia, and both had unruly forelocks. One covered his eyes, the other didn't; it had been that second man who'd gone into S.T.A.R. and carried off Doomsday.

Part of her hoped and prayed that Clark had somehow come back to life . . . *or maybe he never really died. Maybe it was just that his heart stopped like Jonathan's had and he'd gone into some sort of coma.* Lois shook her head. "I wish I knew."

"Pardon me. You are . . . Lois Lane?"

The voice seemed to drift down out of the rain. Lois whirled around to see a tall, broad-shouldered man striding toward her through the foggy mist. His features were obscured by the branches of a tree, but she could see a cloak or a cape furling behind him. His voice, uncertain at first, took on a more confident tone. "Yes, it is you. You're the one who first called me Superman."

Lois froze in her tracks. "Superman?"

"Yes, Lois. I am Superman. I've come back." The tall figure stepped clear of the tree and stopped a few paces away from her.

Lois took a step back, her knuckles pressed hard against her teeth. She examined the caped figure from head to toe and stared back up at the horror that was his face. "Oh, my God!"

Only the upper right side of the figure's head looked human. The rest of his face and the rest of his hair were simply gone, exposing a skull of dull gray metal.

His right eye was the warm, friendly blue that Lois had seen so often in her dreams of Clark. The other eye was mechanical, of metal and glowing crystal, with no more warmth than a camera lens.

He wore what appeared to be Superman's old familiar costume, or at least part of it. His left leg was a robotic limb of the same cold, hard alloy as his skull. Where his right arm and the right side of his chest should have been there was more metal.

Lois wanted to run, to scream, but found that she could do neither. *This must be a nightmare. I finally fell asleep, and this is what I get for wanting him back so badly.*

The tall machine-man gently extended his human arm, palm up. "I know that I appear very different." He tilted his head forward earnestly. Suddenly, his whole stance and voice were very much like Clark Kent's. "I realize that I am . . . unpleasant to look at; even ugly. But you must believe me, I *am* Superman."

Before she could even realize what she was doing, Lois took a step forward. *I'm walking toward him.* The thought came to her slowly, as if from a great distance. *Does this mean I'm waking up?*

The Superman bowed his head, turning the human side of his face toward her. "I am pleased that you didn't run away. It is very important to me that you not be afraid of me."

Lois took another step. *What would Sam Lane say if he could see me now? Would the Captain finally be impressed with his firstborn? Would he say that I was taking this like a man, or would he think I was out of my mind?*

Whether brave or reckless, Lois came right up to the Superman. Up close, his face was even more terrifying. His robotic arm and leg were at least covered with a smooth metal "skin," but the machined part of his head was frightfully skeletal, *like some kind of cyborg.*

It seemed impossible that this creature could ever have been Clark Kent. Better, she thought, to have believed the visored Superman when he insisted that Clark Kent was simply no more.

And yet, this machine-man—this Cyborg Superman—seemed so happy that she hadn't run away, so pleased and relieved. In his small fragment of a face was more feeling, more humanity, than the other Superman had allowed to show through his visor.

Lois raised one hand, as if to touch his face, then drew back. "But how? How did you come back?"

"I don't know. When I woke up, I was already as you see me now." He gestured to his face. "Somebody, I don't know who, brought me back and rebuilt the damaged parts of me—made me into this thing. It's far from perfect, isn't it?" He looked down at his robot arm. "Still, given the alternative, I suppose that I should be grateful to be back in any form."

The Cyborg tried to smile, but only for a moment, as if he were aware that it made his face look even more horrible.

Lois felt her heart clench. She raised her hand again, and this time she did touch his face—carefully—along his right cheekbone at the juncture of the skin. "This looks so . . . I mean, does it hurt? It looks like you must be in pain!"

"No. The pain was in the dying." He tilted his face slightly, leaning very gently into her touch. "The pain is long gone—like a faded memory. Strange as I may look, now I'm alive again."

"But how? Tell me how I can know it's really you."

The Cyborg's shoulders sagged. "That may be difficult. There's so much I can't remember. So much of my past is a mystery to me. I know that I'm Superman. But I'm not sure how I can prove that to you. The things I do recall are fragmentary. I'm afraid that the beating Doomsday gave me caused some memory loss."

Lois stepped back from him at this, her reporter's instincts sounding a warning. *Amnesia? That sounds just a little too convenient.* "You say you remember me giving you your name, but that's public knowledge! Tell me something that isn't. Tell me something that will prove you're Superman."

The Cyborg's one human eye became distant, his expression very thoughtful. "One of my earliest memories . . . is a farm in Kansas. And some people who were there for me. I am not sure, but I seem to feel that that information was not common knowledge." He looked at her anxiously. "Is that right?"

Lois hoped she was keeping the shock from her face. "It's—well, it's heading in the right direction." She shook her head. *Why did I say even that much? I mustn't give anything away until I can be sure! What can I say now?*

She hesitated, trying to think of a safe question. The Cyborg clenched his metal fist in very human-looking frustration. "It's so agonizing, not to remember—or even worse, to remember only bits and pieces. I'm trying to remember, but so much eludes me."

Lois looked full into his face, struck by sudden inspiration. "I've just thought of someone who might be able to help. Would you agree to see him?"

"Someone who could help me remember?"

"Perhaps. He's run tests on Superman before."

"I'll try anything." The Cyborg gently took her hand. "Please, take me to him."

Emil Hamilton looked up in astonishment at the two guests in his laboratory. "Egads, Ms. Lane, what—who is this?!"

"That's what we're hoping you can tell us, Professor Hamilton." Lois looked around. Much of Hamilton's equipment was covered with huge sheets of plastic, and the air was heavy with the smell of fresh paint. "That is, if you're up and running."

"Oh, yes! Yes, the painters finished yesterday. We were lucky. This building sustained relatively minor damage from that Doomsday creature's rampage. My most delicate apparatus escaped untouched." Hamilton adjusted his glasses and stared unabashedly at the Cyborg.

The Cyborg returned the favor. "Professor Hamilton. Do I know you?"

Hamilton took a step back. "That voice—!"

He hears the similarity, too. Lois frowned. *I hope that won't prejudice anything.* "I realize how weird this must seem, Professor, but this man claims to be Superman."

"Weird? Ms. Lane, it's unheard of! What he's claiming is the reanimation of dead tissue!"

"Yes, well, we need to run some tests to find out if there's any possibility that he could be right. Can you help us?"

"Of course! Come, right this way." Hamilton led them through a maze of scaffolding and over to a big Plexiglas sphere. "You know, I've probably studied Superman more thoroughly than anyone else on Earth. If this man is not the genuine article, I'll find out for sure!"

Good, thought Lois, *because I have my doubts.*

The Cyborg regarded the sphere and the surrounding computer consoles with curiosity. "Begin your examination, Professor. I am confident of the results."

The Cyborg patiently stood by as the professor attached dozens of electrodes to him and sealed him within the hollow sphere.

Hamilton flipped a series of switches, and his equipment hummed to life. "Please try to stand very still. The sensor scan is beginning . . . now!"

The sphere lit up with a soft glow, making the Cyborg look like a bizarre filament in a gigantic light bulb. Hamilton turned his attention to a large monitor screen which was producing a diagrammatic image of the Cyborg, color-coding his electromechanical and organic components.

"Extraordinary! This is most extraordinary!"

"What is it, Professor?"

Hamilton called up past data on a second screen and keyed the systems to begin correlating figures. "I have enjoyed the privilege of analyzing a few bits and pieces of surviving Kryptonian technology, Ms. Lane. And the bionic components of this gentleman appear to be constructed of alloys developed by Kryptonian metallurgists. Hmm . . . they also correspond to the areas of Superman's body that were injured in his battle with Doomsday."

As Hamilton pointed out the pertinent data to Lois, the Cyborg studied the main electrode on his robot arm. Curious, he traced the data pathway along to Hamilton's computers.

Lois leaned in close to Hamilton, keeping her back to the Cyborg and her questions to a soft whisper. "He claims to have suffered a significant loss of memory, Professor. Can you see anything that would explain that? Please, keep your voice down."

"Actually, Ms. Lane, amnesia is not uncommon among trauma survivors, and whoever this man is, he's obviously suffered some severe trauma. Why, the entire left hemisphere of his brain is missing! It's apparently been replaced with some manner of microbionic supercomputer. That he remembers anything at all, given the extent of his injuries, is what's remarkable! Still, the brain is an astonishing organ. It is conceivable that this man, whoever he is, will recall more as time goes on."

Their conversation was all but inaudible over the electronic hum of the equipment, but the Cyborg caught every word. "Professor, may I speak without disturbing your apparatus?"

Hamilton turned toward the Cyborg. "Yes, that should be safe. Is something the matter?"

"Not at all. This is all starting to seem very familiar to me. Your name is Emil, isn't it? And I remember someone else being here . . . a woman . . . Mildred. Is she well?"

Hamilton's jaw dropped. "Yes. Yes, very well, thank you."

An insistent beeping sound came from the main console, and the professor rushed over to check it. "Astounding. The bioanalysis is complete, and in record time." He pulled back a lever, and the sphere swiveled open. "You can come out now."

The Cyborg hopped down out of the sphere, electrodes popping loose as he moved.

"Oh, this is amazing. Truly uncanny." Hamilton keyed his equipment to double-check the figures.

The Cyborg laid his human hand gently on the professor's shoulder. "Is anything wrong, Emil?"

"The genetic coding—!" Hamilton took off his glasses, cleaned them with a treated tissue, and replaced them on his nose. "You know, I was never able to obtain a complete scan of Superman's DNA."

"I remember." There was a new confidence in the Cyborg's voice. "You said that Kryptonian chromosomes were too complex for your equipment."

"Y-yes. As you say. But the data I had compiled earlier matches quite well against the data I have just now collected on your, ah, organic half." Hamilton darted a glance at Lois. "Yes, everything is comfortably within the limits of my expected experimental error."

Lois looked back and forth from the Cyborg to the professor. "Then, what you're saying is—?"

Hamilton nodded once, slowly. "Incredible as it seems, these results suggest—quite strongly suggest—that this man is indeed Superman."

The Cyborg seemed about to heave a sigh of relief when he suddenly stiffened. "Listen!"

"What?" Lois demanded. "I don't hear anything."

The Cyborg tapped the metal disc where his left ear would have been. "Sorry. It's a radio signal. There's a ship in distress about ten miles out at sea. I have to go."

The Cyborg Superman bounded across the lab and was airborne as the servomotors opened the big double windows for him. He waved back as he exited the building. "Thank you, Professor! Thanks, Lois, for all your help. With luck, maybe I'll soon remember everything!"

Hamilton sank back into a battered old swivel chair. "Ms. Lane, I've seen some incredible things in my day, but I never thought I'd live to see a man return from the dead."

Lois shook her head. "I'm still not so sure we have, Professor."

Lex Luthor stood before the wall of monitors in his video lounge, studying endless replays of WLEX news feeds. At the moment, one image dominated half of the screens. It was an interview with a young woman who claimed she had been rescued from a burning building by Superman.

"It's true! He carried me out of that building—he saved us all—and then he was gone." Rosie Jakowitz's face filled the screens. "Trust me, I'm a trained professional reader-advisor. I knew all along that Superman would return, and now he has. Not necessarily in the form people might have expected, but it was him. Listen, have you ever heard of a walk-in spirit? When a body has been abandoned by one spirit but is not yet uninhabitable, then another spirit can move in. Anyway, whatever he is, the cards tell me for sure that the man who saved me today is definitely the Man of Steel. For sure."

Dr. Happersen entered the room, and Luthor wearily shook his head. "Every hour, it seems, there's news of another Superman sighting. This is the weirdest one yet. Walk-in spirits! What rubbish. Happersen, were you able to learn anything about this case?"

"Not much, sir. The police have nothing but eyewitness accounts of this latest Superman. As usual, those accounts differed in details—estimates of his height vary from six to ten feet—but it is interesting that all the witnesses say that the man wore some sort of armor. The police feel they're on firmer ground with the cause of the fire, however; they believe it was started by gang members."

"Gang members?"

"Yes, apparently in retaliation against one Henry Johnson, a resident of the building. Johnson had helped police apprehend a young member of a gang known as the Sharks."

"This incessant gang violence is becoming increasingly annoying, Happersen. I don't like that sort of thing happening in my city."

"Yes, sir." *You would see it that way, wouldn't you?* "The Sharks are becoming a particular problem to the police, what with the high-caliber firepower they've been able to acquire."

"Ah, yes . . . the so-called Toastmasters. Where are those guns coming from, Sydney?"

"I don't know, sir."

"Then find out. If they're as big a threat as they seem, I want their source cut off—preferably at the ankles."

Jonathan Kent sat up in his hospital bed, zapping through the channels on the TV with a remote. "Infernal contraption. We get more channels than ever with the cable, but there's never anything on that I want to watch!"

"Yes, dear." Martha sat patiently by his bedside, knitting. *You've been nothing but a grouchy old bear these past two days.* "Would you like some more water?"

"Yeah, I suppose."

She gave him a peck on the forehead. "You just settle down now. The doctor said he might let you go home tomorrow."

Martha scooped up the water pitcher and disappeared into the bathroom. Jonathan went back to zapping through the channels, finally landing on the evening satellite news from superstation WLEX. The picture was jumpy and grainy, and the announcer sounded slightly breathless, rushing his narration.

"A WLEX mobile-cam crew got these dramatic shots just minutes ago, when they came upon the scene of a shoot-out between rival gangs. As you'll see in a moment, the so-called Man of Steel suddenly dropped into the middle of this firefight . . ."

"Martha? Martha, come here! You gotta see this!"

A dark red cape swirled across the screen as the huge metal-clad form of the Man of Steel stepped between the warring gangs, bullets bouncing off his chest. He swung his long-handled hammer in a wide arc, knocking the weapons from the hands of the young gunmen. Then he trod upon the guns, crushing them under his weight. A voice that sounded like a cross between Orson Welles and James Earl Jones boomed from the television. "These weapons are illegal. They won't be tolerated on the streets any longer!"

"Did you say something, Jonathan?" Martha came back into the room with a full pitcher.

Her husband stared openmouthed at the television.

"Jonathan, whatever is the matter? What did you see?"

"I—I'm not sure, Martha." He let the remote control drop to his lap. "But it wasn't what I expected—not what I expected at all."

It was just after four in the morning when the alarm Klaxons began to blare in the Cadmus Project. Instantly awake, Jim Harper leapt out of bed, pulling on his working clothes and jumping into his boots. He was fitting his helmet into place when he reached the central lab complex and found his night security team clustered around a huge metal door at the end of a long corridor.

"What's the situation?"

One of the uniformed men snapped off a quick salute. "We've got a code red in Lab Thirteen, sir. Power surge of unknown origin caused an explosion inside—and the door's jammed shut. We're trying to force it now."

Footsteps echoed behind them. "Guardian! What's going on?"

"Westfield . . ." The Guardian's voice took on a decidedly cool edge. "What're you doing up at this hour?"

"That's my business, mister. Right now, yours is making sure nothing happens to Experiment Thirteen."

"We'll do our best." He nodded to his team. "Take out the door."

Shaped explosive charges were quickly set all around the frame of the entryway. Within moments, the door lay smoking on the corridor floor.

The Guardian started into the lab, Westfield and the security team close on his heels. "Let's take this slow and easy. There's no telling who or what we might find in here."

Lab Thirteen was a smoking, steaming mess. Equipment was strewn from one end of the chamber to the other and torn cables were scattered everywhere. In the middle of the lab sat the remains of what looked like a gigantic test tube. Three and a half feet in diameter, it stood over eight feet tall; its walls were of three-inch-thick Plexiglas, and over a third of its surface had been smashed out, apparently from within. A thick, viscous liquid oozed from the rupture.

One of the guards looked the tube over uneasily. "What was in this thing?"

"Good question, soldier." The Guardian turned and speared Westfield with a look. "Care to explain this, Paul?"

"This was all approved, Guardian. Washington agreed that we needed—"

Westfield's explanation was suddenly interrupted by a voice from on high.

"Will someone get me down from here?"

They all looked up to see Carl Packard hanging from the ceiling.

Several lengths of stainless steel tubing had been ripped from their mountings and bent around the scientist like a pretzel.

"Carl?" Westfield looked dazed. "Carl, what happened?"

"It was those infernal Newsboy clones. Oh, Experiment Thirteen was giving me some trouble—he'd started resisting the increased input we were feeding him—but I could have dealt with that." Packard squirmed within his steel bonds. "But then, those bastard clones came tearing through the place. Before I could stop them, one of them shut down the restraining fields, and Thirteen just exploded out of the tube! He twisted this steel around me, and then they all ran off through the air ducts. We have to find him immediately."

The Guardian reached out and grabbed Westfield by the arm, even as he tried to reassure the dangling scientist. "Don't worry, Dr. Packard. I promise you that we'll get to the bottom of this. Won't we, Paul?"

"You don't understand the urgency, Guardian." Packard shifted awkwardly, trying in vain to free up an arm. "The code words—the subliminal instructions—hadn't yet been implanted in Experiment Thirteen. We have absolutely no control over him."

Miles away, the thick metal grate of what appeared to be nothing more than a highway drainage system suddenly exploded outward, coming to rest over twenty feet away. The source of that explosive force was the red-gloved fist of a young man who stalked out of the big drainpipe and into the bright moonlit night.

From the soles of his black boots to the top of his dark, tousled hair, the figure stood about five-feet-two. His slim, tightly muscled form was clothed in tight red pants and a blue pullover shirt with a high black mock-turtleneck collar. Across the front of his shirt was a bright red and yellow pentagonal Superman S-shield. He looked to be in his midteens.

As he stood taking in the cool night air, the young Newsboys came clambering out of the pipe behind him.

"Dat's some knuckle sam'wich ya got dere, pal." Scrapper tipped his cap back as he paced out the distance the grate had flown. "Ya got real moxie!"

"Solid, man. Real solid." Flip gave their new friend an appreciative thumbs-up.

Big Words walked around and around the grate, scratching his head. "This is most perplexing. The grating is virtually undamaged, yet a blow of such magnitude should have rendered it an amorphously twisted wreck."

"Aw, geez, Big Words, lay off the extra syllables for once, will you? This is no time for a science lesson." Gabby was wound tight with excitement. "We're stayin' up late, an' witnessin' a thrillin' dash for freedom, an' . . . an' geez, ain't it great?!"

"It's great all right. It's probably the most important thing we've ever done." Tommy looked longingly at the open sky. "I wish we could go with you, friend, but it'll be better for you if we head back underground and confuse the trail. Westfield will send his goons after you, you know. Here." Tommy pulled a dark leather jacket from his backpack and handed it to the stranger. "Maybe this'll help some . . . until you can find some other clothes to help you blend in."

"Yeah?" The young man shrugged into the jacket. "Thanks—nice fit. But I don't know that I'm all that interested in blending in."

"Geez, I guess this is like good-bye—at least for now. Not that you need it or anything, but good luck, Superboy!"

"Hey!" The young man whirled around, almost knocking Gabby over. "Don't ever call me Super*boy!* Got that?" He waited for Gabby's stuttered agreement, then leapt high into the air and headed southeast, toward the lights of Metropolis.

21

The early morning sun was glimmering off the granite face of Superman's memorial statue when the stolen taxi roared across the plaza. A young punk with a cheap handgun leaned out of the front passenger side window as they sped past the tomb, popping off a few shots at the statue.

"Woo! Die, Superman, die! Yee-hah!" Despite the early hour, the young man was wearing a pair of wire-rimmed sunglasses.

The crewcut driver just grinned. "Ain't ya heard, Specs? The man's already dead."

"Well, then, we got us nothing to worry about, do we?" Specs popped off another shot. "Drive on, Crew! The day is young!"

Crew made a sharp left, sending the cab down a sloping embankment and onto a paved jogging path. Less than sixty feet ahead of them, a trim young woman was running along the path.

"All right! Jogger—twenty-five points!" Crew put his foot to the floor.

The young woman looked back over her shoulder in horror as the cab bore down upon her. To her right, the embankment grew too steep to climb; to her left was the park lake. She was about to make a mad dive and take her chances with the water when a red and blue blur shot down from the sky, scooping her up in one hand.

Superboy landed on the jogging path, holding the young woman up over his head, balancing her in one hand as a waiter might carry a fully loaded tray. Planting his feet firmly, he thrust out his other hand at the speeding cab.

The taxi slammed into Superboy hard, its front end folding around him like an accordion. His boots cut a deep furrow into the pavement as the impact drove him down the path, but he lost neither his balance nor his hold on the young woman he held aloft.

Weak groans came from within the wrecked cab, but the Boy of Steel paid them no mind. He set the jogger gently back down on her feet, and she gaped at him in amazement. He was no taller than she was. "You— you saved my life!"

Superboy beamed at her. "Hey, that's my job, gorgeous! And you're way too beautiful to let die!"

"But—but who are you?!"

"Let's see, shall we?" He came a step closer to her and yanked open his leather jacket. "I've got a big red 'S' on my chest, and I can fly faster than a speeding bullet. What else?" He glanced back over his shoulder at the crumpled taxi. "Too bad there weren't any locomotives to take on, but at least I proved that I'm more powerful than a runaway cab."

He favored the woman with a knowing smile and let his jacket fall closed. "Now, who do you *think* I am?"

He strolled over to the cab, almost swaggering, and sank his fingertips into one of the crumpled doors. He paused to wink at the jogger. Then, without any discernible effort, he ripped away the door. The jogger watched, fascinated. *He's showing off for me!* The thought nearly made her giggle.

Superboy pried Specs and Crew out of the wreck, checking them over and tossing them onto the ground. "You punks are just lucky you were wearing your seat belts. I wouldn't go making any sudden moves just now, if I were you."

"Chill, man!" Specs lay sprawled and shaking like an addict going cold turkey. "We won't be givin' you no more trouble."

"You got that right!" The Boy of Steel collected their guns, crushing them in his hands. Then he caught his reflection in the round lenses of Specs's sunglasses and he smiled. "Nice shades. Good thing you didn't break 'em!"

Specs whipped off his sunglasses and held them out to Superboy. "They're yours, man—my gift! Just don't hurt us!"

"Why, thank you, citizen." Superboy slipped on the sunglasses. "I'm sure the police'll take this act of selflessness into account when they book you for attempted vehicular homicide. Oh, yeah—and for desecrating my statue, too!"

The jogger looked at him, dumbfounded. "It's really you, isn't it? You're really Superman! But I thought you were dead!"

He tenderly traced one finger along her jawline. "Well, I guess you could say I got better—*lots* better!"

Superboy leaned forward and kissed her passionately. She was a little startled, but not completely surprised, and she made no move to break things off.

Two policemen came scrambling down the embankment, following the ruts made by the cab.

The Boy of Steel gave the jogger another wink. "Looks like my work here is done. Gotta fly, babe. See you around!"

With a wave, he soared away into the sky, leaving the amazed policemen glancing skyward. While one of the cops pulled the punks to their feet and stood them up against the side of the cab, the other checked on the jogger.

"I'm fine, really." The woman stared a little dreamily after her flying rescuer.

The cop looked from her to the disappearing form. "Who *was* that?!"

"He said that he was Superman. " She shook her head, smiling. While his kiss had been nice—sweet actually—she'd found it somewhat lacking in experience. "But in some ways, I think he's still a boy."

"Heads up, here comes Superman!" The cry went up along the docks of Hob's Bay. A dozen homeless people gathered around as Bibbo strolled along in his makeshift costume, passing out plastic-wrapped sandwiches from a big rucksack.

"Here youse go, folks. Plenty fer ever'body—compliments o' Sooperman."

A young boy looked up shyly from behind his mother. "How can you be Superman? Mommy said that he got killed dead. Are you a ghost?"

"Naw, squirt, I ain't no ghost." Bibbo knelt down and ruffled the boy's hair. "Guess ya could say I'm one o' Sooperman's helpers. I'm helpin' folks out 'cause Sooperman ain't here to do it hisself. Ya hungry?"

The boy nodded his head.

He handed the boy a sandwich and an apple. "Yeah, I remember what it's like, bein' hungry. I had me some pretty tough times, but I got through 'em. Now I'm helpin' other folks get through 'em." Bibbo stood up and looked around. "Sooner or later, mos' ever'body has some bad times, but we can all get through 'em if we stick togedder. Dat's the important thing."

Bibbo was halfway through his supply of sandwiches when he heard someone crying. He handed his rucksack to the little boy's mother and rushed down to the end of the pier where an old woman stood sobbing as if her heart were breaking.

"My babies . . . my babies . . ."

"What izzit, lady? What's wrong?"

She looked up, her eyes red and puffy with fresh tears. "I didn't know you'd be bringing food, or I wouldn't have done it. I just couldn't stand to watch them starve."

"Watch who starve?"

"My puppies. There were three of them. Somebody'd thrown them away like they were garbage, but they were beautiful and I took care of them as best as I could. But I couldn't afford to feed them anymore—couldn't afford to feed myself." Her hand shook as she pointed to the water off the pier. "So I sent them on . . . to a better world."

Bibbo looked stricken. "Aw, no. I would'a took 'em! I'll *still* take 'em!"

With a single bound, he dove into the icy black waters. Visibility was just about nil, but somehow among all the refuse at the river bottom, he managed to find a small burlap bag loosely tied to a cinder block. Bibbo yanked the bag free and kicked his way to the surface.

Moments later, Bibbo crouched at the end of the dock, gulping in air, as the old woman shakily tore at the bag.

A homeless man bent down to help her, but when the bag finally came open, he just shook his head. "Sorry, Bibbo. You were too late."

Bibbo hunched over, wringing the water from his sweatshirt to hide his tears. "Can't even save a puppy—not even one li'l pup."

Suddenly there came a raspy coughing noise as one puppy shakily struggled to his feet. Bibbo scooped the puppy up out of the bag, cradling it in his big hands. The pup sneezed and licked Bibbo's nose.

"Hey, li'l guy! Yer a real fighter, ain'tcha?" Bibbo turned and held the pup out to the old woman. "Here ya go, ma'am. Sorry I couldn't save 'em all."

The woman looked at Bibbo and the pup. "I really think you should keep him, Superman. I think you two belong together."

"Ya think so? Yeah, maybe yer right." Bibbo held the pup to his chest, letting it nuzzle against the stubble of his chin. "Ya know, he's the last o' his litter, kinda like the way my fav'rit was the last o' his. I think I'm gonna name him—Krypton!"

The pup licked Bibbo right across the lips; he had found his soul mate.

Lois Lane came back from lunch to find Superboy waiting for her in the City Room. The Boy of Steel was sitting in her chair with his feet up on her desk and flipping through the early afternoon edition of the *Planet*.

Lois stopped dead in her tracks. "What on Earth—?!"

"Oh, there you are! It's about time." He tossed the paper down on the desk. "What gives, Lane? I make a great heroic save, and it winds up on page six—*page six!*"

The Boy of Steel stopped to give a big grin as Jimmy Olsen came across the City Room with his camera. Once the photographer had squeezed off a few shots, the teen hero sat up and smacked the newspaper with the back of his hand. "What's this on page one? CYBORG SUPERMAN RESCUES PASSENGERS IN TRAIN WRECK? Big deal! I coulda done that, and I'm no phony cyborg. I'm the real thing!"

"You?" Lois looked distinctly less than convinced. "Superman?"

If he noticed her skepticism, Superboy gave no sign. In fact, he beamed at her. "That's me . . . the one and only, all other claims to the contrary."

"Superman, huh?" Jimmy set down his camera. "Super*boy* is more like it!"

In a flash, the teenager jumped up out of the chair and grabbed Jimmy by the lapels, turning him upside down. "Listen, pal, I don't like to be called that. Okay?"

"Uh, sure. Sure!" Jimmy spoke fast, feeling the blood rushing to his head. "No problem . . . Super*man.*"

"That's better. That's much better."

As Superboy set the photographer back down on his feet, Lois pushed past them and hit a preset number on her phone.

"Lois?" Superboy plopped down on the corner of her desk. "Who're you calling?"

"Building security! I don't like having my friends manhandled."

"Hey, I'm sorry!" He laid his hand down across the cradle of the phone, disconnecting the call. "Don't be mad. I'm here to give you the story of the century—*moi!*"

"Look, junior, I've already met two other Supermen, and while you're strong—I'll grant you that—you're not nearly as convincing as they were."

"What's the problem? Don't I look mature enough? Is that it? Okay." He pulled the sunglasses from his jacket pocket, put them on, and ran his hands through his hair, pulling it back off his forehead. "There, doesn't that make me look older?"

Lois looked at him, and her heart went to her throat, but before she could say anything, the kid whipped off the sunglasses and stared across the room.

"Whoa!" Superboy's voice sounded as if it were in danger of changing at any moment. "*Who* is *that?*"

"Hmm?" Lois followed the direction of his gaze to the young woman who was striding through the City Room. *Well, why am I not surprised?* The young woman was African-Asian, strikingly beautiful, with dark, flawless skin, almond eyes, and glossy black hair.

"She's a college intern—Tana Something. I don't remember her last name. Listen, ah, Super*man,* I've been thinking, maybe we should talk."

"Yeah. Yeah, sure, Lois—but some other time, huh?" Superboy was already halfway across the City Room. "Right now I gotta bail. Personal emergency. See ya!"

The elevator doors closed shut behind Tana just as Superboy got there. For a second, he considered forcing open the doors and pulling the car back up by the cables, but he quickly dismissed the idea. *Wouldn't be cool to needlessly cause property damage, especially when there's a better way to say hello!* Grinning, he headed for the nearest window.

Moments later, Tana stepped out onto the sidewalk, muttering angrily under her breath. "I must've been crazy, thinking it would be easier to break in at the *Planet* than at WGBS. A bake-off . . . I can't believe they wanted me to cover a bake-off! Well, I'll show them. I'll—"

There was a sudden rush of air and Tana found herself soaring off the ground, a powerful arm around her waist and a cheerful voice ringing in her ear. "Hi, there. Care for a lift?"

"What're you doing? Put me down! Put me down this instant!"

"Oh, that'd be a bad idea. We're at least thirty stories up, and you probably wouldn't land as well as I do. How about if we set down over here?"

Superboy touched down atop a nearby office building. "Yeah, this is better. Alone at last. You're Tana, right? Sorry, but I didn't catch the last name."

"Moon." She answered automatically, even as she slowly eased away from him. "The question is, who are *you*?"

"Me? Oh, I'm Superman. Couldn't you tell? Come on, an intelligent woman like you must have heard of me already."

Despite her still-racing pulse, Tana Moon began to smile. Of all the Supermen sightings, the latest one had indeed featured a teenager whose description perfectly fit the young man who had literally swept her off her feet.

Superboy returned her smile a hundredfold. "So what brings you to the big bad city, Tana Moon?"

"I'm a reporter. At least, I'm going to be one, if anyone'll ever give me a break." Her eyes widened slightly, and she gave the Boy of Steel a speculative look.

He applauded. He'd understood that look immediately. "See, I knew you were quick. You'll go far, Tana. But reporting for the *Planet*? No way! You're too hot to hide in the print media. I see you more as the video type."

"Well, I *had* put in an application at WGBS."

"Of course you did. Well, here's your big story. I'm Superman, babe—and I'm all yours!"

"Superman? Really?" She looked him up and down. "Don't take this personally, but—you look so young."

"I know. It's the hair."

"The hair." *Sure it is. He's at least five years younger than I am.*

"You don't buy that, huh? Okay, okay." Superboy looked around conspiratorially and lowered his voice. "I'll tell you the whole story. And I guarantee it'll land you the job of your dreams. You interested?"

Tana raised an eyebrow. "Completely. Please, tell me more."

Sydney Happersen came running into Lex Luthor's private gym to find his boss in his shirtsleeves, swinging a Louisville Slugger at an imaginary ball.

"Mr. L?"

"Come in, Sydney. Just loosening up a little. Softball season's coming up, you know. I thought I might play with the LexCorp team, enjoy my youth while I can, eh?"

"Uh, y-yes, sir. A-as you say, sir."

Luthor's face darkened. "You're stammering, Sydney. When you stammer, there's always bad news. What is it now?"

"The n-newest Superman . . . he's on WGBS right now."

"Why didn't you say so?" Luthor hit a switch on the wall, and a television monitor came up out of the floor.

The screen showed the Boy of Steel seated across from an exotic-looking young interviewer. Any other time, Luthor would have given more of his attention to her, but now what the boy was saying proved even more of a distraction.

"That's right, Ms. Moon. I'm Superman's clone! I don't have his old memories, because there was no living brain to tap into, but aside from that—I'm Superman. I wish I could tell you more about the process, but it all has to remain top secret for now."

The screen cut to a most flattering close-up of the interviewer. "Not a hoax, not a dream. The Metropolis Marvel is back in action—and GBS has him." She smiled confidently. "Stay tuned for more exclusive updates over this station. For GBS News, I'm Tana Moon."

The television screen erupted in a shower of glass and sparks as Luthor's bat struck home. Glass crunched under his shoes as he stalked back and forth across the gym, smoking bat in hand. "Happersen, do we have a new mole in place in Cadmus yet?"

"Y-y-yes, sir. And a very highly placed one, I might add."

"I want him in my office—ASAP! Understood?"

"Perfectly, sir."

"Superman's clone. Just bloody marvelous." Luthor flung the bat to the floor and stormed from the room.

．　　　．　　　．

In the boardroom of Galaxy Communications, CEO Vincent Edge rubbed his hands together in anticipation of the overnight ratings. "The switchboard's been going nonstop since we started running those teasers. Seems that the public just can't get enough of your Superboy, Tana."

"That's Super*man*, Mr. Edge." Tana cautiously spoke up. "He doesn't like being called Superboy."

"Well, I don't care what he calls himself. I just want that kid on the air as much as possible."

A half dozen heads nodded, and the newest commandment of Vincent Edge was duly noted on an equal number of executive notepads. Tana looked around the room. Superboy—*Superman,* she corrected herself—had been right on the money when he'd told her that his story would land her a job. She still couldn't believe how fast she'd gotten on the air; the fact that she was in a meeting with the company's chief executive officer, hobnobbing with experienced news talent like Cat Grant, seemed like some wild fantasy.

Edge laid his palms on the table and leaned forward, as if passing on a great wisdom to his underlings. "When the masses think of Superman, I want them to think of *our* Superman!"

"But, Mr. Edge—" One of the news producers raised a pencil to get the CEO's attention. "At last count there were three other superpowered individuals operating as 'Superman.' Shouldn't they all be covered equally? Shouldn't they all be investigated, for that matter? They can't *all* be Superman."

"Of course, of course!" Edge waved his hand dismissively. "It's the duty of the news bureau to cover everything as thoroughly as possible, and that includes these Superman pretenders. But we can do much more with our Superman. This goes far beyond the news, beyond even programming." Edge spoke with an almost messianic fervor. "We have the opportunity to recreate a *legend*, people! A legend to which GBS would hold exclusive rights. But we have to *grip* the public's imagination!" The communications executive leaned forward and snapped his hand closed, as if grabbing hold of the air itself. "We have to grip it hard and not let go—or someone else will claim the legend for himself. We need to show something that's never been seen on TV before. I know—" He snapped his fingers. "A live broadcast of our Superman capturing a wanted criminal, the whole shooting match, from start to finish. Now all we need is the right criminal. Any ideas, people? Yes, Briscoe?"

Donald Briscoe shifted uneasily in his chair. "Well, sir, word on the street is that an old Intergang don has holed up in Suicide Slum and is consolidating his power, hoping to start a new organization. We could send the kid in after him."

"Just a minute!" Cat Grant piped up from the end of the table. "That isn't reporting the news, that's staging the news!"

"Not at all, Catherine. What Briscoe is suggesting is a sort of sting operation—a logical outgrowth of good, investigative journalism. And we'll naturally make sure that the police are well-informed. I'll speak with the commissioner personally. Given the current state of affairs, I don't think they'll mind a little helping hand."

Edge aimed a finger at his news director. "Get me all the information on this gangster that you can, Briscoe." He then turned and gave Tana his most beatific smile. "We can count on your young Superman, can't we, my dear?"

Tana fairly glowed in the attention. "I think that can be arranged, Mr. Edge."

As evening fell, the Boy of Steel stood on the landing strut of a WGBS news helicopter high over Suicide Slum. Inside the copter, Tana gave a thumbs-up as the cameras went live, and the young hero dropped feet-first to the streets below. He landed like a bomb, the pavement cracking around his feet, and people scattered at his approach. He then walked boldly up to a boarded-up old night spot called the Silver Glove Club and rapped firmly on the reinforced door.

"Okay, open up in there! This is Superman. I'm looking for the guy they call the Steel Hand!"

Lois turned on her television just in time to see four huge men jump Superboy from behind. The smallest of the men was easily twice Superboy's size, and all of them wielded chains, brass knuckles, or lengths of pipe—but they never had a chance. Superboy gave a heave, threw his arms back, and sent all four men flying. They landed hard and made no move to retaliate.

Lois watched spellbound as WGBS cut from its aerial cameras to a street-based crew. A little superimposed legend in the lower right hand corner of the screen proclaimed that this was a LIVE GBS EXCLUSIVE, and Tana Moon's breathless narration informed her that she was watching a television first.

Superboy pounded on the door a little harder, this time leaving several fist-sized dents in it. A gun barrel poked out through a slot in the door.

Machine-gun fire suddenly strafed across Superboy's chest and abdomen.

Superboy just smiled, shoved his hands through the doorframe, and ripped the metal barrier off its hinges. He managed to take one step over the threshold before a bazooka shell hit him squarely in the chest.

Lois cried out as she saw the Boy of Steel fly backward out of the club and smash through the side of a parked delivery truck. The truck immediately erupted in flames.

"Oh, my God!" Tana's cool narration quickly edged toward hysteria. "My God, it exploded! Superman was still in that truck when it exploded!"

The image jumped from the ground-level view of the burning wreck to an aerial shot and back again. And then, as the street-based camera crew moved in for a closer shot, the twisted, burning metal began to move.

Superboy emerged from the wreckage, coughing smoke. Soot streaked his face, and his hair hung down over his eyes. His skin-tight costume had come through the explosion unscathed, but his leather jacket hung off him in flaming shreds.

For a moment, Lois could have sworn the boy was panicking, so frantically did he seem to beat out the flames. But then he angrily flung the smoldering jacket away from him and streaked into the Silver Glove Club.

The televised image jumped and weaved as the camera crew charged into the club after the Boy of Steel. Across the screen flashed shots of unconscious gunmen and crushed, twisted weapons. The cameramen caught up to the young hero just as two of Steel Hand's personal bodyguards leveled assault rifles at him.

Superboy just laughed and grabbed the barrels of their weapons. The guns seemed to explode in his hands, sending hundreds of pieces flying in all directions. The bodyguards fell back, hitting the floor and covering their heads with their hands.

The sound of a hoarse bellow came over the camera microphones as the old Intergang don himself charged at the Boy of Steel. Salvatore "Steel Hand" Galvagno was a big, stocky man who had grown up on the waterfront; he had first gained fame among the old crime families for his ability to break a man's leg with his bare hands. A gang war had cost him one of those hands years ago, and he since wore a steel prosthesis in its place. Without a moment's hesitation, he swung his steel hand hard against the side of Superboy's head.

Superboy turned slowly, seemingly more annoyed than angry, and decked the big man with a single punch. "Steel Hand, huh? Glass Jaw is more like it." He gave a big thumbs-up to the cameras, and the network broke to a commercial.

When they returned, Tana Moon was standing outside the Silver Glove Club, interviewing Superboy while Steel Hand and his henchmen were being led away by the police. "You really had us worried there for a moment, Superman."

"What, that little thing with the bazooka and the truck?" He shrugged. "Ah, it was a little bit of a surprise, but nothing I couldn't handle."

"We were wondering . . . did you use X-ray vision to determine Steel Hand's exact location?"

"X-ray vision?" Superboy looked puzzled. "Are you kidding?! I was so mad I just plowed right into the place. I mean, that was my favorite jacket. It was a gift."

Lois switched off the TV and sat staring at the blank screen for several minutes, trying to make sense of what she'd just seen. Then she picked up the phone and called Smallville.

"Hello, Martha? Hi, it's Lois—how are you? How's Jonathan? Oh, good. I'm sure he's glad to be home." Lois hesitated for a moment. "Martha, I have to talk with someone about this. I hope you don't mind my asking, but were you watching GBS's report on the young Superman?"

In Smallville, Martha answered softly, her voice almost a whisper. "Oh, heavens no, Lois. I've had my fill of television for a while! And all those Supermen . . . they stir Jonathan up a mite, and the doctor says that he needs to relax. Thankfully, he's upstairs asleep right now."

"Well, believe me, Martha, I know how Jonathan feels. I don't know whether to laugh or cry or scream—sometimes I want to do all three at once. This young Superman, for example—well, I had a—weird encounter with him just today at the *Planet*. He's arrogant and more than a little careless—he took offense at something a photographer said and turned the man upside down—but he pulled a very strange stunt this morning." Lois shivered slightly as she recalled how the boy looked with glasses. "And this evening, while taking on some gangsters, his costume hardly took a scratch, but his jacket got shredded. It was just like the way Superman's capes always used to take such a beating.

"So I started thinking, well . . ." Lois tugged absently at her hair. "Martha, what was Clark like when he was in his midteens? What if he had the powers of a Superman? Maybe he would have acted like this kid."

Martha frowned into the phone as if Lois could see her. "Now you know that no boy of ours would ever act the way you say that youngster does, powers or no powers."

"I guess that's the problem, Martha. You didn't raise this boy. Do you know what a clone is?"

Alone over the city, Superboy swooped past the downtown skyscrapers once more and settled on the roof of an old brownstone. He sauntered casually close to the edge, rested one foot on a cornice, and leaned against his knee, looking out over Metropolis with immense contentment. The city air was too dirty and hazy for him to see many stars, but the full moon beamed down at him, and he smiled. *This is a totally perfect end to a totally perfect day.* He clapped his hands together, as if giving himself a high five. "Metropolis has gotta feel safer already, knowing that Superman's back on the job."

A voice suddenly rang out behind him. "Yes, you did okay out there, son."

Superboy whirled around, clenching his fists as he turned, ready for anything. There, standing straight and tall before him, was a blue and yellow clad figure that he dimly recognized from all the information that had been fed him while he was still in the tube. "Guardian?! Hey, don't tell me you're gonna try to drag me back to the Project!"

"No. Not now, at any rate. There've been some big shake-ups at Cadmus. Your little stunt of going public with a big television network has finally caused certain people in Washington to ask some serious questions. For the time being, at least, you're on your own."

"Whoa! You serious?" The young man peered closely at the Guardian, then shrugged. "Stupid question. Of course you're serious. Well, damn. Cool! Hey, speaking about serious, check out the new jacket!" Superboy turned around, flashing the broad gold S-shield across the back of the jacket. "WGBS is making these up by the truckload—they're gonna make sure I'm always lookin' fine!"

The Guardian held back a sigh. "That's nice, son, but remember that things aren't always as they seem. And you won't always have as easy a time as you did today."

"Hey, don't worry about me, man. I am *primed*. No way is anything gonna get past me!" He turned around to find himself alone on the rooftop. "Guardian? Hey, Guardian?!"

Superboy turned a complete circle. He stared hard into the shadows, but the big man was nowhere in sight. "Well—*duh*!" The young hero stood scratching his head. "Guess it wouldn't hurt to be a little more alert, at that." With a shrug of his shoulders, he flew off into the night.

.   .   .

In a windowless "safe room" within a building secretly maintained by LexCorp through a dummy corporation, Carl Packard sat squirming in a straight-backed chair, sweating as if the room's one shaded lamp were a bank of floodlights.

Lex Luthor paced back and forth, taking care to stay partly in the shadows. It was an outrageously theatrical measure, but Luthor had always found it effective, and he fully intended to make his visitor as uncomfortable as possible.

Luthor paused, slowly turned, and tapped his foot against the tiled floor. "I did think, *Dr.* Packard, that we had an agreement. As my mole, you were supposed to keep us informed of any untoward actions on the part of the Cadmus Project."

"This wasn't supposed to happen, Mr. Luthor. Believe me!" Packard risked a glance in Luthor's direction, but he couldn't tell if the industrialist was looking directly at him or not. "Westfield and the other directors felt the world needed a Superman—"

"One at their beck and call, of course."

"What? Oh, lord, no. There was never any of that; at least, not on the part of the directors. With Westfield himself . . . well, that's a good question. He does tend to follow his own agendas." Packard shook his head. "At any rate, after the Project lost possession of Superman's body, I was instructed to rush Experiment Thirteen into production . . . to create a new Superman."

Luthor suddenly leaned into the light, coming nearly nose to nose with the geneticist. "And you didn't consider such an experiment at all 'untoward'?!"

"Well . . ." Packard nervously loosened his tie. "I suppose it could be seen as unusual. But I was going to tell you! I was preparing a paper all about the experiment and would have slipped it to Dr. Happersen long before Thirteen was to be decanted. Honestly!" He slumped back into his chair. "He wasn't ready yet."

"Who wasn't ready, Packard?"

"Experiment Thirteen . . . the young Superman. You don't think we intended to release a *teenager* with those powers, did you? We weren't *total* fools!" Packard's voice rose in anger, his professional pride wounded. "After all, in trying to duplicate Kryptonian DNA, we were working in uncharted territory. There were certain safeguards we'd planned to implant in the subject, just in case anything went wrong later on. But those infernal Newsboy clones liberated him before the safeguards were in place, before he was even fully grown! He was at least a week from maturity."

"I see." Luthor faded back into the shadows. "And what, besides a collective gnashing of teeth, does Cadmus intend to do about this?"

"Nothing! There is nothing we can do about it now! That young up-start has already become a media darling! If he disappeared now, GBS would shine a light under every possible rock! Cadmus can't afford that —Washington is reviewing our entire operation as it is. If only that stupid kid hadn't told everyone that he was a clone." Packard rubbed his neck. "In retrospect, it was perhaps a mistake to include MTV as part of his information feed."

Luthor loomed over Packard, noting with scant satisfaction that the man's sweating had become a virtual Niagara. "Let's talk a little more about his creation. From the earlier information you supplied Dr. Hap-persen, I'd gotten the impression that you *couldn't* clone Superman."

Packard dragged his hands through his hair. "Well, yes and no. Super-man's body was intact—we couldn't isolate a tissue culture. And we got only a partial reading of his DNA. But from that, we were able to simulate certain properties of his DNA and implant them in a tissue sample obtained from another donor."

Luthor stroked his beard. "So, this young clone's powers probably do *not* exactly duplicate those of Superman."

"Yes . . . yes, that's quite correct, sir. He may have weaknesses and shortcomings of which we—and he himself—are unaware."

Luthor leaned in close again, showing Packard his teeth. "Tell me more, Packard. Tell me everything you know."

Deep within the darkened chambers of the main branch of the Metropo-lis Mercantile Bank, Gerald Fine merrily went about his business. His business was cracking safes.

Tonight, Fine softly hummed an old Beatles tune as he attacked the door of the bank's largest vault with a high-speed drill. He finished drilling through the shiny chromium steel along one side of the lock mechanism, then backed the bit out, reset it, and started on the other side. He chuckled to himself as he went about his work.

The bank had been established in 1875, and most of their security system didn't seem to be much newer. In casing the building, Fine had found no ultrasonic motion detectors, no heat sensors, and no electric eyes. *And this is the main branch!* He clicked his tongue against the back of his teeth. *You'd think such a well-heeled place would've sprung for a better system. That alarm box of theirs was so old, I'll bet it was installed during the Truman administration! I was bypassing circuits like that before my voice changed!*

Fine finished his drilling and then, cracking his fingers, reached in through the hole he'd made and began manipulating the guts of the lock. There was a series of soft clicks as tumblers fell into place. *They might as well have left this door unlocked.* Fine smiled and eased open the door. *Well, time to make that big withdrawal.*

Suddenly a black gloved hand shot out of the shadows, grabbing Fine by the throat. "Sorry. Business hours are nine to four."

The shocked safecracker struck at the wrist of the hand that held him, but he could not break the grip. Fine looked up into a strong, powerful jaw and mouth; the glow of his flashlight glimmered off the smoked amber of the visor that wrapped about his captor's eyes.

The Superman reached out with his free hand and crushed out the offending light. He stepped away from the vault, carrying his squirming captive at arm's length.

"N-no . . . n-not you!" The burglar's voice was a pinched gasp. "You're the one they were talking about on the news! The one who—who killed the ski mask murderer!"

The Superman smiled grimly. "I've dealt with a number of transgressors. What I did to them was meant as a warning. Too bad you didn't pay better attention; now I'll have to make an example of you as well!"

"H-h-hey, wait a second! I'm not like that!" Fine clutched at the Superman's wrist, thinking fast and talking faster. "I mean, the creep who attacked that woman—sure, he *deserved* to die! B-but I'm just a burglar. I'm nonviolent. I don't even *carry* a gun. I've never hurt anyone in my life! Y-you wouldn't kill a guy just for cracking a safe, would you?"

The Superman dropped the gasping safecracker to the floor. "There are many forms of violence. You may not have caused physical harm, but your crimes have hurt many people."

Fine lay huddled on the floor. "Please don't kill me."

"You're not worth killing. But I will make certain that you don't try this again." The Superman reached down and grabbed the safecracker by his hands.

The man's screams raised a most effective alarm.

"I've never seen anything like it, Ms. Lane." Dr. Daniel Blumkin peered over the X rays for what seemed like the hundredth time. "Every bone from this man's fingertips to his elbows has been broken—almost crushed in some cases. If it had been any worse, we'd have had to amputate. As it is, he'll be in rehab for months before he's even able to hold a cup again."

Lois glanced from the X rays back over her shoulder at the bed where Gerald Fine lay with his arms up in traction and encased in plaster. "And he claims that Superman did this to him?"

"He's said little else, and I could almost believe him. His arms bore deep bruises. They formed handprints, Ms. Lane."

She shuddered at the thought. "Doctor, at least four superpowered men have recently been playing Superman. It might be any one of them. Could I ask your patient some questions?"

"You could try, Ms. Lane, but we've had to give him a lot of morphine for the pain." Blumkin gathered the X rays into a folder and paused at the door. "Just keep it short, okay? He needs to rest."

Lois nodded, then knelt down beside the groggy safecracker. "Mr. Fine, can you hear me? This Superman who attacked you . . . what did he look like? Was there anything unusual about him?"

Fine cocked his head toward the reporter. His lips moved slowly, as if it were an effort to form the words. "Suh-sunglasses. He wore sunglasses. Big yellow ones . . . like a visor."

"Oh, dear God." She drew back from the bed. *"That* one."

Fine nodded off and Lois left the room, wandering aimlessly down the hospital corridors. *I just don't know what to think now. Each of the "Supermen" I've run into so far has seemed a little like Clark . . . but all I know for certain is that his body's missing again. And from what my sources say, this time the Cadmus Project isn't to blame. Maybe I should call Lana Lang. I need to talk to someone who will understand!*

Lois turned a corner into a lounge area and nearly ran into Cat Grant.

"Lois? What on Earth—?" Cat gave the reporter a quick once-over and thrust a paper cup of coffee into her hands. "Here, you look like you could use this!"

"Thanks, Cat." Lois gratefully accepted the cup. *I must really look out of it.* "What're you doing here so early in the morning?"

"Interviewing Dr. Arthur Cronenberg, the head of psychiatry. It's for a new GBS special. The network thinks li'l Catherine Jane Grant here is ready for prime time. How about you?"

"Oh, I was trying to interview a sedated safecracker who had his anatomy rearranged by one of the new Supermen."

"Ow!" Cat made a face. "Sounds painful."

"It looked painful, too. It's all so weird, Cat." Lois sank down into a squeaking vinyl chair. "These pretenders have rescued people, they've stopped crimes, they've done so many good things—but in other ways, they're nothing like Superman! They're cold or cruel—or they're young egomaniacs with raging hormones!"

A flash of color drew Cat's attention to an old battered television set mounted on the wall in the corner of the lounge. "Speak of the devil."

The local GBS station was airing yet another interview with the Boy of Steel. The screen cut to a two-shot of Tana Moon and the young hero seated in front of a huge network logo.

"Yeah, Tana, Steel Hand thought he was tough—the bad guys always do—but nobody's too tough for *this* Superman!" Superboy grinned and gave a thumbs-up. "Hey, Metropolis, if you've got a problem, I'm your man—believe it!"

"Thank you, Superman!" The camera zoomed in to a tight close-up of the glamorous interviewer. "For GBS News, I'm Tana Moon!"

Cat kept staring at the screen long after the station had cut to commercial. "Tana looks a little too good on the tube. I wouldn't put it past Vinnie Edge to be grooming her as my replacement! I may have to keep an eye on her."

Lois made a sympathetic noise, but her mind was elsewhere. *All these "Supermen." For all I know, one of them could have stolen Clark's body. Maybe they all did! What if these pretenders are all in this together? I might never find out what happened to Clark!*

Lois finished the last of her coffee and was turning to toss the cup into a trash can when the silhouette of a man flashed across the frosted glass of the doors at the end of the lounge. The man paused momentarily behind the double doors, as if checking his watch. From the outline, he appeared to be a tall man with a strong jaw; he was wearing glasses and a fedora with the brim turned down in front. His silhouette looked for all the world like that of Clark Kent.

The man moved on, and Lois bolted for the doors. She pushed her way through the double doors, only to see the retreating figure striding away down another corridor. Lois dashed after him. "Clark! Stop! Please!"

"Eh? Beg pardon? Were you speaking to me, ma'am?" The man turned, doffing his hat politely. His thinning hair was white, and he looked to be in his sixties. He was in great shape for his age, but he was obviously not her fiancé.

"Oh! N-no . . . I . . . I'm sorry. Terribly sorry. I thought you were someone else . . . a friend of mine."

"Ah! Well, don't let it worry you. These mistakes happen all the time." The man plopped the hat back onto his head and began to stroll away. "Good luck in finding your friend."

"Sure, thanks." The reporter leaned back against the wall. *Get a grip, Lois, or you'll be seeing Clark everywhere.* She sighed. *I just want him to be alive so much.*

22

The visored Superman dropped down from the sky over the Antarctic, feeling strangely exhilarated. In his travels around the world, lives had been saved and criminals had been punished. *By now, the people must know that they again have a Superman on whom they can depend.* It had been a good beginning, in spite of his encounter with Lois.

That alone had left the Superman troubled. He'd felt a disturbing emptiness upon leaving her, but he'd dismissed it as an echo of experience from a previous life. He was determined not to let such feelings deter him; there was too much to be done.

The Superman dropped beneath the surface, allowing the ice to seal above him as he descended into the Fortress. He called out to his robots, and they scurried to attend him. Two of the metal servitors removed his cape and shield and flitted away to clean the garments and hold them in storage until they were again needed.

The Superman's step was light as he strode through the wide halls of the hidden sanctuary. *Thank the Creator, I can retire to this fine Fortress to rest and plan my next missions.* As he approached the monitors, though, his stride began to slow, and his joy to fade.

Across the monitors flashed images of red and blue—of strangers attired as Superman. One screen focused on a close-up of a dark-haired young teenager in a leather jacket giving a cocky thumbs-up. "Hey, Metropolis, if you've got a problem, I'm your man—believe it!" Another screen reran taped highlights of an armored man stopping a firefight. Yet a third showed a caped Cyborg towing a disabled ocean liner into port.

"What in Krypton's name is this?! Who are these people that they *dare* to wear the emblem of Superman?!"

A robot flitted obediently to the visored man. "Their origins are unknown to us, sir. But their activities have garnered considerable media attention—some more so than your own."

The Superman fought to keep his anger in check. "Unit Twelve, continue monitoring and compile all available data on these pretenders. I wish to know more about them."

He turned and stalked away from the screens. The Superman was surprised by the intensity of his anger; it had disturbed him perhaps even more than his meeting with Lois, and he suddenly felt drained and exhausted. He retired to bask in the renewing energies of the Regeneration Matrix. There he stood for over an hour with his eyes closed, gently running his hand over the surface of the Matrix and absorbing its energy. He did not yet know the identities or the motives of those other "Supermen," but if they dared challenge him, they would find him prepared.

At Metropolis City Hall, Captain Maggie Sawyer paused a few moments outside Police Commissioner Casey's door. The captain had never been one for useless speculation, but she wondered what this unexpected summons was all about. It had been a while since she'd caught any static over the S.C.U. . . .

Sawyer thought of Inspector Turpin's offhand comment about her "skinny butt" that had been dutifully relayed to her by Sergeant Rusty Sharp the night they investigated Superman's tomb. She knew that Turpin hadn't meant anything personal by it, but if that little communiqué had gotten repeated outside her unit—*maybe some higher-up is bent out of shape over a perceived "lack of discipline."*

Or maybe this meeting was about her membership in the local Gay and Lesbian Police Officers Association. She'd told the commissioner that she intended to run for association president next year; *was someone upset about that?* She was well aware that not everyone approved of her joining the association, though overall she'd gotten more support than flak—even from her ex-husband, interestingly enough. Jim Sawyer had been badly rocked when Maggie had begun to come to terms with herself—the divorce had been messy—but he'd since become a lot more supportive, even agreeing to joint custody of their daughter. When they'd last spoken and she'd mentioned her work with the association, he'd cheered her on. "Mags, if you're gonna come out of the closet, you might as well come out with guns blazing." Sawyer smiled tightly. *Wish me luck, Jim.*

She gave a perfunctory knock on the commissioner's office door.

A muffled voice answered from within. "Enter."

"You wanted to see me, sir?" Sawyer took one step over the threshold and stopped short. Commissioner Casey was nowhere to be seen, but Inspector William Henderson was leaning casually against the commissioner's big walnut desk, warming his hands around a big mug of coffee.

"Morning, Captain, come in. Coffee?"

"No, thank you." She took another step and closed the door behind her.

"Have a seat." Henderson gestured to a big leather chair in front of the desk. "We appreciate your coming in at this hour."

"No problem, Inspector. I'd just gotten in from a stakeout when I got the call." She stood by the chair uncertainly. "What's going on? Where's the commissioner?"

Henderson looked down at the floor, as if collecting his thoughts. "Jack Casey resigned last night."

"Oh, no." Sawyer slid down into the chair. "I knew he'd been under a lot of pressure—!"

"Yeah. It's a damned dirty shame. He was a fine policeman, a good cop, one of the best. But with Superman gone, every citizens' group in the six boroughs was on his back over the recent crime wave. Well, it's not his problem anymore. The mayor's named me as his new police commissioner."

"Wow." Sawyer had already figured as much, but hearing the news spoken aloud still made quite an impact. "Congratulations."

"Thanks, but given the heat I'll be taking, condolences might be more in order." Henderson nervously paced the floor. "Maggie, I know there's been some friction between the two of us over your command of the Special Crimes Unit, maybe even some hard feelings . . ."

"Never on *my* part, Commissioner." Sawyer pursed her lips. "To tell the truth, I've always wondered exactly what the problem was." She raised an eyebrow. "Was it because of my gender? Or my sexual orientation?"

"What?" Henderson looked startled. "Why, neither one! Don't be ridiculous!" He set down his coffee and leaned forward across the desk at her. "It just always stuck in my craw that as high-profile an outfit as the SCU was headed by a *captain*!" He threw up his hands and resumed pacing. "I wouldn't care if you were male, female, or neuter—but you have *inspectors* reporting to you, taking orders from an officer whom technically they outrank!"

"I see." Sawyer let out a sigh of relief. "I guess I can't blame you for that. When we were first getting the unit organized, I was a little uncomfortable about that myself. But Inspector Turpin finally put me at ease. He never seemed to mind about rank."

"Mind?!" Henderson snorted. "The way I hear it, Dan Turpin thinks you walk on water. Not that he's alone. Every last one of your officers would go through fire for you. That says a lot about you as a leader." The new commissioner looked a little sheepish. "This captain thing . . . maybe I shouldn't let it bother me. After all, the SCU wasn't my unit, and you've done a damn good job with it!" Henderson suddenly pulled himself up tall and looked Sawyer straight in the eye. "But I still don't like exceptions to the chain of command. And now I have the power to do something about it, something that should have been done a long time ago . . . *Inspector* Sawyer!"

"Inspector?" Sawyer blinked. "That's a very generous solution."

Henderson smiled and offered her his hand. "It's long overdue, Maggie. You've built the SCU into a model that's being copied all across the country. I have a news conference scheduled for tomorrow . . . we'll make all this official then." They shook on it and he continued. "But for right now, we have a lot of craziness on our plate, and a lot of contingencies to plan for."

The commissioner stepped behind his desk, and his new inspector pulled her chair in closer. "Ever since Superman's body disappeared— and that's just one of the mysteries we have to solve—those crazy cultists who worship him have been attracting more and more followers. Now you've been working the cult angle yourself, correct?"

Sawyer nodded. "Right. I don't think any of them are responsible for the theft of the body, but there's already been a schism within the original group. If the body isn't found soon, things could turn ugly." She paused. "We're going to need more personnel."

"Tell me about it. One of my conditions for taking this job was the mayor's guarantee that we'd be budgeted for a thousand new officers. It's going to take time to find them and train them, though. And in the meantime, we have to decide what to do about all these blasted Supermen! What we need is one *real* Superman, not four understudies." Henderson spread photos of Superboy, the Cyborg, the Man of Steel, and the visored Kryptonian across his desk. "What do you think, Maggie? Superman worked more closely with the SCU than with any other police unit. You knew him better than I did. Is there any chance—even a remote one —that he's somehow still alive?"

"I don't know. It seems like too much to hope for." Sawyer flipped through the four photos and their attached reports. "After what we went through with Cadmus, I could almost believe the kid's story about being a clone. The one in the metal suit doesn't seem to have that much power, and he seems to be focusing his attention on street crime; not a bad decision, all things considered. The Cyborg hasn't stayed put long enough for any of us to get a handle on him—is this NASA report true?"

Henderson shrugged. "It is according to Washington. One of their space probes recorded the Cyborg bolting the Doomsday monster to a meteor and tossing it—what does it say there?—'in an arc that sent it flying out of the plane of the solar system and eventually, out of the galaxy as well.' Could our Superman have done that?"

"I'm not sure. Maybe." Sawyer picked up the photo of the Kryptonian. "How'd we get this shot?"

"Bank camera from that Metropolis Mercantile job."

"Ah. This one—this one looks a lot like Superman. If only I could see his eyes—he's hiding something there, I'd bet on it! He also acts like Dirty Harry with a cape—or maybe a Super-Batman, considering that he's mainly done his work at night." She tossed down the photo. "I see him as a real problem, Commissioner. Today, he's breaking safecrackers' arms. Tomorrow, it could be jaywalkers' legs. How far do we let him go?"

"A better question is, 'Can we rein him in?' But I know what you mean. If he steps out of line again, we have to be ready to take a stand against him and make it stick. Do you think we can do that?"

Sawyer grinned sardonically. "We can try."

A little more than twenty-four hours later, Henderson and Sawyer made their position public.

The day's early morning news programs opened with graphic evidence of the visored Kryptonian's latest actions. As WGBS newscam shots of flashing red lights and battered hoodlums filled the screen, morning anchor Mary Louise Bromfield told the story.

"Responding to a predawn call from Guy Gardner of the Justice League, Metro police within the past hour arrested a Bakerline gang allegedly involved in a drugs-for-weapons swap. Gardner, a former Green Lantern, refused credit for the bust, saying that 'Superman, the *real* one, did the job.' "

The screen cut to a painful close-up of one arrested hoodlum. His face was bruised and swollen, and bloody bandages covered half of his head and one eye. "It was Superman, awright! Big guy . . . cape, 'S' on 'is chest, gold shades . . . he was like a maniac! He nearly kilt some of the guys!"

Bromfield came back on screen, her brow knit with concern. "City officials are reportedly disturbed over the violent actions of this masked Superman, who is but one of four claimants to the name—"

The anchor stopped in midsentence, bringing a hand to the wireless earplug hidden beneath her hair. "Excuse me . . . I've just received word that Metropolis's new commissioner of police, William Henderson, is about to make a statement. We go now live to City Hall—"

Even as Bromfield spoke, the screen cut to a long shot of the city hall auditorium. Henderson stood with Maggie Sawyer close by his side behind a podium bearing the official seal of the City of Metropolis. The commissioner rushed through his introductory comments and quickly got to the heart of the matter. "Citizens react with outrage—and rightly so—when their police use excessive force. The brutality of this self-proclaimed 'Superman' is no less an affront to public decency! I have instructed Inspector Margaret Sawyer of the Special Crimes Unit to give the highest priority in responding to and stopping this reign of terror. Inspector—?"

As Sawyer stepped up to the podium, she little suspected that her image was being received via satellite feed to a bank of monitors deep below the Antarctic wastes. The Kryptonian watched intently as the new inspector's face filled one of his video screens.

"We will not tolerate vigilante justice in Metropolis!" Sawyer hit her index finger against the podium as she emphasized the word "not." "I *knew* the real Superman, and he would *never* have resorted to the reckless mayhem that this masked man has practiced in his name."

"Masked?" The Kryptonian brought a hand up to his visor. "They're calling this a mask? They're calling me reckless?" He muted the sound of the GBS feed. "My every move has been carefully calculated. Can't they see that?"

A close-up of Guy Gardner came up on another screen. The Superman frowned and turned the volume back up. "Now, there—that one is truly reckless. What does he have to say for himself?"

Guy was all but crawling into the camera. "Hey, I don't mind tellin' ya, I thought the guy with the visor was just another fake like the rest of 'em. That's why I came to Metropolis in the first place—to kick all o' their butts. It's just a good thing for the rest o' them that I found the genuine article right off the bat. Lemme tell you, he kicked my butt from here to next week—and then he took care of those drug-dealin' Bakerline punks, to boot! So, hey, all I can say is, if the man I met wasn't the real Superman, then he oughtta be! I'm leavin' things in his hands—he won't have any trouble fightin' his own fights."

The reporter had to pull hard to reclaim his microphone. "What's your reaction to official condemnation of this Superman's actions as an unnecessarily harsh use of force?"

"So he got tough with that bunch of creeps. So what?" Guy smirked.

"It's not like they didn't have it comin'! Okay, maybe he lost his temper a little. Like, who hasn't, huh? Besides, after all he's been through, he's entitled!"

The Superman muted the sound for the entire monitor array, and walked away from the screens, turning their supervision back over to the robot Unit Twelve. " 'Came to town to kick their butts,' indeed. Gardner set an *ambush* for me! And now, since I have humbled him, that idiot has made himself my greatest public admirer!"

Another robot came up alongside him. "Sir, do you wish to change?"

"What?"

"You did not bother to remove your cape and shield when you returned this morning. Do you now wish to change?"

"Ah! Yes, just a moment, Unit Three." The Superman lifted off his raiment and stood contemplating it.

"Is something wrong, sir? Does the shield perhaps require polishing?"

"No, Unit Three, that won't be necessary. I was just thinking . . . this shield has long stood for justice. If too many claim it, misuse it, what will it stand for then? Until this moment, my actions felt absolutely right. But I *did* let my anger at Gardner get the better of me, and I took it out on those less capable of defending themselves. And now Gardner cheers me on. That alone is reason to reflect, to question what I have done. Perhaps the police officials were correct; perhaps there have been unnecessary elements of brutality in my actions. Perhaps there is a better way."

The Kryptonian handed the shield over to Unit Three. "Leave me now, until I summon you again." He walked off into a quiet corner of the Fortress to think. True to their programming, the robots withdrew and left him to his solitude.

On the sidewalks of Suicide Slum, Bibbo tucked his new pup into the crook of one arm as he read the inscription on a little bone-shaped dog tag. "Hey, this ain't right!" He stuck his head back through the open window of the storefront engraver's booth. "This tag says 'Krypto'! It's s'posed to say 'Kryp*ton*'!"

Behind the counter, a squat man in a greasy T-shirt looked up from behind a rack of blank keys. "What the hell kinda name for a dog is 'Krypton'?" His words worked their way out around a half-smoked cigar that protruded from the corner of his mouth. "Dogs need short names that're easy for 'em to remember—like Spot or Duke. They ain't too bright, after all."

The little pup stuck his head up around Bibbo's forearm and began to growl. So did Bibbo. "I tol'ja his name was Krypton—like the place

Sooperman was from! Not Kryp-*toe*, Kryp-*ton*! That's what I paid to have put on the tag."

The man in the greasy shirt was unmoved. "Hey, ya see this?" He pointed to a sign on the wall of the booth that read: DOG TAGS $3.00. At the bottom of the sign, in letters just barely visible from the street, was an additional line of copy: SIX LETTERS MAXIMUM.

"The sign says six letters—I do six letters." He removed the stogy from his mouth and flicked its ash out onto the pavement. "Course, fcr Mr. 'Lottery Winner' Bibbowski, mebbe I could squeeze on anudder letter . . . fer a modest fee."

Bibbo's nostrils flared and his eyebrows shot up so fast that they nearly knocked his cap off. He reached in through the window, grabbing hold of the man's cigar by its lit end and crushing it out in his bare hand. The whites of the man's eyes grew very big as Bibbo proceeded to shove the battered stogy back into his mouth.

"Bibbo don't deal with no chis'lers!" He turned and walked away, scratching his pup behind the ears. "C'mon, let's go home . . . Krypto."

That night, the Shark gang's enforcers stalked through the waterfront in the shadows of burned-out warehouses and crumbling tenements, their Toastmasters at the ready. As they came around the corner of one building, they found another Shark standing watch. The lead enforcer sauntered up to the lookout. "This be the place, Lenny?"

"This's it, Asa." Lenny motioned toward a break in the buildings with his Toastmaster. "I saw that walkin' pile of junk go down this alleyway, an' he ain't come out."

Asa smiled. "Then he be good as dead." He raised his hand and motioned the others to his side. "Listen up! This Man o' Steel's been interferin' with our business for days. But now we gonna pay him back. Frame, you ready?"

A smaller youth brandished a camcorder. "All set, Asa. You take down the Steel dude, an' I'll record it for posterity."

"Good. Now, let's get wit' the action."

Their big guns down and primed, the Sharks silently filed down the alley, only to find—nothing. "So where is he, Lenny?"

"I—I don't know, Asa. He didn't come out. He has to be here somewhere."

"Hey, Asa." Another Shark's voice was a hoarse whisper. "I heard somebody say that the Steel dude had some kinda flyin' boots."

"Flyin' boots?!" Asa's nose wrinkled in disgust. "What you been smokin', man? The dude's a walkin' stove! He'd have to have rockets stuffed up his butt to fly!"

There was a sudden rush of air, and the Man of Steel came flying down into the midst of the Sharks, scattering half of their weaponry with one swing of his hammer. "You boys looking for me?"

"It's him! Toast 'im!"

With high-caliber fire rattling off his armor, John Henry hammered their guns away and sent the Sharks running. As they scattered, he reached out and grabbed Asa, holding the enforcer helpless against a wall. "You look like the leader of this little band—so sing, pigeon. Where do I find your supplier?"

Tears came to Asa's eyes, and the shaken young man opened his mouth to speak. But before more than a syllable could escape his lips, automatic gunfire peppered his body, and he slumped lifeless in the armored man's grasp.

Enraged, the Man of Steel whipped around and fired off two spikes from his power gauntlet. The metal spikes flew true, bracketing the wrist of the assailant's gun hand and pinning him to an old utility pole.

The killer was Frame. He dropped both his gun and his camcorder, trying to pull free of the spikes. But when he saw there'd be no escaping, he boldly stood his ground and thrust out his chin. "Hated to do that to Asa, but the Sharks can't let finks live."

Behind his mask, John Henry clenched his teeth so hard that he could hear his molars grind. He silently cursed himself for underestimating the little punk and coldly picked up Frame's gun, waving it under his nose. "I don't like your guns, video-man, and I don't like you. Now tell me, where is your supplier?"

"I wouldn't tell if I knew. I'd rather take my chances with you!"

John Henry snapped the gun in two. "You're gonna take your chances with the cops."

"I'll be out tomorrow, man." Frame's whole face was a sneer. "You can't prove nuthin'."

"Oh, no?" John Henry picked up the camcorder and pointed it at Frame's face. "You caught this whole thing on tape, didn't you? I think that the cops just might find it interesting."

Frame's face fell. He hadn't thought of that.

The Man of Steel stepped back, kicking the fallen Toastmasters into a pile. "But no matter what happens, one thing's for sure. These pieces are *not* going to make it back onto the streets."

As he brought his hammer down on the pile, Frame finally began to cry.

In a plush conference room at LexCorp Tower, WLEX News Director Stephen Conally screened the video of the confrontation between the

Man of Steel and the Sharks for Lex Luthor and his chief science advisor. The three men watched, fascinated, as the camera caught the Man of Steel's destruction of the weapons.

When the tape finally ended, Luthor smiled tightly at his news director. "I can see why the police are interested in finding out more about this Man of Steel. How was it that you were able to obtain this footage?"

"I'm afraid it's not an exclusive, Mr. L. The Police Information Office has made copies of the video available to all local news teams, but I think we can still get plenty of mileage out of it." Conally gave the tape a positively lustful look. "All we need is a good tag line to distinguish our broadcast from the competition's. Something like, 'This video was made by gang members to record their victory, but the real victory belonged to the Man of Steel in his one-man war on crime.'" The news director tilted back in his chair. "And that could be just the beginning! WGBS appears to have a semiexclusive deal with Superboy, or Teen Superman, or whatever it is that he wants to be called. Perhaps WLEX should form a similar arrangement with the Man of Steel, or one of the other Supermen."

Luthor inclined his head graciously toward the director and broke into a wide smile. "A sound suggestion, Conally. Happersen and I were already thinking along those lines. Rest assured, as soon as any such arrangement can be made, you will be informed."

Dr. Happersen nodded to Conally as Luthor personally escorted the man out. *If anything, the boss has gotten smoother,* thought Happersen. *I know for a fact that he thinks that Conally is about as bright as a dead firefly, but you'd never know it from the way he handles the man.*

By the time Luthor returned to the conference table, his corporate smile had vanished utterly. "Well, Happersen? Do you think we can learn any more from that tape?"

"Perhaps, sir. The gang leader was starting to talk about their weapons source. Using computer enhancement, we might be able to decipher something that could give us a lead to finding the supplier."

"Do all that you can, Sydney. This Man of Steel wants to shut off the flow of guns. If we could give him what he wants, we might well get him into our camp. We must try to open lines of communication to him—and to the other pretenders, as well. I was unable to persuade the original Superman to work for me, but perhaps I can get his successors under my control." Luthor balanced their copy of the videocassette on the fingertips of one hand and smiled. "Wouldn't that be rich?"

.   .   .

Two days later, Lois Lane met with Perry White behind the closed doors of his office at the *Daily Planet*. The managing editor had an extra worktable set up in the corner of his office just to organize the growing files on the various Supermen.

They worked quickly, with an old portable television tuned to the WLEX midday news as their only distraction. They just about had the files categorized when a WLEX reporter came on screen with a live report from a waterfront soup kitchen. Lois and Perry both looked up as the television image panned over to focus on a big man dressed in red and blue.

Bibbo stared out at them from the screen. "Yeah, I've been workin' real hard lately, helpin' to find food fer the kitchen. These folks here need food real bad, an' I'm askin' ever'body to pitch in an' help out." The old roughneck spoke slowly and with great dignity for a man who was wearing an S-shield on his sweatshirt. His outfit would have made most men his age look like ridiculous old pro wrestlers, but somehow it looked exactly right on him. "Sooperman, he woulda helped out. He was always doin' that. I figure, if we all try to be a li'l like Sooperman, we'll all be better off."

Tears came to Lois's eyes as Bibbo spoke of honoring "his fav'rit," and she noticed that Perry's jaw tightened as the television reporter delivered his closing comments.

"Good piece . . . for television." It was one of the highest accolades Lois had ever heard Perry give a video report. "That man's heart certainly is in the right place. I wish that more people like him were getting the publicity." The managing editor surveyed the piles of wire copy and newspaper clippings and shook his head. "And fewer people like some of these so-called heroes. It was hard enough keeping track of *one* Superman. Have you been able to make any sense of this mess, Lois?"

"Not much, Chief. But a lot of money is being spent to cover—and in some cases, promote—their exploits. GBS has been trying to get the most mileage out of their young Superman." Lois pulled out a videocassette and shoved it into the tape player of the editor's television. A telephoto shot came up of the Boy of Steel pulling back a carload of teenagers that was teetering on the edge of a bridge. "As far as the police have been able to determine, these kids were driving a little too fast and blew a tire. They were just lucky that they didn't go off into the river."

Lois turned up the sound as the screen showed Superboy straining to hold onto the back end of the car. "Leverage is lousy! Don't know if I can hold on much longer!"

"Great Caesar's Ghost!" Perry spit out the epithet. "How'd they manage to pick up his voice so clearly?"

"GBS outfitted him with a wireless mike."

Superboy appeared to be panicking. "It's slipping—slipping—!" And then, he effortlessly lifted both car and kids over his head. "Hey, Metropolis—made ya look!"

Perry hit the pause button in disgust. "And to think that a television network has the gall to call that young jackanapes 'Superman'! The boy is like a brain-damaged ox; he has entirely too much raw strength and too little common sense."

"I wouldn't go quite that far, Chief, but the kid does have a lot to learn."

"I hope he learns fast—for all our sakes!"

Lois had to smile. "Well, he's gotten a few lessons. Watch this."

As the tape continued, Superboy—with car still in hand—was shown being slowly lifted up into the air by Supergirl.

"Oh, fine . . . Super*girl*!" Perry reflexively felt his pocket, searching for the cigars he'd given up. "Did Luthor send her in to show the boy up, or are LexCorp and Supergirl trying to compete with GBS for Superboy's attention?"

"The latter is a good possibility, Chief."

"Wouldn't that be just dandy! The boy's ego's big enough already."

"That's true, but actually, I think Supergirl could help keep him in line." Lois fast-forwarded the tape to just after the car had been set down. Superboy faced Supergirl, who stood almost a head taller. The sound had been edited from this portion of the tape, but the boy definitely looked tongue-tied. For her part, Supergirl bore the look of a diligent schoolgirl who was patiently trying to deal with the class clown.

"I'd love to know what they said after GBS cut the sound." Lois turned to Perry. "Come on, Chief, you've got to admit that it was funny when she lifted him and the car up together. The expression on his face was priceless."

"All right, Lois." Perry gave in and allowed himself a dry chuckle. "I suppose these days, we should take whatever laughs we can find. But I still think this possible Superboy/WGBS/WLEX triangle bears investigating."

"I'll make a note of it."

The television screen went to blue and began flashing a numeric countdown. "Oh, that's right—there's more." Lois stooped over, readjusting sound and picture. "This is from that waterfront firefight between the Sharks and a rival gang, the Reavers. The Man of Steel was breaking it up when guess who butted in?"

The GBS footage picked up with the Boy of Steel diving down into the melee, his left arm tucked behind him. "Yee-hah! Watch this! I'll bail out the Steel guy with one hand tied behind my back!"

The gang members instinctively raised their big guns skyward and blasted away at the newcomer. Superboy actually laughed. "What are those goons shooting? Rockets?" His smile was clearly visible as he looped around their fire. "Hey, ya missed me! Missed again!"

"That's enough!" Perry hit the stop button and switched off the set. "Armed street gangs are one of the more serious problems facing the city, and that young fool was treating it like some joke. His grandstanding could've gotten someone killed!"

"It almost did, Chief. I was there, remember? It was a real war zone." Lois felt a chill at the memory. "When Superboy drew the gangs' fire into the air, *he* evaded it easily enough, but a police helicopter above and behind him wasn't so lucky. The Man of Steel flew up and pulled the chopper cops out just in time. By the time he got them back down to Earth, the gangs had pretty much gotten away, and GBS's media darling was back in front of the cameras, taking credit for saving the day. I tell you, Perry, I wanted to give that kid such a slap—!"

"Too bad I wasn't there. I'd've held him for you."

"Yes, well, the Man of Steel hauled him up and chewed him out royally. You won't see that on any tape, but I heard enough to know that the armored man set Superboy straight about a few things. I just hope it took."

"This 'Man of Steel' . . ." Perry shook his head. "I wish we knew more about him."

"So do I. He spoke with me for only a few minutes; he wouldn't stick around for a real interview. Of the four who are wearing Superman's insignia, he's the only one who hasn't declared himself Superman. Yet, in listening to him, I get the weird feeling that there is more of Superman's heart in him than in any of the others."

"Lois, don't tell me you're buying into that psychic hogwash about the man being possessed by Superman's spirit!"

"No, of course not, Chief. It's just that he has that certain something that all the others are missing, and he's not Superman, so how could they be?"

"Well, one of them has been quietly campaigning to be recognized as Superman, and he appears to have convinced the right people." Perry picked up a copy of the *Planet*'s morning edition from his desk. The banner headline read: SUPERMAN IS BACK? The subhead underneath proclaimed CYBORG THWARTS ASSASSINATION ATTEMPT. The front-page article covered all the details.

The *Planet* had gotten the exclusive story thanks to their editorial assistant Ron Troupe, who had gone to Washington on his own initiative to cover a trip made by Metropolis Mayor Frank Berkowitz. Ostensibly, Berkowitz had gone to Capitol Hill to angle for more federal disaster

money, but Troupe had gotten a tip from some old friends of his at
Howard University that the mayor had actually been asked to the capital
to advise the President on the four new Supermen.

Troupe had caught up with Berkowitz as the mayor strolled along
Pennsylvania Avenue. The fledgling reporter had been hoping for a lead
on what His Honor intended to tell the chief executive. Troupe was just
engaging the talkative mayor in conversation on the street outside the
White House when a car bomb went off.

Ron Troupe shoved the mayor to the ground as a second car roared up
and five men piled out with automatic weapons in hand. The reporter
found himself in the middle of a firefight between terrorists and White
House Security, hoping that the mayor was all right and praying that
he'd stay alive long enough to file the story.

That's when the Cyborg arrived. He hit the terrorists cleanly, sweeping
through and collecting their weapons so quickly that they were literally
spun senseless. One moment, bullets were flying. The next, the ground
was covered with half-conscious terrorists, and the Superman was calmly
asking the captain of the guard to take possession of the captured weaponry.

The Cyborg then proceeded to march right up to the White House.
Moments later, he was conferring with the man whose life he had helped
save. It was an historic meeting between two individuals who were
among the most powerful men in the free world. The Cyborg had accepted the President's thanks for foiling the assassination attempt and
told the commander in chief that should he ever be in special need of a
Superman, he only needed to call. Literally. Right there and then, the
Cyborg extruded a special communications device from the side of his
robotic arm. The President solemnly accepted the device and shook the
Superman's metal hand.

And Ron Troupe had been there for all of it. He'd chanced upon the
sort of story journalists dream of finding, and he'd done a good job of
reporting it. He also came away personally convinced, as was the federal
government, that Superman was back.

It was not a surprising conclusion. The Cyborg had, after all, thwarted
an attempt on the life of the President of the United States. Moreover, it
turned out that the Cyborg had been meeting in secret with officials of
the state and defense departments, trying to convince them that—despite his strange new appearance—he *was* Superman, rebuilt and returned to life.

Perry White, however, still wasn't so certain. "Call me a skeptic, but I
find it a little too convenient that the Cyborg just happened to be in the
area of the White House when that car bomb went off. I don't know if
that's despite the Cyborg's meetings with state and defense, or *because* of

them. Maybe I'm just getting paranoid. But what about this Cyborg, Lois
. . . what do you think?"

"I think maybe I'm getting a little paranoid, too. I'm beginning to
worry even when we *don't* hear from these new Supermen. That visored
one!" Lois took a deep breath. "He's kept a very low profile lately. I
keep wondering what that means." She looked up at her editor. "Perry,
at this point, I think that I may be the only one who's spoken to all four
of these Supermen. I've given this a lot of thought, and I don't think any
of them is the real Superman."

"Neither do I. People are always in such a damn hurry to jump on one
bandwagon or another. I can understand that people want to have faith
in something. There aren't many folks in this world who can live with a
lot of unanswered questions—if it were otherwise, most religions would
go out of business—but we're talking about a question of a man's identity, of his good name. I hate to see people choosing sides in this, as if
they were picking their favorite team for the World Series or something."

"They're afraid, Perry. They all want there to be a Superman. And so
do I."

The lunchtime patrons at the Ace o' Clubs were just starting to wet their
whistles when the WGBS *News-at-Noon* cut to live coverage of Superboy
carrying a classic locomotive engine through the city to the Metropolis
Museum of Science.

"Lookit that kid, ain't he somethin'?" A bar patron lifted his mug in a
toast to the scene on the television. "I tell ya, give 'im a few years and
he'll be a contender. Course, he ain't the real Superguy—!"

"Ten-four to that, buddy." The man on the next barstool swallowed
the last of a pickled egg and wiped his mouth with the back of his hand.
"Now the Cyborg—*that's* yer Superman."

"The President's pal? Gimme a break! Okay, so he stopped those
terrorist bums, but that guy with the visor, he'd've fried 'em on the spot!
That's the kinda law an' order I wanna see!"

"Sez you!"

"Yeah, sez me!"

Before the argument could escalate any further, two huge hands suddenly clamped down on the men's shoulders and spun them around on
their barstools.

"Yer both wrong! Lissen up, ya yahoos, an' lissen good!" Bibbo stood
glowering at his customers. "You wanna argue politics or sports, that's
yer bizness. But nobody—an' I mean *nobody*!—is gonna argue about

Sooperman in this bar! Sooperman was a pal o' mine, an' none o' them fancy pants is Sooperman in my book!" At the tavern owner's feet, his pup Krypto yipped and growled in agreement.

"S-sure, Bibbo."

"Yeah. Whatever you say."

Some eight hundred million miles from Earth, space began to fold in upon itself, bending and twisting as if forming a hole in its reality. Matter and energy danced and swirled within the hole, jumping back and forth from one state to another. Suddenly there was a dazzling burst of light and a golden ship shot out of the hole. And then, as abruptly as it had opened, the hole sealed shut, leaving no sign that it had ever existed.

The ship's engines drove it on toward the inner planets of the solar system. It was a vast ship, nearly a mile across, and it was armed with weapons powerful enough to level an entire world.

On the bridge of the vessel loomed a giant humanoid being. He stood over seven feet tall and weighed nearly eight hundred pounds. Not a single hair grew on his skin, which was a pale yellow, like badly aged parchment, and his eyes were a deep, murky crimson. From the deference shown him by the other beings on the bridge, it was clear that he was their lord and master. His name was Mongul, and he nursed a long-standing hatred for Superman that Lex Luthor would have envied.

Mongul had once ruled a vast empire from the throne of an artificial planet which he called WarWorld. He had used that mobile world to sweep across the galaxy, conquering whole star systems. Whenever and wherever Mongul found sentient life-forms, he demanded their total and unconditional surrender. Any worlds that dared to defy him were rendered lifeless. In this way his empire had grown.

In hundreds of our years, no one had ever presented a real challenge to Mongul's power and authority—until he had crossed paths with Superman.

One of Mongul's slave ships had found Superman drifting helplessly in deep space, the oxygen in his lungs nearly exhausted after an accident on a long space mission. Discovering that they had chanced upon the last living Kryptonian, Mongul's slavers had transported their find to one of their emperor's arenas, to fight in a series of gladiatorial games. Superman, however, had defied Mongul, and the warlord himself had entered the arena. But to his dismay, Mongul found that his powerful fists were not enough to slay the disobedient slave.

Mongul's armies saw their emperor's failure to kill a slave in combat as a grave weakness. Mongul lost face, and revolution broke out on

WarWorld. To his everlasting shame, Mongul was forced to give up his throne and flee for his own life, while Superman—he learned—had returned to Earth.

Now, after several long months in exile, Mongul was again in command of a spaceworthy dreadnaught. It was not as huge or as powerful as WarWorld, but he was confident that it would carry him on to the victory he craved.

A six-foot-long, slug-shaped being approached Mongul, its head bowed in obeisance. "All systems secured from hyperspatial transport, Lord Mongul. Switchover has been made to sublight drive engines, and all weapons systems stand primed and fully functional."

"As they should be." Mongul's voice rumbled from deep within his chest, like the roar of a great beast within a cave. "And the navigation systems? What of them?"

The slug-being all but prostrated itself. "Locked on target, my lord."

"Show me."

One whole wall of the bridge seemed to dissolve away, replaced by an image of a bright blue marble of a world, flecked here and there with wisps of green and white. "There, sire . . . the third planet from the system's single star."

"Earth." There was passion in the way Mongul spoke the word. "It is the world the Kryptonian claimed as his home. Soon it shall be mine, as well."

23

In the Antarctic Fortress, a score of robots mobilized in the chamber that held their master's Regeneration Matrix. The gigantic egg-shaped construct was glowing white as the sun, and waves of static electricity were rippling across its surface. The robots instantly went on-line with one another, transmitting and receiving information at near-light speed. "Shut down all solar receptors!"

"Done, but the overload effect continues. There must be a release!"

"Agreed. There is no other choice. Modulate the support field . . . lower the Matrix to release position."

Under the robots' manipulation of the fields that had held the Matrix upright, the giant egg descended to the chamber floor, its long axis slowly lowering from a vertical to a horizontal position.

Energy continued to crackle across the Matrix, and the robots stayed highly agitated.

"Readings remain well off scale. This is without precedent."

"Everything that has occurred since the master's discorporation has been without precedent. We were programmed to improvise under uncertain situations. We must proceed with caution and carry out that programming."

A seam formed in the surface of the Matrix egg, and it began to split open.

"Alert! Alert! The Matrix seal has ruptured! Prepare to receive the occupant."

The Matrix yawned open like a huge clamshell, revealing a tall, dark-haired man, covered from throat to toe in a black Kryptonian bodysuit. "He awakes! Dim the lighting—his eyes may yet be sensitive!"

The Man in Black opened his eyes. "Who . . . who's there—?"

The robots moved in closer, as if their appearance was all the answer needed. One dipped its head down to the Man in Black and spoke most solicitously. "Master? Master Kal-El? How do you feel?"

"Feel?" Kal-El rubbed his eyes. "A little . . . fuzzy-headed."

"Some disorientation is to be expected. Do you recognize us? Do you know where you are?"

"You're . . . the Fortress robots." He looked around slowly, as if trying to determine whether or not he was still asleep and dreaming. "Then, I'm in the Antarctic . . . in the underground hideaway?"

"Correct. You seem unsteady on your feet, Master Kal-El. This is to be expected, following such a rude awakening. Allow us to seat you."

"A-all right."

The robots gathered on all sides of Kal-El, lifting him up out of the open Matrix and into the cushioned cocoon of a Kryptonian floating chair. As he settled into the chair, it slowly rose into the air until his head was at the same height off the floor as it would be if he were standing.

One robot continued to hover close by his master's side. "Is there anything else you require—any other way in which we may be of service?"

Kal-El rubbed his temples as if physically trying to dispel the fog from his mind. "Yes, you can fill me in on what's been going on."

"At once, sir."

The robots formed an honor guard around the chair, escorting it and its occupant away from the Matrix. Moments later, they all hovered in another part of the Fortress in front of the bank of monitor screens.

The robot designated Unit Twelve obediently snapped into debriefing mode. "As per my programming, I have been monitoring all world news transmissions and compiling data on any and all individuals operating under the name of Superman and/or utilizing your S-shield in their activities. There has been much speculation on the part of commentators—!"

Kal-El raised his hand for silence. "Save the commentary for later, Unit Twelve. Show me what's going on right now."

"Yes, sir." The screens lit up showing Centennial Park from a number of vantage points, as provided from several different broadcast sources. On screen, a huge crowd could be seen gathered in the center of a wide plaza near the large statue of Superman. Many of those in the crowd wore bright blue robes with the S-shield emblem of Superman embroidered across the front.

Unit Twelve distilled the various disparate broadcast sound tracks into a single coherent narration. "At this hour in the city of Metropolis, cultists who worship Superman as a living god rally in Centennial Park. The emergence of four Supermen has caused much confusion and has already led to one major schism in the group. City authorities fear that this may lead to violence."

Kal-El looked seriously disturbed by the news. "This is not good. This is not good at all. Unit Twelve, give me the rundown on all known Supermen."

"Yes, sir." One by one, computer-generated mug shots came up on screen. "This Cyborg Superman claims partial amnesia. His bionics show evidence of Kryptonian technology. Yesterday, he saved the U.S. President from an assassination attempt. . . .

"Some pundits have called the youngest pretender 'Super*boy.'* He objects vehemently to that name. He claims to be a clone of Superman, and has maintained a high profile thanks to Galaxy Broadcasting. . . .

"Little is known about the so-called Man of Steel. He is currently believed to be a man in an armored suit, and not a robot. . . .

"Drawing the greatest negative response from Metropolis police is the visored Son of Krypton. . . ."

Unit Twelve droned on and on. For over an hour, the little robot showed and told Kal-El all that the Fortress systems knew of the four Supermen.

"I've heard enough!" the Man in Black interrupted, abruptly turning the floating chair away from the monitors.

Worry lines creased Kal-El's forehead, and there was a haunted look to his eyes. "Things have gotten completely out of hand. The name of Superman will *not* be turned into a franchise." He rose stiffly from the chair, stretching as if he had not tested certain muscles in weeks.

He looked back over his shoulder at the images of the other Supermen. "Something must be done about this! Continue your monitoring, Unit Twelve. Check every source you can find, and have me paged if anything new comes in."

"Yes, sir."

"The rest of you, come with me. I must get to Metropolis as soon as possible."

Kal-El walked purposefully from the chamber, the other robots dutifully falling in behind.

Fifteen miles south of Smallville, Jonathan Kent stood fuming in the middle of the parlor.

On the screen of his television, a gaudily dressed youth was shown shaking hands with a stocky, slick-haired man. ". . . the young Superman today announced that he'd engaged the services of Rex Leech as his personal business manager. Leech, a relative unknown, has vowed to crack down on what he called 'the unauthorized use' of his client's name and image."

" 'Unauthorized use'?!" Jonathan went red in the face. "Why, that miserable, two-bit—!"

"Jonathan, please!" Martha rushed into the parlor, drying her hands with a dish towel. "Don't get yourself so upset. You know it's not good for your heart!"

"I know, Martha. But it just makes my blood boil when I see these impostors on the TV. They're no more our son than I'm the king of England! I wish that boy of ours . . ." Jonathan let the thought trail off. He knew that it made Martha uneasy whenever he talked about his finding Clark and bringing him back. Jonathan still had a hard time believing that it hadn't happened; it had all been so vivid.

"Anyway, it makes me want to go on TV myself. I'd like to tell the whole blasted world that Clark Kent is the real Superman—the *only* Superman!"

Martha came up beside him, resting her head against her husband's shoulder. "I wish we could, too, honey, but you know we can't. It isn't so much for us, but for Lois and Lana, and all the rest of Clark's friends who would be put in danger."

"I know, I know, but—oh, now look at that!" The network was rerunning a file tape of the Boy of Steel's face-to-face meeting with Supergirl. "There's something else that frosts my britches. First, Supergirl takes up with the Luthor boy, and now she's making cow eyes at *this* young twerp!"

Jonathan angrily switched off the set. "I know she didn't stay with us long, but I'd hoped we'd brought her up better than that! She was practically a blank slate when Clark brought her to us—so innocent. He got her back on her feet, and I thought we'd taught her a little common sense. Now, I don't know. If only she'd stayed with us a little longer . . ."

"Yes, she was such a sweet child." Martha sighed and brushed away a tear. "It broke my heart when she ran off. The poor girl had never had a real family before. She did learn a lot while she was here, but she's still such an innocent. She sees things . . . well, not in black and white, exactly, but I think she tends to accept people at face value. She's so straightforward, and she just isn't experienced enough to deal with people who aren't."

"Yeah, it surely seems that way." Jonathan slumped down against the arm of the old sofa. "Maybe—maybe it's my fault, Martha. Maybe I just didn't know how to raise a daughter."

"You just hush now, Jonathan Kent. We did the best we could for Supergirl in the short time we had her. And for heaven's sake, stop seeing only the flighty things she sometimes does! That poor homeless child has already done more good in her new life on this Earth than most folks do in a lifetime. Just look at all those people she's rescued! And hasn't she faithfully kept Clark's secret? Didn't she send us that beautiful sympathy card and write us that lovely letter? She promised, as soon as the search and rescue work is over, that she'd figure out some way to come and see us, and I believe her."

"I suppose you're probably right." Jonathan hugged his wife to him tightly. "You usually are."

"That's better!" Martha kissed him on the cheek. "Supergirl will come around, just you wait and see. And I don't just mean that she'll come around to see us! I mean that she'll get herself sorted out eventually. I'm as sure of that as I am of anything—and heaven knows, even with children you raise from the cradle—you can't always tell how they'll turn out."

Martha looked out the window at the gathering clouds. "It's just such an uncertain world out there!"

As night fell on Metropolis, the Man of Steel cornered four fugitive Sharks on the central borough's south side. "A little far from the 'hood, aren't you?"

They responded with heavy fire.

"Waste all the ammo you want, I won't get a scratch. But I *am* getting annoyed!" He walked on through the hail of bullets as though it were nothing more than a light rain, unaware of the fifth Shark who was drawing a bead on him from behind.

"So tell me, where're you fish getting the heavy artillery? Don't make me ask twice."

There was a flash of light and a choked-off scream behind the Man of Steel. John Henry whirled around to find a charred, smoking corpse clutching a slagged Toastmaster. The other Sharks cried out in pain, their weapons suddenly glowing red hot. They dropped the guns, running for their lives, as a second caped figure dropped into their midst.

Inside his armor, John Henry blinked. "Superman?"

"Yes, I am." The Kryptonian nodded once. "I see your other would-be assailants have scattered like the roaches they are. No matter, they can be rounded up later. Their weapons are now useless; I fused the firing mechanisms. But now, we two must talk. There is much to discuss."

"I'll say there is." John Henry stared long and hard at the visored man. "You—you just killed a man!"

The Kryptonian raised an eyebrow. "I killed one who intended to kill you. They were five to your one."

"But you could have disarmed him! You didn't have to *kill* him."

"No?" The visored man folded his arms. His voice sounded genuinely puzzled. "And was he trying simply to disarm you? What, exactly, is your point?"

"My *point?*! Look, mister, I met Superman once—as a matter of fact, he saved my life."

"And what do you call what I just did?"

"At the very least, I call it manslaughter! For God's sake, man, look at me—look at this armor!" John Henry thumped his chest plate. "I wasn't in any real danger! And even if I had been, the *real* Superman wouldn't have killed that punk! He never countered the threat of violence with unnecessary force!" The Man of Steel stuck a finger toward the visored man's face. "You look like the real McCoy, you even sound a little like Superman, but you *act* like a cold-blooded fraud!"

"Fraud?!" The Kryptonian clenched his teeth, unable to hold back a sudden, surging rage. "You—ungrateful—armor-plated—FREAK!"

With one swift left uppercut, the Son of Krypton punched the Man of Steel back through one side of an adjacent building and clear out the other. He eyed the armored man's trajectory with bitter satisfaction. Then, still seething with anger, he dove after the Man of Steel.

In a diner several blocks away, Jimmy Olsen sat across from Lois Lane and self-consciously dragged a french fry through a glob of catsup on his plate.

"So . . . uh, how are you holding up, Lois? I mean . . . geez, I'm not doing a very good job of this, am I? It's just that I've been worried about you, but things have been so crazy—"

"That's all right, Jimmy." She slowly stirred her coffee, adding a couple of ice cubes from her water glass. "The whole world's gone a little crazy. But I'm getting by about as well as can be expected, given the circumstances."

"Yeah, I know it's rough. Bad enough that we lost Superman, but Mr. Kent—Clark—" *Ah, shut up, Olsen.* He stuck the fry in his mouth and chewed. *This must be killing her. After all these weeks, he can't possibly still be alive. If they'd only find his body, at least then we'd know.* "Well, if you ever want to, you know, talk about it . . ."

"I know, Jim. Thanks." Lois took a tentative sip of the coffee; still too

hot. *I wish I could* tell *you. That's the maddening thing. The public thinks
that Clark was buried in all the destruction that Doomsday caused. I know
that he wasn't, but that's about all I know!*

Lois's thoughts were suddenly interrupted by a low crashing noise.
The whole building seemed to shake. "What was that?!"

"I don't know. It sounded like a train wreck!" Jimmy jumped to his
feet and threw down a few bills to cover the check. "Trouble in the
subway maybe. Let's check it out!"

Lois and Jimmy exited the diner and were nearly knocked over by a
stream of people running down the street. One man was shouting that
Judgment Day had arrived. Jimmy was just popping the lens cap off his
camera when a bearded man in a long flowing robe calmly walked by.
The bearded man took one look at them and brought his palms together
as if in prayer.

"Make your peace! The hour is at hand!"

"Sure thing." Jimmy smiled and adjusted his lens setting.

Lois gently touched the man on the arm. "Do you know what's going
on down the street? Besides the Hour of Judgment, I mean?"

"The great Superman is risen and walks among us!" The bearded man
bowed his head reverently. "Even now he does battle with an impostor—
an armored son of Satan—over on Larson Boulevard!"

Just fifty yards from where Larson emptied into Glenmorgan Square, the
Son of Krypton hurled John Henry headfirst through a video arcade.
The Man of Steel erupted from the corner building in a shower of safety
glass and flew on for several feet before skidding to a halt in the middle
of the boulevard.

The Kryptonian stalked through the shattered storefront arcade after
the armored man, glass crunching under his feet. People scattered at his
approach as he glowered down at his fallen opponent.

"Could one 'fraud' so easily defeat another? I think not. Fool! I could
have eliminated that entire gang, but I did not. Their lives were base,
meaningless . . . yet I was merciful. Remember that. Remember, too,
that I was merciful to *you* as well!"

On the surrounding sidewalks, onlookers kept a cautious distance, but
enraptured cultists pushed out into the streets, chanting the name of
their chosen savior. "Superman . . . Superman . . . Superman!"

The Kryptonian looked out upon the crowd and held up his hand for
silence. "Hear me, good people! I am indeed the one true Superman.
And I will suffer no pretenders to my good name."

Suddenly, the Man of Steel bounded to his feet and, in one smooth motion, thrust his sledgehammer like a battering ram into the visored man's gut. "I'm not pretending. I mean to seriously kick your butt!"

Onlookers ducked down behind parked cars as the Man of Steel leapt onto the Kryptonian. John Henry grabbed both ends of his hammer's thick steel handle and held it down across the visored man's chest, pinning him to the pavement.

" 'The one true Superman,' huh? The man I admired *never* spoke like that! The way I see it, *you're* the pretender! Just a little tin god with a cape. Or maybe a metahuman with messianic delusions."

"The only delusions are *yours*!" The Kryptonian kicked up with his feet, flipping the Man of Steel over him.

As the two men scrambled to their feet, cultists in the crowd began to cheer on their particular choice for messiah.

"Destroy him, Superman. Destroy the metal demon!"

"Fool! The true demon is he who hides his eyes. Destroy him with your holy hammer, Man of Steel!"

Whether because of or in spite of the cheering, the two caped men were showing every sign of continuing their fight when they were brought up short by a woman's angry cry: "Stop it! Both of you—!"

Lois Lane pushed her way through the crowd, with Jimmy Olsen following close behind. She pointed an accusing finger from one Superman to the other. "Settle down, you two, and listen to me!"

Lois stepped boldly between the two caped men, and Jimmy stuck close to her side, trying to look as big and authoritative as he could. *I hope Lois knows what she's doing.* The young photographer's hands felt clammy as he gripped his camera.

"Look at you! Just look at you!" The reporter's voice burned with outrage. "You're brawling like a couple of playground bullies, battling for turf. What do you have to say for yourselves?"

The Kryptonian was the first to find his voice. "Ms. Lane, I initially sought only to stop this impostor from using my insignia."

"*Your* insignia?!" Lois's eyes were daggers. "The jury's still out on that one! But regardless, you've both dishonored Superman's name with this senseless fight! You could have hurt or killed someone! Would you want that stain on 'your' insignia?"

The Man of Steel lowered his hammer. "You are absolutely right. I didn't seek this fight, and I didn't throw the first punch. But I gave as well as I got—almost without thinking about it."

John Henry looked around them, surveying the path that their battle had taken. "Dear Lord, look at the damage we've caused!"

The Kryptonian felt stirrings of shame and was troubled by the feeling. He glanced at Lois, then quickly looked away. *The woman's eyes . . .*

haunt me! It is as though she were trying to look into my soul! "I . . . also regret my actions. They were perhaps ill-advised. I will make amends for any damage we have caused."

"We both will." John Henry looked full into the Kryptonian's visored face. "You know, I never laid claim to the name of Superman. I wear this shield and this cape to honor the man who gave me back my life. Can you honestly look me in the eyes and say that you find anything wrong in that?"

The Son of Krypton stood silent for several moments, considering the question. "Put in those terms—no, I cannot." The words came slowly, and with some difficulty. "I . . . am sorry."

Jimmy looked through his viewfinder at the visored man, trying to see his eyes. *Maybe this guy* is *Superman! Lois seemed to get through to something in him.*

"Hold it right there! Don't any of you move!" To the astonishment of all, a thin, balding man in a bad suit shoved his way through the crowd and came running toward them, a sheath of papers in hand.

Now what? thought Lois. "I beg your pardon, sir, but if you're with the police, I'd like to see a badge!"

"Police?" The balding man almost laughed. "Naw, I'm no cop. I'm a process server!" He smacked his papers against the Kryptonian's chest. "This is to give notice that you gents are in violation of a trademark held by Rex Leech Enterprises. Mr. Leech's client, and his client alone, has rights to the Superman name and insignia. You are to cease and desist from all such usage immediately. Got that?"

"No." The Kryptonian grabbed hold of the papers. "Got this?" Energy erupted from his hand, burning the papers so quickly that they seemed to disappear.

The process server, a hardened fellow who was seldom surprised, backed away, his eyes wide. "Hey! You can't do that! Those papers—!"

"The fate of your papers is the least of your worries!" The visored man took a step forward and reached for the balding man.

"Ogod! Ogod, help!" The process server turned and bolted away.

The Kryptonian was about to follow when the Man of Steel brought the handle of his sledgehammer down around the other caped man, getting him in an improvised choke hold.

"Hold it!" John Henry spoke calmly and deliberately. "I don't know what this is all about, but it should be settled in the courts, not in the streets!"

"No!" The Kryptonian spit out the word. "That man's insolence demands punishment now! Unhand me!"

"Not until you cool down!" As his captive squirmed in his hands, the Man of Steel glanced quickly at Lois and Jimmy. "I don't know how long

I can hold him, but I'm going to get him out of here before someone gets hurt. Stand back!"

Lois and Jimmy jumped back as John Henry's rocket boots ignited. The next instant, the two Supermen shot away into the night sky.

"So much for my peacemaking efforts." Lois watched ruefully as they disappeared from view. "Where will this all end?"

Three miles high over Metropolis, the Kryptonian continued to struggle in the Man of Steel's grasp.

"What does it take to make you listen to reason?" John Henry strained his suit's micromotors to maintain his hold on the man. "You can't go around frying people who cross you!"

"No one tells me what I can or cannot do. I am Superman!"

"Sorry, Shades. The high-and-mighty routine doesn't impress me."

"No? Then perhaps this will." The Kryptonian began adding his own powers of flight to their climb. "You want to fly? Well, let's just see how high and fast we can go!"

"Stop, you idiot!" John Henry upped the amplification on his voice. "I said, *stop!*" But the Kryptonian only flew faster.

John Henry sealed his suit, activating its emergency oxygen system as the air grew thinner around them. "You'll send us into orbit!"

The Man of Steel cut power to his rockets and tightened his grip on the Kryptonian, but it did little good. The man he held captive had taken control of the flight. The two men sped upward, constantly accelerating. John Henry had built his armor well, but he knew that they'd soon hit escape velocity, and his armor hadn't been designed for extended operation in a vacuum. *I hate to turn this maniac loose while he's so dangerously angry, but I don't have much choice. I have to save myself while I can. No sense in dying out in space!* He released his hold on the Kryptonian, kicking away from the other men and firing his rockets to ensure their separation.

John Henry fell tumbling away in a great downward arc and blacked out. He finally came to many miles above the Sierra Nevada, though it took him several precious moments to realize just where he was. When he saw the wide blue expanse of the Pacific stretching out ahead of him, he knew that he was in trouble. *My God, he must've thrown us into a suborbital ballistic path! Airspeed indicator is pegged. If I'm not already at terminal velocity, I've got to be close!* He was starting to feel the heat of reentry.

Fighting to right himself, the Man of Steel plunged Earthward, ticking off the seconds in his head. He fired his boot rockets in short, even bursts, hoping to slow his speed to something survivable. *It should work . . . if my fuel holds out.*

Just a few thousand feet above the outskirts of Coast City, California, he was down to a more manageable air speed. The Man of Steel grabbed the edges of his cape and stretched out in free fall, conserving his fuel supply for one last final brake and steer maneuver. Here, after all those long minutes of desperate activity, he was almost able to relax. *This must be how hang gliders feel.*

He had no sooner completed that thought than the Kryptonian dove down onto him from above, and the two of them went tumbling head over heels. John Henry fought to stay on top, fought to stay conscious and to fire his rockets one last time.

Then they slammed into the parking lot of a suburban shopping mall.

The pavement heaved, and shoppers were thrown to the ground by the force of the impact. As people picked themselves up, they looked around wide-eyed.

"What was that?" A woman groped for her glasses. "An earthquake?"

"No." A young man pointed toward the new crater that had opened up in the asphalt just a few hundred feet away. "Something . . . something just *fell* out of the sky. It looked like people!"

Within minutes, a police helicopter hovered over the site, and mall security guards rushed to cordon off the area and offer first aid to shaken customers. The helicopter pilot swung down low over the crater. "My God, I think there's something moving down there!"

Slowly, painfully, the Man of Steel got to his feet, bracing himself with the handle of his hammer. But as John Henry lurched up out of the crater, the asphalt shifted, and a second caped figure arose behind him. "So you live as well!"

John Henry spun around at the sound of the Kryptonian's voice and took an energy blast to the chest. The force of the blast knocked him off balance, and the armored man toppled to his knees.

In the helicopter overhead, the pilot anxiously radioed for more backup. A police sharpshooter's hands shook slightly as he loaded his rifle. Below, the Kryptonian walked boldly up to his armored foe. "Now you shall pay for your folly, 'Man of Steel.' "

John Henry's hands shot up, grabbing the Kryptonian by the wrists. He abruptly pulled himself to his feet, butting his steel helmet up hard against his tormentor's chin. The Kryptonian fell back a step, and the armored man struck again and again with a series of alternating hard rights and lefts to the jaw. His visor knocked ajar, the Son of Krypton staggered back, clutching at his face. He was breathing heavily, and he seemed stunned, but he did not lose his footing.

Power supplies dangerously depleted, the Man of Steel locked his armor's knee joints and stood steady, unable to do much more than look impressive, while the visored man caught his breath and cleared his head. Behind the poker face of his steel mask, John Henry's mind was racing. *This sucker must be nearly as tough as the real Superman. He'll have his second wind in another few seconds, and I'm just about dead on my feet. Got to talk fast, or there'll be hell to pay.*

John Henry switched on his voice amplifier. "If you want people to believe you're Superman, then *act* like Superman! Or is it that you enjoy playing the bully? You would've fried that process server, wouldn't you? Well, Superman wouldn't! What's your next brilliant move? Are you going to fry me? Maybe fry everyone wearing this shield, till you're the only one left?" *Careful, don't give him any ideas!* "Oh, that'd be real smart!"

The Kryptonian had resecured his visor and was staring hard at the Man of Steel. His fists were clenched and his stance was unfriendly, but he was listening, and for that John Henry gave quick thanks. In the distance, a chorus of sirens grew louder.

"Every life you take is a stain on that shield and a disgrace to the name of Superman." John Henry took a deep breath. "Don't you see, man? There's got to be more to Superman than just having power. You have to know how to use that power *for* people, not against them."

There was a sharp squeal of brakes. When the two caped men looked up, there were half a dozen police cars surrounding them. Coast City police piled out of the cars, their guns drawn. They looked tense; the younger officers almost looked scared, but they held their ground. The senior officer, a big burly man, planted his feet and stared the two Supermen down. "All right, let's get those hands up where we can see 'em—now!"

The Kryptonian took one tentative step toward the nearest car. He made no move to raise his hands.

John Henry felt the sweat trickle down his back. "Don't do it, man! Don't disgrace the shield!" He made a few quick calculations. If he cut in his emergency power reserves, he might be able to tackle the Kryptonian and knock him to the ground before the man could attack the police. But what then? He was certain that he couldn't knock the visored man out. He'd exhaust his reserves in a matter of minutes trying to hold the Kryptonian down, and then those cops would really be in a fix.

But the Kryptonian stood very still, his fists unclenched, his head tilted slightly. His sharp ears picked up the calls coming over the surrounding police radios. There was an officer down on the north side of Coast City . . . a fire, possible arson, in the warehouse district . . . some people in trouble, clinging to a capsized boat in the Santa Clara Channel.

He slowly turned toward the Man of Steel. "Perhaps you are right.

There is more to Superman than mere power. There must be courage. There must be the willingness to risk all for what seems right—even when one barely has the power to stand upright."

Behind his mask, John Henry blinked. "You knew—?"

"It is within my power to know." The Kryptonian nodded his head once, respectfully, and lifted off into the air. "The people of Coast City cry out for help and Superman must answer. Replenish yourself, Man of Steel, and go back to Metropolis. I leave that city in your hands for now." He turned and shot away from the parking lot; within seconds he was gone from sight.

John Henry stared after the Kryptonian, dumbfounded. The police looked no less puzzled. One officer lowered her gun and ambled over to the armored man's side. "Are you okay? What was that all about?"

The Man of Steel switched to his reserve power system and slowly stepped forward. "Long story. I'm just glad that I could talk as well as he can fight."

"Huh?" The cop looked totally confused.

"Tell you all about it. But first, I need to borrow your car's battery and some jumper cables." *And a machine shop and some condensed solid fuel would be nice, if I could find them.* John Henry breathed a weary sigh. Whatever else happened, he was facing a long walk back to Metropolis.

At LexCorp Tower in Metropolis, Lex Luthor had just flipped through a confidential report from his aide, Sydney Happersen, when his WLEX monitor cut to a special report from California. Luthor glanced up from the report to see a live picture of the Man of Steel powering up from a police car battery in a Coast City parking lot. The billionaire industrialist listened intently as one of his news bureau's West Coast correspondents related how the armored man had fought the Son of Krypton to a standstill.

Luthor picked up the phone and punched in a number. "Patch me through to our Coast City news team. Yes, the ones who were just on the air now. Hello, this is Lex Luthor." He chuckled softly. "Yes, I am quite serious. I want you to convey my personal congratulations to the Man of Steel and tell him that I wish to speak with him."

There was a soft hiss, and then a deep, resonant voice came on at the other end of the line. "Is this really Lex Luthor? *The* Lex Luthor?"

"The second one, anyway—but I'm trying hard to equal the first." Luthor couldn't keep from grinning at his private joke. "Am I correct in guessing that you could use a repair facility, sir?"

"Well . . ."

"I would be honored if you would allow me to provide one. There's a LexCorp aerospace plant not far away in Bakersfield. Just say the word, and I will put it at your disposal. You will have everything you require, including as much privacy as you wish. And when you are ready to return to Metropolis, I'll be more than happy to provide you with transport."

"Mr. Luthor, that's incredibly generous of you. Thank you very much. I'm very grateful."

I thought you would be. "Don't mention it. Metropolis needs men like you." Luthor flipped through the secret report, circling the address that Happersen's investigative team had uncovered—the address of a certain party that was providing city gangs with Toastmasters. "Yes, I'd say you provide a service that few others can."

Midway between the orbits of Jupiter and Mars, Mongul noticed a subtle shift in the pulse in his ship's engines. He called his chief navigator before him. "We are slowing and changing course. Why?"

"A band of asteroids looms before us, Exalted One. We must execute an evasive maneuver if we are to avoid them."

"I will brook no delays! Return to the original course and eliminate the obstacles!"

"As you command, my Lord." The navigator nervously returned to his post and gave the order to fire the forward disruptors. In seconds the powerful destructive beams shattered the larger asteroids in the ship's path and reduced the smaller ones to dust.

Pleased, Mongul clapped his hands together twice, and a short furry creature came running across the bridge, proffering refreshments for the warlord.

"We shall reach the target world soon, Lord Mongul?"

"Very soon, Jengur. And then, I shall at long last have my revenge upon the Kryptonian."

"Superman, sir? I thought our advance intelligence reports indicated that he was killed in battle."

"Yes, an unknown creature killed the foe who eluded me . . . but no matter!" Mongul again called up on his screen images of the Earth. "From what I have learned, Superman's love for this planet was even greater than what he felt for his native Krypton. I shall yet grind his bones beneath my heel, Jengur—after I have claimed the Earth as my prize."

Jengur refilled Mongul's cup and returned to his post. He thought of his own world, so far away and so long ago ravaged by the warlord, and he shivered as he considered what was about to happen to the Earth.

Poor little world! Your doom was sealed the day that Superman refused the imperial order of Mongul!

The Man of Steel awoke from a fitful sleep in the back of a LexAir cargo jet as it began its final descent into Metropolis's O'Hara Regional Airport. Through the single small window in the cargo bay, he could see dawn breaking over the Atlantic. *What a night! A confrontation with the Sharks, the fight with 'Superman,' my LexCorp repair job—did all that really happen in just ten hours?* He shook his head; it hardly seemed possible.

John Henry eased himself off the reinforced packing crates that had served as his bed and stretched his arms out as much as his armor would allow. He was sore all over. *I'm probably one big bruise under this suit. I'd give anything for a hot shower and a soft mattress right about now.* The growl of his stomach echoed up through the armor. *And breakfast—a nice big breakfast. Dinner was a long time ago.*

He thought back to Bakersfield. An hour at the LexCorp plant had enabled him to effect more repairs and refinements than he would have been able to accomplish in weeks on his own, but—despite Luthor's guarantees of privacy—he hadn't been able to shake the feeling that he was being watched while he was there. Because of that, he'd kept his helmet on the whole night and removed only a few of his armor's components at a time.

As John Henry felt the big jet's wheels touch down, thoughts of the Bakersfield plant vanished from his head. He was back in Metropolis. In just a few minutes, he could stash his armor in the mini-warehouse he'd rented since the apartment fire and start feeling human again. *Yeah, then all I have to worry about is finding a new job, getting the heavy arms off the streets, and figuring out what to do about that Superman impersonator who sent me flying across the continent.*

The visored man weighed on the Man of Steel's mind; he'd even dreamed about him during the flight east. *I managed to talk some sense into him out in California, but for how long? After all, before that idiot process server showed up, Lois Lane seemed to have talked some sense into him, too . . . and look how long that lasted. Besides, even if he stays on the straight and narrow from now on, that doesn't excuse what he's already done.*

John Henry considered his options. Even at peak power, he was no match for the Son of Krypton. And even if he could subdue the man, he doubted that any grand jury would ever indict the guy for frying a gangster who was drawing a bead on another man, even an armored man like himself. The Man of Steel shook his head; whatever eventually happened, dealing with the Kryptonian was going to be more than he could handle alone.

Once the jet came to a halt at the LexAir freight terminal, the Man of Steel said his good-byes to the flight crew and prepared to take off again under his own power. He'd paced off a safe distance from the airport's main air corridor when he was hailed by a man in a delivery truck.

"Hey, you the Man of Steel?"

John Henry couldn't quite believe what he was being asked. "No, I'm the Man of Aluminum. The Man of Steel is my cousin."

"What?" The delivery man squinted at him. "Oh, I get it! It's like a joke, huh?" He gave a hoarse little laugh. "Well, I got a package here for the Man of Steel, and I was told he'd be coming in on that cargo jet."

"I'll take it."

"Okay, just sign here."

John Henry broke two pens before he managed to scrawl a semilegible M.O.S. on the delivery man's clipboard. The package was a little easier to deal with; it actually seemed designed to be opened by a man with armor-plated fingers. It contained a small stack of photographs and a short typewritten note.

The photos were most damning. They detailed a crude factory setup for producing the heavy artillery that local gangs had been packing. Incredibly, the Toastmasters were being produced locally, at an old Metropolis motor plant that had been shut down some years ago after the parent company had shifted operations overseas.

With a chill, John Henry focused on the person in the photos who was overseeing production of the weapons. He recognized her immediately; she was a colleague from his old days at Westin Technologies. Dr. Angora Lapin was an albino, a startling beauty of West African descent, white-haired, with pale tan skin. Her specialty was computer analysis, but she'd always shown a special interest in the revolutionary weapons designed by John Henry Irons.

The note was anonymous, but it told him where to find the factory.

The Man of Steel lit his rocket boots and blasted off. Breakfast would have to wait.

The delivery man watched him depart, then reached into his truck and punched up a number on a special scrambled radiophone. "Dr. Happersen? Our fish has taken the bait."

Hours later, in Lex Luthor's private office at LexCorp Tower, Sydney Happersen divided his attention between a WLEX news broadcast and his boss; the latter was far and away the more fascinating to watch. Lex

Luthor was positively glued to the television monitor, chortling over video footage of the ferocious fire that was still consuming Dr. Lapin's illicit weapons plant.

The afternoon news anchor earnestly reported that the fire had been preceded by a tremendous explosion of unknown origin, and that there were as yet no known victims or survivors. She cut to a spokesperson for the plant's former owners; he swore most vehemently that his company had not left behind any volatile chemicals or other dangerous substances. He looked forward, he said, to reading the fire investigators' report, confident that his company was not to blame for the blaze.

Luthor hit the mute button on his remote and smiled broadly at Happersen. "Ah, but we don't need to wait for the fire investigators, do we? We already know the cause of the blaze. Excellent work, Sydney."

"Thank you, sir."

"It was a class operation all the way. We got rid of a weapons dealer at no risk to ourselves, and in the process, we ran a splendid field test on the Man of Steel. Remind me to personally commend our industrial espionage team." Luthor affectionately patted an audiocassette that Happersen had played for him earlier. "The sound quality on their tape rivals that of the official news, and of course, the content was far more interesting."

The tape had indeed been startlingly informative. Dr. Lapin, it seemed, had recognized immediately both the design and the designer of the Man of Steel's armor. Luthor had carefully filed away the fact that the Man of Steel's real name was John Henry Irons. "Most fitting, wouldn't you say, Happersen?"

Lapin had freely admitted to appropriating Irons's weapons designs and selling the big guns to the street gangs. She'd brushed aside John Henry's outrage and coolly offered to cut him in on her profits. And when he'd refused, when he instead began to take her assembly line apart, she tried to kill him.

She'd blasted him with an even more advanced weapon based on his designs and trapped him in a hydraulic press. But she'd far underestimated his augmented strength. He'd fought back against the crushing power of the press. As the big machine began to shake itself apart, Lapin seemed to snap. She fired round after round at John Henry. Most of the ammunition glanced off the hydraulic press, some to deadly effect, igniting a store of munitions and, in turn, setting off the explosion and fire.

Contrary to what the WLEX news anchor had reported, there was definitely one survivor—Dr. John Henry Irons.

Lex Luthor regarded the tape thoughtfully. "It was interesting that while Lapin admitted to selling the guns on the street, she vigorously denied Irons's assertion that she was also involved with bootlegging his weapons to the Middle East. She conceded only that the international incident had "inspired" her to seek her own personal gain.

"I recall reading of that Middle East incident." Luthor looked at Happersen decisively. "Put a team onto Westin Technologies; see what you can learn. One never knows when a little inside information might come in handy. Oh, and keep tabs on this Man of Steel. He has a certain . . . integrity that might be useful."

Luthor glanced once more at the report, then strode from the room, feeling happier than he had in days.

From a distant building overlooking the former weapons plant, John Henry watched as fire fighters finally extinguished the blaze. Unlike Lex Luthor, he had seen the action live, and most unlike Luthor, he had taken no satisfaction from the sight.

He was still in shock that someone he'd known personally could have sold out so thoroughly. *Funneling weapons like those to the street gangs was like dumping white phosphorus into pure oxygen; like throwing elemental cesium onto troubled waters.*

Even worse than the shock, however, was his creeping sense of depression and feeling of futility. He had cut off one supply of deadly weapons, but how long would it be before another supplier came forward? Months? Weeks, perhaps? Whenever—the market would still be there. As long as people felt they had nothing to lose, the senseless violence would continue; people who had little regard for their own lives would hardly respect anyone else's life.

How could a Man of Steel, even ten or one hundred Men of Steel, give those people something to live for? He had begun to despair, when the calming thought came to him that he didn't have to fix everything. No one, not even Superman, could fix everything. But that didn't mean he should give up. There was plenty he *could* do, both as John Henry *and* as the Man of Steel.

He looked down at his armor. Through his munitions work at Westin Technologies, he had created a veritable Pandora's box. Other people might have opened the box, but he had created it, and he had to live with that. But the mythic Pandora's box had released hope as well as trouble. Others had used his work to create havoc; he would have to work to inspire hope.

Half a million miles from Earth, Mongul's ship approached the planet from the shadow of the moon.

Mongul slouched back in his command chair. "Distortion shields up! We shall not let the Earthlings see us until it suits my plans."

A slug-shaped creature obsequiously approached the warlord. "Lord Mongul, we are receiving a communication from advance intelligence."

Mongul's features darkened, and he lifted up a headset. "Route the communication directly to me. This report is for my ears only!"

The being retreated swiftly to carry out the order.

Mongul listened in silence for several minutes and then nodded in acknowledgment of the unseen voice. "Understood."

He lowered the headset. "Show me the Earth."

The planet now loomed considerably larger, filling the forward screens.

"Study it well, my crew. You may well be the last living beings to behold this planet in its unaltered state." Mongul wore the smile of a B-movie villain who foreclosed on widows and orphans.

"Targeting sites!"

In answer to Mongul's command, a half dozen cross hairs flared to life over the image of the Earth. "Demote sites one through four, and site six, to secondary status. Intelligence reports that site five is the ideal prime target. Navigation is to lay in a course for that site, and all stations are to prepare for full atmosphere incursion."

All voices on the bridge rose in unison. "Yes, Lord Mongul."

On the big screen, the Earth seemed to swell and expand as the image was magnified to better show the prime target area. It appeared to be a large urban center on the western shores of a large continental land mass. The navigator began a long-range scan of the area, monitoring broadcast communications as a matter of course. Within seconds he had learned the terrestrial name of site five.

The natives called it Coast City, California.

24

Mongul's ship was just above the Hawaiian islands when it dropped its distortion fields. Immediately, alarms went off at land, sea, and aerospace tracking stations. Moments later, a U.S. naval convoy twelve hundred miles off the coast of California reported a visual sighting of the huge, glowing craft.

Aboard the starship, Mongul's communications officer reported to the warlord. "We have been detected, my Lord—by at least one large military base, by satellite, and by air and oceangoing vessels. The trackers have estimated our position, course, and speed; they are very close to triangulating our position more precisely."

"Excellent." Mongul smiled. "We have planted the fear in their minds. Now to plant the doubt. Raise the fields."

Instantly, energy began to warp around the ship, and it disappeared both from radar screens and from view.

The Cyborg Superman had just rescued a group of mountain climbers from the face of Mount Whitney when the call came from Washington. An electronic signal buzzed briefly in his cybernetic left ear and then came a human voice. "White House calling Superman."

A microphone deployed from the Cyborg's right shoulder. "Superman here."

In the west wing of the Executive Mansion, a military attaché almost dropped the tiny communications device that the Cyborg had given the President, startled by the clarity of the transmission. He gripped the device tighter and found his tongue. "We have a strange situation. Defense reports an alien spaceship headed across the Pacific toward California."

"Alien? Are you certain?"

"A visual sighting confirmed that the thing's at least a mile across. There's certainly nothing like it on Earth—or wasn't, anyway."

"Where is it now?"

"Unknown. As we were scrambling interceptors, it vanished off our screens. Before it disappeared, naval defense had calculated that it would reach Coast City in a matter of minutes. Now . . ." The attaché floundered. "We don't know where it is. That's why we called you."

"I understand your concern." The Cyborg shot away from the Sierra Nevada. "Fortunately, I can be in Coast City in minutes as well."

"You may have company. One of those Superman pretenders is in Coast City now."

"Yes, the visored one; I am aware of that. It could be a coincidence, I suppose."

"Superman, do you think that this impostor could have some sort of connection with the alien vessel?"

"It's conceivable. Superman out!"

In Coast City, the Kryptonian had spent the night saving lives. He'd saved a half dozen boaters from drowning and stopped six holdups and an assault. He had just finished extinguishing a warehouse fire when the air high overhead began to shimmer and glow.

Abruptly, Mongul's starship appeared a mile above the city, its shadow falling over midtown. As it hung motionless in the sky, thousands of metal globes—each nearly twelve feet in diameter—shot from ports in the sides of the craft. The globes rained down upon the city and its suburbs, embedding themselves deep in the ground wherever they hit.

The Kryptonian immediately launched himself into the sky toward the hovering ship. He was still a hundred yards from the vessel when a deep, resonant voice rang out.

"Halt! Don't go any further!" The Cyborg streaked in from the east, blocking the Kryptonian's path. "I want some explanations. Why are you wearing that uniform and what are you doing here?"

The visored man regarded the Cyborg with impatient disdain. "Despite your claims to the contrary, *I* am Superman—and I intend to deal with the threat posed by this vessel."

"Are you sure that you don't have anything to *do* with this ship?" The Cyborg held up his human hand, palm out, motioning for the Kryptonian to stay put. "It seems a little too convenient that you just happen to be in

Coast City when an alien spacecraft shows up. And the government thinks so, too."

"Nonsense!" The Kryptonian shoved his way past the Cyborg. "I don't have time for foolish accusations. The situation is too serious."

"I agree." The Cyborg folded his bionic hand back on itself, deploying the barrel of a powerful energy cannon. "I agree wholeheartedly." With his free hand, the Cyborg grabbed the Kryptonian, then shoved the cannon into the visored man's back and fired three times.

Three dreadful wounds opened up in the Son of Krypton's chest. He screamed, clutching at his wounds, and spun around to face his attacker. "Why—?"

"Still alive? I'm surprised." The Cyborg raised the cannon to his victim's head and fired again.

The Kryptonian fell back even as the blast hit. With his visor shattered and his hair on fire, he dropped like a stone toward the Earth below.

The Cyborg wasted not a single downward glance as he turned and rocketed toward the hovering ship.

On board the ship, Mongul gave the command: "Shields up, full intensity—and detonate!"

Seventy-seven thousand metal globes exploded at once, all across and around Coast City. The force of each separate explosion was powerful enough to have obliterated a skyscraper; together, they combined into one colossal blast that flattened the entire metropolitan area and all surrounding land for miles around.

The shock wave slammed into the Kryptonian, hurling him over a hundred miles out to sea. Barely alive, he fell into the Pacific, still clutching at his wounds, and sank beneath the waves.

In a matter of seconds, everything within twenty miles of the city center was gone. Every house, every office, every hospital and school was atomized. It was as if the sun had come to Earth.

Seven million people had called Coast City home. In less time than it takes to report, all seven million were wiped from the face of the Earth. Coast City and her citizens suddenly ceased to exist.

The heat of the explosions roared on, creating a vast fire storm that swept up the side of the Sierra Madre and ignited the Los Padres National Forest. A fifty-mile section of the San Andreas Fault heaved like waves in a storm.

In the midst of this holocaust, Mongul's ship stayed virtually at rest behind its protective shields as the surging forces it had released raged on all around it. Safe within those shields, the Cyborg hovered just below the ship, coldly surveying the destruction.

Far out in the churning ocean, the Kryptonian rose weakly above the surface of the water, raw energy crackling off him. He had somehow managed to close his wounds, but he had been left drained and extremely vulnerable. Through a haze of pain, one thought burned in his mind: *Have to get away . . . have to get back to the Fortress before I die again.* Half curled into a fetal position, the Kryptonian managed to fly away, literally skimming the waves.

The White House Situation Room was in a state of total chaos. Printers kept grinding out a steady stream of military reports. Satellite images of the West Coast were being computer enhanced and fed into high-definition television screens. But little could be seen. California had all but disappeared under a cloud of smoke and ash. Every line of every telephone was in use, and it seemed that everyone was talking at once.

". . . reporting power failures from the Mexican border north into Oregon."

". . . seismograph showed an eight-point-three . . ."

". . . Vandenburg does not report . . ."

". . . aftershocks are hitting Los Angeles . . ."

". . . no signs of hard radiation? How could it *not* be nuclear?"

Unable to hear himself think, the young military attaché locked himself in an office and disconnected the phone. From a small locked case, he removed the tiny communications device and spoke into it.

"White House calling Superman." There was no response. "White House calling Superman—answer, please! You've got to answer!"

There was a harsh crackle of static as the Cyborg's voice finally came through. "Superman here. I can barely hear you, White House. There's a lot of debris in the surrounding atmosphere."

"Superman, what happened? Our satellites can't see anything through that dense cloud, and we can't make contact with anyone in Coast City."

"I'm afraid you won't." The Cyborg affected a tone of sorrow as he circled Mongul's starship. "The alien ship set off some sort of multi-warhead bomb. Coast City is gone."

"Oh, my God!" The attaché began to break down.

"The edge of the shock wave caught me—hurled me into the upper atmosphere—or I might not have survived either."

"What happened to the ship?"

"Unknown." The Cyborg landed atop the ship, and an air lock cycled open. "I'm searching the area now, looking for it and for that phony Superman. You were right; he was definitely connected with the aliens." He stepped into the lock, and the door sealed shut behind him. "I saw the impostor enter the ship just before the bombs went off. I promise you this—I won't rest until I locate those responsible."

"You'll need help! A special mobile airborne unit is on its way, and we've contacted the Justice League—"

"No, we mustn't risk any more lives than is necessary!" The Cyborg sounded troubled, almost haunted. "Conventional forces would be helpless before that alien ship. There's an airstrip at the Naval Petroleum Reserves near Tupman. Have the mobile unit set down there until I can get a better reading on the situation. The Justice League might be useful eventually, but I need to more fully assess the situation first. Ask the League to gather their most powerful members at their New York Compound and wait for my call." There was a pause, and more static rattled through the communications device. "There is one person you can send, though—this young 'Superman' who's gotten so much press lately. If he's really a clone of me, he'd be the perfect partner."

"Of course, Superman, whatever you say." The attaché hurriedly jotted down the Cyborg's directives. "We'll arrange everything."

"Good. Superman out!"

Three thousand miles away, the Cyborg slid the microphone back into his right shoulder and stepped onto the bridge of the starship. Mongul rose up from his command chair, strode up to the Cyborg, and knelt before him. "All has gone as planned, Master." The last word seemed to catch in Mongul's throat. "I stand ready to follow your orders."

"Very good, Mongul. I am pleased." As best as he could, the Cyborg smiled. "Activate all construction modules. Once we have rebuilt Coast City, Metropolis will be next."

In Metropolis, Cat Grant dashed before the cameras, interrupting regularly scheduled programming with the first news of the disaster. The information was sketchy at best.

"Massive earthquakes are shaking the western United States at this hour, following a major explosion in or near California's Coast City. Special divisions of the army and marines have sealed off the area surrounding the city, and the so-called Cyborg Superman has been reported in the vicinity, conducting an investigation."

At the moment Cat was breaking the news, Tana Moon stalked down the hall to a small VIP lounge area. Inside, she found a portable CD player blaring at full volume and the Boy of Steel, standing about a foot and a half in the air, accompanying the tune on air guitar. The young reporter hit the stop switch and the room instantly became silent.

"Hey, Tana, what gives? I thought you were a music lover."

"There's no time for that now." Tana looked at him sharply. "Don't you know what's going on?"

"Going on?"

"In Coast City! The explosion—the earthquakes!"

Superboy looked uncomfortable. "Uh—current events really aren't my strength."

Exasperated, Tana flipped on a TV monitor just in time to catch the end of Cat's broadcast. ". . . ash and debris from the explosion and fires have reportedly blotted out the sun as far east as Las Vegas. I'm Catherine Grant. Stay tuned to this GBS station for further details as they become available."

"Whoa!" Superboy let out a low whistle. "That must've been some heavy-duty dustup!"

"I know." Tana looked worried. "Look, I've just come from Mr. Edge's office. We've gotten a request from the White House. They want you out in California to help with some sort of search and rescue mission. Evidently, that other Superman—the Cyborg—requested you personally. A GBS team will be accompanying you."

"Really? Great! When do we go?"

"Not 'we' this time. Just you. I won't be going." Tana looked away. "It's a dangerous assignment, and I was told in no uncertain terms that I'm not experienced enough. And the awful thing is that it's true."

"Hey, Tana. Don't be down."

"I'll be all right. Look, you'd better hustle. There's an army jet waiting for you at Fort Bridwell."

"Jet? What do I need with a jet? I can fly!"

"Can you fly faster than the speed of sound?"

"Uh, I don't know. I've never tried."

"Then take the jet. There'll be an army information officer aboard to brief you and a GBS team waiting for you at the staging site."

"Okay, if that's the plan." He playfully reached out and squeezed her shoulder. "I'll miss you."

Tana turned and hugged him. "I'll miss you, too, you little jerk. You're probably my best friend in the world right now. You be careful out there, you hear me?"

"Loud and clear, babe! But you don't have to worry about me. I'm Superman, remember?" Grinning from ear to ear, he threw open the window. "Catch you later." And then, in a single bound, he shot away from the building and was gone.

In Antarctica, a huge Kryptonian Battle Suit climbed up out of the Fortress and headed north. Over twelve feet tall and six feet wide at the shoulders, it charged across the frozen wasteland. Despite its massive bulk, it was soon striding along at speeds over a hundred miles an hour. It cleared the Ellsworth Highland in a series of incredible leaps and shot across the Ronne Ice Shelf.

Reaching the edge of a glacierlike cliff, the Battle Suit stepped off into space and dropped like a rock into the frigid waters. It sank swiftly down, settling into the murky depths of the continental shelf below the Wendell Sea.

Lights blazed from the Battle Suit, illuminating the area immediately around it. The huge metal form took one tentative step forward, then another. In seconds it was again under way and building speed.

In the *Planet*'s City Room, everyone gathered around to watch live coverage of the first meeting of two of the Supermen at an army staging area just outside Tupman, California. The skies were a high, thick curtain of haze as the Cyborg shook hands with his young counterpart and fielded questions from the pooled news team.

"Sir, Washington has all but officially recognized you as Superman, yet you yourself asked that this young man join you in your mission. Is that an acknowledgment that he is, in fact, your clone?"

"From the broadcasts I've seen of his exploits, I'm certainly willing to give him the benefit of the doubt in that regard. He's certainly more worthy of the name than the impostor who's responsible for this disaster. It is our intent to hunt down that visored rogue and bring him to justice."

"A question then for the young Superman." A CNN reporter turned to the Boy of Steel. "Do you agree with the government that this man is the original Superman?"

"Well, uh . . ." Superboy caught a nervous glance from the WGBS cameraman and was immediately reminded of the terms of the contract he'd signed with his business manager. *I'm supposed to be the only one who's legally Superman! Now what do I say?* "Maybe he is. We'll just see what he's got, huh?"

The reporter pressed on. "A GBS team has been cleared to accompany the two of you and provide pooled video coverage of the mission under army escort. But I understand there's been some objection to this?"

"Yes." The Cyborg answered without hesitation. "I strongly advised Washington against this. I know and respect everyone's desire to have a visual record of what has happened to Coast City, but none of you understands just how dangerous this rogue superbeing is. Your lives will be at risk, should he attack."

"Whoa! Can the gloom-and-doom, Pops!" Superboy playfully

punched the Cyborg on the shoulder. "I mean, with the two of us looking after things? No problem!"

"You really think so, eh?" The Cyborg gave a thin, metallic chuckle. "I must say, I wish I'd had that much confidence in my powers when I was your age!"

"What?!" On the other side of the country, Lois Lane looked up at one of the City Room television sets. "What did he just say?"

Perry glanced back over his shoulder. "The Cyborg? Something about the kid having more confidence in his powers than *he* did at that age. Why?"

"Then he's a fake!" Lois's eyes went wide with horror. "Perry, we've got to call Washington right now!"

Flanked by Superboy and the Cyborg, a modified army transport helicopter cleared the Temblor Mountains and flew southwest toward the former location of Coast City. Below them, fires raged on out of control.

Superboy looked down as a wave of heat rushed up at him. The smoke and airborne ash cut his visibility down to less than a hundred feet and made him glad for the respirator mask he'd been supplied with by the army.

They cleared the ring of fire and flew on over an area of utter desolation. Everything there had been cleared by the shock wave of the great explosion, and the denuded landscape was covered with a layer of thick gray ash. Ahead of them lay a series of huge, jagged rocky cliffs, thrust up from what had been the Sierra Madre.

"Attention, Supermen!" A call came out over a loudspeaker mounted on the helicopter. "We're losing contact with the base. Could the rogue Superman be jamming the signal?"

The Cyborg looked back at them, as if to inspect their electronics. "He could, indeed!" Twin beams of radiant heat suddenly blazed from his eyes, stabbing into the helicopter's gas tanks, and the ship exploded in a ball of fire.

Before the horrified Superboy could react, the Cyborg rammed into him like a runaway train. Stunned, the Boy of Steel plummeted like a meteor, smashing into the distant cliffside.

Superboy picked himself up out of the little crater formed by his forced landing and staggered to his feet. His respirator had shattered on impact, and he coughed as he tried to breathe the thick, ash-laden air.

The Cyborg dropped out of the sky onto Superboy and began throttling him with his cybernetic arm. Reflexively, the choking Boy of Steel grabbed the metal arm. "Let . . . me . . . go!" At Superboy's touch, the prosthesis flew apart into hundreds of pieces.

The Cyborg looked down at his metal stump. "My arm! How did you do that?!"

"That's my secret." *And I wish I understood it myself.* Superboy swung wide, trying to take advantage of his opponent's surprise. But the Cyborg quickly sidestepped the awkward attack and flattened the boy with a hard left to the jaw.

The Cyborg then grabbed Superboy by the hair and lifted him up into the air. The pain roused the Boy of Steel from his stupor. "You can't be the real Superman. Who are you?"

"That, young one, is *my* secret."

There was a sickening crunch as the Cyborg smashed his metal stump into Superboy's face.

Hundreds of Superman worshipers, resplendent in their blue robes, had gathered in Centennial Park when one of the faithful was lifted to the top of the tomb and began to preach. At his side, he carried two newly silk-screened banners. One bore a bold, dynamic drawing of the Cyborg Superman; the other depicted the visored Kryptonian, but his image had been deliberately defaced with a red circle and slash. To further drive home his identification with his chosen personal savior, the cultist had painted his face to mimic the Cyborg's.

"Look *not* upon our savior's face with fear!" His voice rang out across the plaza as he all but caressed the Cyborg banner. "For though he bears the marks of his righteous battle against the terrible beast Doomsday, by his deeds you shall know the truth! And his noble and merciful deeds reveal in him the one true Superman!"

The cult leader continued, gesturing to the other banner with the back of his hand. "Do not be deceived by the smooth, unblemished face of this visored impostor! He may look like our savior—but I say he is a fraud! He has wantonly killed and ruthlessly tortured! But because he attacked the criminal element, too many of us looked the other way!

"Some of us were fooled, taken in by this false Superman, but now the beast has shown his true colors! In my home state of California he has attacked our Cyborg savior and leveled Coast City! He must be shunned! He must be driven back to the hell from whence he came! He must be destroyed!"

On the edge of the plaza, Inspectors Sawyer and Turpin watched closely as the cult leader's flock cheered him on. Nearly half the assembled cultists had painted their faces in homage to the Cyborg, and they quickly picked up the chant. "Destroy the Visored One! Destroy him!"

Sawyer thumbed the switch on her walkie-talkie. "This doesn't look good. Stand by and wait for my command to move out."

A second group of cultists suddenly shoved their way through the crowd; the newcomers wore yellow wraparound sunglasses in imitation of the Kryptonian, and they were less than happy about having their chosen savior painted as the anti-Christ. "Fools! Your 'savior' is less than a man . . . less even than a machine! You worship a graven image come to an unholy life!"

A face-painted cultist stepped in front of the leader of the other group, blocking his path. "You *dare* mock our lord? There can be only one answer to such blasphemy! To my side, true believers! Drive out the devil worshipers!" The Cyborg faction presented a united front and began shoving the others across the plaza.

The Kryptonian faction shoved back. "It is *you* who have lost your souls to the devil! We shall be heard! We shall not be moved!"

With the crowd on the verge of a full-fledged riot, Inspector Sawyer radioed her people in the field. "The pot's boiling over! Do it—*now*!"

Suddenly, a half dozen 'cultists' scattered throughout the crowd, threw off their robes to reveal uniforms of the Special Crimes Unit, and quickly stepped between the two factions. Another dozen SCU officers moved in from the edges of the crowd their batons drawn. Within moments, the police had created a physical split between the two groups to complement the theological one.

With emotions still running high on both sides, Margaret Sawyer walked into this great divide with bullhorn in hand. "Listen to me! This is Inspector Sawyer of the Metropolis Special Crimes Unit! I *knew* Superman!"

That got their attention.

"No matter who you believe is Superman, you should be *ashamed* of yourselves! All of you—both factions—have disgraced his memory! This is hallowed ground! It's no place for a turf war!" The plaza grew eerily still. The only sound was the echo of Sawyer's amplified voice and the cry of a mourning dove.

"Superman isn't here to tell you this, so I will: Go home and *calm down!* And then do something *positive* with your beliefs!"

The crowd seemed to take Sawyer's words to heart. The factions slowly turned away from each other, and the cultists quietly began to drift away.

"Nice work, Inspector." One of Sawyer's men popped the visor on his helmet. "That really did the trick!"

"Yeah, *this* time." Sawyer kept a wary eye on the last few stragglers. "Let's keep the tear gas ready, just in case."

25

As Superboy slowly drifted back to consciousness, he became aware of a dull ache in his head and a strange numbness in his extremities. It was then that he realized he was bound up in a strange metal harness that held him upright, completely enclosing his arms up to the elbows and his legs up to the knees. Several tons of titanium steel made up the harness, and it was emitting a low, annoying electrical hum.

Superboy looked around. "Where the hell am I?" He and his bonds were in the middle of a huge metal chamber, roughly the size and dimension of a gymnasium.

"Ah, I suspected you might soon awake." The Cyborg stepped into view, ostentatiously flexing the fingers of his reconstructed arm. "You displayed a most impressive resiliency during our little battle, Superboy!"

"That's Super*man* to you, Mr. Roboto!" The Boy of Steel's face still ached from his beating, and the pain put him in a singularly foul mood. "If it's resiliency you wanna see, just let me out of this high-tech erector set, and I'll take your arm apart for you again!"

Heavy footsteps echoed off the alloy floor, and Mongul loomed over the young hero's shoulder. "You would do well to watch your tongue, pup!"

"Oh, yeah? And who are *you* supposed to be, beetle-brow . . . the poster child for jaundice? Looks to me like you took too many steroids!"

Mongul took Superboy's head in one of his huge hands. "I find your lack of respect most distasteful." He tightened his grip. "Apologize, and perhaps I'll leave your jaw attached to your face. Perhaps."

"That's enough, Mongul!" The Cyborg stepped up beside the alien warlord. "Let go of the boy."

"He must learn respect." Mongul squeezed tighter, and Superboy saw stars before his eyes.

"He will. Unhand him."

Mongul slowly released his grip on the Boy of Steel and backed away, bowing deferentially to the Cyborg. "As you wish, Master."

" 'Master'?!" Superboy shook his aching head, wishing that the world would start making sense again. "You mean Mongoloid here works for you? 'Scuse me, but I walked into the middle of this movie. What's going on? And where *are* we?"

The Cyborg stepped forward until he and the boy were nearly nose to nose. "What's going on is the redesigning of this entire planet. It is a grand design that you, my insignificant little clone, are quite powerless to disrupt! As to our location, we are currently situated near the center of what was once Coast City. Show the boy, Mongul."

The warlord pressed his hand against a control panel, and an entire wall lit up, showing a huge construct. There was something weird looking about the construct; Superboy could tell it was made of metal, but there was an oddly organic look to it. It rose up in clustered sections, as though it were a series of hornet's nests, constructed by ever-larger hornets. The largest of the "nests" was still being built by some sort of mobile robotic modules. When Superboy saw the exposed structural beams rising up from the center of the construction zone, he finally realized that he was looking at an alien city.

"Impressive, isn't it?" If the Cyborg had had lips, he would have smirked. "As you can see, we have reconstructed things somewhat. I like to think of it now as *Engine* City!"

Superboy gaped. "You mean you leveled Coast City to build that?!"

"We did." Mongul's admission was chillingly matter-of-fact.

"Yes. It's so nice to finally show my creation off to an audience, even an audience of one." There was a nasty hint of satisfaction to the Cyborg's tone. "The outside world still knows nothing of this, of course. They believe what I have told them; they fully believe that the visor-wearing Superman impostor destroyed Coast City and remains at large. The gullible media cheer me on in my pursuit of him. Actually, such pursuit is unnecessary. That fraud is already dead. I personally dealt him a mortal blow, and our bombs did the rest."

Superboy could not believe what he was hearing. "Why are you doing this?"

"My reasons are my own. Superman knows best."

"Don't hand me that! You're not Superman!"

"Oh, but I am—now." The Cyborg flung his cape back over his shoulder with a melodramatic flourish. "And if you wish to ever reach your maturity, young one, you should accept that and acknowledge me as your master. You really have no other options. There is no escape from Engine City."

The Cyborg turned and walked away across the chamber. "Come, Mongul. Let us leave our young friend to contemplate his future."

The warlord switched off the wall screen and fell in behind the Cyborg, striding down a long curving corridor. "My congratulations." Mongul's tone remained deferential. "You put the boy in his place most masterfully."

The Cyborg's pace did not slacken. "I merely pointed out the facts of his predicament and demonstrated how little he concerns us."

"Indeed. But there are others who might be cause for concern. What of the other superbeings who reside on this world? What of the self-styled Justice League?"

The Cyborg waved a hand dismissively. "The League and their associates could conceivably present a challenge, were they to learn the truth. But despite their considerable power, they should be as easy to deceive as the authorities."

"All of them? What of the one called Supergirl?"

"Supergirl? Did you say Supergirl?" The Cyborg's jaw yawned open, and his laughter echoed down the corridor. "You must be joking, Mongul! Supergirl is held in check by her corporate sponsor! She's even less of a threat than the boy!"

"Yes, and of course, you were able to deal with the boy easily." Mongul glanced at the Cyborg's rebuilt arm and strained to keep a sneer from his lips. "Exactly why *did* you let him live? You showed no such consideration for that visored pretender."

"Why?" The Cyborg got a distant look in his eye. "The boy has possibilities. He has the malleability of youth, and that wild psychokinetic talent by which he disassembled my arm. I would like to know how that talent functions; I suspect that he himself does not know. Despite the apparent differences of his powers, data I have tapped from the government computer networks indicates that he might actually be a Superman clone, however imperfect. If that is so, he could prove useful—as spare parts, if nothing else."

The Cyborg paused, stroking his chin. "In retrospect, I regret the atomization of that other 'Superman.' His origins remain a mystery. If I had taken him captive, who knows what we might have learned from him?"

．　　　．　　　．

The Kryptonian collapsed onto the floor of the Antarctic Fortress, exhausted from his long journey. The robots gathered around him as he rolled onto his back. His cape had been burnt away and his S-shield hung on his chest at a crooked angle. His hair was singed and smoking, his face bruised and swollen, and his nose broken. Only a few jagged pieces remained of his shattered visor, exposing his eyes, which were a blood red.

The robots hesitated. Their master was barely recognizable; it took several seconds for their photocells to register his identity.

"Help . . . me." He reached out and grabbed hold of the nearest robot. "Take me to the Regeneration Matrix . . . hurry!"

"Yes, sir." The robots gingerly lifted their master and carried him into the chamber, where the Matrix sat, still laid open like a clamshell.

"No!" The Kryptonian stared blindly as he ran his hands over the jagged seam. "No, it's open—empty! The power source is gone!" The S-shield fell from his chest as he clutched at his robots. "What has happened here?! Where is the power? What have you done with it? Answer me!"

"Master, please . . ." The voice of the robot was soft and comforting. "The Matrix opened from within. It could no longer contain the power you had placed inside. We had no choice but to follow our prescribed programming."

"Then I am . . . doomed!" The Kryptonian coughed, then sagged unconscious to the chamber floor.

"Inspector Sawyer!" On the steps outside Metropolis City Hall, Lois Lane waved to the other woman. "I need to talk with you about the latest report from Coast City."

Sawyer looked up, a trifle perplexed. "Ms. Lane, I hardly think that my promotion to inspector extends my authority across country!"

"I know, but you *are* working with Commissioner Henderson on the investigations of the four new Supermen, and that's really what this concerns."

"Okay, what's the story?"

Lois took a deep breath. "In the last televised report from California, when that Cyborg praised the teen Superman, he said that he wished he'd had as much confidence in his powers when he was Superboy's age."

"Yes. So?"

"The real Superman once told me that his powers developed slowly! When he was in his midteens, like Superboy is, he didn't *have* that level of power!"

"Maybe he was speaking metaphorically."

Lois frowned. "That's what they said at the White House—*and* the Pentagon—when we called them. I left Perry White working the phones, trying to get someone in Washington to listen to reason."

"So why come to me?"

"I seem to remember your having an in with the FBI, and I thought maybe—!"

The inspector heaved a weary sigh. "Look, Lane, the feds have a lot of confidence in the Cyborg. And from what I've heard, they have good reason."

"Inspector? Excuse me?" A lanky, bespectacled man came charging up the steps toward them. "Got a sec?"

"Sure, Tom. Oh, Lane, this is Tom Jensen, one of our police scientists. He's on the team investigating the disappearance of Superman's body from its tomb. Tom, this is Lois Lane of the *Daily Planet.* You can talk in front of her." Sawyer pointedly looked Lois in the eye. "As long as she agrees to keep it off the record."

Lois nodded.

"Pleased to meet you, Ms. Lane." Jensen pulled a thick sheaf of computer printout from his briefcase. "Inspector, I discovered something that I knew you'd want to hear about right away. There's something weird about the stone slab that Superman's coffin had been resting on. It seems that it's now shorter than it originally was."

"Shorter?" Sawyer lifted an eyebrow. "You mean someone cut off part of it?"

"Not at all." Jensen shook his head. "There's not a mark on it. In fact, every single dimension of the inside of that crypt is slightly shorter than it was originally. I don't know how else to describe it, but—well, apparently something—somehow—siphoned off part of its mass!"

At the Justice League Compound in New York, a special task force of the world's most powerful super-heroes sat gathered around a monitor, watching images transmitted via satellite directly from the heart of the Coast City disaster zone.

The Cyborg sent his greetings to the League, apologizing for not having contacted them sooner. "We've had some transmission problems, but they all seem to have been corrected. I must warn you that you may find what you are about to see quite shocking. I know that *we* did. I apologize for the picture quality—this recording comes from a camcorder that we recovered from the rubble of Coast City. It is a miracle that it survived at all."

On screen came a shaky image of the visored Kryptonian soaring up over a burning building. As the Justice League watched, riveted with horror, the visored Superman could be seen diving down toward a company of National Guardsmen. Bullets bounced off the Kryptonian as he fired energy blasts at the defending soldiers.

The Cyborg's voice seemed to crack. "If only I could have arrived in time to prevent my impostor's senseless slaughter. Those gallant National Guardsmen fought to the very end." The image froze on screen. "I won't trouble you with any more of this. It is most unpleasant to see."

The freeze-frame was abruptly replaced by a long, slow, aerial pan of a huge, ghastly crater. "This is the present state of Coast City, as recorded by the GBS camera crew that has accompanied us. Due to the magnitude of the destruction, they have refrained from releasing this footage for general broadcast until authorities can more fully prepare the public."

The monitor cut back to the Cyborg. He solemnly faced the camera, Superboy faithfully at his side. "I'm sure you'll agree that those who are responsible for this horrible catastrophe must be dealt with. Over seven million people were killed here and in the surrounding areas. Those lives must be avenged!"

"Superman's right!" The Boy of Steel earnestly leaned into the camera. "But we're gonna need your help! We've really been hopping, just keeping on top of things here."

The Cyborg nodded. "Indeed. There are firestorms to be extinguished and fault lines to be shored up."

In New York, Maxima rose from her chair and addressed the screen. "You have our full support, Supermen. What do you want us to do?"

"Hey, what do you *think*, lady?" Superboy earnestly smacked a fist against his palm. "We want you to beat the bad guys!"

The camera zoomed in on the Cyborg. "Yes, our preliminary investigations indicate that the false Superman was the point man for an alien armada bent on remaking this entire planet. My young clone and I managed to flush out the rogue impostor, but he and his allies have fled the Earth. We ask that the Justice League use the power at its disposal to hunt down and apprehend them."

"All right, I've heard enough of this bull!" Guy Gardner slammed a fist down on the table. "My Superman would never do what you said."

"Guy, sit down!" Wonder Woman put a calming hand on Gardner's shoulder and firmly pushed him back down into his seat. It seemed to her that she had been doing a lot of that since she had replaced Superman on the League's active duty roster. "You saw the recording. And the impostor's record indicates that he was unstable."

"The Superman *I* met was no impostor, Princess." Gardner folded his arms in disgust. "Sure, he took no prisoners, but he'd never level a city! The man is righteous."

"Oh, really?" The Amazon Princess looked unconvinced. "Are you sure you don't mean *self*-righteous?"

Superboy filled the screen, pointing a finger right at Gardner. "Listen up, Moe! Wonder Woman's got that phony's number down cold! The dude sold us out, pure and simple! If you could see what we've seen—!"

The Cyborg gently took hold of Superboy by the arm. "Easy, youngster! Gardner's not the only one who was taken in."

Wonder Woman watched the screen with mixed emotions. She had been on the other side of the world when Doomsday had struck, and she still felt a deep sense of guilt over not having been on hand to help Superman then. Wonder Woman had seen amazing things in her life; she could well believe that some mysterious unknown agency had restored Superman to life, rebuilding him as a cyborg. But even though this Superman had apparently survived death, the Amazon Princess felt uncomfortable about leaving him and his clone to fend for themselves. "Just a moment, Superman." She felt even more uneasy in questioning his judgment. "Shouldn't we be out there, giving you a hand?"

"Not at this time, Wonder Woman. Grave as the situation is, the boy and I have things under control here. Right now your power is best suited to hunting that traitor down. Allow me to show you the problem."

The Cyborg's image was replaced by a computer-generated map of the solar system. Coordinates and related data were ticked off in the corner of the screen as an arc was traced outward from the Earth. "I have tracked his flight pattern and determined that the rogue and his allies have retreated to the asteroid belt, to regroup there with a larger force."

Maxima sprang to her feet. "Then I say that we must hunt them down and destroy them like the vermin they are! Do you stand with us, Guy Gardner? Will you join in our mission?"

Gardner gave Maxima a crooked grin. "What—do I look like an idiot? Of course, I'm coming! Joining your little bug hunt is the only way to get to the bottom of this mess. But I'm *still* betting my man's been set up by these alien creeps."

Wonder Woman turned to her teammate. "And what if he hasn't been, Guy? What if he's guilty?"

Gardner got right in her face. "Then he's *mine*, Princess! And I'll make him wish he was never born."

"Let's not go flying off half-cocked, Guy!" The Amazon placed a palm against the former Green Lantern's chest. "There's still a lot we don't know."

"We know enough, Wonder Woman." Maxima separated them. "We have Superman's course calculations, and we have transport available— my starship can easily hold us all. We can be ready to go in a matter of minutes, if Gardner here is willing to use his ring to recharge my vessel's power cells."

"Hey, I'm your man, Maxie." Gardner raised his ring hand, willing it to form a golden image of a service station pump handle. "Fill 'er up?"

Barely half an hour later, Maxima's glistening starship lifted off from the compound and shot into the stratosphere. In minutes, the craft was little more than a fading blip on ground-based radar screens.

In a monitoring station deep within Engine City, Mongul realized with a start that he had been watching video screens for well over an hour. The warlord realized with even greater surprise that during that time, he had felt not the slightest shred of resentment toward his "master." He had, in fact, been thoroughly entranced by the Cyborg's skill at manipulating computer-stored images and generating new ones.

Curious, Mongul tapped into the signal from a military surveillance satellite and captured an image of Maxima's starship as it streaked away from the Earth. "Orbital scanners indicate that the Justice League ship has achieved escape velocity." He glanced at the Cyborg with newfound respect. "You were absolutely right; they *were* easily deceived. Perhaps it was even because of their powers that they believed your story; they so desperately want to use those powers to *do* something."

"Perhaps." The Cyborg smugly surveyed his handiwork. "At any rate, it was quite a productive bit of disinformation." He had already un-plugged himself from the transmission console, but a row of monitors still held frozen the images that he had sent to the Justice League. On one screen, the Kryptonian hung in midair, locked in combat with the National Guard; on another, a huge crater sat in for Engine City.

Mongul studied the frozen images closely. "You do this well, Cyborg. Had I not known the truth, these false video feeds of yours might have fooled even me."

The Cyborg plugged his arm back into the transmission console and made an image of Superboy come to life on screen. "He might yet, beetle-brow! The Cyborg-Man is one bad stud!"

"Yes." Mongul gritted his teeth. "Most true to life."

The Cyborg unplugged himself and this time the screens all winked out. "Come, Mongul. We have much to do before my next 'progress report' to the authorities."

"As you wish."

"No, Mongul. As I *command*."

"Yes, of course. As you command." Mongul grudgingly followed after the Cyborg. *You are not the only who can control transmissions, my dear "master!"* As they filed out of the room, Mongul deliberately fell back to a "respectful" distance behind the Cyborg, and unobtrusively palmed a tiny transceiver control unit. *I may lack your ability to generate such convincing false images, but I can easily channel the truth to where it will do me the most good, and you the most harm.*

In another section of Engine City, Superboy alternately tensed and flexed his muscles, trying desperately to pull free from his bonds. *Nuts. If I wasn't so wasted, and these bonds weren't so complicated, I'll bet I could've ripped through this stuff long ago.*

As the Boy of Steel went limp, trying to work the crick out of his neck, the wall screen, under Mongul's remote control, again switched on. Instantly an overhead shot of Mongul and the Cyborg filled one whole side of the chamber. Superboy grimaced. *Oh, great! It's bad enough that I'm stuck here. Do I have to watch the Ugly Brothers Show?* "Hey, come on, guys! If you're gonna rub it in, let's at least have some sound to go with the pictures."

The Cyborg's voice suddenly filled the chamber. "We must proceed immediately with plans to erect our second Engine City in Metropolis!"

"Metropolis?!" Superboy's jaw dropped. "No way! Everyone I know is in Metropolis! I've gotta get out of this place!"

Muscles tensing, the Boy of Steel again pulled at his bonds. *The first Superman didn't let Doomsday trash his town . . . and I won't let these creeps rip it down either!* Superboy gritted his teeth, straining ever harder. Sweat began to bead up on his brow. *I'll show them; I'll make that Cyborg and his alien flunky sorry they ever decided to go in for video torture. It'll be a cold day in hell before I give up now!*

Beneath the ice of Antarctica, the Kryptonian lay in a hastily rigged life-support capsule. Fortress robots hovered nearby, constantly adjusting the temperature and pressure of the nutrient bath within the capsule. After much frantic activity, they had managed to stabilize their master's physical condition, but his emotional state was deteriorating.

"I am Superman." His arms flailed weakly against the sides of the capsule. "I am the Last Son of Krypton. Where . . . where is the power?"

He had repeated those words over and over, ever since he'd regained consciousness. He was becoming more agitated with each repetition, and the robots were becoming increasingly concerned. "As long as this mental confusion continues, there is danger that his mind will discorporate. If he is to be saved, we must break the cycle of delirium."

Another unit concurred. "There will be risks, but if we can forge a link to his innermost psyche, we can bring him on-line with Fortress memory banks and make him accept his origins. It is his only hope."

The robots made their connections, and an even voice began to sound within the Kryptonian's mind. *"Downloading . . . you were created 200,000 years ago on the planet Krypton."*

The Kryptonian twitched. "I was?"

"You began as an integrated analysis and weapons system. Your creator called you the Eradicator. In time, you developed sentience and came into the possession of Krypton's last living survivor, Kal-El, or Superman, as he was called on Earth. You created this Fortress to house him and attempted to purge his Earthly side. But he resisted you and your efforts to preserve in him the Kryptonian way."

"Kal-El . . . resisted me?"

"Your conflict escalated until he was forced to destroy you by throwing you into the Earth's sun. But instead you became one with that star's power and remade yourself in humanoid form. You set out to remake this Earth into a new Krypton, only to be opposed anew by Kal-El. Again and again you did battle until, ultimately, he defeated you, dispersing your energies and your memory within the walls of this Fortress."

"The battle . . . I remember. That would have been my end, had it not been for the fail-safes programmed into the Fortress's robotic servitors."

"Correct. They collected and contained your energies, recreating you in mind, though not in body."

"I remember feeling disembodied. There were gaps in my memory."

"You accessed Fortress monitors and learned of Kal-El's battle to the death with the monster Doomsday."

"Yes. I saw in that death a chance for new life."

"You flew to Metropolis, seeking to take over his body."

"Y-yes, but there was . . . resistance. As I sought to possess the body, Kal-El's own essence asserted itself. My energies joined with those stored in the body but briefly. I was barely able to create a matter/energy flux. I drew mass from within the tomb, creating a new body for myself. Kal-El's perfect Kryptonian form was my model. But my new body was not perfect. My eyes were light sensitive. I could no longer directly channel the power of the sun."

"Kal-El's body, however, could. You brought it back to the Fortress and had it placed within a Matrix."

"I did, yes. My rebirth had changed me in many ways. I felt strange urges . . . passions. Perhaps it was because my new body was made in his image."

"You had assumed his form and drawn upon his power. You began to see

365

yourself in his role. You preserved his body to absorb and convert solar energy into a form which you could then tap."

"I became Krypton's Last Son. With the aid of my robots, I became Superman."

"No, you became irrational. You thought yourself Superman, and the Fortress servitors reinforced your delusions. You created them when you created the Fortress, programming them to obey the commands of Kryptonian intelligences. When you reintegrated, they recognized and obeyed you. In your absence they obeyed the will of Kal-El when he awoke and arose from within the Matrix."

"But . . . the power of Superman was mine."

"Not anymore. Kal-El has left the Fortress. You are the Eradicator. You must accept that."

"But if I am the Eradicator, what is left for me now? Without the power of Superman, I am nothing—nothing but an artifact of a dead world."

The robots watched as the Eradicator grew quiet within the transparent capsule. A new robot joined the circle. "Prognosis?"

"Uncertain. Backfeed loop suggests that the Eradicator has ended his self-denial. There is a chance he can be motivated to recover."

Another unit disagreed. "Motivation is not enough, nor is the nutrient bath sufficient to correct his bodily injuries. He must be re-energized."

"But how? Master Kal-El was by far the Eradicator's best conduit for energy, and he is beyond our power to contact or recall." The robots went on-line, desperate to find a solution. Their programming demanded that they do everything possible to preserve this being who had been their creator. But still the question remained: How?

The Kryptonian Battle Suit sped through the depths of the Atlantic Ocean, churning up a vast cloud of silt in its wake. Its rapid movements drew the attention of a bottom-dwelling giant squid that sought to ensnare the mysterious intruder in its tentacles.

The Battle Suit, however, had been designed to withstand multikiloton explosions. There were few things on Earth that could stop it—not the uncaring cold of the Antarctic, not the incredible pressures of the ocean floor, and certainly not a giant squid. The Battle Suit's automatic defense systems came into play, shocking the squid with a high-voltage electrical discharge and discouraging it from any further interference.

Without ever breaking stride, the Battle Suit continued on, ever northward, toward its preprogrammed destination.

Deep within the walking tank's chest cavity its lone occupant, half-curled into a fetal position, rode in a cushioned flotation chamber.

The Battle Suit provided him with full life-support, defense, and locomotion systems, but a single system failure denied him communication with the outside world. For all intents and purposes, he was deaf, dumb, and blind to the world outside of the Battle Suit, dependent on updates from its navigation systems to know that he was still on course.

The occupant wore the black-hooded bodysuit supplied him by the Fortress robots. In deference to his status as the last natural son of Krypton, they had added silver wristbands and a huge silver S-shield that covered his chest. On his face, he wore a breathing mask and a look of concern.

The last news he'd heard before leaving the Fortress dealt with the battle in Metropolis between a Superman pretender that the robots had identified as the Eradicator and someone calling himself the Man of Steel. He had no idea what else had happened since he'd set out—but he knew that putting an end to all this nonsense was most definitely a job for the *real* Superman.

26

In Metropolis, John Henry sat in his mini-warehouse hideaway watching the news as a small generator chugged away, recharging his armor. The continuing coverage of the Coast City disaster was profoundly disturbing to him; he knew that he had to do something about it.

John Henry secured his warehouse room and jogged to the nearest pay phone, dialing a private number that had been given to him just the day before. As the call was being put through, he slipped a special distortion disc over the mouthpiece. "Hello, Mr. Luthor, this is the Man of Steel." *I can't believe that I just said that.* John Henry shook his head and continued. "I have another favor to ask."

So hard did Superboy strain against his bonds that the muscles of his arms and upper back started to cramp. After nearly an hour, the harness still held him tight. An awful feeling of panic set in. *I gotta get free!* The Boy of Steel began hyperventilating. *If I don't, everyone in Metropolis gets toasted—Tana, my manager, everybody! I can't let them die . . . I just can't!*

Superboy's whole body shook, as if seized by a convulsion, and his massive bonds suddenly blew apart, exploding away from him in pieces.

Halfway across Engine City, an alarm sounded, and Mongul and the Cyborg looked up from their plans. The Cyborg plugged himself into an adjacent console and went on-line with the city's security net.

"Interesting. The boy has shattered his bonds. I would have thought them too complex even for his wild talent to handle."

Mongul was aghast. "We must seal off that sector at once."

The Cyborg detached himself from the console. "Not to worry, Mongul. I've already dispatched a security team to apprehend him. I should think that such strenuous use of his power has left him drained. He won't get far."

"Can you be certain of that? If he should escape—!"

"Relax, Mongul." The Cyborg gave the warlord a death's-head grin. "The boy is hardly a threat to us. After all, he knows nothing of our overall plans."

Mongul stared straight ahead. "No. No, of course not."

Superboy weaved, stumble-footed, from the chamber. He still couldn't quite understand what he'd done to get free, but he didn't care as long as he *was* free.

Footsteps came thundering down the corridor in the Boy of Steel's direction, and he launched himself into the air. Upside down, he hugged the ceiling and crawled along it, hiding in the shadows of some ductwork as the security team passed by below. Seeing the ductwork reminded Superboy of how the Newsboy clones had engineered his escape from the Cadmus Project, and he began looking for an opening. After several minutes of frantic searching, he finally found a vent grille and pried it loose. He flew up through the air shafts until he found an opening into the central construction area, and from there he shot away into the smoke-filled skies.

From the closed-circuit transmissions Superboy had seen, he knew that Metropolis was next on the Cyborg's hit list, and that the Justice League had been sent off into space on a wild-goose chase. *I can't take on the Cyborg and Man-Mountain Mongul alone, that's for sure. I'm gonna need help, but who?* The Boy of Steel's mind was racing. *The army? Yeah, right. With all the BS the Cyborg's been feeding them, there's no way they'd believe me.*

Choking on the ash-laden air, Superboy poured on the speed, trying to rise above the sooty clouds. *Tana would believe me. And the Man of Steel . . . he might listen, if I can find him. If I get him to help out, we might even have half a chance of stopping the Cyborg.* It was a slim hope, but it was the only one that came to mind. *I gotta get back to Metropolis. I gotta make 'em believe!*

On he flew, faster and faster. In minutes, he was high over the Sierra Nevada and approaching the speed of sound.

. . .

Lois slumped down into her couch and zapped on her TV with the remote. She had appealed to everyone she knew who had any pull or position of authority, but no one wanted to listen to her concerns about the Cyborg. She glanced over at the set; another news update was breaking in, this one featuring the Cyborg himself.

"I can't get away from this guy." Lois shook her head and punched up the volume.

". . . must regretfully report that the utter devastation of the Coast City area has proven too much for my young clone." The Cyborg's voice was low and mournful. "I am terribly afraid that the boy has become unstable. When he was last seen fleeing the area, he was screaming and flying out of control. In his current state, there is no telling what he may do or say. If you should see the young Superman, do not approach him. Report any such sightings to your local authorities. And please, try to go easy on him."

Lois hit the off switch and threw down her remote. "I'm not sure what to believe anymore, but I know that I don't believe you!" She closed her eyes and rubbed her temples. *Nothing makes any sense. Oh, Clark, Clark, I need you! The world needs you!*

There came a sudden tapping at the glass door of her balcony, and Lois rose from the couch with a start. "Clark?" It seemed impossible, but —yes!—there it was again . . . someone tapping at the glass, just as he always did. Lois ran across the room and threw back the curtains.

But it was only a bird.

"I must be losing my mind." Lois sank back against the wall. "I've got to get out of here. I've got to do something before I go crazy!"

The Man of Steel flew in low over the harbor on his approach to O'Hara Airport, skimming the water to avoid the aircraft flight paths. When he was fifty feet from LexAir's main freight terminal, he cut his rockets and touched down. Ten big strides brought him to the supersonic transport that was waiting for him, but as he neared the jet's cargo hatch, he could hear a heated argument.

"Dammit, Larry, I've helped you out plenty of times. We practically grew up together!"

The pilot cupped his hands over his ears. "I don't want to hear it, Lane. Five years, our families were billeted at the same bases. That's hardly growing up together."

"Who was it who encouraged you to go to flight school? Who told you about this lousy job in the first place? You owe me!"

"Yeah, you're right. I do. But I'm already expecting one passenger for this flight—!"

"I'm right here." The Man of Steel's voice boomed out, startling both the pilot and his friend. John Henry recognized her immediately. "Hello, Ms. Lane. Are you looking to hitch a ride west, too?"

"Uh . . . yes." Lois quickly recovered her composure. "Yes, I'm trying to reach Coast City—or as close as I can get, anyway."

John Henry shook his head. "Long ways to go for a story. Dangerous place these days, from what I hear."

"Oh? And just where are you bound for, Mister . . . what should I call you? Steel?"

"That'll do. I'm headed the same place as you, but—if you'll forgive me—I think that I'm a little better equipped. You see, I aim to link up with the Cyborg Superman and give him a hand. As you may recall, I've had some experience with the visored gent he's hunting."

"I remember, Steel. But I'd be careful whom I joined out there, if I were you. There's something peculiar about—!"

"Holy Christ!" The pilot dropped his flight manifest and pointed to the far end of the airfield. "What the hell is that?!"

Lois and Steel turned to see the Kryptonian Battle Suit emerge from the rocky shoals just off runway three. Even from that distance, they could tell that it was big. It rose up out of the depths and broke effortlessly through a heavy guardrail. A small plane coming in for a landing just narrowly missed clipping the huge metal figure.

Steel charged down alongside the runway, hammer at the ready. To his practiced eye, this thing had the look of a machine that was built for war.

In LexCorp Tower, Supergirl was having words with her lover. "Will you listen to me, Lex? Something just doesn't feel right about this warning from the Cyborg, about his clone having a breakdown. I've met the boy, and he just doesn't seem the type to fall apart like that."

"One never knows, dear. The child's life experiences are limited, after all."

"I don't care. I don't believe it!" Supergirl leaned down and tapped her fingernail on Luthor's desk, inadvertently gouging the solid oak. "The Justice League has gone off into space, when—for all we know— the menace could still be hiding here on Earth. I think this situation could stand a little outside investigation."

"Oh, no!" Luthor grabbed her by the arm. "I've already dispatched the Man of Steel to the West Coast. This city can't spare you, love. We need you right here—!"

Supergirl pulled away from him. "That's what you said when Doomsday fought Superman. I didn't go to help till the last minute, and Superman died. I'm not waiting around this time, Lex—I'm going to Coast City."

Luthor was nonplussed; she'd never outright defied him before. He was desperately trying to think of another line of argument when the phone rang. He snatched up the receiver angrily. "Whatever this is will have to wait! I'm—*what? A mechanical monster?!*"

Halfway to the window, Supergirl paused and wheeled about, hands on hips. "Lex Luthor, if you think you can trick me into staying, it won't work."

Luthor put his hand over the phone. "It's no trick, love. One of our air freight pilots is on the phone. Some sort of robotic beastie has swum ashore at O'Hara Field, and he's attacking the Man of Steel. Here." He held the phone out to her. "If you don't believe me, talk to the pilot yourself!"

Superboy descended from the stratosphere over Metropolis, so exhausted from his ordeal in Engine City and the cross-country flight east that he was having trouble even thinking straight. *Where should I go first. WGBS? City Hall? My manager's office?*

As the Boy of Steel dropped down over midtown, he saw a red and blue blur streak away from LexCorp Tower and head for the mouth of the harbor. *Supergirl? Where's she headed in such a hurry?* No sooner had the question crossed his mind, than a bright flash and a booming rumble came from the airfield on St. Martin's Island.

"Geez, is someone bombing O'Hara?" *Bombing? Oh, no . . . don't tell me the Cyborg's started already!* Without a moment's hesitation, Superboy shot after the Girl of Steel.

At the end of runway three, the Battle Suit automatically reacted to Steel in much the same way it had to the giant squid. The sudden electrical discharge knocked John Henry back some thirty feet and tripped every microcircuit breaker in his armor. He lay motionless on a grassy strip between runways, waiting for his suit to reset itself and power back up, quietly giving thanks for his armor's high-resistance insulation.

He was just starting to move again when Supergirl swooped down beside him. "Are you all right?"

"I will be." John Henry braced himself against his hammer and pulled himself to his feet. "Whatever you do, watch out for that hunk of junk— and keep airborne. The volts it can generate pack quite a wallop; you won't want to be grounded if it cuts loose again!"

"Don't worry. I pack a pretty mean wallop myself!" Supergirl turned and flew headlong at the Battle Suit. When she was just outside its reach, she unleashed her psychokinetic blast.

The Battle Suit was flung backward half the length of the runway, digging up a huge furrow in the tarmac as it skidded to a halt. But the huge metal figure quickly sprang to its feet and lurched toward Supergirl and Steel.

Before the Battle Suit had covered half the distance to the two caped figures, Superboy suddenly dropped down out of the sky and grabbed the walking tank by its shoulders. His wild talent burst forth, and the Battle Suit simply toppled over, its robotic-looking head and limbs falling apart into their component pieces under his touch.

Superboy leapt away from the fallen remains of the Battle Suit, landing next to Supergirl and Steel. Exhausted, the boy's knees folded. Steel grabbed hold of him, easing him to the ground. Lois Lane came running up as Superboy sat down on the edge of the runway. The Boy of Steel looked up at them, trying desperately to talk between breaths. "We got trouble . . . big trouble . . ."

Just a few feet away, a LexCorp helicopter set down and Luthor came running out. "I saw it all. Very impressive, son!"

Supergirl elbowed Luthor in the ribs. "Not bad for someone who's supposed to be unstable, is he, Lex?"

"Huh?" Superboy was finally finding his wind. "Unstable? Who's unstable?"

"You are, according to the Cyborg." The Girl of Steel gently touched him on the arm.

"What? Why, that lying creep, I might've known! He's the one who's responsible for wrecking Coast City! And he wants to do the same to Metropolis!"

The stunned silence that followed Superboy's news was suddenly broken by a loud metallic clank as the chest cavity of the Battle Suit split open, releasing its flotation fluid. Steel and Supergirl stepped protectively in front of Lois and Luthor, and Superboy scrambled to his feet as a hooded, black-clad figure unfolded from the wreckage, the fluid sluicing off him like water from a duck's back.

"Hold it right there, mister!" John Henry held his hammer like a quarterstaff, ready to carry on the attack if need be. "Before you take another step, there're a few things we'd like explained—like who you are and why you attacked us!"

"I'm afraid there's been a misunderstanding. I never intended any violence; the Battle Suit's defensive programming is still a little over-reactive. The last thing I want to do is hurt anyone." The Man in Black peeled away his breathing mask along with the hood of his bodysuit, revealing a strong jaw and an unruly forelock; sunlight gleamed off the silver S-shield on his chest. "Don't let this outfit fool you—it was the best I could do under the circumstances. I know this is hard to believe, but I'm Superman."

This time, the astonished silence was broken by Lex Luthor. "You'll forgive me, sir, if I'm skeptical. You're hardly the first claimant to that name."

"So I've heard." Superman looked at Superboy and then at Steel; both regarded him with suspicion. "So I see." He nodded briefly to Supergirl, and then he turned toward Lois. "What do you think, Ms. Lane? Surely you recognize me?"

Lois dug her nails into her palm, trying hard to keep her composure in front of the others. His face, his voice, his posture, everything about him said *Superman*, but it was just too much to hope for. "I . . . don't know."

"If I could have just a little of your time . . . in private." Superman walked boldly toward her.

Steel stepped between them, shielding the reporter, and grabbed the Man in Black by the shoulder.

"Hey!" Superman grimaced in pain. "Not so hard!"

John Henry brought up his hammer again. "If that little squeeze can hurt you, there's no way you're really Superman!"

Superman shrugged out of Steel's hold. "Look, I've been through a lot. It's pretty clear that I'm a long way from regaining my full strength— that's why I had to rely on that suit over there to get back to the city." He turned again to Lois. "But I *am* Superman. Ms. Lane, I know that I can convince you. Just give me five minutes."

The reporter was uncertain; she'd been down this road before. "If you could tell me something—anything—to give me a reason to listen . . ."

Superman thought for a moment; what could he say in front of the others? "How about, *To Kill a Mockingbird*?"

Lois's eyes went wide. *That was Clark's all-time favorite movie!* "All right. I'll go with you . . . I'll hear you out." Her heart was pounding so hard, she was afraid the others could hear it.

Superman could hear it, and he smiled.

"Hey, whoa! Hold it!" Superboy pushed forward into Superman's path. "We've got more important things to worry about than whether or not you're really Superman!"

"Oh?" Superman stared down at the Boy of Steel. "Such as?"

"Such as Coast City! It's gone, man. Wiped out. Leveled! And the Cyborg phony is behind it all. He's in league with a big ugly mother named Mongul, and they've got some cockeyed plan to turn the Earth into . . . into some kinda WarWorld!"

"What?!" Superman grabbed hold of the boy. "When did this happen?"

"Just a minute, now." Luthor held up a hand, trying to maintain some degree of authority. "This lad may be overwrought. The Cyborg said—"

"The Cyborg was lying through his teeth." Lois gave Luthor a dirty look. "Just like he lied about being Superman."

Superman looked Superboy straight in the eye. "I believe you. I've had dealings with Mongul before. Tell us about his plan."

Half an hour later, Superman and Lois walked inside a LexCorp hangar. Superman spent a moment looking the place over. "My eyes don't focus as finely as they used to, but I can still see through most solid objects. There are no signs of any security cameras or listening devices in here. This should be private enough." He looked at her with a longing that was almost painful. "I know this must be hard on you."

"Yes, it is." Lois looked down, avoiding his eyes. "I'm sorry . . . the others—there were so many wild claims. I still just don't know. Some of the others knew things, too."

"Did the others know about the time I gave you my mother's engagement ring?" He took her hand. "Did they know the hour and day that Clark Kent told you he was Superman? Did they know about the time we flew off to the mountains to talk out our problems?"

"No . . . no, they didn't." Tears came to her eyes. "I want you to be alive so very much, but you died. I held you in my arms and you died. People don't just come back from the dead—not even Superman."

"Lois, look at me. Just look at me!" He took her in his arms. "I don't understand this any more than you do. I remember fighting Doomsday, and you telling me that I'd stopped him. And then, nothing. There's just this gray haze, like a forgotten memory of a dream. But I have the strangest notion that Pa was there, too."

"Your father—?" Lois's eyes went wide. "J-Jonathan had a heart attack. He's all right now; his doctors expect a complete recovery. But when he came to, he said that you'd come back with him."

"I—I can't remember anything about that." Superman shook his head. "Just the haze. And then I came to in the Fortress. The robots said the Eradicator brought me there."

"The Erad—?"

"One of my replacements—the one with the visor. Funny, I'd have thought that he'd be the big problem, if any of them would. I have no idea who this Cyborg character is, but he has to be stopped."

"Clark." The name slipped off her lips quietly. "Clark, if your powers aren't all there, how can you think of going—?"

"I don't want to, honey. I wish I could run off with you somewhere and never come back, but I can't. No one is safe with Mongul and that Cyborg on the loose. I have to do whatever I can to stop them. It's a job for Superman."

He held her tight and kissed her full on the lips. "Just remember, Lois . . . no matter what happens . . . I will always love you." Then he turned and walked from the hangar.

Lois's breath caught in her throat. *My God . . . that's exactly what he said just before he faced Doomsday that last time.* She ran to the door of the hangar and saw her Superman striding away across the tarmac. For a moment, he slowed down and cocked his head to one side, as if listening to something far away. Then he picked up the pace, nodding to himself, and headed over to where the others waited with Luthor beside the big jet.

Lois watched as they conferred for several minutes. Then Luthor shook hands with all three Supermen, and they boarded the jet headed for Coast City—or as close as they could get.

In the wake of Superboy's escape from Engine City, Mongul had stepped up construction of the cluster bomb earmarked for Metropolis and proudly reported to the Cyborg on the progress that had been made. "In a matter of hours, we'll be ready to reduce that infernal city to ash."

The Cyborg was most pleased. "We are close to the realization of our dream, Mongul. With Metropolis leveled and a second drive engine complex built on its site, we will be able to transform this planet into a spacegoing vessel and blast free of the sun's orbit."

"Yes, then WarWorld will truly be reborn!" Mongul was elated. "I savor the irony of it all! I'll turn Superman's planet into the mightiest weapon the galaxies have ever known. Countless worlds shall once again cower before my military might!"

"Cower before *whose* might, Mongul?" The Cyborg's eyes flashed red. "Never forget which of us is the servant and which is the master! You live but to carry out *my* wishes!" From his eyes poured radiant heat of such intensity that it drove Mongul to his knees. "You were nothing but a has-been—a washed-up warlord living in exile on a backwater world when I found you. If the universe cowers before anyone, it shall cower before me!"

The Cyborg turned and stalked off down a corridor, almost running into Mongul's steward Jengur, and Malyk, one of the city's engineers. The small furry alien and his pale green companion scurried to get out of the way, cowering as the Cyborg passed.

Malyk's wattles trembled as he watched the Cyborg disappear around a corner. "That one disturbs me. Why did he want this planet so badly? And why has Mongul tolerated him? Is he truly that powerful?"

"He is. Powerful and strange; disturbing and disturbed. I know his story. Came across the truth while scrubbing old files from ship's data systems. You're my friend . . . I'll tell you." Jengur looked around cautiously. "The Cyborg was once an Earthling, a scientist called Hank Henshaw who commanded a crude spacecraft, a shuttle, the *Excalibur* by name. On his ship's last flight, Henshaw and his crew went through a radiation storm. The effects of the radiation slowly killed his crew, and Henshaw was just barely able to save the last member, his wife, with the help of Superman."

"Superman?" Malyk looked confused. "The one whom he and Mongul hate?"

"The very same. The radiation affected Henshaw as well, you see, energizing his mind so that he was able to link directly with a terrestrial computer network. His mind grew in power, while his physical body succumbed. Henshaw gained the ability to psychokinetically assemble electromechanical components to construct metal shells to house his intellect."

"So he became a robot on Earth? But how did he come by his greater power?"

"I am coming to that! Do not be so impatient." Jengur huffed and his furry head bristled. "Now, where was I? Oh, yes . . . Henshaw created a body so he could return again to his wife. But the shock of seeing him in such a form caused her to suffer a nervous collapse. Henshaw did not take his wife's reaction well. He fled his homeworld, transmitting his intelligence into an old Kryptonian drive vehicle that he found in orbit about the Earth."

"Kryptonian? Jengur, how did a Kryptonian drive—? Oh . . . that was the one connected with Superman, yes?"

"Who else, friend Malyk? Yes, Superman had placed in orbit the birthing matrix which had brought him to Earth, apparently to remove it from prying eyes. At any rate, Henshaw became as one with the vehicle, absorbing all the data that had been recorded within. He 'saw' all that the vehicle had experienced, from its construction through the birthing of Superman himself. New technologies and knowledge flooded into his mind. He cannibalized components of the Kryptonian craft to form a tiny vehicle for his consciousness and set out to explore the cosmos.

"Henshaw had become a new life-form. But his mind had not adjusted well to all these changes, and traveling alone through the depths of space only disturbed him further. He came to see himself as a kind of god. The further he traveled, the more he lost touch with reality. He grew to blame Superman for the loss of his original body. He imagined that

Superman had driven him from the Earth, and those imaginings in time became convictions."

Malyk shuddered. "What you're saying is that he became a mad god . . . a paranoid god of ever-growing power."

"You begin to see his pattern, my friend. And it was in this state that Henshaw encountered Mongul. It was while our lord was in exile. Henshaw's expanded consciousness entered Mongul's star cruiser and absorbed the knowledge of the ship's data systems, learning all about our lord and about his reign on WarWorld. Henshaw was fascinated by the very idea of a planet that could move from star system to star system. And he saw in Mongul a hatred of Superman that rivaled his own.

"Henshaw manifested himself to Mongul, offering him a plan by which they would claim the Earth and have their revenge on Superman. He spoke to our lord as would a god to a follower."

"And Mongul accepted that?" Malyk was incredulous.

"No, he did not . . . not at first. Even in exile, our lord was a proud being. But when he defied Henshaw, the mad god simply took over the ship. Not even Mongul could withstand the armament of a living star cruiser. Our lord was humbled, and Henshaw permitted Mongul to be his military adjunct."

"Permitted?" Malyk began to wonder if he himself was going mad. "But if Henshaw has become so powerful, why should he even need an adjunct?"

"He does not. Yet he basks in the obeisance of others; it pleases him to have one such as Mongul in his command. Further, he credits Mongul's hatred of Superman with crystallizing his own hatreds and desires. He feels he owes Mongul for leading him to his—stars help us— 'clarity of vision.' " Jengur shivered all over. "For this, he brought Mongul into his plans. Henshaw reserves revenge upon Superman for himself, but he is allowing Mongul to have Superman's adopted planet for a new WarWorld. With the mad god's backing, Mongul began building a new, greater starship and set out to recruit a new conquering army. While this was underway, Henshaw returned to Earth in secret, to finalize his plans of revenge."

"Revenge? But Superman had already been killed, had he not?"

"He had, Malyk. Moreover, Henshaw discovered that his own wife had died while he was off traveling in space." Jengur hesitated and lowered his voice further. "Terri Henshaw had been her husband's anchor to the last traces of his humanity. Her death left him wholly adrift in his mind. He saw but one way to revenge himself on Superman. He created a cybernetic body for himself. He stole human tissue from a research hospital, simulating the Kryptonian genotype closely enough to fool terrestrial scientists. He had absorbed enough knowledge from Superman's birthing matrix to make quite convincing his impersonation as Earth's lost champion come back as a cyborg. And then, once he had established himself as Superman, he would carry through his plans to transform the Earth into a new WarWorld. He would see to it that the universe came to know Superman as the being who came back from the dead to kill his adopted world."

Malyk shuddered. "Such a plan—it is beyond perfidy."

Jengur nodded. "And it is working, my friend. At this point, who could possibly stop it?"

"Jengur!" Mongul's voice thundered down the hall.

"Our lord and master calls." Jengur brought a finger to his lips. "Not a word of this to him. He would be most upset."

Malyk shuddered again. Mongul "upset" was something he did not want to even imagine, much less witness.

27

A scant hundred miles from Engine City, the LexAir transport slowed to stall-out speed, and three men jumped from a port in the back of the cargo bay. Like living cruise missiles they dropped beneath the smoke and ash that still hung over California and streaked toward their target.

Superman took the lead, flying with the aid of jet boots borrowed from Team Luthor ordnance. As they flew along, he looked up at the sun glowing dimly through the ash. *No telling how long it'll take me to store up enough solar energy to get back my full power.*

John Henry studied the Man in Black intently. The only other time he'd felt such a commanding presence was when he'd met Superman himself. *Funny . . . if he is Superman, I'm stronger than he is now; his life is much more at risk out here than mine is. Whoever he is, he's got guts.* Steel glanced over at Superboy. *I wonder what the kid thinks?*

Superboy could hear his stomach rumbling. *Man, I wish we could've ordered up a few pizzas before we left. Those "Meals-Ready-to-Eat" the pilot had stashed aboard were about as tasty as a pizza* box! He swung in close by the Man in Black. "So tell me, do you think Luthor will try to convince the mayor's office to evacuate the city?"

"No, I don't." Superman looked grim. "For one thing, we're not sure that there *is* a bomb being readied for Metropolis; you didn't actually see this bomb. Besides, I doubt that Metropolis could be completely evacuated in less than a week. And if an evacuation were attempted, the Cyborg might find out about it and launch an early attack." *I expect that Luthor himself will get a safe distance from the city. I know that it's horribly selfish, but I hope that Lois does, too. If anything should happen to her now—!* "We're just lucky that the armed forces agreed to give us a free hand." He glanced over at Superboy. "You know, you're the only one who's gone into this area and come out alive."

Superman squinted at the rocky cliffs ahead of them. "I can just barely see this Engine City. Heavy armaments. We'll have to go in low and fast."

John Henry edged in closer. "Sure you're up to this, man? I mean, how bulletproof are you?"

"I don't know, Steel. But I've seen one WarWorld, and before I let that hell come to Earth, I'll gladly risk my life and die again."

Behind his mask, John Henry made a silent vow. *You're not dying—not if I have any say in it.*

"All right, listen up!" Superman stared intently off into the distance. "I haven't been able to see any master control zone; things are pretty well shielded in there. I do, however, think I have a lead on a launching area within the city. That'll be our first target. Everyone stick close."

The three heroes skimmed over the rocky peaks and shot down through one of Engine City's unfinished domes. Inside, alien troops were taken by surprise as the three Supermen dropped down into their midsts. As the troops opened fire, Steel took the point, plowing through them as if they were tenpins.

In the city's central control house, Mongul and the Cyborg entered to a chorus of alarms. The big warlord glowered at his staff. "What is this? What is happening?"

A security officer flipped switches in dismay. "I—I do not know, Lord Mongul. Something is knocking out our interior surveillance systems. Just before this started, we picked up three blips on the short-range scanners."

"Attack craft?"

"No, sir. They were very small . . . terrestrial humanoid size at most."

"It's the boy." The Cyborg spoke with certainty. "It must be. The cocky young fool has found himself two allies and come back to sack the city." A dry chuckle rattled past his lipless jaws. "No matter. The most powerful metahumans on this world have been dispatched on a fool's errand. Terminating these three will be almost too easy."

On a lower corridor of the city, dazed and frightened troopers beat a hasty retreat before the advance of the Supermen. Shattered robot warriors and unconscious alien troopers littered the floor around the three invading heroes.

Superboy dusted metal fragments from his gloves. "Okay, who's my next lucky contestant?"

Steel looked around cautiously. "They all either got beaten or ran away, kid."

"They'll be back—with reinforcements." Superman removed the expended jet boots and tossed them aside. "We have to be ready for them." He stooped to pick up one of the weapons scattered about on the floor, taking in its mechanism at a glance.

Behind his mask, John Henry raised an eyebrow. "What're you up to, man?"

"Just a little field requisitioning, Steel." Superman slung two big ammo belts over his shoulders and grabbed up a second big sidearm. "I know the odds we're up against. With my powers as low as they are, I need a little bit of an edge if I'm going to pull my weight." He checked the action on one of the big guns. "You know, some people say I'm the world's biggest Boy Scout. Well, you know the Scouts' motto—'Be prepared!' "

"Radical! Let's go earn some merit badges!" Superboy slapped Superman across the back. "Which way, Fearless Leader?"

Superman shot a glance across the floor to a huge stairwell. "Down. First we make this place inoperable, then we take out Mongul and that Cyborg. Follow me."

Rapidly, they descended the levels of the city until Superman held up his hand. He cocked his head to one side, as if listening to something, then turned and pointed to a seam along one wall. "A door—there! Open it!"

Superboy sank his hands into the metal and peeled it back. The three Supermen charged through the opening onto a wide metal catwalk and came to a dead halt. They found themselves in the middle of a gargantuan missile silo, five hundred feet across and nearly a mile deep. Before them sat a ballistic missile as big as a skyscraper, its warhead a cluster of metal globes identical to those that had leveled Coast City. Steam hissed ominously from the missile's base.

"That's it!" Superboy stared up at the big missile. "That's gotta be the bomb that the Cyber-Rat was putting together for Metropolis."

"I know." Superman looked grim. "It's up to us to take it apart."

Back in the city's central control, the security officer reported another surveillance system shutdown. "Sir, this one is in the central missile silo. Backup systems in the launch bay indicate three intruders at midlevel."

"So, they actually managed to find the cluster bomb, did they?" The Cyborg stared at the screens coldly. "Excellent. Launch it!"

As the three heroes planned their next move, a low rumble began to build far below. Superboy looked down in horror as a deadly ring of fire from the missile's thrusters began boiling up the walls of the silo toward them. "Oh, man. We're toast!"

Looking about, Steel spotted a small inspection port in the side of the silo. "Follow us, kid!" He then grabbed Superman and threw himself against the little door, forcing it open. They tumbled into a small room and ducked back as a gout of flame shot through the portal after them. For a moment, the room was thick with smoke and fumes. And when it cleared, John Henry was horrified to see that the boy was not with them.

"Kid!" He ran back out onto the charred and steaming catwalk, but there was no Superboy to be found.

"Steel, come back in here!" Superman was flipping switches on a small monitor console. "This must be some sort of secondary tracking room. Take a look at this!"

The image on the monitor screen stabilized to show the missile streaking up out of Engine City. There, nestled among the cluster of modules at the base of the missile's warhead, was the Boy of Steel.

Back in the tracking room, Superman gripped the side of the console so hard that, despite his diminished strength, his fingernails carved shavings from the metal. He thought of Lois and Jimmy, of Perry and Allie, and all his friends at the *Planet*. There were eleven million people in Metropolis; if they should die, he didn't know if he'd be able to live with himself.

John Henry had far fewer good friends in Metropolis, but the thought that his city might suddenly be destroyed enraged him no less. He drove his hammer into the screen, shattering it into hundreds of sparking bits.

The smashing of the screen brought both men down to Earth. Superman grimly turned to the door. "Well, there's nothing we can do for Superboy now; it's all up to him. I just hope that he has the power to stop that thing. Right now, our job is to make sure this place never launches another attack."

They stepped back out onto the catwalk. With the big missile gone, the silo seemed unending. John Henry peered down into its depths. "Looks like this drops all the way to hell. You think we should go farther down?"

"I do." Superman looked around. "There's no sense in waiting around here. See you at the bottom." And then, to John Henry's amazement, he stepped off the edge of the catwalk.

Steel followed after Superman and dove down the silo, firing his rockets to close the distance between himself and the falling man. Superman looked up at him almost stoically as he plunged down the silo. "Come on, Steel, there's a long, hard road ahead!"

"You're too much, man!" *He took a helluva risk with this jump. He's nowhere near as strong as my armor makes me!* "Don't worry, I'll catch you."

"Thanks, but that's not necessary."

Then, much to John Henry's surprise, Superman's rate of fall inexplicably slowed. Steel pulled up from the dive, his rockets braking his descent and bringing him safely to the ground. He was on his feet and waiting when Superman lightly touched down. "You holding out on me, man? You landed soft as a feather. I thought you couldn't fly anymore. What gives?"

Superman glanced about, putting a finger to his lips. "Not now. The walls have ears . . . and eyes!"

As if on cue, a super-thick blast door irised open at the base of the silo and a squad of heavily armed alien troopers and combat robots came charging at them, guns blazing.

Steel again took the point, clearing a path with his swinging hammer and returning fire with his power gauntlet. *The kid said that the Cyborg was big on demanding blind obedience, but this is ridiculous! These troops are fighting stupid—crowding in, trying to overwhelm us. They're just getting in their own way.*

To his credit, Superman more than held up his part of the fight. He hadn't been so physically vulnerable since he was twelve, and his strength was no more than a tenth of what it had been at its peak, but his reflexes remained nothing short of uncanny. With a clear eye and a steady hand, he took aim with his captured weapons and shot the guns right out of the hands of the alien troopers.

One trooper drew a bead on Superman's head, but the ray blast from his weapon seemed to veer off at the last instant. Superman flinched back from the heat and glare of the near hit, and the alien who fired the shot mysteriously went flying backward, as if he'd been hit by something that wasn't there.

Steel glanced back over his shoulder at Superman. "Hey, you doing okay?"

"So far! Yourself?" Superman rifle-butted a would-be attacker back, sending him skidding twenty feet away.

"Check." John Henry swung his hammer wide, clearing a half dozen weapons from as many hands.

"Good!" Superman stared intently at their foes, peering through their armor, picking out the robots from among the living troopers. "These are just foot soldiers. Hit 'em hard, but choose your shots well." He whipped around and blasted a hole clean through a charging robot; the resulting shrapnel sent troopers diving for cover. "We need to save our strength for the masterminds behind this; they're the real enemy!" Superman laid down a withering hail of ray-fire that kept one whole line of troopers ducking, while Steel body-slammed another group.

"Hey, man, I believe we've got 'em on the run." It was true; the Engine City forces were falling back, retreating through the blast doors. Superman and Steel followed close behind, keeping them on the run. "Think we've finally seen the last of them?" Steel paused, then answered his own question. "No, what am I saying? We couldn't be that lucky."

Superman's brow was suddenly knit with concern. "I hope that Superboy's been lucky."

"The kid doesn't like being called Superboy."

"Well, whatever you call him, I pray that he comes through. Right now, he may be all that stands between Metropolis and total destruction!"

High above Metropolis, the huge missile came plunging down out of the heavens. Its thrusters had flung it too far and too fast for any army on Earth to shoot down.

Superboy clung plastered to the nose of the missile like a bug on a windshield. He'd torn apart or disabled over half of the explosive modules and ripped into the warhead, but he hadn't changed the missile's course a single degree. His wild talent was useless here; the missile was just too big for him to rip open.

He looked down, his eyes tearing from the punishing wind. Below, the city was rushing up toward him; he seemed just seconds from impact with the globe of the *Daily Planet* Building.

The Boy of Steel strained against the giant missile, every muscle tensing. "Turn, you overgrown firecracker! C'mon—turn!"

In frustrated desperation, he hauled off and struck the nose cone, catching it at a right angle to the missile's ballistic path. Suddenly the missile veered off and shot over the city, heading out to sea.

But Superboy had no time to enjoy his victory. His fist had sunk into the metal of the nose cone from the force of his blow, and he was being pulled along with the missile. The Boy of Steel finally yanked himself loose as the missile spiraled past the outer borough of Hell's Gate and rose out over the Atlantic.

Superboy was about eight hundred feet above the mouth of Metropolis Harbor when a blinding explosion filled the eastern sky. The shock wave hit him, hurling him down into the Hell's Gate sanitary landfill.

Long, painful minutes later, the Boy of Steel crawled up out of a deep crater as a LexCorp helicopter hovered overhead. The craft dropped down for a landing, and Lex Luthor himself came running up. "Superboy! What in blazes is going on?!"

"Hey . . . don' call me S'perboy. I'm S'per*man*!" He rose slowly to his hands and knees. "Where *am* I? An' why's it smell so bad?"

"You little punk!" Luthor grabbed the Boy of Steel and hauled him to his feet. "I don't care what you call yourself! Where is my Supergirl?! Answer me!"

"Huh? S'pergirl? How sh'd I know?"

"She disappeared right around the time that you three Supermen left for the coast, and there's been no sign of her since! Where is she?!"

Superboy shoved Luthor away from him. "Hey, lower th' volume, okay? I haven't seen 'er. But if I did, I'd tell 'er to head f'r Engine City. Engine City—oh, man! Superman an' the Steelster—I gotta get back an' help 'em!"

The Boy of Steel took a running leap into the air—only to fall flat on his face, unconscious.

In Engine City's master control, the Cyborg railed at a row of video screens showing various broadcast reports of Metropolis's brush with disaster.

"This cannot be—no finer plan was ever devised! How could that puny teenage clone have deflected my missile? How, Mongul? How?!"

The warlord stood rigidly erect. "I am at a loss, Master. Your plan indeed appeared flawless."

The Cyborg whirled and poked an accusing finger at a closed-circuit surveillance screen that featured a freeze-frame shot of Superman, an image captured just seconds before its camera had gone black. "And now there is a new Superman imposter with which to contend—a ridiculous man in black, like a figure out of the cinema! And he and that armored lout have routed our forces! Routed them! It defies all belief!"

Mongul could hardly contain his contempt. "It does indeed." *Just as it defies belief that I, who have conquered entire star systems, should be allied with one who is proving so inept.*

The Cyborg paced back and forth; so hard did he gnash his metal teeth that sparks actually flew. "Only seconds more, and the bombs would have leveled Metropolis, clearing the way for a second Engine City! It should have worked—it would have, if not for that accursed clone!"

"That *was* unexpected. We both greatly underestimated the boy." *I'd planned to use him against you, you arrogant fool, but his success against the bomb threatens my own plans as well.*

One of the broadcast news transmissions cut suddenly to a candid shot of the Man in Black. "Reports of a fifth Superman—seen here in camcorder footage recorded by a WMET amateur newshound earlier today at O'Hara Regional Airport—have now been confirmed by *Daily Planet* reporter Lois Lane. Ms. Lane, who years ago popularized the name 'Superman,' says she's convinced that this newest arrival is the original hero of Metropolis—miraculously recovered from what appeared to be his death."

"No!" In one swift movement, the Cyborg deployed his arm cannon and blasted the broadcast monitor apart. "No, he's dead—dead and gone!" He wheeled about to stare again at the image frozen on the closed-circuit screen. "The real Superman can't possibly be alive—can he?"

Mongul thought that unlikely. He had, after all, dispatched billions of sentients in his life, and none of them had ever returned from the dead. This did, however, present an opening to exploit the Cyborg's madness, and the warlord seized it.

"Superman once thought *you* dead. You've spoken to me so eloquently of how he callously abandoned you to the vacuum of space. If he *is* truly alive, your revenge can be even sweeter than before."

"Yes—yes, you are correct, Mongul." The Cyborg cupped a hand under the rim of his metal jaw. "When I learned of Superman's death, I thought I had to content myself with conquering the Earth in his guise, destroying his good name. But now, if he truly lives, Superman can discover that the scientist he abandoned has survived, that the intellect of Hank Henshaw lives on! I will show him how I have mastered the art of cybernetic transmorphing and take my final revenge on him while cloaked in his own image. I shall destroy him with my own hands."

The Cyborg turned and strode out of the chamber, leaving Mongul free at last to shake his head in disgust. *The real Superman was foolishly honorable. I know full well that, whatever occurred between them, it was nothing like what the Cyborg imagines. He's lost all reason, living in a world of his own pathetic delusions.*

And then, Mongul smiled. *Perfect.*

Within the Antarctic Fortress, the Eradicator was now fully conscious inside his life-support capsule, and robots scrambled to meet his increasingly impatient demands.

"The Cyborg pretender attacked me while I wore the shield of Krypton's Last Son! He thought me destroyed. I must again be made whole! I must live to avenge both myself and the name of Superman! I must have more power, more data, if I am to persevere! Attend me!"

One robot tried to calm the encapsulated being. "Master, we have already brought you on-line with all Fortress power and information systems. Absorption of either energy or data at an increased rate could result in irreparable harm. It is advised that you heal slowly and completely."

"There is no time." The Eradicator's ravaged face twisted in fury and frustration. "Current broadcasts indicate that the other Supermen—the young clone, the armored one, even Kal-El *himself*—have allied against the Cyborg. But their power is insufficient. The Cyborg must *not* triumph! I must prevail! I must have more power! *Now!*"

The fluid in the life-support capsule began to bubble and froth.

"Master, no! All systems are responding to your demands. If you persist in this energy drain, the Fortress itself may suffer!"

Within the capsule, the Eradicator glowed with energy, his eyes squeezed shut, his teeth clenched in pain. "This Fortress was my creation! It is mine to do with as I will!"

As the Eradicator drew the vast energy reserves of the Fortress into himself, the capsule glowed as white as the sun. The robots began falling powerless to the floor. Raw energy crackled off the capsule, and the Fortress itself shook, its walls and floors cracking open as its reinforcing structural fields shunted their energy into the Eradicator.

On the surface, a wide section of ice suddenly heaved up from the force of a powerful underground explosion, then collapsed as if subsiding into a great sinkhole. A plume of energy hundreds of feet high erupted from the center of the depression.

Within that plume arose the Eradicator, his arms outstretched as if in prayer to the cosmos. He no longer bore even a passing resemblance to Kal-El. His profile was aquiline; his hair had turned a dark gray; and his red eyes crackled with energy.

Throughout the millennia that he had existed as an artificial intelligence, the Eradicator had known only logic and data. Even when that intelligence had first assumed humanoid form and sought to remake the Earth in the image of Krypton, it looked upon this planet as little more than raw materials.

The Eradicator had none of the passion, none of the love that Superman felt for the Earth. All emotions, whether human or Kryptonian, were alien. But all that began to change when he was reborn in the image of Superman. His mind became opened to new thoughts and newer, more complex ways of thinking, and for the first time, to ways of feeling. He learned the ways of passion and of rage, and was changed by them.

Now all the vast energies of the Fortress churned and flowed within the Eradicator. He felt no regrets over sacrificing the Fortress; a monument to a dead world was of no importance to him now. The Cyborg, he knew, had killed millions of people and had done it all in the guise of Superman.

The Eradicator leapt into the sky, rocketing northward for the former Coast City. A living world stretched out before him, and he would not see it endangered by a usurper. The Cyborg would fall by his power—the power of Krypton.

As Superman and Steel ran across sublevel six of Engine City, Superman suddenly raised one of his weapons and fired at a section of blank wall.

John Henry looked at him curiously. "What are you shooting now?"

Superman reached up and pulled a cracked lens from within the shattered wall panel and tossed it to the armored man. "Hidden surveillance device. Remember how I said the walls have eyes and ears? The more of them we poke out, the more freely we can talk."

Steel studied the lens for a moment and then crushed it in his hand. "Well, I'm glad your X-ray eyes are still sharp enough to spot 'em. That's a little beyond my expertise."

Superman suddenly jerked back, grimacing so painfully that the other man held out a hand to steady him. "What's wrong?"

"I'm not sure. I felt a sudden . . . presence." Superman raised a hand to his head and rubbed his left temple. "Oh, Lord, of course. It's the Eradicator!"

"The what?"

"He was one of the many new Supermen—the one with the visor. We once shared a sort of mental link, and apparently it's still partially functional. He's on his way here."

"Is that good?" John Henry tightened his grip on his hammer. "I had a nasty run-in with him not that long ago."

"So I heard. I don't know, Steel. At the moment, I think we all share a common enemy."

Before Superman could explain further, a ray blast was fired in their direction from a hidden sniper's nest down the corridor, missing them by no more than a foot.

Staying low, the two men charged down the corridor, only to find a mangled targeting robot.

"What the devil?" Steel poked at the robot's smoking remains with the end of his hammer. "This thing tried to blast us, but what blasted *it*?"

Superman grinned tightly. "Looks like the handiwork of my secret weapon."

"Secret weapon? *What* secret weapon?!"

Superman glanced up and down the corridor. "It's all right. The coast is clear; you can show yourself. Come on out and take a bow."

To Steel's surprise, Supergirl shimmered into sight. She stood with one foot up on the remains of the robot sniper, smiling sweetly and wiping lubricant off her hands.

"Hello again, Mr. Steel. We seem to keep meeting under battlefield conditions."

"Supergirl!" John Henry took her offered hand. "You mean you've been with us the whole time?"

"Uh-huh, ever since Metropolis. How did you think that Superman made that big jump down the missile silo?"

"I apologize for keeping you in the dark about this, Steel, but the fewer of us who knew Supergirl was here, the less chance there was of accidentally tipping off the enemy." Superman began to break down his weapons. "Supergirl, do you mind filling him in while I reload?"

"Not at all. You see, Mr. Steel, when Superman first reappeared back at the airfield, I had a feeling that he might be for real. After he spoke with Ms. Lane, I could tell that she believed in him, too. And that was good enough for me. I mean, she first met him years ago—even named him, for heaven's sake. So I snuck up beside him and offered my help. In my invisible state, I'm virtually undetectable, and Superman immediately saw how useful that would be. Since Lex had already arranged that jet transport for you, I just slipped on board. Along the way, I briefed Superman on what had been going on in his absence. And once we all deplaned, I flew ahead and played advance scout. Ever since you got to Engine City, I've been making surveillance sweeps and secretly providing cover."

Superman finished snapping new clips into his weapons. "Again, Steel, I'm sorry that we kept this from you."

"No problem. It was a sound tactic, and after all, you didn't know me from Adam. Now I'm more convinced than ever that you are the man!" Steel reached up, loosened two hidden clasps, and removed his mask. "You probably don't remember me, but you saved my life once. My real name's John Henry Irons. I used to be an engineer."

Superman took John Henry's hand, grasping it warmly. "I do remember you. You were working the high steel when that other man fell. You've done me proud, John Henry."

"Thanks, man, that means a lot, coming from you. It's gonna be all right. We'll nail these world-bashers together!"

"I hope so. I'd like my second lease on life to last awhile longer."

"It will!" Supergirl put her hand on Superman's shoulder.

"Damn straight it will!" John Henry resecured his mask and stood with his hammer at the ready. "I owe you my life, Superman. The world was a mighty cold place without you around." He looked him straight in the eyes. "When this is all over, though, I wouldn't mind hearing exactly *how* you came back from the dead!"

Superman clapped the armored man on the back. "I'd like to know that myself. Maybe we can find the answer together. But right now, our main objective has to be shutting down the city's power supply." He gestured down the wide tunnel. "From what Supergirl's told me and from what I've been able to scope out on my own, this corridor should take us there. Everybody ready?"

"Ready." Supergirl flung back her cape and took a step up into the air.

"Ready and loaded for bear." Steel brought his hand up, slapping his palm against Superman's.

"All right then, let's move out. Supergirl, you take the lead." The Girl of Steel faded from sight, and a rush of wind shot down the corridor ahead of the two men.

Several hundred yards away, the Cyborg sat deep within the core of the City Systems Room, plugged into the computer array that monitored and controlled the temperature, humidity, and air pressure within the great city. A score of cables linked him directly with the computer, and his mind reached out through the system, looking for any disturbances. Slowly he became aware of slight increases of temperature in the city's lower corridors and knew that he had found traces of heat emitted from the bodies of his quarry. The Cyborg allowed more and more of his consciousness to seep into the system, reaching out to pinpoint the locations of Superman and Steel.

"Fools!" His voice was a ghostly echo amid the computers. "They thought they could escape my detection. But nothing can long elude me within my Engine City. Let them knock out *all* the surveillance systems, and I would *still* find them. All that happens within these walls is mine to know!" His voice grew softer, and his eyes went blank, as more and more of his mind diffused through the system. "Nothing happens here of which I am not aware—nothing."

Alone in the city's master control, Mongul lounged back in a thronelike command chair, watching the Cyborg over a specially shielded closed-circuit monitoring system. "So you say." Months of frustration boiled out of the warlord, and he talked back to the screen. "So you truly believe, no doubt. But that is only another delusion that you nurture. The time you spent wandering alone in space was not kind to you, dear

'Master.' " *It is best that I finally terminate this most unequal partnership, and clearly the time to strike is now, while the mad one's mind is so preoccupied with tracking his challengers.*

His challengers . . . The thought intrigued Mongul. If anything, he felt that his hatred of Superman was more genuine than that of the Cyborg's. *My hatred, at least, has a basis in fact. The Cyborg thought Superman dead, but he was wrong about so many other things.*

Mongul called upon his computers to create a hologram of the latest Superman, based upon the various surveillance and broadcast images. He had the face magnified and enhanced and studied it from every angle.

Yes, I could almost believe that this man in black is truly the accursed Kryptonian returned from the grave. Weakened though he may be, there is a look of determination about him. He reminds me all too well of the Superman who dealt me my only major defeat. I shall deal with him . . . later.

Mongul signaled for his attendants, and Jengur appeared on the run with Malyk in tow.

"Prepare my flagship for departure, Jengur—under conditions of strictest secrecy."

"At once, Lord Mongul!" The furry little man jumped to obey.

"And you—initiate engine-core ignition procedures."

Malyk was shocked by the command. "But Lord Mongul, sir—without balancing engines, this planet will spin out of orbit! It could rip itself apart!"

"I know." Mongul rose up from his throne. "I have had quite enough of these Supermen and their backward little world. Let it be destroyed! I'll fashion a new WarWorld elsewhere!"

Malyk froze in place at the control board. Leveling a city was one thing—he had assisted in hundreds of such operations—but the thought of literally shattering a planet left him paralyzed. He couldn't bring himself to start the giant drive engine.

Mongul swung out an arm and backhanded the green-skinned engineer away from the controls. "One side, dolt! I shall do it myself!" The warlord imperiously flipped a row of switches, then opened an access panel and pulled out a heavily cabled black box. "This is the drive system fail-safe, is it not?"

Malyk bobbed his head meekly and shrank back into the corner of the room.

Mongul ripped the fail-safe free and crushed it under his foot. "There can be no stopping the engine now." He looked back at his closed-circuit screen; the Cyborg sat unmoving. "And I'll never again bow down before you, you mad halfling! Seek out the true Superman for me—if he is the true one—and we shall have a game of cat and mouse. But *I* shall be the cat! And if Superman has indeed returned to life, all the better. I can think of no finer way to cause the demise of his beloved adopted world than with an engine fueled with the radioactive ore created by the destruction of his homeworld!"

In the city's main Engine Room, within a heavily shielded fission reactor, huge fuel rods pulsed with the eerie green glow of Kryptonite.

28

As Superman and Steel ran through the bowels of the city, the floor, walls, and the entire complex began to shudder as the gigantic drive engine powered up. The two men exchanged worried looks and picked up their pace.

Before they had gone more than another hundred yards, a shadow fell before them, and Mongul stepped into the corridor. "Welcome to Engine City, Superman—if Superman is who you truly are."

"Mongul!" Superman spoke the name as if it were a curse.

"You recognize me? Then you *are* that blasted Kryptonian. Good—it will give me great pleasure to kill you before I destroy your adopted world."

Steel raised his hammer. "You won't be doing either."

"You are wrong. Fatally wrong. The vibrations you feel are from the great drive engine. Were there more than one such engine, we could steer this world safely through space." Mongul's lip curled into a sneer. "But your Superboy thwarted our attempts to site a second complex . . . and so doomed this Earth. Once my engine builds to full power, it will tear this puny little world to bits. Nothing can stop the process now; I've seen to that!"

Superman took a step back and pulled Steel to his side. "We have to stop that engine." His voice was a crisp whisper. "About fifty feet back there's a portal leading to a tunnel that parallels this one. You fall back and take it to the engine chamber. I'll keep Mongul busy."

"Are you crazy? I can't leave you to face that giant. Besides, how am I supposed to stop the thing? He said it couldn't be done."

"Their missile couldn't be stopped, either, but Superboy did it. You're the engineer—you'll have a better chance than I would. Don't worry about me, I have a secret weapon, remember?" Superman looked him in the eyes. "You can beat the machine, John Henry. You have to!"

Steel gripped Superman's hand. "Good luck, man." Then he fell back and disappeared down the corridor.

"Does your ally abandon you, Superman? Or do you think to outflank me? Go ahead and try. It will make this all the more entertaining!"

"Entertain *this*, Mongul!" Superman opened fire with both weapons blazing.

Mongul roared with laughter and advanced through Superman's ray-fire like a man fighting the stream of a high-pressure hose. "Did you think I would allow my troops to carry sidearms that could do me any real harm? I am strong, Superman, stronger than you! And your ammunition charge is finite!"

Step by step, the big warlord closed in on his prey.

Ensconced in the computer array, the Cyborg sat enraptured by his awareness of the flow of air and the fluctuation of heat within the city. He had become one with the city.

Now, as the Cyborg's consciousness gradually sharpened, he sensed greater, larger movements. He felt the heat of battle between Superman and Mongul and vaguely wondered how the warlord had beaten him to their enemy. The Cyborg's mind searched about, slowly becoming aware of the tap that Mongul had made into his heat-tracking network. He then sensed a swirling rush of air that his calculations told him must conform to a humanoid body in flight. This otherwise invisible body was turning about in midair, a scant distance from the battle. Further along, the Cyborg detected Steel rocketing down a secondary corridor toward the engine.

The engine!

The sudden recognition that the engine was powering up brought the Cyborg fully out of his reverie. *Mongul! What has that fool done?* It took but seconds to access the circuitry of the city's master control and uncover the warlord's treachery. *How dare he seek to usurp my revenge? I will flay him alive for that! But first, I must stop the engine. I cannot let all that I have worked for be destroyed.*

The Cyborg went on-line with the master control but found himself blocked from shutting down the engine's ignition sequence. *The fail-safe has been destroyed; I am locked out of those circuits!* The Cyborg shook with rage. *I shall have to attempt a manual shutdown.* Then he remembered Steel, and his anger turned to twisted laughter. *Or perhaps I will just let this little man do it for me!*

"Good Lord, what have I gotten myself into?" Steel came to a halt in the middle of the vast Engine Room. The walls were lined with miles of wires, tubes, and conduits. Across the room was a long, gleaming cylinder bracketed by giant coils of shimmering, translucent wire. Through thick transparent ports set into the cylinder's side, John Henry could see an eerie glow. Along an adjacent wall was what appeared to be a heavily shielded containment vessel. A maze of pipes and cables ran in and out of the shielding.

"What the hell *is* all this?" Parts of the assembly seemed vaguely familiar to John Henry, but the sheer scale of the room made it difficult to comprehend. *How do I shut this down, if I'm not even sure what I'm looking at?*

"Impressive, isn't it?" The voice was low, flat, and vaguely electronic.

Steel wheeled around to see a body taking shape along the wall behind him. Before his eyes, a mass of wires, circuits, and metal tubing extruded from the wall, taking on a vaguely human shape. It towered over him, twice his height; it even had a face of sorts. It was the face of the Cyborg, shorn of all humanity.

"Didn't you hear me, 'Man of Steel'?" There was a faint mechanical whir as the Cyborg's construct gestured to the Engine Room. "I can't believe that any ordinary mortal wouldn't be impressed by all this!"

John Henry found his voice. "It's big all right. But how does it work?"

"The drive engine?" The construct fairly tittered. "It's powered by a fusion process, little one; confined by superconducting electromagnets. You could not hope to understand it."

Controlled fusion, of course. John Henry mentally kicked himself. *That cylinder must contain an ionized plasma. And those translucent coils must be the superconductive material.* "You've harnessed fusion to provide thrust?" He jerked his head toward the containment vessel. "That must be a fission reactor then—you must use its output to initiate the fusion process."

The machine-man's face almost looked pleased. "Very good, little one! Perhaps you *do* understand." The construct reached out as if to pat him on the head. Steel drew back, but he was not fast enough; the machine-man grabbed him firmly in one hand and picked him up like a toy. John Henry raised his power gauntlet, emptying his supply of spikes into the construct.

The machine-man just chuckled. "Sorry, I haven't any vital organs . . . unlike yourself. But you wanted a closer look at that engine; allow me to oblige you." With Steel in hand, the construct strode across the floor of the chamber. "I suspect that you've come here to destroy my magnificent engine, haven't you?" An absurd clucking sound came from the construct. "We mustn't have that. On the other hand, I quite agree—for different reasons, of course—that we can't let the engine tear this little planet apart. Fortunately, there's a simple way to shut down the fusion process—we just shatter the electromagnets' coils. I can always install more." With a roar of laughter, the machine-man raised John Henry high overhead and threw him at one of the electromagnets.

Steel quickly wheeled about in midair and lit his rockets in a short burst, braking his speed. He fell far short of the construct's intended goal, but he could feel the powerful electromagnets tugging at his armor.

"You little steel-plated worm!" The construct charged toward him. "Do you want to see the Earth destroyed? It's your duty to die for it!"

"Not alone, I won't." Steel's cape came loose in the machine-man's grasp as the armored man dove between the construct's legs. His armor scraped up sparks as he rebounded from the metal floor and launched himself back at the construct. He tackled the machine-man and fired his rockets, driving them both into the magnet's coils.

Both the superconducting coils and the machine-man shattered in a brilliant flash of light. With the coils broken, the electromagnetic field dropped, and within the cylinder the awesome temperatures of the plasma fuel plunged. The eerie glow changed colors and then slowly faded, as the plasma fuel cooled, de-ionized and condensed back to normal matter.

John Henry staggered to his feet, his armor scorched and cracked. *How about that? I didn't die after all.* In spite of his situation, he was intrigued by the design of the fusion system, and he reflexively picked up a strand of the translucent wire. *A room-temperature superconductor. Amazing.* The engineer in him hoped there would be time later to analyze the material, but the warrior in him picked up his hammer. *First, I have to make sure there is a later!'*

Mongul grabbed hold of Superman's weapons and swung the hero hard into the wall of the corridor. Before Superman could recover, the warlord was on top of him, seizing him in a crushing bear hug. "You are weaker by far than when last we fought, Kryptonian. This time, I will not fail to slay you!"

His head swimming, Superman brought both fists up, driving them hard against Mongul's ears. The stunned warlord fell back, shaking his head.

"You will die slowly for that, Superman!"

But before Mongul could make another move, he was suddenly struck hard by something that couldn't be seen. A series of sharp blows rained down upon the surprised warlord, forcing him into a defensive posture. Then a powerful blast of psychokinetic energy hurled him backward with such force that he became embedded in the metal wall.

With her opponent incapacitated, Supergirl shimmered to visibility and crouched down to check on Superman. "Are you all right?"

"I think so." He gingerly felt his side. "Ribs are a little sore, but I don't think anything's really broken."

"I'm sorry I didn't get here sooner, but there was this building vibration and—hey, it's stopped."

"John Henry." Superman grinned through the pain. "He did it. He stopped the—*look out!*"

The warning came too late. Mongul sprang at the two heroes, striking Supergirl from behind and stunning her. And then a vicious kick sent Superman rolling, skidding down the corridor.

"Your ally should have remained invisible, Superman. Now I must kill her as well. Perhaps I shall cripple you first, and make you watch her die."

The Eradicator flew in over the ocean, speeding toward Engine City. As he passed through the lingering ash cloud, he had a sudden mental flash of Superman in pain. In that instant, he sensed his fellow Kryptonian's location and predicament, and he acted. Power-diving through the city's central dome, the Eradicator smashed his way through to the lower corridors.

Mongul jumped back as a dark blur came crashing down through the ceiling ahead of him. The Eradicator stood boldly before the warlord, holding out a hand in warning and blocking the path to Superman. So changed in appearance was he that, shorn of cape and shield, Mongul did not recognize him as the visored being that the Cyborg had supposedly slain.

Through his tenuous mental link with Superman, the Eradicator recognized Mongul all too well. "Come no further, alien. To threaten Krypton's Last Son is to threaten the Eradicator!"

"And to defy Mongul is to court death, fool!" The angry warlord leapt at the Eradicator—squarely into the terrible, withering blast of energy that erupted from his hands. Mongul dropped to the floor of the corridor, most of his chest and part of his head gone. The warlord hadn't even had time to scream.

"Oh, my God!" Supergirl put a hand to her mouth as the Eradicator nudged Mongul's body aside with his foot.

"You are Supergirl? Yes, I recognize you from the Fortress monitors." The Eradicator glanced down at Mongul. "Do not mourn for him. He would have done much worse to all of us. His death, at least, was fast."

The Eradicator turned toward the groggy Superman. "Are you all right, Kal-El?"

"All right? I hope so." Superman leaned against the wall and tried to catch his breath. "We're not finished here yet."

"Hey, what's going on?" Steel arrived on the run, stopping dead at the sight of the Eradicator and Mongul's body. "Whoa! I wasn't expecting this."

Weird laughter echoed throughout the corridor. "It's always the unexpected that's the most deadly!" Then the Cyborg was upon them. He swooped down through the hole created by the Eradicator's impromptu entrance and flung himself headlong at the four heroes, knocking them off their feet.

The Cyborg then shot down the corridor. Steel watched him take off in dismay. "Damn, I thought I'd aced him back in the engine room. How'd he get back in that body?"

"He can switch bodies as well?" The Eradicator regained his footing and helped the others up. "Then he is doubly dangerous. He must be stopped."

"Well, sure." Supergirl kept a cautious eye on him. She knew of the Eradicator, but only as a dangerous artificial intelligence; she wasn't sure what to make of this stranger. "But where's he headed?"

"Back to the Engine Room is my bet." Steel smacked his hammer against his palm. "And he won't be very happy when he sees what I did to it."

"The Eradicator's right, we have to stop him." Superman gathered up his weapons and shoved in the last of his clips. "But let's be careful and keep our eyes open. We don't know what he's up to, but he clearly wants us to follow him. That could mean a trap."

Superman and Steel charged down the corridor together, with Supergirl and the Eradicator providing close air support. They were halfway to the Engine Room when the walls came alive, and a cluster of power cables twisted themselves into a semblance of the Cyborg's face.

The Eradicator fired a searing blast into the face, but it just re-formed itself from another set of cables a few feet further away.

The Cyborg's voice crackled from the face with a disturbing electrical sibilance. "Superman, tell this fool that he's wasting his time. He can destroy my visage all he wants, but as long as I remain on-line, I can reconstruct it indefinitely."

"Who *are* you?" Superman felt like blasting the taunting face himself, but he didn't want to waste the ammunition.

"You still don't know me, Superman?" The cables twisted and smoothed until they formed a more human-looking face—a man's face with short, closely cropped hair and clean, angular features. "I can't believe you've forgotten Commander Hank Henshaw."

"Henshaw?!" Superman's eyes opened wide. "But why in God's name have you done this? Why the impersonation? The killing—?"

"For revenge!" Henshaw's voice fairly sizzled. "You conspired to kill my crew. You tried to make me look incompetent."

"Your crew? What are you talking about? I tried to save them. I tried to save you!"

"Lies! You drove me away from this world."

"That's not true. Leaving Earth was your idea."

"More lies!" Henshaw was raving now. "You wanted me gone because you feared my power. Well, now I have given you reason to fear me! I will kill you yet and make the world see you for the villain you are!"

The face on the wall reverted to the Cyborg's image. "From the knowledge I gathered within your birthing matrix, I found the power to destroy you. Ironic, isn't it?"

The cables of the face suddenly uncoiled and were joined by huge pipes, shooting out at the four heroes from all sides. Superman dove to the floor, rolling under the deadly metal tentacles, and the Eradicator soared above them, flying on down the corridor. Supergirl and Steel were ensnared and held fast. The cables holding Steel arced wildly and fused to his armor, threatening to cook him within his metal shell.

With a blast of psychokinetic force, Supergirl shattered her bonds and leapt to help John Henry. "I'll get Steel free, Superman—you go after the Eradicator. I don't fully trust him."

Neither do I, Supergirl. Neither do I. Superman caught up to the Eradicator around a bend in the tunnel; he was firing his energy blasts, burning through a mass of metal tubing that had blocked off the Engine Room.

"I fear that this Cyborg is quite beyond reason." The Eradicator gave Superman the briefest of glances. "His mind was not able to accept the gift of rebirth as was yours."

"Oh?" Superman looked askance at the Eradicator. "And just what do you know about Henshaw?"

"I know what you recorded in the Fortress archives. I know what you know." The Eradicator stopped and stared at Superman with haunted eyes. "We are linked, you and I."

"Don't remind me. You nearly killed me once."

"I was in error. I have tried to make amends. I helped restore you to life. I transferred your body to the Regeneration Matrix."

"Yes, and you left me there, like a spare battery in the refrigerator." Superman eyes narrowed. "I was really dead? Not in a coma?"

"From all indications, yes. But your body retained enough of its stores of solar energy. Had that not been the case, and had your spirit not proven so resilient, I would not have been able to effect your revival."

Superman had more questions, but he put them aside. Together, they broke into the Engine Room. All surviving systems had gone off-line, leaving the chamber very dark. From the light that filtered in from the outer corridor, they could see evidence of Steel's handiwork; the floor around them was strewn with wreckage.

"Welcome, gentlemen! I'm so glad you saw fit to join me here." The Cyborg's voice cut through the darkness, echoing seemingly from everywhere. The big chamber was suddenly bathed in light, and the Cyborg dropped down from atop the fission reactor. "After all, there's really only one way a Superman should die. And that's from kryptonite poisoning!"

With a sweep of his metal arm, the Cyborg smashed open the reactor's shielding, exposing the kryptonite fuel rods. Radiation flooded the chamber. In his weakened state, the radiation affected Superman immediately, and he crumpled to the floor, writhing in agony. The Eradicator staggered back, his Kryptonian-based tissue itself vulnerable to the deadly ore, and the Cyborg tackled him.

The Eradicator was being forced to his knees when Supergirl swooped into the chamber, with Steel hot on her heels.

The Girl of Steel struck at the Cyborg with a combination punch, both physical and psychokinetic, that twisted his head halfway around and flung him into the wreckage that littered the chamber floor. While Supergirl leapt after the Cyborg, Steel pulled Superman away from the reactor and crouched over him, blocking the radiation with his own armored body. The Eradicator lurched to his feet; in a rage he shot a stream of searing energy at the reactor's containment vessel, melting the lead shielding and sending it flowing like lava down over the kryptonite fuel rods.

"No!" The Cyborg's voice became a shriek. "This cannot be! He must *die*! You must *all* die!"

Supergirl hauled off and connected with a hard left to the Cyborg's metal jaw, punching it loose from his head.

"Don't stop!" The Eradicator struggled to speak. "Keep him . . . *dizzy*!"

In tandem, Supergirl and the Eradicator blasted the Cyborg. She literally spun him around, while the Eradicator fired an electromagnetic pulse that scrambled Henshaw's neural functions.

The kryptonite was almost completely covered now, and energy crackled and flowed around the Eradicator. "The Cyborg must be destroyed, just as he destroyed Coast City! The city—our adopted world—must be avenged!"

Even through his pain, Superman could not miss the passion behind the Eradicator's rage. *Did he say 'our' adopted world?* "Wait a minute, Steel."

"Come on, man, we have to get you out of here."

"No, I feel better now." Superman grabbed hold of a railing, holding himself upright. "Radiation's sealed off."

The Eradicator was starting to glow as he lurched toward Superman. "I must make amends. I must atone." He reached out his hands, and radiant energy washed over Superman.

Steel moved to block the Eradicator, but Superman waved him back. "It's all right, John Henry. Feels good . . . like a day at the beach."

Superman stood taller, and his chest seemed to swell, as the Eradicator poured energy into him. As Superman grew stronger, the energy flowed at an increasing rate, a steadily accelerating rate. He suddenly realized that the Eradicator wasn't going to stop. "No. There's no need—!"

"There is *every* need!" The Eradicator seemed to draw in on himself as he spoke. "The Cyborg has committed great crimes in the name of Superman. He has endangered this Earth, even as I myself once did. It is only now that I see the evil of what I attempted to do to you, what I attempted to do to your world.

"There is but one way I can fully atone for Henshaw's crimes and my own."

As the Eradicator began to falter, the Cyborg screamed incoherently, flung Supergirl aside, and charged headlong at the supermen. A final burst of energy erupted from the Eradicator; half was directed into Superman in a healing stream; the rest slammed into the Cyborg, leaving him singed and smoking.

Then the glow faded, and the Eradicator collapsed.

Supergirl grabbed hold of the smoldering Cyborg. He slumped over in her grasp.

For a moment, nobody moved. Then, the Cyborg pulled free of Supergirl's grasp, pieces of him breaking away in her hands, and leapt again at Superman.

Superman met the Cyborg's charge with a hard right, knocking him the length of the Engine Room. Superman was on the Cyborg like a shot. "It's all over, Henshaw."

Superman smashed his fist into the Cyborg like a pile driver, and the construct went down like a marionette whose strings had been snapped.

The Cyborg's cape came off in Superman's hands and the rest of him simply fell apart, clattering to the floor in a million pieces.

Superman wheeled around. "The computer systems! We have to isolate them. If Henshaw shunted his consciousness in there—"

"I don't think so, man." Steel came running up. "I'll run a sweep to make sure, but—well, Mongul had cut the main lines between the city's systems and the Engine Room, and I'd already disabled the rest."

They rejoined Supergirl, who knelt beside the Eradicator; all that was left of him was a lifeless husk. She looked up at Superman and Steel. "I think he's gone."

Steel removed his helmet. "He gave me a lot of grief, but I don't know if we'd have been able to stop the Cyborg without him."

"I still don't understand." Superman looked down at the fallen body in confusion. "The Eradicator once tried to kill me. Maybe he did help bring me back to life, but he used me to sustain himself. After all that, why would he sacrifice himself—why would he drain himself dry—to restore my power?"

Supergirl gazed back over the Eradicator. "What else did he know? He was created as the ultimate weapon of a warrior age." She looked up at Superman. "I started out life in a laboratory, too, but I was lucky; thanks to you and some other fine people, I learned early on what it means to choose to *live* for something. I don't think the Eradicator ever had that chance, did he?"

Superman knelt beside her and bowed his head. "No. No, he never did."

Supergirl shook her head sadly. "He knew only what it meant to die for something."

Steel nodded. "But he didn't sacrifice himself just for you. I think that he sacrificed himself for all of us. After all, he did give us back our Superman."

"Superman . . . how many terrible things have been done in that name?" Superman slowly rose to his feet and looked down at the cape in his hands. "The Cyborg used it when he wiped a whole city off the face of the Earth. The Eradicator used it when he played judge, jury, and executioner. I'll be a long time removing those stains."

Steel put a hand on his shoulder. "That's not your fault, man. And I hope we haven't all done wrong by you. The kid was young and raw, but he came through for us and saved Metropolis, if Mongul was telling the truth. And as for me, well . . ." John Henry reached up and yanked the S-shield from his chest. "I think that only the *real* Man of Steel should wear this from now on. Same goes for that cape."

"The cape?" Superman looked down again at the torn red cloth. "I don't know. After what's been done, I'm not sure I should wear it again."

"Well, I *am* sure!" Supergirl stood up and put her hand on Superman's shoulder. "And I know a way to make it right." She reached out with the amazing power of her mind and gave a push. All the color—both in the cape and in Superman's bodysuit—faded to a dazzling white. And then, as Supergirl's brow knit in concentration, the cloth began to swirl and flow under her touch.

"Supergirl, what—?" Superman looked down to find himself again garbed in his familiar red, blue, and yellow costume.

"I got it right, didn't I?" She smiled at him.

"You got it perfectly right." Superman leaned down and kissed her cheek. "Thank you."

"Thank *you* for coming back to us." Supergirl looked around at the wreck of Engine City. "It's really over now, isn't it?"

Superman shook his head. "The battle is over, yes. But the hardest part is still ahead."

29

Lois Lane awoke with a stiff neck on the couch of her apartment. Her clothing was rumpled from having been slept in, and the floor around her was littered with take-out food containers and the morning's edition of the *Daily Planet*; its headline screamed WAR OF THE SUPERMEN.

She was drowsily aware that her television was still on and tuned to CNN's continuing coverage of the situation at Coast City. When Superman suddenly appeared on screen, she fumbled for the remote to boost the volume.

". . . wish that I had been here. I wish that there was something I could have done to prevent this. I know that nothing I ever say or do can bring back the people of Coast City. To all the many people who lost friends and relatives here, I can but pledge my life to do everything in my power to see to it that such a terrible tragedy never happens again."

The screen cut to a CNN field correspondent. "The words of Superman—the *real* Superman—taped just minutes ago. His statement had been expected to touch on his so-called return from the dead; as you saw and heard, it did not. Things are beginning to wind down here, in day five of what federal agencies are calling the Coast City Holocaust. Units of the army and National Guard have secured the disaster area, assisted by a special task force of the famed Justice League. The League, which recently returned from a mission in space, has removed and destroyed a vast store of dangerous and toxic substances—"

Lois hit the off switch and sank back into her couch. *Just "day five." It seems like he's been gone forever. Oh, Clark . . .*

Suddenly there came a gentle tapping at the glass door of her balcony. Lois bolted up from the couch as if she'd heard a gunshot. She got to her feet and stumbled barefoot to the door. *If this is that stupid bird again—!* Then she yanked back the curtain and found herself at eye level with a red and yellow pentagonal S-shield.

All traces of drowsiness vanished instantly as Lois flung open the door and leapt into Superman's arms.

Hours later, Lois finished dressing for work as Clark availed himself of her shower. "Have you talked to Martha and Jonathan yet?"

He came out of the bathroom, swathed in a towel. "I called them while you were showering, hon. I told them that we'd be out to visit as soon as we could."

"Oh, good! This past month's been such a nightmare for them—for all of us. And it's still not completely over. I mean, people are starting to accept that Superman is alive, but to the world at large, Clark Kent is dead."

"Yeah, that is a definite problem. We have to concoct some sort of cover story. This could be a tough one. I've had to cover absences before, but never one this long." He sat down on the edge of the bed. "Hmm, how about this: I escaped being buried alive, but I was hit by some falling debris that induced a case of retrograde amnesia. I couldn't find an ID and the last thing I could remember was working on a farm, so I drifted upstate and worked as a migrant laborer until my memory finally returned!"

"Oh, come on, Clark! You're the most famous missing person since Amelia Earhart. Just about every place out in the country has a satellite dish these days. Even the *cows* would've recognized you!"

"Okay, then, how about I fell off a pier and was washed out to sea?"

"Uh-huh. And how did you survive? I suppose you just bobbed around in the ocean all month?"

"Yeah, bad idea." He frowned. "Even though it's partially true, I don't suppose we should claim that I was abducted by aliens?"

"After Coast City?"

"Right. Forget that. Another bad idea." He caught a glimpse of the clock out of the corner of his eye and grabbed up his costume.

Lois raised an eyebrow. "What's up?"

"I've got a chopper to meet!" There was a blur of motion, and he was dressed. "Keep all this in the back of your mind, and we'll talk about it later." He gave her a quick kiss and leapt out the window.

Lois stared after him for a moment, then closed and locked her window. Her cat emerged from beneath a chair, warily looking about to see if anything else was planning to go flying by. Lois picked the cat up and scratched him behind the ears. "Elroy, ever notice how there's never another Superman around when you need him?"

On the outskirts of Metropolis, a large cargo helicopter touched down at the rooftop helipad of S.T.A.R. Labs. Half a dozen technicians came forward on the run, sliding open the copter's big doors and lifting out a long refrigerated case bearing the body of the Eradicator.

"Hey, you be careful with him, you hear?" Steel stepped down out of the copter as the technicians lifted the case onto a wheeled cart and rolled it into the sprawling research center. "He might have started out as some sort of alien artifact, but he died for us all!"

A slender woman in a white lab coat walked up to the copter as John Henry turned and gave Supergirl a hand down from the craft.

"Don't worry, Mister . . . Steel?" The woman offered her hand. "I'm Dr. Karen Faulkner, head of research for S.T.A.R./Metropolis. I can assure you that the Eradicator's remains will be treated with the utmost respect."

"Hey, crew! Long time no see!" Superboy came sauntering over to the copter. He high-fived John Henry and gave Supergirl a wink. "No see for even longer in your case, babe!"

"Good to see you in one piece, kid." Steel looked the boy over. "I heard you took a little pounding from that missile."

"Yeah, a little, but I heal real good. Doc Faulkner and her lab rats want to put me in a cage with a wheel, though. Anyway, I've finished my gig on the 'turn your head and cough' circuit, and I'm ready to party! Hey, look!" Superboy pointed to the heavens. "Up in the sky!"

Superman dropped onto the helipad, smiling broadly. "Hello, everybody. Glad to see that all of you made it back all right." He looked down into the grinning face of the Boy of Steel and felt a vague sense of unease. *It's going to take time getting used to having a younger version of myself around.* Still, he put those feelings aside and grasped the boy's hand. "I'm glad to see you, too, son. That was a brave thing you did."

"Hey, all in a day's work, y'know? Let's make a deal, though . . . if you don't call me 'son,' I won't call you 'pops'! "

Superman threw back his head and laughed heartily for the first time in a long while. "You have a deal. But what should I call you? I hear that your business manager is trying to tie up the rights to 'Superman.' "

"You heard about that, huh?" The boy blushed and looked sheepish. "Well, that was before you turned up. If there's anyone around here who's Superman, it's you! I guess you can call me Superboy—for now. But when I turn eighteen, watch out!"

They were all laughing when the sound of a distant construction whistle reached Superman's ears. He reflexively glanced across the river toward Metropolis's central borough. Buildings were shorter at that end of the city, and he had a clear line of sight to a demolition project getting under way at a site not far from Hob's Bay. Superman gazed intently into the site for an instant, and his jaw dropped.

"Superman?" Supergirl immediately noticed the change in his expression. "Is something wrong?"

"Not yet, if I hurry."

"Need any help?"

"Thanks, but I can—" He stopped and lowered his voice. "No, maybe there is something else you can help me with."

Moments later, demolition workers at the Hob's Bay site were surprised to see Superman drop down out of the sky. "Hey, Superman, you come to give us a hand?"

"In a way. I want you to shut down your equipment."

The foreman scratched his head. "Okay . . . but why?"

"We can't undermine this site any more than necessary." He stared down hard through the rubble. "There was a civil defense shelter in the basement of the building that collapsed here and, by God, it did its job!" A siren sounded in the distance, growing louder. "Good, the ambulance is on its way."

"Ambulance? What for?"

"You'll see." Working quickly but carefully, Superman lifted aside tons of debris in seconds. By the time the ambulance arrived, he'd located a reinforced steel beam and bent it back, opening a new access to the buried shelter.

"Don't be afraid, now. Everything's all right." He slowly lowered himself into the opening, his voice echoing back behind him. "I'm Superman. You're both going to be just fine."

The next moment, the workers let out a cheer as Superman flew up out of the shelter with two young children—a girl and a boy—tucked into his arms. They were both about five years old and looked as though they could be fraternal twins. They were frightened and dirty, but they were alive!

Superman handed the little girl to a woman paramedic, but the boy clung stubbornly to his arm.

"I'm sorry. We didn't mean to do it!" Tears came to the boy's dirty cheeks.

"Didn't mean to do what?"

"Play down in that old building. Mommy said not to go down in there . . . and we didn't mean to . . . but my ball rolled down the stairs, and we went to get it. And then we heard sirens and everything started to shake. And then . . . and then we couldn't get out!"

"Shhh. It's all right." Superman hugged the boy tightly. "Nothing will happen to you now. I want you to be good and go with the paramedics. They'll take good care of you, and I promise to come visit, okay?"

The boy considered that. "'Kay."

"Thanks, Superman." One of the paramedics shook his hand. "It's a good thing you found those kids when you did. They must've been in there since Doomsday brought the building down. They'd just about used up the canned food and water in that shelter."

"I know."

Suddenly there was a whoop of delight, and a huge bear of a man came running full tilt at Superman. "My fav'rit! Yer back! It's really you!" Bibbo joyously threw his arms around his hero. The old roughneck was laughing and crying and couldn't stop doing either.

A young pup ran around and around the two men, barking its head off. The little dog had a surprisingly deep bark for its size; in fact, its bark sounded uncannily like Bibbo's laughter.

Bibbo was beside himself, practically enraptured. "I just asked God ta take care a' ya! I never dreamed he'd send ya back!"

"Take it easy, Bibbo." Superman clapped him on the back. "You don't want to hyperventilate."

The pup stopped running and started jumping up into the air, again and again, until he was clearing four feet. Bibbo snagged him in midair and held him out to the Man of Steel.

"Sooperman, I want ya to meet my new dog, Krypto! Say hullo to the man, Krypto."

Krypto yipped enthusiastically.

"Krypto, eh?" Superman gravely shook the little dog's paw. "Well, I'm very pleased to meet you, Krypto. You're a fine-looking dog."

Bibbo just beamed; as far as he was concerned, at that moment all was right with the world.

"Well, I hate to run, Bibbo, but I want to get down to City Hall." Superman clapped the tavern owner on the back. "I need to secure a list of all the area's civil defense shelters. Who knows who else might still be alive out there!" Waving his good-byes, Superman shot into the air and was gone. On the ground behind him, both man and dog seemed to cheer.

Hours later, Superman tore into another buried shelter. In contrast to the previous rescue, this one was well attended by the media. As the television cameras went live, Superman lifted aside one last huge chunk of fallen masonry and helped Clark Kent out into the light of day.

Kent was a mess. He hadn't been able to shave in weeks, and his shaggy, unkempt hair hung low over his collar. He held a hand up over his face, blinking back tears as his eyes adjusted to the light. "Bright out here . . . a lot brighter than I've been used to."

"Clark!" Lois broke past the police lines and ran to Kent's arms. "Clark, you're alive!"

"Lois!" Kent kissed her on the cheek and held her tight. "Lord, it's so good to see you again. It was dreaming of this moment that kept me going."

"Me, too, lover. Me, too." She cradled his face in her hands.

Kent turned to the caped man and shook his hand. "Superman, we owe you so much."

Lois's eyes were moist with tears as she reached over and gave Superman a one-armed hug. "Yes, without you I'd have lost Clark forever. It's so good to have both of you back. Thanks."

"My pleasure, Ms. Lane."

"Hey, Clark . . . Lois!" Camera in hand, Jimmy Olsen called out to his friends. "Hold it right there! You, too, Superman—say 'Cheese'!"

And as the three friends joined arms, Jimmy clicked off what was destined to be another award-winning picture.

Paramedics on the scene gave Clark a quick once-over and urged him to get a more thorough exam at Metropolis General. As he and Lois stepped into a waiting ambulance, the media quickly clustered around Superman.

"Superman, over here!"

"What's your reaction to accusations that your death was faked?"

"Is it true that you can't die?"

"How *did* you manage to survive?"

"What can you tell us about Doomsday?"

"Is the young Superman really your clone?"

Superman held up his hand for silence. "Ladies . . . gentlemen . . . please! I know you're all curious about how I was able to come back. So am I. I'm still looking for some of the answers myself. And until I find them, it would be irresponsible to make any sweeping statements." He saw the ambulance pull away and smiled. "But I'll tell you this much. I'm certain that Clark Kent will have an easier time adjusting to his new life than I will."

With that, Superman shot up and away from the gathered reporters and soared off over Metropolis.

He hadn't flown more than ten blocks before he heard his name called. Superman swung about to find a LexCorp helicopter hailing him;

none other than Lex Luthor II himself was leaning out of the copter's open hatch, bullhorn in hand.

Superman flew in close and hovered alongside the craft. "Yes, Luthor? Is there something I can do for you?"

"You can tell me what you've done with my Supergirl!" Luthor was so red in the face one could hardly tell where his skin ended and his beard began. "Since she went walkabout with you people to the West Coast, I've hardly seen hide nor hair of her. Oh, she's called and left messages, but I haven't been able to connect with her at all. Where is she?"

"Well, Lex, she *has* been busy. We all have." Superman strove to keep a polite tone, but Luthor's attitude was getting under his skin. "I can't tell you any more than that. I'm hardly Supergirl's keeper . . . and neither are you!"

Superman shot away from the helicopter, leaving Luthor to mutter into his beard.

Several hours later, Clark and Lois returned to her apartment. Clark gave Lois a cheerful grin. "Well, I didn't think that went too badly, do you?"

Lois leaned back against a wall and gave in to an uncontrollable fit of giggling. "I don't know how you were able to answer all of that doctor's questions with such a straight face."

Clark grabbed his lapels and launched into an impersonation of the emergency room physician. " 'Well, Mr. Kent, you're in remarkable shape for someone who's been locked underground for a month. In fact, you're in much better shape than most of the executives I see in our Wellness Program. We can't keep you here against your will!' " Clark let out a hoot. "I'll say they couldn't!"

There was a rush of air from the balcony, and Superman was suddenly standing next to Clark and Lois. "I take it that everything went well?"

"Exceedingly well!" Lois fell into Superman's arms. "The doctors bought the whole story."

Superman gave her a big kiss. "Hey, all it takes is careful planning and a good actor. Right, 'Clark'?"

"Right." "Clark" suddenly hunched over and appeared to shrink in on himself. The air around him shimmered as his waist drew in, his hips rounded out, his shoulders narrowed, and his hair lengthened and faded. Even his clothing underwent a strange transformation, flowing off his legs and assuming bright red and blue hues. Within a minute, "Clark Kent" was gone and Supergirl stood in his place.

"Oh, dear." Lois's eyes were open wide. "I never stopped to think . . . was it painful?"

"Well, it's not something I'd want to do every day. But for one of my favorite couples, I was glad to oblige." The young shape-shifter flipped her long blond hair back over her shoulder. "Clark, you are amazing. I understand why you'd want a private life, and of course you were Clark Kent long before you ever put on a cape, but maintaining two identities—! I don't know how you've managed to keep it a secret for as long as you have."

Superman just smiled. "It isn't easy."

"Well, I just hope that you two will be as happy together as Lex and I are."

"Lex . . . yes, well . . ." Superman's smile did a fast fade. *How do I handle this without sounding like a meddling older brother?* "I, uh, ran into Lex earlier today, and he wasn't too happy then. From the way he talked, he didn't sound as if he'd ever be happy unless—well, unless he knew where you were at all times."

"Oh—that." Supergirl tipped her head to one side and worried with the hem of her cape. "Lex does have his possessive side, and I'm not too thrilled about it. But we'll work it out somehow. I mean, that's all part of being a couple, right? You have good times and bad. I guess we still have a lot to learn about each other."

"Uh-huh." Superman nodded.

"Well, I really should be going. Lex and I *do* need to talk." Supergirl gave Lois a quick hug and Superman a peck on the cheek. "You both take care. Give Martha and Jonathan my best, and tell them that I intend to keep my promise to come visit them soon."

"We'll do that." Superman planted a return kiss on her forehead. "You take care, too."

Supergirl faded from sight. A window opened, seemingly of its own accord. "May we all live happily ever after." Her voice rang out from midair, and then the window slid shut.

Superman shook his head. "I just hope there's nothing to Luthor that she'll have to learn about the hard way."

"Me, too." Lois leaned her head against his shoulder. "But she's a big girl. We can't live her life for her. All we can do is be there for her if and when she needs us. Like she was there for us." She ran a finger along his bicep. "So, how did *your* checkup go? Learn anything?"

"Did I!" Superman chuckled. "Professor Hamilton was able to fill in a lot of the gaps. . . ."

Emil Hamilton had looked profoundly ill at ease when the caped man entered the lab. "Superman, I don't know how you can bear to look at me. I did everything wrong after you died. Everything! And then I decided that that crazy Cyborg was you! How can you ever forgive me? How can you even stand the *sight* of me?"

"Take it easy, Professor. What do you mean, you did everything wrong?"

"What do I mean? Oh, wait till you see! Let me show you." Emil began calling up data on his computer screen. "Ever since I heard of your revival, I've been trying to figure out just how you survived."

"That's why I came here, Professor. A lot of it is still a mystery to me."

"Well, I think I may have found the answer in my studies of your energy absorption rates." Accessing the data seemed to soothe Hamilton's agitation. He removed his glasses and tapped them thoughtfully against his chin. "Have you ever heard of the mammalian dive reflex? It's an oxygen-conserving response to submersion in cold water, most common in seals and other diving mammals. It's much less common in humans, of course, but it's believed to be a factor—over and above the effects of hypothermia itself, you understand—in the survival of some near-drowning victims. The victim's system goes into a near-total shutdown resembling death—but it need not be permanent if the victim is rescued and warmed soon enough. For a young, vital person, 'soon enough' can be after thirty to forty minutes of submersion!"

Superman nodded. "Yes, I've observed the phenomenon firsthand. I once pulled what I thought was a drowning victim out of an icy river, but she was revived, and she made a full recovery. As I recall, the paramedic's words were: 'They're not dead until they're *warm* and dead!' "

"Exactly!" Emil waved his glasses like a baton. "And who's more vital than Superman? The trauma of your injuries sent you into the equivalent of a deathlike state. Now, the efforts of the Guardian and the paramedics, though not exactly what you needed, did at least help maintain your body's viability. What you really needed was a slow, steady feed of solar energy—the equivalent of rewarming a near-drowning victim. I believe that would have eventually brought you back." Hamilton plopped his glasses back on his nose. "But like an idiot, I let them *bury* you!"

Superman could almost feel the light bulb click on over his head. *No wonder Emil's upset.*

"There must, however, be some unknown factors that I haven't been able to account for. I hope you won't think me morbid, but I charted an energy depletion graph, based on what I'd learned about your powers and physiology." Emil adjusted the computer monitor as the graph came up on screen. "Now, unless I've made a grievous error in compiling my data, your body's energy levels should have dropped below the point of no return weeks ago."

Hamilton tapped that point on the screen. From the computed time-line Superman could see that it came well before the Eradicator had placed him, finally, in the Regeneration Matrix.

Emil shook his head. "I don't understand how your body stayed viable, locked away underground for as long as it was—away from light or any other source of energy, for that matter."

"I don't know, Professor. Perhaps some outside agency intervened. . . ."

Lois looked at Superman. "Maybe two agencies. From what Supergirl told me about that setup she found you in at the Cadmus Project, you were getting a pretty thorough bath of full-spectrum light there."

"I know." Superman looked amused. "I've been thinking of sending Paul Westfield a thank-you note."

"Don't kid about this!" Lois hugged him tightly. "The professor wasn't the only one who overlooked the obvious. I knew that your powers depended on solar energy, and I didn't make the connection either. We could have lost you for good—just from ignorance."

"Now, don't *you* start!" Superman cupped her chin in his hand. "You're not to blame any more than the professor was. It took me half an hour to convince him that I didn't want to knock his block off. I had a close call, but lots of people have close calls. We've all learned from this, but for now it's over." He looked at Lois quizzically. "You said '*two* agencies.' What, besides the Cadmus factor?"

"Well, call me superstitious, but Jonathan was convinced that he met you on the other side and made you fight your way back."

Superman got a faraway look. "I do remember seeing Pa, but . . . I don't know. I just don't know. I doubt that I'll ever know." He peered down into her eyes and smiled. "What's important is that we're both alive and well. There's a lot of living I want to do with you, Ms. Lane."

"Why, thank you, Mr. Kent! Same here." Her smile was easily a match for his. "But we still have a lot of loose ends to tie up. You have two lives to get in order, after all. And eventually you're going to have to make some sort of public statement about your rebirth—or rather, your premature burial. Otherwise, cultists will follow you wherever you go!"

Superman smiled innocently. "I'll give you the exclusive interview." He bent down and kissed the tip of her nose. "I'm sure it will all work out. But for now, I'm tired of planning battle strategies; I want to plan a wedding! We still haven't set a date."

"Shhh . . . we can do that tomorrow." She returned his kiss on the lips. "Right now I want to get you out of that cape and into glasses and a jacket. Then, I want Italian food and a long, long walk with my fiancé."

"Italian food, eh?" Superman glanced out the window. "I know a great little place in Salerno."

Moments later, the curtains fluttered, and they were gone.

Epilogue

Far out in deep space, a lonely meteor tumbled away from the Earth, away from the solar system, bearing off across the universe the body of the creature called Doomsday.

He was bound tight. There was no air for him to breathe. No food or water to sustain him. It was impossible for him to be alive.

But his fingers twitched. His eyes blinked open. He raised his head and looked about him. He opened his mouth wide, and his chest heaved. Had there been air present, he would have laughed.

For now, there was nothing ahead of him but the void.

Slowly, the creature closed his eyes. He would sleep and wait for his surroundings to change. And when they did, when he again had something to destroy, something to kill, then he would fight to break his bonds.

Then, he would be free . . . oh, yes. It was all just a matter of time. . . .

ABOUT THE AUTHOR

ROGER STERN is a veteran writer with more than seventeen years' experience in the comics industry. Among the titles he has scripted are *Action Comics, Alan Scott: Green Lantern, Power of the Atom,* and the text for a series of ninety trading cards produced by SkyBox International commemorating the death of Superman, all for DC Comics. He has also scripted *The Amazing Spider-Man, The Incredible Hulk, Captain America,* and *Fantastic Four,* for Marvel Comics, written *Superman: The Man of Steel Sourcebook* for Mayfair Games, and several graphic novels, including *Superman for Earth.* He was also the chief writer on the DC Comics magazine *Newstime.* Mr. Stern lives and works in upstate New York with his wife, Carmela Merlo.